"*Ten Thousand Charms* is a moving story of love and redemption as its diamond-in-the-rough characters struggle with faith to leave behind a dark past for a brighter future."

LINDA WINDSOR,
author of *Blue Moon*, #3 in her Moonstruck Romance series

"*Ten Thousand Charms* is a terrific debut for writer Allison Pittman, a tale of love and redemption that grabs you and won't let go. It will leave you like it left me, anxious to see this author's future work."

JAMES SCOTT BELL, bestselling author of *Presumed Guilty*

"Once I started my *Ten Thousand Charms* journey, I couldn't turn the pages fast enough. Pittman's literary eloquence provides a sidesaddle perspective into one woman's life journey, love struggle, and eternal conflict. 'Gloria' is so *real* you not only cringe along side her pain, you writhe with emotion as her internal struggle to find a love worth holding on to is companioned with a desperate desire for the eternal love promised through Christ. Definitely a keeper! This will be a suggested read for all of my listening audiences."

LINDA GOLDFARB,
syndicated talk-radio host, speaker, and writer

"If you took Francine River's classic *Redeeming Love* and merged it with Janette Oke's quaint prairie style, you could almost envision the masterpiece Allison Pittman has created with her poignant tale of God's redemptive power. If you're in need of a fresh touch of God's grace, *Ten Thousand Charms* is the story for you."

JANICE THOMPSON, author of *Hurricane*

"Are you thirsty, weary, or heavy laden? Come—rest and let Allison Pittman take you to another place and time where you will find joy resting in the arms of Jesus."

LAUREN L. BRIGGS, author of *The Art of Helping*,
What to Say and Do When Someone is Hurting,
Making the Blue Plate Special, and *The Joy of Family Legacies*

A NOVEL

ALLISON PITTMAN

Multnomah® Publishers *Sisters, Oregon*

TEN THOUSAND CHARMS
published by Multnomah Publishers, Inc.
© 2006 by Allison Pittman

International Standard Book Number: 1-59052-575-2
Cover image by PixelWorks Studios, www.shootpw.com

Background cover images by MacDuff Everton/Corbis and
Gary Crabbe/Alaney
Interior design and typeset by Katherine Lloyd, The DESK

Unless otherwise indicated, Scripture quotations are from:
The Holy Bible, King James Version (KJV)
Other Scripture quotations are from:
The Holy Bible, New International Version (NIV)
© 1973, 1984 by International Bible Society,
used by permission of Zondervan Publishing House

Multnomah is a trademark of Multnomah Publishers, Inc.,
and is registered in the U.S. Patent and Trademark Office.
The colophon is a trademark of Multnomah Publishers, Inc.
Printed in the United States of America

For information:
MULTNOMAH PUBLISHERS, INC.
601 NORTH LARCH STREET
SISTERS, OREGON 97759
Library of Congress Cataloging-in-Publication Data
Pittman, Allison.
Ten thousand charms : a novel / Allison Pittman.
     p. cm. -- (Crossroads of grace ; bk. 1)
ISBN 1-59052-575-2
1. Prostitutes--West (U.S.)--Fiction. I. Title.
PS3616.I885T46 2006
813'.6--dc22   2005035675
          06 07 08 09 10 11 12 — 10 9 8 7 6 5 4 3 2 1 0

For my brother, Chris,
who knows better than anyone
the joy of resting in the arms of Christ.

Acknowledgments

I praise God for His wisdom, mercy, and grace. He gave me answers before I could formulate questions; He guided my steps when I didn't know I was on a journey; He lit my path when I thought I had found my resting place.

I thank God for the amazing family He has seen fit to give me. For my husband, Mike, and my sons, Ryan, Jack, and Charlie— thanks guys for all the camping trips! For my parents who have been such an example of strength in Christ. For my sisters who make me feel so special. And for Martha, who made my brother's life complete.

Finally, I must give thanks for all of those people who made this book possible. Thank you, Rod, for being such an amazing editor. Only you could make me feel at peace in blue socks and black shoes. Thank you, Monday night group—you read every page of this and gave such great advice about trees and talking heads. Most of all, my sweet sister in Christ, Brenda, for never letting me forget Who I know, and Who knows me.

COME, YE SINNERS, POOR AND NEEDY

Joseph Hart (1759)

Come, ye sinners, poor and needy,
Weak and wounded, sick and sore;
Jesus ready stands to save you,
Full of pity, love and power.

Refrain:
I will arise and go to Jesus,
He will embrace me in His arms;
In the arms of my dear Saviour,
O there are ten thousand charms.

Come, ye thirsty, come and welcome,
God's free bounty glorify;
True belief and true repentance,
Every grace that brings you nigh.

Come, ye weary, heavy laden,
Lost and ruined by the fall;
If you tarry till you're better,
You will never come at all.

Let not conscience make you linger,
Nor of fitness fondly dream;
All the fitness He requireth
Is to feel your need of Him.

Come, ye weary, heavy laden,
Lost and ruined by the fall;
If you tarry till you're better,
You will never come at all.

1

Wyoming Territory

*G*loria forced herself to take another step. Then another. And another. For most of the journey, she'd been lucky enough—and pretty enough—to ride along with supply wagons and men migrating to another promised land. But her luck ran out at the opening of this narrow, winding pass.

"Ain't nothin' up there to go to," her latest anonymous bene-factor had said. "There's a little camp called Silver Peak, but it don't have no future. Prob'ly gonna close down next year."

"I have friends there," Gloria said.

"I just bet you do." His leer gave Gloria a momentary hope that he would take her up the pass, but he insisted that the jour-ney was too dangerous for his rig.

"Ain't but about seven miles," he said, dismissing her from his wagon seat. "Get started now and you might make it before dark."

For once, a man's promise turned out to be true, because it was nearing dusk as Gloria rounded the last bend. In fact, there was just enough light for her to get a glimpse of something red.

"Jewell."

The red-shingled roof was the trademark of any Jewell Gunn fancy house, and the closest reference Gloria had to a home. Now it served as a beacon, guiding Gloria's steps until the entire establishment—huge and gaudy compared to its rough-hewn neighbors—came into view.

As she approached, the closest thing Gloria had to a friend, Jewell herself, leaned out a second-story window. Dressed in a silk robe wrapped haphazardly at the waist, Jewell planted her elbows firmly on the sill.

Gloria shifted her bag to a fresh hand, straightened her shoulders, and forced a spring into her final steps as she set her eyes firmly on the door.

She needs to be the one to call to me.

Within minutes, Jewell's distinctive whiskey voice filled the yard.

"Well, Glory-be it's Glori-A!" It was the phrase Jewell coined whenever she paraded the young Gloria through a crowded parlor. "Lord, girl, if I hadn't seen your feet movin', I'da swore you was the mangled mess of a bobcat snack."

"Is that right?" Gloria set her case down, planted her hands on her hips, and tried to keep the quaver out of her voice. "And if I didn't know you were the richest woman in Wyoming Territory, I'd swear you were some old whore seein' the first light of day."

There was a beat during which Gloria wondered if she had gone too far, but then Jewell leaned further out the window and said, as if shouting a secret, "All us rich women are whores, honey. I'm just not one who needs to hide it."

The first thing Gloria did upon entering the house was drop her bag in the hall.

"Would you like to sit down, miss?"

It was an impossibly small voice, one Gloria might have missed altogether if there had been a breeze to rustle the curtains.

"Some water, please, would be nice," Gloria said. She sank gratefully into overstuffed cushions, feeling guilty for asking this little person to fetch anything. The girl was every bit as slight as her voice.

"Nothing to eat? Some bread? Cheese? An apple? One of the

men shot a goose. We're roasting it, but it won't be ready for hours."

Gloria ignored the now familiar rumble in her stomach. "Just water, thanks."

The little one turned to leave, and in her haste ran headlong into a newly dressed and coiffed Jewell.

"Fetch a light supper for our guest, Biddy," Jewell said once she'd set the reeling girl straight on her feet again.

"She says she just wants some water, ma'am." Biddy's voice grew smaller with each syllable.

"Nonsense," Jewell's voice addressed Biddy while her eyes remained fixed on Gloria. "Boil some tea. Toast some bread and open that last jar of marmalade."

Biddy scuttled out of the room.

"Sorry we don't have a fatted calf," Jewell said, "but then you're not exactly the prodigal son, are you?"

"The what?"

"Darlin', you are ignorant."

Gloria nodded in the direction of Biddy's exit. "So is this a whorehouse or an orphanage?"

"You tell me," Jewell said, wedging herself into a chair just opposite of Gloria.

"I'm not exactly an orphan."

"When'd your ma die?"

"It's been a few years."

"She held on a long time."

"Too long."

Gloria ran a fingernail along the edge of the dried mud on her boots sending crumbs of her journey onto Jewell's braided rug. Out of the corner of her eye she saw Jewell's reaching hand and stopped.

"You coulda stayed with me," Jewell said. "I could have made you something special."

"As special as Mama?" Gloria looked up at Jewell.

"It's not my fault she got sick."

"She got sicker after you kicked us out."

Just then the door opened and Biddy made her way into the room, carefully balancing a tray, which she set on a small table in front of the parlor's sofa.

"We can talk some more later," Jewell said. "Right now, eat."

She woke up naked and nestled underneath a heavy down coverlet. Her mind struggled through fog to capture memories from the previous night. She ate toast. She drank tea. And then black.

"Your little journey must have wore you out." Jewell was sitting once again at her open window; the early morning chilled the room. Jewell closed the window, crossed the room, and sat on the corner of the bed.

"I tried shakin' you, callin' you, but you'd have none of that. I figured freezin' would be the gentlest way."

Gloria tried to croak out a response, maybe an apology, but her tongue was like cotton in her mouth. No noise.

Jewell took a glass of water from the nightstand and watched Gloria struggle to one elbow before handing it to her.

"We had a slow one last night," Jewell said while Gloria forced the water down her throat. "I actually had a chance to get some rest." She leaned toward Gloria in a gesture of conspiracy. Her breath reeked of coffee and sleep. "I hope you don't mind sharin' a bed with some old whore."

"That depends," Gloria rasped, testing the taste of words. "Who else was invited?"

Jewell snorted and snatched the glass away. "I've got a house full of healthy girls. Why would I waste my reputation on a half-dead path rat like you?"

"Sorry." Gloria turned her back and drew the coverlet over her shoulders.

"Especially one in your condition. How far gone are you?"

Gloria turned back to face Jewell, clutched the coverlet to her chin.

"Is that why you're here? Did you expect me to get rid of it for you?"

"Can you?"

"Not until you start tellin' me the truth," Jewell said. "How far gone did you say?"

"Four months."

"That's what I figured. You're stick-thin except for that little bump. Ain't you been eatin'?"

"I've been traveling." Gloria sat up again and reached for the water. "I thought you might, well, help me with it."

"You mean get rid of it."

"You did it for Mama once."

"Yes, I did. And for others, too. Some lived, some died. But none were as far gone as you, at least not that I knew goin' into it. So, now that that's off the table, what's your next plan?"

"I don't have a next plan. I was counting on—"

"Well stop countin' on that. So who is he?"

"Who?"

"The King of France," Jewell said. "Who do you think? Who's the father?"

Gloria chuckled. "The King of France."

Jewell did not chuckle back.

"I could pay you. I have money, nearly—"

Jewell brought up a hand. "Biddy checked your bag last night. You don't have a dime. I checked your clothes while you were asleep. Couldn't find a dollar."

"It's sewn up in the hem of my dress. Some of it, anyway."

"So that's how you trust me?"

"No," Gloria said. With each sentence her voice became stronger. "That's how I trust the world. I came here on foot remember? You think I'm going to walk from camp to camp toting my money like a picnic lunch?"

A slight shrug granted that point to Gloria, but the next breath brought back the voice of accusation.

"So I ask you again, who's the father? Better yet, what makes you think he's here?"

"I didn't come here looking for any man," Gloria said. "I came here looking for you."

Now Jewell did laugh. "Listen, missy. A girl like you could pull in five hundred a night in Virginia City. Why would anyone walk away from that to hide out in the woods? You're runnin' away from somethin'."

Jewell got up from the bed and crossed the room. A brocade dressing gown was strewn across a chair. She picked it up and held it out to Gloria, who took it and shrugged her arms into the sleeves before emerging from the bed.

"Leaving's not the same as running," she said, wrapping the warm material around her and cinching the belt with a determined knot.

"I ain't so sure of that," Jewell said, heading for the door. "Let's go downstairs and get some breakfast and we'll see which it is."

A fire was already burning in the large cookstove that dominated one wall of the kitchen. Along a second wall, a washbasin overflowed with dirty dishes. The odor of the previous night's roasted goose lingered, the smell of it colliding with the early morning nausea somewhere near the top of Gloria's throat.

Jewell walked over to the stove and lifted a burner to stir the embers within.

"Eggs? Coffee?"

"Sounds fine," Gloria said. Her hunger was nearly unbearable by now.

"I'll cook, you talk," Jewell said.

Gloria took a deep breath and began the story she'd rehearsed with every step up this mountain.

"Just after Mama died, I left California. Went straight to

Virginia City. I walked right up to the biggest, fanciest house in the district and said, 'My name's Gloria. I'll have them lined up at the door.' The first two places turned me down, then spent the next two years fighting to get me back."

"Who'd you work for?"

"Ellie Dennison."

"Cat House Ellie? She's a tough one."

"Not if you're bringing in money."

"Is it true what I hear about the money in Virginia City? I heard some gals could bring in a thousand a night."

Gloria flashed her perfected sly smile. "It's true."

Jewell stopped in mid-whisk and gave Gloria a look full of suspicion and resentment.

"What can I say?" Gloria assumed a dramatic pose. "I inherited my mother's charm and it paid off handsomely."

"Knowin' Ellie, she was the one gettin' paid. She always took more of a cut than I ever thought was fair."

"That's if she knew how much a girl was bringing in."

By now the coffee was brewed, and its aroma filled the warm kitchen. Gloria inhaled the smell of breakfast and let out a small sigh.

Jewell scooped a pile of scrambled eggs out of the iron skillet and onto a clean blue plate. Next to the eggs she plopped two biscuits fresh from the oven. This she set in front of Gloria with a steaming cup of coffee.

"Sugar? Don't have no milk."

"Black."

"So, when did you get caught?" Jewell poured herself a cup of coffee and settled across from Gloria with her own plate of food.

"What makes you think I did?"

"You're here. You're broke."

Gloria popped a bite of piping hot biscuit into her mouth and savored the sensation as it crumbled, melted, and found its way to her waiting stomach. She allowed herself one more bite, plus a forkful of eggs and a sip of coffee before continuing.

"We all got caught," Gloria said, gesturing with her fork. "All of us in Ellie's house. Everyone in the district, really. The wives of the town went on a rampage."

"They got to put their upturned noses in everything, don't they?"

Gloria continued to eat, making every effort to remember to chew.

"Ellie said we all had to pay our fines out of our own money. I knew if I sent her to my stash, she'd find out I'd been cheating her, so I told her I'd used all my money ordering a silk gown custom made in France. She let me sit in jail for a month."

For a minute the only sound was the scrape of Gloria's fork.

"I was in jail when I realized I was pregnant," she said, not looking up. "I knew when I got out Ellie'd never keep me on, and eventually she'd learn that there wasn't any dress coming from France. So one night I just left."

Jewell had been steadily eating throughout Gloria's story. Now she set down her fork and reached for a small tin in the middle of the table. From it she drew out a pinch of tobacco and a small white rolling paper. Neither woman spoke again until the paper was licked, sealed, and lit with a match struck across the bottom of Jewell's shoe.

"Why here?" She puffed a bit of smoke, grimaced, and plucked a bit of loose tobacco off her bottom lip. "Why me?"

"Where else? I needed someplace where I could be safe."

"From?"

"Everything," Gloria said.

"And you think you're safe with me?" Jewell's voice was a mixture of curiosity and insult.

"As safe as anywhere, I guess."

Jewell stubbed the rest of her cigarette out in a half-eaten biscuit just as Gloria made a move to snatch it off the plate. "Where's the money?"

Gloria made every effort to hold Jewell's gaze. "Locked up in a bank back in Virginia City. But I have a little with me. I just need to hole up here for a while. I can pay."

"Forget pay. You plannin' to work?"

Gloria looked around the kitchen. Dirty dishes were piled everywhere.

"I can clean up."

"That I expect. You know what I mean."

"Maybe in the spring. I figure my time will come in March, so…"

"I got two little one-rooms out back. I was hoping to expand this spring. Looks like I got my wish. You can take one of those."

Jewell heaved herself up from the table and walked toward the kitchen door. Gloria got up, too, and searched for a bucket to take to the pump outside. When she found it, she turned to leave and was surprised to find Jewell hadn't yet left the room.

"One more thing, missy," Jewell said, pointing an accusing finger. "Don't for a minute think you're gonna saddle me with this kid while you skip off back to the big money."

Gloria let her mouth fall open. "Jewell!" she exclaimed, bringing a hand to her heart. "What makes you think I'm capable of that?"

"'Cause that's what I'd do if I was in your boots." Jewell pointed to Gloria's bare feet, winked and walked out the door.

2

The snow came in earnest in November. There had been hints and teases of winter, short-lived flurries that dusted the trees with a temporary glaze; the hard frost each morning left icicles that melted long before noon. But on the day that Gloria counted to be the first of her fifth month of pregnancy, Silver Peak spent three days in the clenches of a ferocious blizzard. When the wind stopped and the last flake fell, the little settlement found itself buried under a solid blanket of winter. The trees now groaned under the weight of frozen batting. The miners who hadn't abandoned the camp to work the mines in the more temperate California left their tents and crowded into makeshift cabins, sometimes five men to a single room, and prepared to wait out the winter. They made only the most occasional forays out to meet the party sent with pack mules to get supplies, or to pass an evening in Jewell's warm and welcoming house.

But if Jewell was counting on her red-roofed house to make her fortune, she was destined for disappointment. Those few men who remained to brave the winter often wanted little more than good whiskey or a warm meal after tramping through the snow to her door. Gloria spent many evenings alone in the kitchen, tidying up or just sitting by the warmth of the stove, listening to the conversation on the other side of the door.

"Now come on, gents," Jewell's voice boomed, "I know you got a little something extra in those pockets to spend upstairs."

And some anonymous male voice would answer that if Jewell was going to charge fifty cents for a shot of whiskey, he'd better save his money to get through winter, and the parlor would rumble with laughter and agreement.

Sometimes the door separating the kitchen from the parlor would bang open, and Sadie, one of only two girls besides Biddy who stayed to hold out the winter with Jewell, would burst through.

"Liebling, why stay in here all alone? Come talk with us." Her voice held the faintest trace of a native German tongue, giving every statement the air of a command. Even Jewell had been known to bend herself to Sadie's whim, but Gloria felt no compunction to obey.

Later on the door might crack open ever so slightly, and the round soft face of Mae, the third of Jewell's girls, would poke her head around the corner, saying, "Gloria? Are you sure you don't want to come out? Sadie's about to tell more stories about New York. Wouldn't you like to hear?"

But Gloria could hear the stories just fine through the door, and as long as she listened through the door, nobody would ask to hear her own stories. She didn't have any she was willing to tell.

But late, late at night, after the last of the whiskey-warmed miners had stumbled into the snow or had been tumbled, with a rental rate taken from their pockets, into an empty bed upstairs, Sadie, Mae, Biddy, and Jewell would wander into the kitchen where Gloria still sat, reluctant to leave its warmth to make her way to her little cabin in the back. Mae took charge of boiling water for tea, and Jewell passed her flask, dropping a jot of brandy into every cup. Sadie poked the fire in the stove, sending a final blast of warmth into the room, and Biddy sat silently in her chair, the expression of terror that normally filled her face temporarily masked with an air of contentment.

This is when the table came alive with stories. Jewell regaled them all with tales of the colorful men of the untamed country. Mae had few tales to tell, but her absolute delight with any amusing tidbit was just as entertaining. Biddy's tragic tale was common knowledge, but she sometimes softened the room with a contribution only she could bring—memories of a home, a family, a loving mother and father who hadn't sold her into this life.

"Your mother would be glad to know you're safe. And warm," Sadie said one evening, placing a strong hand over Biddy's tiny one. "There's worse than this."

Jewell was downing a swig from her heavily laced tea and chuckled as she wiped her mouth with her sleeve and gave Gloria a nudge with her elbow. "She's got that right, eh, missy? She ain't seen the half of what she's bound to."

"*Ssshht!*" Sadie hissed. "She's a child, Jewell."

"A young woman alone in this world ain't got time to be a child," Jewell said. "Besides, this one here was one of my girls when she wasn't much older than Biddy, weren't you Gloria?"

Gloria's face burned, and she focused her gaze on the stray tea leaves floating in her cup.

"But was that what you wanted?" Mae asked.

"Who knows what they want?" Gloria said, shrugging. She brought her steaming cup to her lips to stifle any further conversation.

"Well," Sadie said, slamming both of her big hands on the tabletop loud enough to rattle the cups and startle the women out of their melancholy, "when *I* was little, I wanted to be a hot corn girl."

Gloria gulped a bit too much of the hot liquid and choked it down.

"A what?" Jewell asked.

"A hot corn girl. Where I grew up, we had all kinds of vendors out in the streets. They had little carts that they pushed up and down, calling out to everybody. But I loved most to see the hot corn girls."

"What were they?" Biddy's eyes matched the wonder in her words.

"Oh, they was beautiful. They chose young girls, the pretty ones, and they wore these great skirts that looked like layers and layers of rags. And a blouse on top that was open, like this." She used her finger to draw a line from one broad shoulder to the next. "And they would walk, barefoot no matter what the weather, pulling a little cart and calling—" At this, Sadie scooted her chair away from the table. She clutched a handful of her skirt in one hand and held the other aloft as she sashayed around the kitchen.

"Hot corn! Hot corn! Here's your lily-white hot corn. Hot corn! All hot! Just come out of the boiling pot!"

Her voice took on a charming and innocent quality as she filled the room with its song.

"Why didn't you do it?" Mae asked.

"Oh, only the prettiest girls could get that work." Sadie settled herself back into her chair. "I have never been a great beauty."

"Nonsense," Mae said.

Gloria looked up from her tea to study Sadie's face. There was no hint of embarrassment at her statement or any sense of begging for a compliment. And she did not acknowledge Mae's attempt to give her one. Rather, she turned to young Biddy at her right and, cupping the young girl's face in her strong hand, said, "You, Liebling, would make a beautiful hot corn girl."

Biddy's face burst into a smile.

"And you," Sadie directed her glance to Jewell, "are so powdered and puffy you look like a beautiful pot of hot corn."

The room exploded in laughter that dwarfed any ever heard in that house. All five women were left speechless, breathless, holding their sides and wiping their eyes. Biddy declared it was the first time she'd laughed since before her brother died. Mae's body seemed to ripple. Jewell herself was not immune to the infectious humor.

And Gloria thought she was going to die. Or the baby was going to die. Or both. She had never in her life experienced laughter to the point of pain. She held herself and doubled over, anxious for the return of her breath so she could cry out for help, but every breath just fueled another spasm.

Then, suddenly, with one sharp gasp, she stopped. The look of shock on her face brought the other women around the table to a halt, too. Except for Mae, who continued to quiver silently.

"Gloria," Jewell said, the first syllable spoken like a chuckle, "you all right?"

"We're fine," Gloria said, returning her hand to her stomach. "The baby just laughed back."

Baby.

It was the first time she'd voiced the word.

Just after midnight, the brandy took its toll and Jewell hoisted herself up from the table saying, "Night, ladies," before ambling upstairs to her room. Mae left half a step behind her, ready to lend a steadying hand at the slightest stagger. Biddy followed, yawning.

Sadie and Gloria sat in comfortable, sisterly ease for a while.

"You think March?" Sadie spoke into the silence.

"Hm?" Gloria said.

"Your baby. It will be here in March?"

"Oh, yes. 'Round there sometime. It's hard to know for sure."

"March is nice. A spring baby."

"I don't want to think about it."

"Scared?"

"Not so much scared," Gloria said. "More like sad."

Sadie ran her finger around the edge of her empty cup. Said nothing.

"I can just imagine," Gloria said, "this baby sitting around a table some night telling stories about how her mama was a—"

"Might be a boy," Sadie said with a smile.

"That doesn't change who I am," Gloria said. "I just don't want this baby to have the life I had."

"So change your life."

"To what?"

"Find the father. Bat those big blue eyes of yours and say, 'Darling, today's your lucky day.'"

"I wouldn't know who to bat my eyes at."

"You did not come here to find the father." It was a statement, not a question.

"I thought Jewell could get rid of it."

"This far along? You could have died."

Gloria stared into Sadie's eyes and let the depth of her desperation sink into the silence.

Sadie reached for Gloria's hand, holding it firm, despite Gloria's attempt to pull it away. "It is a baby," she said, "not the end of your life."

"I don't care about my life," Gloria said. "I never have."

"But now you share it."

"Not for long. Not for a minute longer than I have to." Gloria snatched her hand free and drummed her fingers on the table.

"So Jewell was right."

"About what?"

"She thinks you are planning to drop the baby here and leave in the spring."

Gloria didn't deny it.

"Listen to me, Gloria. Things will change when you see that baby. You cannot help but…care."

"Like my mother did?"

"No," Sadie said. "Like I did. Every one of them."

Odd, but Gloria's first reaction was to look around the room, as if somehow during the weeks she'd been living here she had overlooked the presence of Sadie's children running underfoot.

Sadie seemed to read her mind and laughed. "Well, of course they are not here," she said warmly.

"Where are they?"

Sadie's plain face took on a dreamy expression, and her smile wavered for just a moment before she said, "Now, that is a question. I had a little boy, then a little girl. Both born just perfect, but…" The wistful pain in Sadie's eyes kept Gloria from asking for details. Right there at Jewell's table, Sadie seemed to get younger and younger, revealing the girl she had once been. Not pretty, exactly, but softer, innocent.

"The next one came too soon," she continued. "I wasn't much farther along than you are now. After that—" she stumbled, as if searching for the precise thought—"well, I suppose I was not meant to be a mother. But still, in here," she tapped her breast, "I still long for my children. I still carry a love for them."

"That's just it," Gloria said, beating her own heart. "I don't feel anything here."

"You will," Sadie said. "Trust me. And when your time comes, I'll be there to help you. I helped bring lots of babies into this world. Never lost any that weren't my own." She chuckled. "Guess I was meant to be on the other end."

Gloria shared her smile and felt a need to comfort and reassure this woman who always seemed stronger than herself.

"I'll be glad to have you with me," she said. "I guess I am a little scared." She gave Sadie a pat on her hand and stood to leave. "G'night." She drew her shawl tight around her and braced herself to face the late-night cold.

"Why don't you just stay in one of the rooms upstairs?" Sadie asked. "With just the three of us in the house, there is plenty of space."

"No, thanks. I've spent most of my life in somebody's upstairs room. I like having my own little house." She glanced out the window at the tiny shack. "I like being alone."

The baby made another lurch within her, strong enough to call her attention and bring a protective hand to her abdomen.

"Well," she forced a smile, "almost alone."

~ 3 ~

The fire in the little stove died during the night. The pile of quilts and blankets kept Gloria warm enough, but one poke of her nose outside the mound of covers was enough to let her know it would be a long, miserable walk to the outhouse.

"Maybe I can wait," she murmured to herself before burrowing deeper into her nest. Five minutes later, though, waiting was no longer an option.

The first step was always the worst. Even though her feet were wrapped in thick woolen socks, the sharp chill of the floor was painful to her feet. Her body was wracked with chills, and her hands shook so much that she couldn't fasten the hooks of her boots.

"Oh, bother with the buttons," she finally said. She wrapped herself in a generous wool coat and headed outside.

There hadn't been a fresh snow in over a week, and Gloria easily traversed the well-worn path from her door to the outhouse. Having relieved herself, she faced a choice between taking the same path back or branching right to follow the path to Jewell's back door.

"Well," she said, "let's see what the girls have for breakfast."

There was the usual bustle of activity in Jewell's cozy kitchen, but food wasn't a part of it.

"Girl, we ate near an hour ago," Jewell said. She was pulling all the jars and tins from the shelves and assembling them on the table. "There's some coffee you can warm up."

29

"Oh, let me fry her up some grits," Mae said. "Poor thing in her condition, she needs her sleep."

"Thanks, Mae," Gloria said with a grateful smile.

Just then Sadie poked her head through the door. "One of the men just rode up. He says the supply wagon is about halfway up the pass. Should be here before dark."

"A supply wagon?" Gloria said. "With all this snow?"

"Aw," Jewell said, "this ain't nothin'. It's the mildest winter I can remember."

"It is unusual." Biddy peered into the sugar canister. "Looks like we'll have enough for at least two dozen. Maybe three."

"Three dozen what?" Gloria asked.

"Cookies," Biddy said. "We've only got a handful of currants, but I can chop them up real fine to make them stretch."

"What's the occasion?" Gloria touched her finger quickly to the coffeepot to test its temperature.

"Supplies," Jewell said. "Come noon this place'll be crawlin' with men. They're holed up in their cabins now, but once that wagon shows…"

"It's like a party," Biddy said, her voice excited. "Everybody gathers around and waits. Once the wagon's here, we unload it together to see what we've got."

"Not much of a party with just cookies and coffee," Mae said over her shoulder. She was patting a handful of cold cooked hominy into a cake to fry in a shallow pan of drippings. "We got about a dozen potatoes left. We could slice 'em thin and fry those up. Sprinkle with a little vinegar…" Mae's mouth twisted in anticipated delight.

"Now it's sounding like a party," Jewell said, granting the girls a rare smile. "I got about four bottles of whiskey left. We start pourin' that, and those men oughta start wantin' some more *friendly* company."

"Land sakes, Jewell," Mae said. "With just me and Sadie?"

Biddy busied herself measuring and sifting flour and did not look at the other women in the room.

"Relax, Mae," Jewell said. "There ain't but twenty men left here for the winter. And let's face it, they'd probably rather have a good cookie than... Just my dumb luck, tryin' to strike it big in a mine camp full of monks."

"Maybe," Mae said, "we should count our blessings. There's worse things in life than nice men."

"Much worse," Gloria said. "Like hunger. Can we spare any molasses for those grits?"

It was, indeed, like a party. Jewell had all but abandoned her makeup during the slow winter months, but when she walked into the parlor, she was aglow in powder and rouge. Mae brushed Biddy's hair until it shone, then braided it into two coils that she wrapped around Biddy's head, securing them at the nape of her neck with a large red bow. Mae bundled as much of herself as she could into an unwilling corset, causing her bosom to billow up into an impressive display. Sadie wore blue velvet, trimmed in black lace. Her ash-colored hair curled into long coils, caught together at the nape of her neck and draped over her shoulders.

And Gloria. The dresses she brought from Virginia City had been long abandoned. Now she wore blouses borrowed from Sadie and one of Mae's skirts cinched above her expanding belly, which made the skirt ride up a little in the front, revealing unbuttoned boots and thick wool socks.

"I'm not quite the belle of Virginia City anymore, am I?" Gloria said.

"Oh, I don't know," Sadie said. "You are shaped rather like a bell."

"Very funny."

"Maybe we can do something with your hair," Sadie said.

"If you can, you're a better woman than I am."

"No argument there." Sadie took a brush and went to work on the mass of blonde curls that fell just below Gloria's shoulders. The result was a simple thick knot ornamented with a jeweled comb.

"It's beautiful," Gloria said, referring to the comb.

"It was a gift," Sadie said. "But you can keep it."

The first men showed up just after noon, the products of their own special care in grooming. Their hair was slicked back with Macassar oil. Beards were trimmed and tamed; many were clean-shaven for the first time in months.

Soon after they arrived, under Jewell's pointed instruction, they began laying planks across wooden barrels in Jewell's yard for makeshift tables.

The thermometer read forty degrees—an unseasonable warm spell in January—and everybody seemed to revel in the respite from bitter winter winds. Biddy's cookies were laid out on plat-ters, but they were soon bolted down by the hungry miners. Likewise were Mae's fried potatoes. Sadie poured cup after cup of coffee; Jewell served shot after shot of whiskey.

Gloria watched it all from behind her blue flowered curtains.

After the refreshments were gone, the men tossed horseshoes to pass the time. Soon, heralded by shouts of "It's here! It's here!" from scouts stationed at the mouth of the pass, a single wagon, burdened with crates and barrels and boxes and led by a team of sturdy oxen, made its way into the clearing.

"Gloria! Come join us!" Sadie was yelling from the middle of Jewell's yard.

Gloria parted her curtains and gave a jaunty wave.

"It is *Weihnachten!*"

Gloria crossed to her door, opened it a crack and peeked her head out. "What?"

"*Weihnachten!* Christmas!"

"Little late for Christmas, don't you think?"

"Better late than never," Sadie said.

It was, in a word, bounty. There were sacks of flour, corn-meal, sugar, tobacco. Two barrels of beer were immediately tapped, and coffee cups overflowed with foam. One whole plank was lined with tins of oysters, crates of apples, sacks of potatoes, and boxes of crackers. There were five smoked hams, links upon links of sausages, onions, herbs, beans, bacon, coffee, tea, and whiskey.

The wagon's master, a jovial man named Ernie, set up his scale at the head of a table and opened for business. One by one, orderly, the men of Silver Peak lined up, their pockets full of gold and coin and cash, and prepared to pay Ernie's inflated prices.

Gloria left her cabin and took her place with Sadie and the girls off to the side.

"Jewell always lets the men go first," Biddy whispered. "They don't take much, don't cook much. Then she buys up whatever's left and cooks it up to sell to them later on."

"Smart woman," Gloria said.

The sun continued to spread a certain warmth, and the jovial mood of the crowd grew with each purchase. Jewell broke away from the girls and worked her way through the crowd, greeting the men, pouring beer, telling jokes.

"Now, Sam, what're you gonna do with that coffee? From what I hear, your coffee'd make a horse go blind. Bill, you know you need an onion to go with them sausages. What's this, Mason? My whiskey ain't good enough for you, you gotta buy your own?"

The men, slicked and dandy, blushed and hemmed and hawed under her attention. The same men who thought nothing of tossing her a twenty-dollar gold piece before heading upstairs with Sadie turned into jelly when Jewell tickled their chins and called them handsome. Gloria envied her ease in conversation.

Jewell's whiskey-rough voice was such an integral part of the party's noise, Gloria's attention was drawn when it abruptly stopped.

Two people—a man and a woman—had slipped into the supply line. The man was well over six feet tall with shoulders broad enough to span a doorway. His hair, parted down the middle, hung nearly to his shoulders. He clutched his hat in one hand; the other hand rested on the back of a woman who could only be his wife.

"MacGregan," Jewell said in a tone of extreme, exaggerated politeness. "Mrs. MacGregan."

"Good afternoon, Miss Gunn," MacGregan said. Gloria detected a faint Irish brogue in his voice. The wife said nothing.

"You don't make it down here too often," Jewell said, seeming to enjoy his discomfort.

"Been cooped up in that cabin too long," MacGregan said. "Never know how long a warm spell like this is gonna last."

"It is nice, isn't it? Can I get you a drink?"

"No, no thank you. I'm not a drinkin' man."

"Ah, yes, of course. I forgot. Perhaps some tea for your wife?"

"That would be—" He was interrupted by a brief, fierce shake of his wife's head. "No, but thank you."

"All right then." Jewell reached up to give MacGregan a hearty pat on the arm—much to his wife's obvious consternation—before taking up with a group of four men who needed her to settle some kind of bet.

"Who is that?" Gloria asked Sadie.

"John William MacGregan. He and his wife got here about a year ago. They have a cabin pretty far up the mountain. Don't come down here much."

"Why not?"

"Can't you guess?" Sadie said. "The wife. Look at her, the prude. I suspect she doesn't care much for us."

"How does Jewell know him?"

"I think she knows him from before she got here. Maybe he has some wild, mysterious past."

"The wife doesn't look too wild."

Mrs. MacGregan was tall, though not as tall as Sadie, and thin. Gaunt, really. She wore a heavy dark coat, and her narrow face popped out of it like a pale flame. Wisps of black hair clung to her cheeks. Most of the party had abandoned their heavy wraps, but Mrs. MacGregan not only wore hers, but continued to clutch it close to her. Gloria noticed something familiar in the posture and leaned over to tell Sadie.

"She's pregnant, too."

"You think so?"

"Look at her," Gloria said.

"You are right," Sadie said. "Poor thing. She looks so sickly, too."

"You should talk to her, offer to help."

"But of course," Sadie said, "Then maybe we'll drink some tea and tell each other secrets."

"Listen," Gloria said. "She's going to need a midwife."

"All right," Sadie said, "but you go with me to talk to her."

Mrs. MacGregan's eyes narrowed with each step Gloria and Sadie took. Finally, she took a step back as if to hide herself behind her massive husband.

"Mrs. MacGregan?" Sadie spoke to the woman as if she were a child hiding in a coal closet. "Hello, Mrs. MacGregan. My name is Sadie, and this is Gloria."

Sadie held out her hand, but Mrs. MacGregan made no attempt to take it.

"Katherine," John William said, "don't be rude."

Katherine MacGregan emerged from behind her husband and offered the women a timid hand. "Pleased to meet you," she said without unclenching her teeth.

There was an uncomfortable beat of silence, the four of them standing, staring. Sadie rocked back and forth on her heels. Gloria looked just past Katherine MacGregan up into the trees dripping with melted snow.

Sadie took a deep, deep breath. "So, Mrs. MacGregan, when are you due?"

"Excuse me?" Her voice was full of indignation.

"She's askin' about the baby," John William said. He turned to Sadie. "This spring. Probably April."

"Gloria is due in March," Sadie said, pointing to Gloria's obvious mound.

"Well, congratulations." John William's voice was tinged with discomfort, but it seemed to stem from embarrassment rather than disapproval.

Gloria tried to coax a smile of camaraderie from Mrs. MacGregan, but was disappointed.

"I just wanted you to know," Sadie said, "that we are here—I am here—if you need us. Me."

"And why," Mrs. MacGregan asked, "would I need you?"

"I am a skilled midwife." Sadie said.

When Gloria looked at Sadie, she seemed to have grown another inch. The top of her head came nearly to John William MacGregan's chin.

"When your time comes, just send your husband down, and I'll be right up to help you."

"That's good to know," John William said. He held his hand out to shake Sadie's. When Sadie grasped it, though, Mrs. MacGregan slapped Sadie's hand away.

"He will *not* be darkening the door of your house."

"Now, Katherine," John William said, his voice tinged with warning.

"I only meant—" Sadie said.

"I don't care what you *meant*," Mrs. MacGregan said. "We don't need you or your kind."

"Katherine!" His voice was harsh, but then gentle as he turned to address Sadie. "Excuse her. She hasn't been feeling well. What with…well, everything."

"Well then, good day to you," Sadie said. "And good luck."

"Good-bye," Mrs. MacGregan said.

"It was nice to meet you," John William said. "Both of you."

Sadie turned Gloria toward Jewell's house full of smiles and laughter, but Gloria stepped back and grabbed Mrs. MacGregan's cold hand, refusing to relinquish her grip even when the woman tried to yank it away.

"Listen, Mrs. Mac—Katherine," she said. "We're all just women here. Just women." Her mind tumbled with more words, but something in Katherine MacGregan's face stopped her from speaking further. The vacant, dismissive stare that first greeted Gloria altered, slowly. The captive hand gave a nearly imperceptible squeeze, and Katherine's clear blue eyes emitted just a hint of warmth. Gloria thought she sensed a nod, but didn't want to force the issue or prolong the discomfort.

"Let's go," she said to Sadie, and together they walked into Jewell's house.

They made their way up the mountain, slowly, stopping often for Katherine to catch her breath or rest a spell on a boulder or fallen tree. He helped her as much as he could—gave a supporting arm, cleared the branches, carried the bundle of supplies—but still she complained of exhaustion.

"I thought the trip might be too much," John William said. "Should I take the supplies up and come back? Maybe carry you?"

"Don't be foolish," Katherine said. "I needed to get out of that cabin. The fresh air is lovely. Just let me sit a spell here, if you don't mind."

He did mind, a little. He wanted to get her home and settled, safe and comfortable. She didn't look well. The brisk afternoon air did nothing to add color to her pale, sunken cheeks. Her breath was coming in short, shallow spurts. But he settled himself on a fallen tree trunk, she on a wide, smooth rock. They sat, still and quiet, the surrounding branches heavy with melting snow.

"I'm just worried about the baby," he said after a while.

"You're always worried about the baby. If you worried about me half as much as you worry about the baby…well, you wouldn't have to worry about the baby at all."

The woods were winter-silent around them. The air so temperate he couldn't see his breath. Warmed by the walk up the mountain, he stripped off his coat and let the slight breeze chill through his shirtsleeves. Katherine gave him a chastising look, and he waited for her to tell him that he'd catch his death, but she didn't.

Instead she asked, "How do you know her?"

"Who?"

"The fat one. The one with the painted face."

"You treated her badly," he said. "All of them."

"You didn't answer my question."

"I met her. Before."

"Before?"

"Before you. Before prison."

"Where?"

"Katherine, you know I was everywhere. We were in a different town every week. I don't know where I met Jewell Gunn. I don't even know why I remember her name."

"She seems pretty hard to forget."

"Maybe so."

"What about the girls?"

He sighed. "What about them?"

"Did you know them, too?"

"I'm not—"

"I don't mean these girls, specifically," Katherine said. "But that Jewell's a brothel keeper. She's had other girls. Did you know any of them?"

"Now listen." John William stood and walked over to where his wife sat. He knelt beside her, one knee in a slush of melting snow and mud, and took her face in his massive hands, forcing her to look at him. "You knew who I was and what I did when you married me. I kept no secrets from you. Am I right?"

"I suppose."

"Suppose nothin'. You know the man I was, and you know the man I am now. I'm not gonna sit here and confess my sins to you. I confessed them already. To God. You know that, you were there. And He wiped 'em clean."

"I know, I know—"

"So you got no reason to call 'em up again. God has forgiven me. And while I never did any real harm to you, I thought you had, too."

He dropped his hands, stood, and brought himself up to sit beside her. His hip touched hers, but they sat as if a wedge kept them from turning toward each other.

"I did forgive you—do forgive you—but it's just so hard when you have to meet them face to face."

"Them? What them?"

"Those women."

"It's just like that one said, Katherine. They're just women. Just like you."

"They're nothing like me."

"You know what I mean."

"And that one, the pregnant one. Spilling her condition out for everyone to see. It's positively indecent."

"You've got no right—"

"I have every right." Katherine stood up and wheeled to face him. The abruptness of her motion caused her to reel a bit. John William reached out to her, but she stepped away from his steadying hand. "Every right in the world," she said, her voice weaker. "This place is just so wild. So uncivilized. So, so…"

"We can leave, Katherine. You know that. We can leave any time you want."

"And go where?"

"Anywhere. You got no roots here. No family."

"Just you," she said with a weak smile.

John William waited for her to include the babe she was carrying, and when she didn't, he spoke again.

"What kind of life did you think we were gonna have?"

"More than this," she said. "More than a one-room shack on a mountain. In South Pass, it seemed the men could hardly walk for all the money in their pockets."

"You know I couldn't stay in South Pass." John William stood and walked close to her, but she took a step away. He didn't follow. "Not after the trial, anyway. Things seemed promisin' here at the time."

"Well, there's no promise now, is there?"

John William stared at his wife. She had always been reserved, even cold at times, but he had never seen her this bitter. Her face was set like flint, her pursed lips so hard he wouldn't have been surprised if they produced sparks when she spoke.

Then, slowly, her expression began to soften. There was just the hint of a pleasing smile. Katherine took back the step she'd taken away and reached out to him. Her hand was thin and red-raw, and she ran it up and down the length of his arm; the chapped flakes of her fingers snagged the material.

Her touch caused him to tense every muscle in his body. Instinctively, his hand clenched. She saw this and smiled again, bringing her hand to rest on his, her fingers curled over his fist.

"Maybe," she said, "you could go back—"

"No."

"Not forever. Just once. Maybe twice. There's a lot of people who'd like to see—"

"Katherine, I made promises. You know that." He drew his hand away from her, then took her into his arms. He felt the funny little bump of their child pressed against him and knew he would do whatever he had to in order to make this woman happy. He leaned back and hooked his finger under Katherine's chin. She offered no resistance as he lifted her face to his.

"We'll leave in the spring," he said, "after the baby's here. I'll keep workin' right from when production starts up again until you and the baby are ready to travel. Then we'll go."

He kissed the end of her nose.

"You haven't said where."

"I haven't decided. Right now, all I want to do is get back to the cabin."

With that, he bent his knees, scooped his pregnant wife into his arms, and began walking toward their home.

"John," Katherine said with a giggling lilt to her voice, "what about the—?"

"I'll come back for everythin' later."

"But that's our food! What if a bear gets it?"

"Well, then," he said, nuzzling into her neck, "I'll get the bear, get us a rug."

Katherine laughed at that, and he tucked her a little closer. He loved to hear her laugh. Treasured it, really, like any other rare thing.

❧ 4 ❧

The first pain surprised her. She'd felt contractions on and off for weeks, but Sadie had assured her that they were nothing. Just her body practicing for the real thing.

"How will I know when it's real?" Gloria had asked.

"You will know."

And with that first pain, she did.

It wasn't particularly strong. It didn't bring her to her knees or make her cry out. It simply tugged at her back, like a child with an apron string, and told her, "It's time, mama. It's time."

She had been in Jewell's kitchen, a rare visit these days. March was a fickle time in Wyoming. One day the snow would be so deep, Gloria's pregnant stomach prevented her from stepping high enough to get through it. Then would come days where slush and mud made walking a treacherous path for a woman who couldn't see her feet. For weeks now, Gloria stayed mostly to the bed in her cabin.

But today the air was crisp, the wind reasonable, and the path a perfect surface of shallow crunchy snow.

The women sat around their familiar table, sipping their familiar coffee. The difference was that now Gloria was so big she could hardly reach her cup.

"*Ach!* Why don't you move in? Upstairs?" Sadie asked, just as she had countless times.

Jewell never offered such an invitation, and this evening was no exception. She simply looked at Gloria and waited for an answer.

"I've told you. I like the little house. I like to be alone. I've never been alone before."

"You're spendin' a lot of time here for someone who likes to be alone so much," Jewell said.

Gloria made a face. "Besides, I think it might be better if—if the baby isn't born in a whorehouse."

Jewell laughed out loud. "Darlin', what do you think you're livin' in now? Just because I'm not sendin' men out there don't mean that I put up that shack to be a guest room."

"It's just that, it's never been—I've never had—"

"And don't be thinkin' that you're gonna take up residence in the Taj Mahal permanent. Once that baby's out, I expect to get some work outta you."

"Of course," Gloria said, soothing. "But for now, I think of it as a home. My home."

They'd finished an early supper and Gloria stood to clear the table.

"Let me do that," Biddy said, taking the plate from Gloria's hand. "You should rest a bit. You look tired."

"Don't be silly," Gloria said. "I'm fine. Besides, if I don't do the clearing, I'll have to do the cooking."

Mae, Sadie, and Jewell all assumed an expression of mock horror and urged Biddy to please, please, let Gloria do the dishes.

"I'd waste away to nothin' if I had to eat your cookin'," Mae said.

"Wouldn't do you no harm," Jewell said. "Frankly, I don't care who cleans up the mess, just get it done. It's a nice day, gonna be a nice night. You girls all look a bit haggard. Finish the kitchen, then get yourselves ready."

When the door finished swinging behind Jewell, the atmosphere in the room changed to one of light, lively fun. Sadie poured steaming water from the kettle into the washbasin. Mae scraped the plates into a slop can before handing them to Gloria, who submerged them in the hot, soapy water. Once clean, they were handed to Biddy, who dried and stacked them on the table to be put away later.

"I like doing dishes," Gloria said. "It makes me feel like I'm putting everything back in order again. A new beginning."

"Listen to her," Sadie said, scrubbing a heavy cast-iron skillet, "a regular philosopher. Too bad your mama didn't work back East—you could have gone to college."

"Might have to learn to read first." Gloria's voice held all the humor of Sadie's, and there was the familiar layer of laughter that accompanied much of the women's conversation. Although she'd been a part of it for nearly five months, it still managed to warm Gloria's soul in a way she never could have imagined.

"I can see what Gloria means," Mae said. "There's something satisfying about standin' at the window, lookin' out at the sunset."

"You know what would be even better?" The dream-filled voice of Biddy made them all pause and turn to her. "It would be even better to know that you were standing at your *own* window in your *own* house looking at your *own* yard and doing your *own* dishes."

That feeling settled among the women, and while nobody said anything at first, the sense of agreement was strong. After a few seconds, Sadie's voice broke the melancholy in the room.

"What would be best," she said, "would be to be at your window, doing your dishes, and have the man of the house come up behind you, nuzzle your neck, and say 'Tut, tut, darling. You look tired. Why don't you sit down and let me finish up?'"

The laughter was back. Not loud, not raucous, but soft and complete. It was a sound that filled every corner of the room. Gloria enjoyed her contribution to it, loved the feeling of it bubbling up from deep within her. She was just finishing a long soprano sigh when she felt it.

That first pain.

That first tug.

She handed the last clean cup to Biddy, used the end of her apron to wipe her hands, and grabbed her coat.

"I've got to get home now, girls," she said and closed the door on their good-byes.

The single window faced the east, so she couldn't watch the sunset, but Gloria did look through her blue flowered curtains as the shadow of her cabin stretched across the yard. All the lights were on at Jewell's, the windows open. The crowd Jewell was expecting didn't arrive. From what she could tell, there were just a few men over, playing cards and buying drinks. The house sounded full, not loud, and Gloria knew that if she ever did have a place in it, she wouldn't after tonight.

The pains progressed with the darkness. First erratic and inconsequential, they grew in intensity and regularity. She'd almost laughed at the first ones. "Ooh, that's a big one!" Or, "Yep, I think this is it!" Laughing, she thought, was better than screaming—not that they'd been strong enough to make her scream. Besides, laughter meant strength.

But as the shadows lengthened and the darkness crept in and around her home, the laughter died.

"I should have told Sadie," she said to the empty room. "She should be here. She said she'd be here."

There was a little fire in the stove, not much more than embers right now, and still she felt hot. She'd taken off her clothes earlier, and now sat on her bed wearing one of Mae's nightgowns. The room was encased in darkness. Her only lamp sat on a little shelf that jutted out from the windowsill. She rarely lit it, preferring to lie in the darkness and concentrate on feeling the movement of the baby within her.

The life within her.

Left in the dark, she could imagine the trappings of a home surrounded her. She could conjure the breath of a sleeping mate. She could pretend that this child was coming into a world where it would be loved and cared for in a way she never was. She tried to imagine herself, an unborn mass in her mother's womb, tried to see her mother lying in darkness eagerly awaiting Gloria's arrival. A single flame in the lamp would make all of that disappear. A solitary strike of a match would light the whole room and reveal its bed, its bureau, its chair, its stove. Worse, it would reveal the small green leather case, the legacy her mother left her. The rootless existence handed to her. The mere presence of light was not worth the dashing of a dream, not on any ordinary evening, anyway.

But this was no ordinary night. With a shaking hand, she lit the lamp, turned the flame high, and waited for someone to notice.

Another pain seized her.

Why hadn't she told Sadie? Why didn't she call out to her now? Why not risk the few steps across the yard? The pain that gripped her made Gloria feel as though the muscles in her body were about to rise against her and squeeze out her own breath, her own life. Without Sadie's help, she felt she might not live through this night at all.

Maybe that's why she'd kept silent.

Last week she lived through two days without feeling the baby move. Not at all. She'd stayed awake all night, not wanting to miss a single kick. But nothing. She knew it was dead, just knew it. She remembered the sadness in Sadie's face as she talked about her stillborn children, yet she felt a tiny sense of relief at the thought of escaping motherhood. She congratulated herself on the confirmation of her inadequacy.

But when she woke up that third morning to the insistent stretching of arms and legs within her, she experienced pure joy. Silently, alone in her bed, she had rejoiced at the child's determination and strength. The baby wanted her, and it wasn't until this night, this moment, this pain that she wanted it, too.

If the baby could decide to live, so could she. But not alone. She needed help; she needed Sadie. She needed—

To walk. Maybe she could make it to the door. A breath of fresh air. She was a little unsteady, stooped over. It only took about three steps to go from her bed to her door, and by the time she made it through the third step, she felt as though her body were engulfed in shards of glass. She fell against the door latch and took a stumbling step outside. Sometime during the seconds that had passed since she left her bed, it had started to snow. Fat, soft, silent flakes. Gloria turned her face up toward the sky and opened her mouth. The snowfall was so new, so irregular, that it was some time before she felt a flake fall onto her tongue. But she did, then another, and another as the snowfall increased in intensity.

Then pain.

She held onto the doorframe even as she fell to her knees. She knew she would never make it across the yard to Jewell's back door, so when the grip of this last contraction eased, she called to the open window.

"Sadieeeee!"

The wind wasn't howling or strong enough to whisk her voice away, but the thickness of falling snow seemed to absorb sound.

"Sadieeeee!" she called again.

Still no tall silhouette in Jewell's doorway. No bustle of broad shoulders and ash-colored hair. No friendly voice, no ready joke. No capable hands to deliver one life and keep another.

She had to try one more time. Just one more. If Sadie didn't come, she would crawl to her bed and wait to die. She straightened her back as best she could, took a deep breath, and screamed into the growing sheet of snow.

"Sadieeeee!"

Still nothing. Still on her knees, she allowed her weight to settle on her feet. She felt a chill begin to spread throughout her body. Then she felt something else.

Warmth.

It was coming from within her. Slowly her feet and ankles were drenched in liquid warmth.

"Oh, dear God," she said. "I've killed it. I'm sorry," she called in the general direction of Jewell's house. "I'm so sorry."

Gloria let loose of her grip on the threshold, felt her face hit the mud, and sank into blackness.

Somebody was telling her to wake up. Insisting, really.

"Come now, Gloria," said the voice at the edge of the fog. "Wake up now. We got some work to do."

"Mama?"

"Sure, if that's what it takes. You ready to have this baby?"

"Mama...mama, I'm sorry."

"Not as sorry as you're going to be if..."

The rest of the sentence dissolved in a grunt. Two strong hands grasped her under her arms and suddenly she was being lifted to her feet.

"Let's get you to the bed."

"I killed it," Gloria said, sobbing. She did her best to shuffle her weight in the direction that the hands were dragging her. "I felt it, just pouring out—"

"That was just your water breaking."

"What water?"

"Your water. It happens. It is natural and right."

Gloria felt the edge of her bed behind her knees and began to sink down upon it.

"Not just yet. Your gown is soaked and we need to get it off."

The fabric was tugged off her shoulders and she felt it fall at her feet. She convulsed a bit at the sudden chill, but the warm, strong hands guided her to lie down. Soon she was engulfed in the warmth of her quilt pile.

"You warm yourself up, Liebling." The hair was brushed off Gloria's face with the softest caress she could remember. "I need to get some help."

Gloria reached up and gripped the hand that stroked her cheek.

"Don't leave me, please. Not again."

"It's all right, Gloria. I'll be back. Right back. I won't leave you."

The haze dissipated, and Gloria felt the clear, strong presence of love. This wasn't her mother. This was her friend.

"Sadie. You're here."

"Yes." Her voice was deep and warm and full of promise.

"Sadie, I killed the baby."

"Darling, relax. You are fine. The baby's fine."

"I don't want it to die. I don't want to die."

"Nobody is going to die tonight," Sadie said, her voice strong and authoritative. "But I need another set of hands in here."

"You'll be back?"

"Of course."

"Sadie?"

"Yes, honey."

"How did you know to come here?"

Sadie laughed. "Biddy made a spice cake, and you didn't show up. We knew something had to be wrong."

Gloria's body embraced her laughter.

"Now stay put," Sadie said. "I'll go get one of the girls."

Sadie stood up and crossed the room.

"Sadie?"

A sigh. "Yes, Gloria." She kept a hand on the door's latch while turning to face her friend.

"I never laughed until I met you."

"Of course you did."

"No, I didn't. I really don't think I did."

"You just don't remember. Now, I've got to go get some help."

"All right. Sadie?"

Another sigh. This time she let go of the latch, walked back to the bed, and knelt beside Gloria.

"What?"

"Could you bring me a piece of that spice cake?"

"Not until you're through," Sadie said.

Gloria started to voice her disappointment, but it turned into a moan. Right away, Sadie was at the foot of the bed, lifting the quilt from Gloria's legs and repositioning her body.

"On second thought," Sadie said, "the girls will figure it out. I am staying right here."

Gloria wanted to say "thank you," but the haze was back. She felt Sadie's hand between her thighs.

"I can feel the head. It won't be long now."

"It has a head?"

"Of course it has a head. No creature runs around on this earth without a head. Except maybe you sometimes."

More laughter…

"Sadie?"

"Yes, Gloria."

"It doesn't hurt anymore. Why doesn't it hurt?"

"Because I am here. I'm helping you."

"I don't feel anything."

"You will. It is almost time to push."

"Push?"

"You'll know. Your body will tell you when to push the baby out."

"I don't want to push it out. It's safe with me."

"It will still be with you. It will always be safe."

"But I don't know…"

Faces appeared in the doorway. Voices popped into the room. Mae brought fresh water for Gloria to sip and coffee for Sadie. Biddy brought fresh linens and firewood. Jewell wondered when it would all be over. So did Gloria. Sadie knew…

> *"Deserted by the waning moon,*
> *When skies proclaimed night's cheerless noon,*
> *On Tower Fort or tended ground,*
> *The Sentry walks his lowly round*
> *The Sentry walks his lowly round…"*

"Sadie?"

"Yes, honey."

"You're singing?"

"Yes."

"I've never heard you sing before."

"I don't do it very often."

"You should. It's beautiful. What is it?"

"Just a song I remember growing up. Sailors sang it."

"Where did you grow up?"

"New York."

"How did you get here?"

"Long story."

"Will you sing some more?"

> *"And should a footstep haply stray*
> *Where caution marks the guarded way*
> *Stranger quickly tell, a Friend*
> *The Word good night all's well*
> *All's well, all's well..."*

"It's time, Gloria. Now. It's time to push."

"I don't know what—"

"Your body knows. Now push."

Gloria brought herself up on her elbows and bore down. Hard. She gritted her teeth and felt her head grow tight with pressure. Her eyes closed tight, and the image of her single burning flame lingered, now blue and dancing.

"Good girl. Good girl." Sadie's voice faded in and out of Gloria's ears. "I can see the head now. Rest a minute, then we'll push again."

Clouds cushioned Sadie's words, so Gloria had to ask, "Now? Push?" when Sadie said, "Push! Now!"

"Are we almost done?" Gloria cried.

Bits of conversation were abandoned, at least Gloria thought they were. She spoke without hearing, heard without knowing—just a constant wash of sound as if she'd been plunged into a river that lapped and rolled inside her head.

So Gloria pushed. Again. Again. And again. Each one a little easier than the one before it until—

"'S here!" Sadie's voice sounded triumphant.

Gloria was vaguely aware of precise, deft movements before Sadie spoke again.

"He's here." Sadie abandoned her post at Gloria's feet and now sat at Gloria's side. She laid a warm, wet, squirming thing on Gloria's breast.

"*Er ist perfekt. Er ist schön.*"

"What?"

"It's a boy, Gloria. A beautiful, healthy boy."

"A boy?" Gloria brought her arms up to trap the baby next to her skin.

"Yes, and he's just perfect. Just needs a little cleaning up."

Sadie took the baby from Gloria, who was surprised to find her arms reaching for him. Mae had been instructed to set some water on the stove, and now Sadie dipped a hand in it to test its warmth. Satisfied, she soaked a rag in the warm water and began to wash the baby's skin. The newborn let out a wail of protest.

"He's a real boy all right," Sadie said. "Already he doesn't like to take baths."

Gloria watched the bathing of her son. It seemed an impossibly long process—each little arm, each little leg, the protruding little lump on his belly.

"Can I see him again?" she asked.

"Of course you can, silly. He's your son. He is yours. Just let me get him presentable."

Sadie wrapped a tiny scrap of cloth around the boy's bottom and then swaddled him in a little blanket she and the women had pieced together during the darkest days of winter. The warmth of the blanket stilled his cries, and when Sadie brought him back to Gloria, he was pink and wide-eyed.

Somehow, Gloria knew just how to crook her arm to cradle her son. Somehow he knew to wriggle a tiny hand free to reach for his mother's finger. His eyes were deep and brown; his head covered with long silky blond strands. The day was just dawning, his first day on earth, and already it was impossible to imagine a world without him in it.

Sadie continued to bustle around the room, tidying this and straightening that. She held out a robe that Mae brought during the night.

"Let me take him a minute so you can put this on."

Reluctantly, Gloria handed her son over to her friend. She managed to turn, let her legs fall over the side of the bed, and shrugged into the warm wrap. She was about to ask Sadie to help with the belted tie when she looked up. Sadie was holding the boy close, closer than Gloria had. Her face was twisted in pain, and tears—the first Gloria had ever seen her shed—fell onto the baby's head.

"Oh, Sadie," Gloria said.

"Mine were beautiful, too. Just so still, so quiet."

"I'm so sorry, Sadie. I wish I could—"

"Well, you can't." Sadie squared her broad shoulders. "What you need to do now is get yourself cleaned up. The girls will want to come over here and meet the young prince. Let's see if I can get a comb through that hair of yours."

The baby once again nestled in her arms, Gloria allowed Sadie to gather and brush and braid her hair.

"He is blond, like you."

"Yes," said Gloria, losing herself in his face.

"So what are you going to call him?"

There was a brief pause in the brush's task, and Gloria turned and looked into the eyes of her friend.

"Did you name your son?"

Sadie's eyes clouded for just a second. "We named him Daniel."

"That's a beautiful name," Gloria said. "May I take part of it?"

Sadie said nothing, only nodded her head as her eyes brimmed with tears.

"Danny. I'll call him Danny."

Just then there was a brief knock at the door, and before either woman could utter a "come in!" the door swung open and

Jewell, Mae, and Biddy bustled into the room.

"Well, it ain't exactly Madonna and Child," Jewell said, "but it ain't such a bad-lookin' picture."

"Oh, oh, oh!" Mae said over and over, her hands made little fleshy claps.

Biddy stood shyly in the background. "May I see the baby?" she asked in her tiny voice.

"Of course," Gloria said, reaching her free arm out to the girl. "You can even hold him if you'd like."

"Him?" Jewell said. "Well, that's a good thing at least. This ain't no life for a girl."

He is able, He is able,
He is willing, doubt no more;
He is able, He is able,
He is willing, doubt no more.

A miserable freezing sleet hammered John William and Sadie as they made their way to the MacGregan's cabin. Her long legs matched his stride all the way from Jewell's house, but as they approached his home, he pulled ahead to reach out and open the door as he would for any other woman. She brushed past him and entered the room.

"Well, this is a cozy little nest," Sadie said, shrugging her shawl off her shoulders and dropping her bag to the floor. Her presence filled the cabin. "Where do you plan to put the baby? On the roof?"

"I've made…" he lost the word, "somethin'." John William made an apologetic gesture toward a small box lined with soft woolen blankets. It sat on the floor close to the fire.

"Are you expecting a baby or a litter of puppies?" Sadie asked, laughing.

John William turned from her to look at the little box. It was all he knew to do. He was about to offer an apology for it when he felt Sadie's strong hand grip his shoulder.

"Listen, I'm sorry. I was just—"

But she was cut off by a muffled cry coming from the bundle on the bed.

Katherine was where he'd left her, curled up on the mattress in the corner of their home. She was whimpering now, a welcome sound to John William's ears. He crossed the room and knelt beside the bed.

"I think she's doin' better," he said.

"Oh, you think so, do you?" Sadie knelt down to rummage

through her bag, taking out an assortment of linens and strips of cloth. These she deposited at Katherine's feet. She saw the washstand in the corner and made her way toward it, rolling her sleeves to the elbow. "And what makes you say that?"

"You should have heard her before I came to get you. She was screamin', howlin' even." He took Katherine's hand, brought it to his lips, and spoke into her palm. "I really think the worst is over."

Sadie made her way back across the cabin, her newly washed hands dripping with water.

"Until that baby is born," Sadie said, "the worst can't be over. Now I'm going to try to get this gown off her. You get every lamp and candle you own. It is getting dark."

Sadie whisked the quilt off Katherine's body and into a heap on the floor. "Fold that and set it near the fire to warm. You might want to build it up. The storm is bringing quite a chill."

John William's head reeled with instructions. Candles, light, fire. Through the fog generated by his fear and confusion, he barely heard the conversation between the two women as he bustled about in obedience.

"All right, Mrs. MacGregan," Sadie was saying, "let's get that gown off."

"Something's wrong…something's…"

"It is never easy the first time. Now just help me here. Are there buttons?"

"The baby…" Katherine's voice was thick and weak. "The baby's not moving…something's wrong…"

"I am sure the baby's fine. Now, if you can't lift yourself up, I will just have to tear this off of you."

John William was returning the glass bowl to their only lamp when he heard the tearing of the fabric and the sharp gasp that followed.

"*Mein Gott.*" This in a whisper, sharply contrasted to the confident stream of commands from the same voice.

He stopped in his busy task and turned toward the bed.

His wife lay there, repositioned from the curled comfort he'd left her in. Now she was flat on her back, her swollen body centered on the white muslin gown she'd worn to bed on their wedding night. It was torn, straight up the middle. Her arms, still in the sleeves, were flailed out on either side of her, and the fabric draped beside her like angel's wings.

Bloody angel's wings.

"Get over here," Sadie commanded. "Hold her up against you. It's going to be too hard for her to push the baby out if she's lying straight down."

John William lifted Katherine's body with all the gentleness he could muster and slid behind her. Her head lolled against his shoulder. Her breathing was ragged. Her mouth slack.

Sadie had one hand on the rounded mound of Katherine's stomach; the other reached inside Katherine's body.

"Is she going to be—"

"Hush."

John William couldn't bear to look. He buried his face in his wife's damp hair and prayed. *Heal my wife. Carry my child. Guide her hands. Keep me strong.* He listened for God's voice to come through with words of comfort and assurance, but all he heard was Sadie.

"The baby is alive. I feel it. But we have to get it out. Soon."

When he opened his eyes he saw Sadie standing at the plank balanced across two whiskey barrels that served as their table. She had a knife in her hand and was pouring water from the steaming teakettle over its blade.

"You must have put the water on before you came to get me."

"She told me to." Strands of Katherine's hair clung to his lip, but he was powerless to brush it away, even if he wanted to.

"Smart woman." Sadie held the blade against her thumb as if to test it and, satisfied, crossed back over to sit on the bed at Katherine's feet. The sight of her, brandishing the knife in one hand while the other rested on the heap of child within his wife was too much for John William to bear. He once again closed his eyes and prayed. This time out loud.

"Heal my wife. Carry my child. Guide her—"

"Listen. She has bled a lot. Too much, really. Losing all that blood will leave her weak. Make it hard to push out the baby. So we must help her. Understand?"

"How?" He directed his question to the blade in Sadie's hand.

"First, try to rouse her. Talk to her. Right there in her ear tell her to wake up. To push."

John William brought his hands up around Katherine's shoulders and shook her gently.

"Wake up, Katherine. Wake up. We need you…."

"Now," Sadie spoke almost in harmony to John William's urgent cooing. "We'll need to help her. I'm going to make a tiny, tiny cut here, to give the baby a little more room."

"Will it hurt her?"

"At this point," Sadie said, refusing to continue until he met her gaze, "that can't be our first concern." Then, softer, "I don't think she's feeling much of anything right now. But she has to be alert. She has to push."

Katherine rolled her head back and forth against John William's chest.

"No…no…no…" she moaned. "Get her out…get that woman—"

"Good," Sadie said. "That's good. She is awake. Now talk to her. Tell her to push down. Push that baby."

"Katherine, darling, you need to—"

"Get her *out!* Get that whore out of my house!"

"I'm not a whore right now, darling." Sadie's attempt at a soothing touch along Katherine's leg was rebuffed by an amazing display of strength and anger as Katherine kicked it away while attempting to lunge from her husband's embrace.

John William pinned her to him, his arms crossed over her clammy bare skin. He burrowed his face into her neck and whispered streams of hushes and platitudes until, limp with exhaustion, Katherine lay still.

Sadie hadn't moved an inch. Perched on the side of the bed,

she captured Katherine's flailing foot with one hand and forced it back to the mattress. The other leg was pinned to the wall by Sadie's body.

"Let me go…let me go…" Katherine's voice trailed of in a haze of delirium.

"She feels trapped is all," John William said with a hint of apology.

He remembered how much she hated that feeling. All winter, trapped in the tiny cabin by the winter's snow, she'd paced the perimeter of the room. Ten paces. Eight paces. Ten paces. Eight paces. She swore each week of pregnancy that the place got smaller. She could barely turn from one task to the next without brushing against a wall or piece of furniture. John William had slept on the cabin floor for the past month; she couldn't stand his proximity in their bed. And now, here she was, pinned like some wild beast, tended by a stranger and enemy, all in the name of the life they'd created together.

"She'll be fine," he said.

The look in Sadie's eyes gave no indication that she agreed. She squared her shoulders, sighed, and resumed her instructions as if the past few seconds never happened.

"When I say so, Katherine, I need you to push as hard as you can."

"…can't…"

"I know you're tired, Mrs. MacGregan. I know it's been hard. But just a little more, *ya*? We will help you all we can, but you need to push. Ready?"

John William watched the knife disappear behind the mound of Katherine's stomach. Sadie's face took on a look of furrowed concentration. Then Katherine's body seized again, not in anger but in pain. She let forth a cry that pierced his very heart. Her hips bucked up off the mattress, her back arched in defiance.

"Push!"

Sadie placed the hand that had been restraining Katherine's

foot on top of her distended stomach and worked in a way that made John William picture his wife kneading bread.

"What can I do?" he asked.

"Put your hands on her stomach. Yes, right there." Sadie's hands, nearly as large as John William's and stained with Katherine's blood, guided his to rest on the mound he'd monitored over the past few months. Katherine had never been comfortable with her changing body, but John William was constantly curious and amused. Many nights, after Katherine collapsed into exhausted sleep, he laid his head against his child, reveling in the bumps and patterns of its hidden play. Now it was alien. Frightening. A threat to the life of its mother.

Heal my wife. Carry my child. Guide her hands. Keep me strong.

"And just a little pressure right where she's pushing…" Sadie's voice hung on the edge of his prayer.

"I can't…I can't…" Katherine's anguished cry punctuated the earnest cries of his soul.

"I've got its head, Katherine! Push again!"

Heal my wife.

"…no…"

"You can. You're strong. Again, push."

Carry my child.

"I've got the shoulders. Almost out. One more time, Katherine."

Guide her hands.

"…no more…"

Keep me strong.

Katherine's final piercing scream was deafening, and it didn't stop. Not even when she fell back against him in exhaustion. Then John William realized the wailing he heard wasn't coming from his wife, but from the thing that squirmed in Sadie's bloody hands.

"It's a little girl," Sadie said. "Let her go and come help me with the baby."

John William eased himself from behind his wife's limp body.

His legs cramped momentarily beneath him, and he wondered just how long he'd been sitting there.

Sadie's voice resumed the tone of a patient instructor. "Take some of that hot water from the kettle and put it in a bowl. Add some cool until you barely feel it being warm. We need to wash her."

Her voice prattled on about blankets and towels while his head reeled with questions he dared not ask. Once again he busied himself with compliance, until he found himself facing this tiny creature on the table, no bigger than the loaf of bread next to her. When Sadie put a warm wet washcloth into his hand, he turned to her and said, "I can't do this."

"Of course you can. Just take the cloth and wipe—"

"I'm afraid I'll hurt her."

Sadie put her own hand on his, her palm barely grazing the back of his hand and guided the pressure of his touch.

"You know, MacGregan," Sadie said softly, withdrawing her hand, "it is a good thing for a little girl to have such a strong papa."

John William worked the cloth between the tiny fingers, maneuvering around the hand that barely spanned his thumb. He pinched the tiny ankle between his fingers and gently wiped the thrashing foot.

"Be careful of her head most of all," Sadie said. "Hold it gently and just squeeze the water over it."

The tiny head was covered with soft brown hair that fell to curling as it dried. The face, however, continued to scrunch itself in protest of every ministration.

Proud of his final product, this beautiful shining little girl, he looked over his shoulder at the women on the bed. One lay motionless; the other was caught up in the business of cutting, kneading, cleansing.

"What do I do now?" he asked, beaming.

"Get something clean to wrap her up in."

He scooped the little girl up, her body nestled perfectly in the crook of his arm, and held her as he rummaged to find his best Sunday shirt.

"Will this do?" he asked, uncomfortable with his uncertainty.

Sadie smiled. "It's perfect. Just the thing. Now lay it out on the table and wrap her up."

He did so, putting the little head where his own thick neck would be and brought the wide shoulders to wrap around her delicate ones. He then folded the shirt up to the tiny one's chin and lifted her up, wrapping the excess fabric around her back. The baby's cries diminished with each fold and tuck.

"How's that for swaddlin'?"

"*Gut.*" Sadie's voice was distracted. "Fine."

"What now?"

"Sit down with her." Sadie's head motioned to one of the two chairs in the room.

John William backed against it and sat down, then studied the face of his baby girl. Minus his scars, the badly healed nose, and the lank hair, she looked just like him. But when the infant opened her eyes, he saw the clear blue soul of his wife.

Thank you, God, for carrying my child to me. Now, please, heal my wife.

The baby let out an enormous yawn, stretched against the confines of her swaddling, and settled herself to staring into her father's eyes. Much as he longed to lose himself in his daughter's gaze, John William could not ignore the sounds behind him. The rustle and rip of fabric. The occasional whimper followed by soothing, unintelligible words. The occasional question.

"Do you have another...? In this trunk?"

Guide her hands.

Once out of the corner of his eye he saw Sadie cross the room for a cup of water. Then he heard the familiar sound of Katherine's silver-handled brush making its way through long black hair.

"Better?"

No answer.

Then the baby started to squirm. To cry.

Keep me strong.

"Um," John William's voice seemed loud and unwelcome in the newly peaceful atmosphere. "I think she's…"

"Bring her to her mother," Sadie said.

John William was afraid to turn around, not sure of what sight would greet him. But when he did, he saw his wife—pretty, though pale—propped up against the wall, cushioned by their pillows. She wore the sleeveless gown reserved for hot summer nights; the row of buttons undone. Her hair lay in a thick braid over one shoulder, fastened with one of the blue scraps of cloth she usually used to make her curls for fancy dress. Under the pattern of their worn blanket, taken from its storage in the trunk in the corner of the room, he could see the shapes of her splayed, bent legs. He remembered the hushed conversation about packing the wound and changing the dressing. He forced it from his mind and stood to bring his wife and daughter together. Katherine had never been one to break into an easy smile, and he nearly lost his heart as he saw the effort it took.

"We need to see if she will suckle," Sadie said. "Katherine's too weak to hold her, so you will need to."

John William held his newborn daughter to her mother's breast, and the tiny girl latched on immediately, her instinct for survival manifested in the first hint of appetite. Her clear blue eyes searched her mother's face. Katherine returned the gaze, and then both mother and daughter closed their eyes in contentment.

"When she's finished," Sadie said, shrugging into her shawl, "wrap her in that quilt you set over by the fire. Keep her warm."

She walked around the room, pinching out the candles and lowering the lamplight until the cabin was encased in comfortable shadows. All was silent except for Katherine's shallow breaths and the baby's hungry smacking.

Just before walking out the door, Sadie scooped up a bloody bundle and stuffed it in her bag.

"Keep praying," she said, "if you think it helps."

"Thank you," John William said, tearing his eyes away from his family to glance first at Sadie's face, then down to her hands.

"If you need us, you know where we are."

He didn't see her leave, but he heard the latch of the cabin door fall into place.

Heal my wife.

His arm ached, trying to keep the baby attached without leaning on his wife's pain-wracked body.

Keep me strong.

At some point the baby's mouth went slack, the sucking stopped. John William pulled her away, and a few drops of milk drooled out of perfect pink lips. Tiny snores came from the bundle of calico. Sadie had placed the warm quilt in the makeshift cradle, and he opened the folds of it and laid the child within, then carried the cradle and set it down on the floor just below Katherine's sleeping head. Kneeling by the side of his marriage bed, he took Katherine's hands in his and continued his simple fervent prayer.

Heal my wife. Keep me strong.

At some point, fatigue overtook him. He awoke to a mewling sound coming from the folds of the quilt. His head lay on Katherine's stilled breast, her hand dropped from his grasp.

He spoke his last remaining prayer into the daylight that flooded his home. "Dear God, keep me strong."

ᵐ 6 ᵚ

*G*loria looked up sharply at the sound of the knock. No one ever visited her. No one who knocked, anyway. She crossed the small room and pressed her ear against the wood.

"Who is it?"

The first response was a masculine rumble, muffled by the steady beat of the storm outside. Then Sadie's voice rang clear.

"Open the door, Gloria."

Within seconds, the small room was full of people and rain. Sadie had braved the short distance between the main house and Gloria's room without donning any sort of cover, and her face and shoulders were dotted with raindrops.

The man, however, looked as if he had waded through rivers to get here. His drenched hat was drawn low on his face, the collar of his coat tugged up to his chin, but Gloria recognized him immediately as the man she had met at the supply wagon. The man with the pregnant wife. MacGregan.

Danny's basket was close by the small stove in the corner. Gloria lifted the basket, set it on her bed, and drew her only chair close to the stove.

"Here," she said. "Sit down."

"Let's take off that wet coat first," Sadie said.

She removed the drenched garment from his shoulders and hung it on the hook by the door. Sadie then led him to the chair and said, "Give her to me."

That's when Gloria noticed the bundle in the sling across his chest. It had the shape of a baby, but it was deathly still and quiet.

Sadie held the child while MacGregan reached behind his head to pull the sling from his neck. Once relieved of his burden, he collapsed into the chair. Gloria stepped back, sat on the edge of her bed, and placed a grateful, protective hand on her sleeping child.

"What have you brought here?" Gloria asked.

"You remember Mr. MacGregan. John William—"

"I know who he is."

"His wife died last night." Sadie cradled the baby in her arms and lifted the quilted cover from its face. "You remember her from that day at the supply wagon."

Of course Gloria remembered. The wife. Respectable, married. Gloria thought back to the look of withering disdain and tried to conjure an appropriate emotion.

"She had a real hard time of it." Sadie sat next to Gloria on the bed, the baby on her lap. She peeled away layers of damp swaddling, then bent her head down close and whispered, "*Wachen Sie auf,* sweetie. Wake up."

"What are you doing here?" Gloria asked. "Why is *he* here?"

"We need your help," Sadie said, looking up from the baby for the first time.

"We offered to help," Gloria replied. "We offered to help and she said no. Not from us."

"Well, she cannot refuse now. This baby needs to nurse, and you're the only one who can do that for her."

"Why should I?"

By now Sadie had the baby completely uncovered and Gloria saw the tiny body. A little girl silent and cold. Without thinking, Gloria took a blanket from her son's coverings and held it out in silent offering. Sadie lifted the little girl, and Gloria spread the blanket on Sadie's lap. As Sadie drew the warm corners across the tiny shoulders, Gloria sensed a now familiar tugging at her breast.

"I'll answer that," came the gruff voice from beside the stove. Gloria looked at him, but he wasn't looking at her. His face was firmly fixed on the hands clenched in his lap. His lips barely moved. If he hadn't been the only man in the room,

Gloria wouldn't have been sure he was speaking.

"First off," he said, "I'll apologize for my wife's rudeness. She wasn't a happy person. She didn't want to be here."

Sadie spoke up. "There's no need for—"

"And maybe I don't have the right to ask. But I'm not askin' for my wife. I'm not askin' for myself. It's for my little girl."

He looked up, and Gloria saw his face for the first time since that January afternoon nearly five months before. He ran his fingers through his wet hair, raking it from his face. She saw his piercing, pleading eyes, the color lost in the shadows. His nose was large and, she guessed, had been broken at least once. His jaw was strong, as was his chin, which now quivered in betrayal of the strong front he seemed determined to maintain.

"It seems," he continued, "that God brought you here and brought me here for a reason. He took my wife, but he saved my child."

Gloria snorted. "If God can save your child, why do you need me?"

"Because, sometimes God needs a little help."

There was a brief moment of almost complete silence broken only by the sound of Sadie softly patting the baby girl's back.

Then, in an instant, everything broke free.

A boisterous cry burst from the bundle at Sadie's shoulder.

John William leapt from his chair and rushed to Sadie's side. "She's alive!" he cried.

"Well, now," Sadie said, bringing the baby back to a cradle in her arms and smiling into the scrunched, screaming face. "It wasn't ever a question of her being alive. She is a strong girl. She was just a little sleepy. A little cold. And now," Sadie looked pointedly at Gloria, "she is a little hungry."

Gloria felt an unexpected rush of milk. Her fingers fumbled with the buttons on her blouse and then with the ribbons of her chemise. She looked up at John William, who flushed and turned his back. His shyness made Gloria smile. She couldn't remember the last time she'd seen a man blush.

"Give her to me," she told Sadie.

Soon, without further question or conversation, the little girl was in Gloria's arms, rooting impatiently as Gloria worked to uncover her breast. The impatient cries continued until Gloria guided the tiny face to the nipple and the hungry mouth latched on as if for life. She looked down at the baby's face, now pink and flushed, and asked, "What's her name?"

John William didn't turn around when he answered.

"We—she wanted to name a little girl Celestia."

"Celestia?" Gloria said, her voice tinged with amusement. "Such a big name for such a little girl." She took the blanket that had been used to wrap the baby, draped it over her shoulder, and told John William it was safe to turn around. "What was your wife's name?"

"Katherine," John William replied.

"Well, then, how about Kate?"

"Yes!" Sadie chimed in. "Celestia can be a middle name. She can be Katherine Celestia, and we—well, you—can call her Kate."

"Well, that would be fine, I guess," John William said. He seemed confused, overwhelmed, relieved. "Katherine Celestia MacGregan."

Just then, another sound joined the room—a soft stirring from the basket on the bed.

"That," Gloria said, "is my son. His name is Danny—" she stopped short, startled by the emptiness of his name. "Just Danny."

John William reached behind Gloria and took her child up in his arms.

"Hello, Danny," he said. "Do you mind if I hold you for just a minute? Your mama's busy right now."

Little Danny replied with a contented coo, and John William returned with him to the chair by the stove.

Soon a new quiet settled in the small room. One of peace, of life. Nobody spoke, not even to Sadie when she silently slipped out the door.

*S*pring ushered life into the small camp of Silver Peak. As snows grew scarce and days grew warm, more and more men arrived to find their fortune in the mine. Two more girls came to claim their piece of that fortune in Jewell's house. Yolanda, a beautiful, dark-eyed spitfire from the Mexican Territory, brought added spice to the group. Donna was a stunning quadroon trained in the brothels of New Orleans. Shortly after she arrived, arrayed in finery and accompanied by five trunks of dresses, Jewell staged an impromptu welcome party complete with sandwiches and beer.

Gloria did not attend the party. The cozy meals the women had shared around the table in the house's kitchen were a thing of the past. Yolanda and Donna brought new life to the house, and with it new customers. Men began to litter the parlor shortly after sundown and stayed in a steady stream late into the night. Under Jewell's watchful eye, a small piano was brought up the narrow mountain roads, and music pounded steadily whenever someone could play. The budding friendship Gloria had established with the girls faded as she became what Donna called "the mammy behind the curtains."

Biddy and Mae visited occasionally, but they much preferred the jovial atmosphere of Jewell's bawdy parlor over the subdued mood of Gloria's cabin. Jewell herself rarely darkened Gloria's door, except for the occasional reminder of what Gloria owed her, and she soon made it clear that Gloria was welcome in the big house only when she was willing to work upstairs.

But Sadie remained a true friend. She brought trays of food from the kitchen and watched the babies so Gloria could get out for an occasional walk or breath of fresh air. She helped Gloria keep up with laundering the endless stream of diapers and dresses, the tiny scraps of cloth strung to dry right alongside rows of petticoats and stockings.

One afternoon, as the women hung the wash on the line, Sadie turned to Gloria and said, "Just how long do you think Jewell is going to put up with this?"

"What do you mean?" Gloria forced a note of innocence in her voice.

"Staying here. Not working."

"I work." Gloria clipped a diaper to the line. "I'm in there every morning tidying up while you all sleep. I've been doing my part."

"You know what I mean," Sadie said. "You are a good-looking woman. You have your figure back. It's spring. The men have come back. They ask about you." She took a step closer and lowered her voice. "Jewell asks about you, too."

"I'm just not ready yet," Gloria said. "MacGregan comes in the evenings to see his girl. I can't very well ask him to watch the babies so I can go entertain a few of his friends. What would he think?"

Sadie stared at her. "What do you think he thinks? He thinks you're *eine Dirne*. The girls are starting to talk, Gloria. This is a whorehouse, not an orphanage."

"Danny and Kate aren't orphans. They have—"

"Parents? Do you think you're that girl's mama? Do you think MacGregan plans to be Danny's new papa? He is using you, Gloria. You are his cow until he can get a real one up here."

Gloria wrenched her arm from Sadie's amazingly strong grasp. "What do you know about it?"

"I know enough. I know he is planning to leave as soon as he can get a wagon and supplies together."

Gloria felt as if she'd swallowed a rock. True, she and John William didn't talk much when he came to visit Kate. The times were often awkward and silent, consisting of his holding his daughter, head bowed low over her tiny body, and low, whispered phrases Gloria could not understand. Then he would leave, tipping his hat and saying, "Thank you, ma'am." But surely, Gloria thought, if he planned on leaving Silver Peak he would have said something.

"Did he tell you he was leaving?"

"No, of course he did not tell me." Sadie moved to a second line and started hanging bed linens. "He never darkens the door of the house. Not since that night. But he talks to his friends, and his friends talk to me, and they say he is leaving after the next payout. They say he has promised his cabin to Bud Lindstrom in trade for some tools."

Gloria looked at Danny and Kate, nestled together in a large basket on the ground. The basket itself sat on a strip of oilcloth so the dampness of the earth wouldn't seep through. They were both awake, and four tiny fists swung aimlessly in the air. They emitted tiny, grunting, happy noises. Gloria estimated that it had been about two hours since they last nursed, and she could feel her breasts growing heavy in anticipation of the next feeding. Kate first, since Danny was a little more patient, a little less pushy than the seemingly insatiable Kate. At first, Gloria worried that Kate would take all the milk, leaving none for her son, but through the weeks she became more and more amazed at the capabilities of her body to meet the needs of both children.

Now, as she looked at baby Kate, her tiny fist brought up so she could suck on her knuckled finger, Gloria was hit with a feeling of loss.

"Why wouldn't he say something about leaving?" Gloria said, more to the sheets than to Sadie. "What about his daughter?"

"Well, I have my theory," Sadie said.

"Of course you do," Gloria said, amused.

"I think he is a good man at heart. But he cannot know what to do, alone with a baby. He is the kind of man that—well, let me just say this. Be careful."

"Careful? Why?"

"Careful that he doesn't take off in the middle of the night and leave you with both of those kids. A man on his own has got no use for a baby girl."

"He wouldn't do that."

"Oh no? Men do it all the time. Where is your baby's father? For that matter, where is your own?"

Gloria remembered searching the faces of the countless men who frequented her mother's room, studying their features, trying to find a small bit of herself in them.

"This is different," Gloria said. "Danny's father is out there somewhere with no idea he has a child. My mother didn't know who my father was."

"You think because he has made a few visits and held that baby, MacGregan is going to take her off to a farm?"

"He doesn't just hold her. It's like he—" Gloria searched for a word, "like he worships her."

"Well, he can worship her all he wants, but he cannot feed her and she will not be any help on the farm. Is he coming to see her tonight?"

"I suppose. He comes most evenings."

"Well, then," Sadie said, clipping the last of the sheets on the line, "you must tell him what you know."

～ 8 ～

$\mathcal{Y}$ou're early," Gloria said as she opened her door to the heavy persistent knock. "Danny and Kate are still sleeping."

John William normally arrived just at dusk, freshly washed after a day spent in the mine. Often Gloria caught the scent of a harsh soap as he breezed past, barely acknowledging her in a rush to take his daughter up into his arms.

But now it was just late afternoon. The girls hadn't even called her over for supper yet, and the babies were still down for their afternoon nap. She realized that this was a part of her life John William had no concept of. He took no part in the day-to-day routine of caring for two infants. As far as he knew, Kate spent her days nestled in her makeshift cradle waiting for the hour or so she would spend in her father's arms.

"They'll probably sleep for another hour or more," Gloria continued, "and then it'll be time for Kate to nurse and then, of course, Danny, so if you'd like to—"

"I need to talk to you," John William said.

"All right." Gloria was glad for the interruption of her nervous chatter. She motioned to his accustomed chair in the corner of her cabin.

The earlier conversation with Sadie played over in her mind, and Gloria braced herself to be strong. She perched on the edge of her bed, faced him, and assumed an expression of what she hoped came across as curiosity.

"I'm leavin'," John William said. "I can't stay here anymore."

Gloria considered her options for reply—anger, sadness, indignation—but she was shocked at John William's next statement.

"And I need you to come with me."

"What?"

"I know it seems sudden, but it's not, really. This place is dyin'. There's no fortune to be made here."

"It's just a dry spell," Gloria said, not quite sure if she was trying to reassure him or simply buy time. "It happens all the time. The next mother lode might come tomorrow."

"No it won't." He stood and took the few steps necessary to cross over to the window. He pulled aside Gloria's curtain and spoke as if to the camp as a whole. "There's no water to sluice the veins. We've just about tapped it out. They've just about decided to close down production."

"When?"

"Probably not till end of summer. But I can't wait that long."

Gloria looked around her little room. Her four walls. In it was the only bed she'd never had to share. Hanging from the window were the only curtains she'd ever owned. This was a home, her first.

John William's voice continued to linger at the margins of her thoughts.

"If I wait until they officially shut down production," he said, "they can claim my property. That means my goods, as well as any of the gold I have."

"How much do you have?" Gloria asked.

"Enough to start over," John William said, turning to look at her for the first time. "To build a new life."

"And just where would this new life be?"

"Oregon."

"Oregon? Since when is there gold in Oregon?"

"There isn't," John William said. "There's land. I don't think I was ever meant to do this," he gestured vaguely at the gritty world outside of Gloria's cabin. "After I—well, married Katherine—our plan was to farm. We just got wind of the silver here and my— Katherine wanted us to make a go of it."

"So why not try to make a go of it again? Try South Pass, it's not ten miles from here, and I know it's still going strong. Or maybe Virginia City. I've been there. It's still spitting silver faster than a man can spend it."

As she spoke, Gloria's voice was rising. There was a tiny rustle from the basket atop her bed, and the tiniest squawk came from little Kate's mouth. John William scooped up his daughter and held her, cradled in the crook of his arm. He bent his head to hers, whispered a greeting, and looked at Gloria again.

"I don't want her livin' where the land spits silver," he said. "There's nothin' good for her here. I don't want her to be wild, to grow up around—"

"People like me?"

"I didn't say that."

"You were about to."

"No, I wasn't."

Kate was fully awake now, her blue eyes taking in the full vision of her father's face. A contented gurgle escaped her mouth, and another escaped her other end. The tension in the room was immediately broken, and both Gloria and John William laughed.

"I think she needs a change," Gloria said, reaching to take the baby.

"I think you're right. Should I leave?"

"Leave?" Gloria said. "Listen, MacGregan, if you're planning to take this little one off to the Oregon Territory, you're going to have to learn to change a diaper. Open that top drawer and fetch out a clean one."

John William pulled a clean square of linen from the top drawer of the bureau in the corner.

"You're forgetting somethin'," he said, handing Gloria the clean diaper and watching, fascinated, as she deftly removed the soiled one. "I asked you to come with me. I need you to take care of Kate."

Gloria was thankful to have the task at hand to command her attention. She couldn't decide if she felt gratitude or fear. She'd never been needed before, not for any noble cause, anyway. How many evenings had she sat around various parlors with her fellow prostitutes, talking about the moment when some man would come along and offer to take them away from that life? Rescue by marriage had never been Gloria's longing, but from the dreamy expressions of younger girls and the hardened expressions of the older women, she knew that any life with any one man was preferable to life with hundreds of them. Now, here she stood, on the threshold of an opportunity to take her away from the shame she'd created, and she was gripped with crippling inde-cision. This was no leap she was willing to take without being certain of just how and where she would land.

"What about Danny?" she asked. Kate was freshly diapered, and Gloria handed her back over to John William.

"What do you mean?"

"Well, how does he figure into the picture?"

"Danny's your son," John William said softly. "He figures in with you, of course."

"What about his father?"

"His father?"

"Yes. Or didn't you think he had one?"

"I guess I never—"

"No, of course you didn't. I know I'm a whore, but I do have some sense of…" her voice trailed in search of a word. "I mean, it wouldn't be right to just take off in the night with another man's child, would it?"

"Do you know, then, wh—um, where his father is?"

"You meant to ask if I know *who* his father is. And the answer is yes to that one. *Where* he is is another story."

"Is he here, do you think? Is that why you came here?"

"Here seemed just as good a place to look as any," Gloria said. "I came where I had friends."

"No family?"

"Not until Danny." Gloria turned her attention to the baby boy, still asleep despite the rise and fall of the voices in the room.

"And while I appreciate your offer, I just don't think I'm ready to go off and become some farmer's wife."

There was a beat of silence in the room, then John William said, "I'm not askin' you to be my wife."

The life Gloria led to this point offered few opportunities for her to feel embarrassment. Shame, sometimes, but true embarrassment was a reaction she wasn't sure she was capable of. Until now.

"Oh," was all she could reply.

"Don't get me wrong," John William said. Kate was beginning to fuss, and he jostled her a bit to comfort her. "I just—"

"You just what? Figure I have no life so I can just pull up what I got and haul off with you? You think I got no better future than to play wet nurse to your brat until she takes herself off and you can drop me off in some God-forsaken ditch in the middle of the wilderness?"

Gloria's voice swelled with anger even as her breasts swelled with milk for the now crying Kate. She was infuriated at her body's betrayal, wishing she could refuse John William the help he needed. With a sound of impatience, she took the fussy girl away from this man who, all of a sudden, seemed too clumsy and inept to hold a child much less comfort one. Gloria made a soft shushing noise as she placed the knuckle of her first finger into the baby's mouth. Little Kate's powerful gums gripped her finger, and Gloria knew this child would not be appeased for long.

This cozy picture of maternal comfort seemed out of place with the glare of pure hatred she leveled at John William, who met her gaze head on. The previous air of bumbling apology was gone. When he spoke now, it was with a voice of authority and resolve.

"Look, I meant no harm in askin' you to come with me. I didn't figure I had a choice but to ask you, and it ain't no kind of life living without choice. And as much as I need you, I didn't want you to feel locked into anythin' you didn't want. I need you now," he said, reaching across to stroke his daughter's face, "but I won't need you forever."

Gloria took a few deep breaths, composing herself and allowing her heart to resume its normal, steady beat.

"How much do you have?" she asked.

John William looked confused.

"You said you had enough to start over," Gloria said, her voice low and calm. "Just how much is that?"

"In ounces or dollars?"

"Dollars. Ounces don't mean anything north of California."

John William raised his eyes as if in calculation before replying, "About nine hundred."

"That's it?" Gloria said. "You weren't meant for this, were you?"

"I've done some tradin'. A wagon, a team, some supplies."

"Here's our deal," Gloria said. "I'll come with you, me and Danny that is, and I'll do my part." Gloria felt as if she truly had the upper hand for the first time in her life.

"And?"

"And when I'm no longer *needed*," she felt a twinge of triumph when John William winced, "I'll be on my way."

"Sounds fair."

"With five hundred dollars—"

"Hey, now—"

"For my services."

"I'm not interested in your *services*."

"Maybe not," Gloria said, "but men pay me for the use of my body, and you're using my body. You'll pay for it. Oh, and one more thing."

"I can't imagine."

"When I leave, I leave Danny with you."

"You can't mean that." John William's eyes darted over to the tiny boy nestled in slumber. "You can't think of abandonin' your son."

"Think of it this way," Gloria said. "I save Kate's life, you save Danny's. I don't plan to live any kind of life that a child should be a part of."

"What about his father? Is it right for you to leave another man's child with a stranger?"

Gloria looked at John William with the expression that practically guaranteed any man's compliance. "I guess I owe you the truth. I don't really know who Danny's father is."

"I'm sorry."

"Don't be," Gloria said. "It's nothing to do with you. It's just like my own mama used to say: 'Darlin', I could marry myself to the king of France about as easy as I could name your daddy.'"

Gloria had never spoken these words aloud, and was shocked that they held none of the humor they always seemed to when her mother spoke them to her. Maybe it was the whiskey slur that had lent them warmth all those years ago.

"So you see," she continued, "I got no reason to stay. And nowhere to go. I got no choice, either. When do we leave?"

"How soon can you be packed?" John William awkwardly brushed the hair from his face. It was the same gesture he'd done that first night he brought Kate, and Gloria noted that it was a telltale sign of nervous resolve.

"How soon do you need me?" she asked.

"The next payout is Friday. I'd like to leave the next mornin'."

Three days.

Gloria took a quick mental inventory. Three dresses; two babies. Everything else—the furniture, the bedding—all of it belonged to Jewell. Just as her mother had done, Gloria would fill the little green suitcase with all her possessions, hers and the children's, and migrate to the next place.

"How early?"

"First light."

"We'll be ready. Now go, I need to feed this little one before she chews through to the bone."

John William smiled and said, "Thank you, Gloria." He looked up and said, "Thank you, God."

Then he bent to kiss his daughter before leaving. As he did so, long strands of his brown hair brushed Gloria's chemise. She looked down and realized she'd never, in all her years, felt this close to any man.

It terrified her.

John William opened the cabin door to the spring afternoon, but before leaving he turned to say one last thing.

"By the way, France doesn't have a king."

Gloria stared, puzzled.

"You said you couldn't marry the king of France any more than you could name Danny's father. Well, from what I've heard, France doesn't have a king right now, so I guess you're no worse off than any other woman. See you at dawn on Saturday."

9

*I*n her life, Gloria had never said good-bye to anyone, but there would be no sneaking away from Silver Peak. Sadie was at Gloria's door the minute John William left, peppering Gloria with questions about their plans.

"What makes you think we have plans?" Gloria asked. Sharing her life was a new experience, and not one she was completely comfortable with.

"Oh, everybody knows you have plans," Sadie said. "A man doesn't sell off his tools and buy a team unless he is planning something."

"That doesn't mean—" Sadie shot Gloria such a look that she sighed in resignation. "We're leaving on Saturday."

"I knew it!" Sadie poked Gloria's shoulder. "I knew he would take you with him."

"It's not forever," Gloria said.

"Nothing is. But it's for now, and that's enough. Let's go tell the girls."

Then came the flutter of activity. Gloria found herself in the center of such bustling and care, she didn't know whether to be grateful, humble, or annoyed. A dozen petticoats were sacrificed to make diapers and dresses for the babies. Jewell's kitchen was combed through, and any spare dish or utensil was packed in a straw-lined crate. Sadie took the quilt from her own bed, cut it in half, and created a soft, downy lining for the babies' makeshift cradles. Mae took stock of Gloria's wardrobe and decided that none of it would do. After giving Gloria a sly wink and a pat on the shoulder, she secluded herself in her room.

The night before Gloria was to leave, the women gathered in her cabin, sitting where they could find space and nibbling some of Biddy's delicious apple spice cookies.

"I made an extra batch for you to take," Biddy said shyly. "I hope Mr. MacGregan thinks they're good."

"Of course he will," Gloria said through a mouthful of cookie. "It'll be nice to have a treat when we're out in the wilderness."

"Wilderness?" Sadie said, laughing. "Where do you think you are now?"

Gloria and the others joined in her laughter. True, Silver Peak was nothing like the larger cities where Gloria had lived, but she'd heard about the vast miles of loneliness on the trail to Oregon, and she wasn't sure if she was up to the hardships of such travel.

"Well, you certainly can't wear *that* out in the wilderness," Mae said, gesturing broadly toward Gloria's dress. Although Gloria had worn some of Mae's much larger skirts during the final months before Danny was born, her slim figure had returned and she was again wearing her own dresses.

"What's wrong with this?" Gloria asked. She had never worn flashy clothes, but she did insist on rich, quality fabrics. Now she wore a two-piece dress, peacock green with black velvet trim.

"It's just a bit…"

"Fancy?" Biddy's tiny voice filled the awkward silence.

"That's the word," Mae said. "Fancy. You'll need clothes that are just a bit more…"

"Ugly?" Sadie chimed in.

"Serviceable," Mae said, tossing Sadie a disdainful look. "Simple clothes. Looser, easy to clean." As she spoke, Mae was delving into the satchel she'd brought with her to the cabin. Out of it came heaps of fabric that, with a flourished snap, were seen to be blouses and skirts.

"Mr. Brady brought such lovely bolts in the last supply," Mae's musical voice continued. "I've been working on these since you told us you were leaving."

The cabin was filled with excitement as Gloria tried on the new clothes. They were a perfect fit, the blouses lightweight and long sleeved, each one dressed with a row of pretty wooden buttons. There were three in all, and two skirts of a solid, sturdy fabric to go with them. Mae fussed over every seam, and the women giggled with each new outfit, declaring that Gloria looked like quite the "farmer's wife" despite her protests that she was nothing of the sort. When their giggling escalated, Gloria hushed them, lest the sleeping babies wake.

"Let me just take up the hem on this one," Mae said. It was a third skirt, made from the same fabric as one of the blouses—dark brown littered with tiny red flowers. "I'm afraid it will just get dragged through mud and ruined. I'll have it ready by morning." These last words were spoken as Mae headed toward the door, skirt flung over one arm.

"Mae," Gloria called after her, "that's really not—"

"Let her do it," Sadie said softly, her hand on Gloria's arm. "It will make her feel good."

The window was open, and the fresh spring evening floated past the curtains. The absence of Mae's chatter left a comfortable silence in the room. Gloria, Sadie, and Biddy sipped steaming mugs of tea and made a collected effort to ignore the wave of masculine laughter drifting across the yard that separated them from Jewell's parlor.

"Sounds like a crowd," Gloria said.

Nobody spoke.

"Brisk night like this," she continued, "brings them out of the woods, it seems."

Still no response.

"Reckon Jewell's gonna be tearing over here lookin' for—"

"The new girls can handle it," Sadie said. "Tonight, I just…"

Silence returned for a moment until Biddy's tiny voice said, "You are so lucky."

"Who's lucky?" Gloria asked.

"You are." Biddy lifted her eyes and forced Gloria to meet her gaze. "You don't have to go over there."

"Listen, Liebling," Sadie said, "none of us has to go over there tonight. Tonight, we are just sitting here talking. Like old friends."

"That's just tonight," Biddy said. "What about tomorrow night? And the next? Gloria's getting a home. A family. She'll never have to do this again."

"Now wait just a minute," Gloria said. "I'm going to be back, you know."

Biddy looked at Gloria with a wide-eyed, incredulous stare. "Why would you come back?"

"Because the alternative is spendin' the rest of her life dirt poor and pregnant, stompin' kitchen mice with her bare feet."

The three women turned, startled as Jewell's husky voice invaded their conversation. Her pudgy hand reached in through the open window, grasped the curtain, and snatched it aside to reveal her puffy, rouged face.

"Jewell, you dog," Sadie cried, blotting at the tea she'd spilled in her lap. "You scared us to death!"

"Hush!" Gloria hissed. "You'll wake up the babies."

"In case you ladies of leisure hadn't noticed," Jewell continued, her lowered voice taking on a more menacing quality, "we're getting quite a crowd gathered over at the house. Rumor has it they're looking for some company. And here I see some lovely ladies who would be just perfect for the job." She perched her elbows on the windowsill and seemed to be settling in for a long conversation. It was the same pose Gloria had seen her in when she first arrived at Silver Peak.

"Please, Jewell," Sadie said, "we are just having a nice evening here."

"Yeah. And there's some gentlemen with pockets full of money who want to have a nice evening, too."

Biddy seemed to be shrinking into her chair. Her head drooped down until her chin touched her chest.

"So break out a bottle and give them some cards," Sadie said, one hand drifting protectively to Biddy's shoulder. "These men are pretty easily entertained."

"They don't *pay* to play cards," Jewell said. "I think it's time you girls remember that you work for me. I ain't exactly runnin' a tea room."

"Why don't you come in and join us?" Gloria asked, gesturing toward the chair recently vacated by Mae.

"Aw, I don't know," Jewell said. "I've got some company to tend to."

"Come on, Jewell," Sadie said. "Sit and have a drink with us. It is Gloria's last night."

"I'll get you some tea," Biddy said, scuttling from her chair.

But the next second Jewell burst through the door holding her slim silver flask. "Never mind the tea, little one. I brought my own drink."

Jewell settled her generous bottom into the chair. Her breathing was labored, and each puff carried the tiniest whiff of pungent gin. Baby Danny let out a little yelp and stretched himself into a state of full wakefulness.

"So, the little prince is up, eh?" Jewell said before taking a generous swig from her flask. "I don't wanna listen to him scream."

Gloria scooped Danny up from his bed and held him to her shoulder, delighted at the way his face nuzzled into her neck.

"You know," Jewell continued, a slight slur invading her speech, "I sure ain't gonna miss listenin' to them kids wailin' all hours."

"Not much of a mother type, are you?" Sadie said.

"No more'n you are. I'm the mama to all my girls. That's enough for me."

Gloria noticed a slight shudder from Biddy.

Jewell leaned forward in her chair and pointed with her flask. "And from what I know, your mamas weren't no different from me."

"You're not like my mother," Biddy said quietly. "You're not like her at all."

"Well, listen, little missy," Jewell said, "you're more than welcome to head on out and make a life on your own. Like our little friend here."

Gloria held Danny closer. "Stop it, Jewell," she said.

"But she really isn't on her own, is she? No ma'am. She's living every whore's dream."

"And just what dream is that?" Sadie asked. "Getting stuck with some man's baby? Or getting hauled off to some God-forsaken wilderness to churn butter and watch crops shrivel in the sun?"

"I'm not going to churn butter," Gloria said, but neither woman acknowledged her.

"It's the dream," Jewell said, leaning forward, "of some man comin' along, sweepin' you off your back, and takin' you to be the little wife."

"You are forgetting," Sadie said, "that lots of us have been the little wife. I have been the little wife. It is not my dream."

"It's my dream," Biddy said. Jewell shot her a look that sent her skittering back into silence.

"If you must know," Gloria said, standing to walk the newly restless Danny, "it isn't my dream, either. And it isn't his."

"He is a good man," Sadie said. "He will marry you. I know he will."

"I don't want him to marry me. Besides, he won't *because* he's such a good man."

Jewell let out a gasping expletive and settled back into her chair. "Just what is that supposed to mean?"

Gloria didn't know how to explain it. Every time John William came to visit, he prayed. Every time he held his daughter, a reverent calm came over him. He had a presence of strength and peace about him, making him so unlike any man she'd ever known. He had loved his wife. He loved his daughter. He had never shown Gloria any measure of disrespect, but treated her with such distanced politeness that she felt like a piece of furniture in the room. Other religious men made her feel dirty, unworthy. John William just made her aware of all she was lacking in her life. He also made it clear that he had no interest in making her anything other that what she was.

"It means men like him don't marry women like me," Gloria said.

"So you think you're just going to come crawlin' back here *again* when this one's had enough of you?" Jewell gestured with her open flask. "Tell me, is that what happened with Danny's pa?"

"I came here," Gloria said, "because I thought you'd be able to help me. Give me a place to stay until I figured things out. Well, I've figured things out and I'll be gone in the morning."

"And just what," Jewell said, staggering to her feet to confront the now pacing Gloria, "do I get out of this whole deal? Men been climbin' the walls for you and I got to tell them, 'Oh, no, she just had the baby. Give her time. Give her a few weeks.' Well, it's over two months now, you eatin' my food, takin' up prime space, and tomorrow you go traipsin' off with some man without earnin' or payin' me one red cent."

The last of these words were spoken so close to Gloria's face that the sour smell of whiskey was overpowering. Danny balled up a little fist and was working up to a wail until Gloria switched him to the other shoulder to distance him from Jewell.

"She's earned her keep," Sadie said. "She has done her share."

"Of what?" Jewell swung around to face Sadie, nearly losing her balance. "Of dishes? Washing? Servin' drinks? She's givin' this little one ideas that you can earn your place in my house without doin' the very business my house is here for."

Biddy cringed further into her chair, avoiding the hand that gestured so near her face.

"Look, Jewell," Gloria said, "I gave you everything I—"

"Don't start with that, sweetie," Jewell said. "I know what a piece like you goes for in the big towns, and I know you had to walk out of there with more than what you gave me."

"I told you I—"

"And I get nothin' in return. Nothin' for givin' up such a nice place for you and that little bas—"

"Don't call him that," Biddy said. She stood and held her arms out for Gloria to hand the baby over to her. "He's a sweet little boy, and he's going to have a father."

"Ah, yes," Jewell said. "The sainted John William MacGregan. Tell me, Gloria, how much of your little fortune did you promise to this man?"

"That's a terrible thing to say," Sadie said, standing now, too. "MacGregan doesn't need her money."

"I don't have any money," Gloria said. "Besides, I don't think he'd take it if I did."

Jewell snorted. "Why, ain't it good enough for him?"

"I didn't say that."

"Good Glory, girl," Jewell said, her voice thick with exaspera-tion. "*You're* not good enough for him? Your *money* ain't good enough for him? What kind of saint do you think *he* is? Because I know a few things about this man, and he don't have much right to tell you—"

"Stop right there, Jewell." Sadie placed herself between Jewell and Gloria. Biddy sat, quiet in her chair, shielding Danny from the confrontation.

"No, I got to say this, Sadie. I can put up with a lot of things, but I just can't stand a hypocrite."

"He's not—"

Jewell threw up a hand to hush her. "This one," she pointed to Biddy, "thinks a baby ain't illegitimate just because it's sweet. This one thinks that she ain't really a prostitute if she hides her cash and plays at bein' a pioneer. You think a man can have him-self a little family and make everyone forget that he's a—"

"Stop it, Jewell!"

"A what?" Gloria asked, concerned.

"Nothing," Sadie said, looking at Jewell intently. Sadie faced her head on, squaring her shoulders and pulling herself to her full height, a full head taller than Jewell. As she spoke, she took step after step, forcing Jewell to back up to the door. "He's a good, honest, kind man. He'll be a kind, gentle, loving father."

"I just think she should know," Jewell said.

"Know what?" Gloria asked.

"Tell me, Jewell," Sadie said, "is this the concerned mother coming out? Or is this just a bitter old woman who can't stand the thought of anybody being happy?"

By now, Jewell was up against the door. Sadie reached around behind her to grab the latch and push the door open.

"Get out," she said.

"Gloria invited me. It's still her house tonight."

"Jewell," Gloria said, "I'll be back. I'll make it up to you, everything that I owe you. I promise."

"You just be careful," Jewell said, straining to see around Sadie. "You just remember who you are and don't let anyone tell you different. He ain't no better than you, not by a mile."

With that, she left, and Sadie shut the door. By now little Danny was beyond comfort, and Kate was beginning to stir.

"What did she mean?" Gloria asked, taking Danny away from Biddy and settling down to nurse.

"Nothing to concern yourself with." Sadie crossed the room and took baby Kate into her arms. "I'm really going to miss this little one."

"What aren't you telling me about MacGregan?"

"It's nothing you need to know. Listen, Gloria, he is a good man. You know that. But he isn't perfect. Nobody is."

"Jewell seemed—"

"Jewell doesn't want you to be happy. Jewell doesn't want you to leave. You can't trust her to tell you anything."

"But I should trust you?"

"Trust her," Biddy said. "He might not be a husband, but he'll be a good father for your little one. Which is more important?"

Gloria looked down at the beautiful face of her son, tugging hungrily at her breast. Right now she was all he needed, but she couldn't imagine what kind of man she could possibly groom him to be.

"Do I need to be afraid?" Gloria asked.

"Absolutely not." Sadie knelt at Gloria's feet. She laid baby Kate in her skirts and smiled down into the tiny face. "I would never let anyone hurt you. Or them."

"Look," Biddy said, her voice excited. She was looking out the window. "Ben Danglars is coming to visit." She turned and smiled, flushed. "I think he fancies me."

"Go talk to him," Sadie said, her voice full of affection for this young girl. "Just talk to him. Don't go upstairs."

"What if he wants to go upstairs?"

"Most of these men are just lonely," Sadie said. "They want someone to talk to just as much as anything. Talk to him."

Biddy's face beamed a picture of excitement and relief. With more life than Gloria had ever seen in her, she skipped to the door.

"Wait, take that with you." Gloria nodded her head toward the green dress with black velvet trim she had been wearing earlier in the evening. "You'll have to get Mae to cut it down a bit, but it's yours."

Biddy ran over to hug Gloria's neck and bent to kiss the baby. Then, clutching her new treasure, she bounded from the room.

"Well, that's a fine thing," Sadie said with mock reproach. "Maybe I wanted that dress."

Gloria laughed at the idea of this burly woman trying to fit into her clothes. "I have a better present for you, Sadie. You can have my curtains."

"Your curtains?" Sadie said, as if Gloria had promised her all the gold in California. "You would really give me such a treasure?"

Gloria smiled at the sarcasm. "Trust me. You'll get a lot more use out of them than you would any of my old dresses. Besides, they're very special to me. They were part of the last room I shared with my mother."

"So, why don't you want to take them with you?"

"Because I don't want to take any part of that life with me. Because I want them to be a gift. To you. Promise to take them down right after I leave. Don't let Jewell have them. Take them to your room and keep them for yourself. Will you promise me that?"

"I promise."

The evening darkened steadily as Gloria sat, sometimes in conversation, sometimes in silence, with the only friend she'd ever had. Late in the night, Sadie left so Gloria could have a good night's rest. But Gloria did not sleep. Silent in the darkness, she moved about the tiny cabin getting her things together. She would take only the new outfits Mae had sewn for her; every other dress she owned she draped carefully over the room's two chairs. She opened the green case that had become her mother's legacy and prepared to fill it with her meager possessions. But, before she did, there was one final thing to do.

Working by moonlight, Gloria gently pried the fabric lining from inside the lid of the case. She groped around inside the opening; small notes crumpled in her hands. She counted them in the pale silver square of light that fell just below the window until she knew it was all there. One thousand dollars. Cash.

Carefully, making sure to keep her head clear of the window, Gloria used the tiny scissors of her sewing kit to snip the hem of the yellow sprigged curtains. Then, two by two, spread evenly to disguise any bulges, each note was tucked into the hem, and the hem meticulously re-stitched. It was the only feat of sewing Gloria had ever attempted. The kit itself had been a gift from Mae.

Satisfied, she fell across her bed into a restive, uneven sleep.

In just a few hours, moonlight became dawn, and John William MacGregan arrived, sitting high in a wagon driven by a strong team of horses.

He tipped his hat to her, and she knew he was a gentleman.

He showed her the space in the back of the wagon he had cleared for the babies' makeshift beds, and she knew he would be a kind and loving father.

When Mae came bustling out of the house to bring Gloria the newly hemmed skirt, he sent her right back inside to wrap it in paper to protect it from any trail dust.

When Sadie and the other girls ceremoniously presented her with the calico bonnet and laughingly proclaimed her "Queen of the Oregon Trail," he went down on one knee and cupped his hands to make a step for her to climb up into the wagon.

Gloria had never considered her feet to be small, but once John William's massive grip enveloped her foot, she had the distinct impression that if he were to apply even the slightest pressure, he could crush every bone. But she knew just as well that the same strength could lift her, effortlessly, into this wagon and into a new life. When she looked at him for reassurance, his mischievous grin gave no indication which of the two he was more inclined to do.

Saints and angels, joined in concert,
Sing the praises of the Lamb;
While the blissful seats of heaven
Sweetly echo with his name.

10

John William woke up, amazed again that he'd been able to sleep at all. The previous night, with his body stretched to its full length on the makeshift bedroll, he swore he'd not see a minute's rest. The length of the oil-skinned tarp was barely six feet long, so he had to choose between subjecting his head or his heels to the damp of the bare ground. All of the bedding he'd brought from the cabin he shared with Katherine was inside the wagon serving as a comparatively luxurious bed for Gloria. He himself was covered with a coarse, small wool blanket that would not cover him completely if he lay flat on his back. When he did so, his shoulder blades rested on different levels, and a pebble lodged itself into the base of his spine. But the exhaustion of the day soon overtook him, and his physical discomfort was lost in waves of sleep.

Now, opening his eyes to the familiar gray just before dawn, he gingerly flexed his legs as if unfamiliar with their function. Then, just as he had for the past two weeks since leaving Silver Peak, he coaxed his limbs into doing his bidding and began to prepare for another day's journey. He rose slowly, working out the kinks and cramps as he stretched to his full height. He'd slept in the clothes he wore the day before, and now he stripped off his shirt and made his way to the stream they'd made camp next to. He knelt to splash his face with stinging cold water and scoop handfuls of it over his arms, chest, and back. He allowed the last of the night air to dry his body on the walk back to camp. Once there, he took a clean shirt from the satchel lashed to the side of the wagon and pressed an ear against the canvas to see if there was any stirring inside.

There were no sounds coming from within, save for the deep steady breathing of Gloria and the babies. He vaguely remembered hearing a few muted cries and whispers sometime during the night, but the depth of his fatigue kept him from rousing fully. Gloria slept in a nest of quilts, Danny and Kate within an arm's reach. John William had never been invited into that sanctuary, but every night he peeked in to see that they were settled comfortably.

Now he stood outside the canvas and whispered, "Gloria?"

No response. He cleared his throat and spoke again, a little louder.

"Gloria? Are you awake?"

When there was still no answer, he opened the flap at the back of the wagon and peered into the warm, dark space. He saw the tangled mass of blond curls just inches away and debated whether to reach in and nudge the shoulder hidden beneath it.

"Gloria. It's almost daylight and—"

"Shhh." The sound was almost imperceptible.

"You need to—"

"Shhh!"

Now the blond mass was moving as Gloria raised herself to one elbow and turned to look at John William. Her hair was loose and covered her face at such an angle that only one eye, barely blue in the dawning light, could be seen. He got just a glimpse of a bare, white shoulder and quickly turned away.

"If you say another word and wake up those babies I'll kill you," Gloria said, no hint of humor to her whispered tone. "Danny just went back to sleep."

"Those babies can sleep as long as they like," John William said, "but the sun's near up and we got to get breakfast and hit the trail before the day's gone."

"I don't cook, remember?" Gloria said, burrowing into her nest.

"Maybe you don't cook it," John William said, "but you sure do eat it and you sure will clean up the mess, so you best get yourself out here before I start bangin' the skillet till those babies holler."

He dropped the tent flap, wishing he had a door to slam, and wondered, as he had just about every day since that first morning when Gloria climbed up on the wagon seat with her little green case, just how his life had taken this turn.

He strode to the front of the wagon, hauled the cook box off the front seat, and rummaged through it. There were biscuits left from last night's supper wrapped in the blue tea towels that had been a wedding gift from Katherine's sister, a few slices of salt pork, and three eggs. This meal would just about exhaust their food supply, leaving just a few apples and a hefty wedge of cheese for lunch. He fully expected to make Fort Bridger before sundown.

The coffee was simmering on the little cookstove on the campfire when Gloria emerged from the wagon. Her hair was pulled back in a single loose braid that dangled to the small of her back. She wore a white cotton chemise, loosely laced, with a heavy green shawl draped over her shoulders. Her eyes were still half-closed, and her steps unsteady. She took a tin cup from the hook where it dangled, drying after last night's washing.

"Coffee," she mumbled.

John William answered with a rough gesture toward the pot. Gloria remained, immobile, holding her cup in front of her. After a moment, she gave up, huffed, and reached for the pot herself.

"Use a towel," John William said. Burning her fingers on the coffeepot handle had become an almost daily ritual.

"I know," Gloria said, her voice tinged with resentment. She reached for the blue tea towel, and the leftover biscuits tumbled into the dirt. She whispered a curse and squinted up at John William.

"Sorry."

"Not a problem," John William said, his voice a mixture of amusement and annoyance. "We can just dust 'em off."

He watched Gloria blink and shake her head, apparently

trying to focus on pouring the coffee. This morning it was a fairly successful accomplishment; only a few drops sloshed over the edge of the cup and onto the biscuits at her feet. John William, deciding it was worth the risk, held out his cup.

"I'll take some more of that."

"Certainly," Gloria said, her voice filled with exaggerated courtesy. She angled the pot over the cup and filled it just to the top.

"Very good, Miss Gloria," John William said, carefully bringing the cup to his lips. "You've made quite an improvement. Do you feel up to fryin' a few eggs?"

"Listen, MacGregan. The deal was that I feed your daughter, not that I feed you."

Gloria settled onto one of the campstools and wrapped both her hands around her cup.

"Right, then," John William said, trying to keep the annoyance out of his voice. "Do you think you can bring yourself to clean off the biscuits you dropped?"

"I think I'm up to that." Gloria picked them up one by one, swiped them across her skirt, and deposited them on the plate they had fallen from.

"Better?"

John William took a biscuit from the plate, dunked it into his coffee, and popped it, whole, into his mouth. They passed several minutes in comfortable silence, sipping coffee and listening to the sizzling of salt pork in the frying pan. When it was cooked through, John William drained most of the fat into the drippings jar, leaving some in the pan to fry the eggs. He broke them one at a time, careful not to let the whites run together.

"I'll fry them hard," he said. "Don't want to waste the yolks."

Gloria made a contented-sounding noise through a sip of coffee.

"Plates?"

Gloria rose dutifully to get the plates from their drying rack at the back of the wagon. She handed one to John William, and on it he placed a slice of salt pork, two eggs, and two biscuits.

"Eat up," he said. "We're in for a long day."

Gloria took the plate from him and returned to her seat. She dug in with her fork and didn't look up until John William was settled across from her. He bowed his head over his plate and sensed that Gloria stopped chewing mid-bite.

"Dear God," he prayed, "we thank You for this food You have provided for us. We thank You for the strength it will provide for us as we journey this day. Bless our journey. Keep me on the path You would have me follow. Give us the strength to overcome our obstacles. Watch over me and Gloria and little Danny and Kate. Amen."

He opened his eyes and looked at Gloria and waited for her to echo his "amen." She didn't. She never had. Instead she swallowed the bit of food sheltered in her mouth during the blessing and gestured toward his plate with her fork.

"You don't want the other egg?" she asked.

"No, no. You eat it."

"What about our long day?"

"It'll be longer listenin' to you complain all day about being hungry."

"You know," she said, dunking a biscuit into her coffee, "if you ate more you might not need to pray for strength."

"I could eat an ox a day and still need to rely on my Lord," John William said with such an air of finality that Gloria returned to her breakfast, eating with a little less relish.

When they'd finished, John William harnessed the horses while Gloria went to wash the dishes in the stream. When she returned, John William was struck by the difference in her appearance. Her pale face was tinged with pink, he guessed from a cleansing splash of the cold water. Her hair was damp, smoothed away from her face. The loose braid was now a tight plait, twisted and secured to the back of her head. She wore a pale blue blouse, tucked into her gray skirt. A wide leather belt emphasized her slim waist. She looked proper, almost severe, like a woman who would promptly throw away a biscuit that landed on the ground.

He watched her approach, the sun now full up and strong. When he saw her raise her hand, he lifted his to return the greeting, only to realize that she was shielding her eyes and did not see him in the early morning glare. Feeling foolish, he dropped his hand and returned to his task.

Just then, a lusty cry came from within the wagon.

"Somebody's awake," he said.

"Sounds like Kate." Gloria loaded the clean dishes into the cook box, and together they hoisted it to its place below the wagon's seat.

"Can we get started? Or do you want to feed her first?"

"It's late, isn't it? I can feed her in the wagon. Danny will be up soon, too."

Gloria grasped the wagon seat and began to climb up.

"Let me help you," John William said. He took her elbow and held her steady as she climbed over the wheel and settled herself on the wooden seat. Once settled, she turned, reached through the canvas opening at the front of the wagon, and plucked the impatient Kate, now fairly screaming, from the little wooden crate that served as her crib for this journey. She began unbuttoning her blouse, and John William turned away, running his fingers over the harnesses. Satisfied, he walked one more circuit around the wagon, checking to be sure that the fire was out and all their belongings were gathered and secured.

"Ready?" he asked, glancing up at Gloria.

"Could you hand me my hat?" she said. "It's just in the back."

"Of course. Wouldn't want you to burn."

He walked to the back of the wagon and found the calico bonnet.

"Here you are," he said, holding it up to her.

"Could you help me?" Gloria shrugged in gesture to the greedily nursing Kate. "My hands are full."

"So they are."

When he joined her on the seat, she bowed her head for him

to put the bonnet on. He hadn't been this close to her since the day he asked her to join him on this journey. The top of her head was just inches from his eyes, and he marveled for just a moment at the myriad colors that nestled against each other before blurring that vision with blue calico. Once the bonnet was settled on her head, Gloria lifted her face, and John William looked down the shadowy tunnel into her eyes.

"Don't choke me."

"What?" Her question jarred him from his brief reverie.

"When you tie it. Don't choke me."

"Don't tempt me," he said. But as his fingers grazed the softness of her throat and cheek, he knew that choking her was not the temptation he would need to guard against.

"That's good," Gloria said. "That feels right."

"So the princess is ready to proceed?" Just then, Kate gave a happy little kick that thrust a foot outside of the blanket she was wrapped in. John William caught the tiny foot in his hand, brought it to his lips. "Excuse me. Are the *princesses* ready to proceed?"

"We are, sir," Gloria said. "Drive on."

John William hopped down, picked his own hat off the peg on the side of the wagon, and shoved it onto his head. He gave the horse a friendly slap on its flank and took the first steps of the thousands he would take that day.

Lead me not into temptation.

The words had never had such meaning before.

Deliver me from evil.

But the glance over his shoulder yielded a vision that didn't seem evil. A woman, yes. But a woman demurely covered, face hidden, nourishing his child.

Katherine's child.

Katherine.

John William had been awake for nearly two hours this day, and this was the first time her name entered his head. He found himself pushing away blond tangles to make way for a picture of

Katherine's dark features—plain, but beautiful in their own way.

Lord, I rely on You for my strength. Give strength to my thoughts. Give strength to my heart. Give strength to my body.

"Especially my body," he said aloud.

"What was that?" Gloria asked from her wagon perch.

"Just praying."

"Again?"

"Always."

hen the sun hit full noon, John William cooed a gentle "whoa" to the team and brought the wagon to a halt.

"Time to rest," he said, as he'd said every day at this time. The horses were unharnessed and allowed to drink from a stream if they were near one, from water poured from their drinking barrel into the washtub if they weren't. A cold lunch was assembled from whatever bits and pieces of food were available. A measure of canvas was laid out on the grass, and the babies, free from their diapers and gowns, were allowed to lay and roll and squirm, their naked bodies exposed to the fresh summer air.

Often, once the horses were taken care of, John William would pluck a flower or a long stem of grass and run it, lightly, up and down the babies' bodies. He delighted in burying his face in baby Kate's belly and blowing as she kicked and squealed with laughter. This was a game he enjoyed with Danny, too, even after learning the hard way that it's much more fun when a little boy has his diaper on.

Gloria didn't play. She busied herself with putting away the lunch things, wiping down the plates. But the corner of her eye never left the frolicking scene on the canvas.

She marveled at the controlled strength of this man. She'd seen him use his bare hands to snap branches into kindling, and now those same hands gently held her infant son aloft in thrilling flight. The man who could walk alongside the wagon for hours in total silence now seemed a fountain of noise. Gibberish and song poured from his lips. His uneven features—misshapen nose, scarred skin—seemed to soften, giving him the appearance of a lovable monster, an overgrown troll.

He set Danny down and turned his attention to Kate. She lay on her stomach, struggling to hold her head up and view the world. He loomed, like a giant bear set to maul. He even made a comic growling sound before pouncing, his body creating instant shade for the little one, and running his beard up and down her spine.

His beard.

He didn't have one back in Silver Peak. Gloria wondered just when the whiskers took over his face.

Then, as it happened every afternoon, the yawn. It started always with a squinting of his eyes and a scrunching of his nose. Then his mouth opened as if the jaw were about to unhinge. He brought his fists to his shoulders, stretched his arms and arched his back, all in accompaniment to a massive, primordial yawp.

"Those babies wear me out," he said, as he did every day. "Think I need to rest up a bit. Close my eyes."

"You do just that," Gloria said, as was their routine. "I'll wake you in a little while."

Today they were stopped near a little grove of trees, and John William sought out the one with just the perfect roots to cradle his head. Once that spot was found, he stretched flat on his back and almost instantly began snoring into the heavy silent afternoon.

Gloria dampened a soft washcloth and brought it over to where the babies played. One by one, each little body was washed and let to dry in the warm summer air. Then Gloria tied a fresh diaper around each tiny belly and settled in to nurse. This afternoon, Danny was first. She brought her son to her breast; baby Kate lay in the nest of her skirt. She leaned herself against another tree, where she wouldn't be in full view of John William should he suddenly wake, yet keeping him well within her sight.

With one hand she held Danny firmly; the other hand played gently across Kate's soft, clean skin. Gloria ran one finger from the top of Kate's brow to the middle of her tummy then back up for a *bop!* on the tip of Kate's button nose.

"What a pretty, pretty girl," she whispered. "You're such a pretty girl. Do you look like your mama?"

Gloria spoke to the wide blue eyes that seemed so entranced by Gloria's own face. She'd only met Katherine MacGregan once. Now she tried to recall the woman's features, to see them in this little one's face. Gloria had never seen Katherine smile; Kate's face was constant, toothless joy. Katherine's eyes were dead, distant; Kate's eyes danced with searching curiosity. Katherine's hair was shiny, blue-black. Gloria ran her hand over Kate's soft head— perfectly bald since her second week of life.

"Or do you look like your daddy?" At this, Kate emitted a moist gurgle and kicked her little feet in delight. Gloria laughed, softly, and glanced over at the sleeping form a few feet away. The man Jewell wanted her to fear.

Her hand abandoned its job of tickling Kate and came to stroke her own son's face. Danny's eyes were closed in the contentment of suckling, but they opened wide at his mother's touch.

"And you? Do you look like your daddy?" Danny's eyes held her gaze, almost as if demanding an answer. Having none for him, Gloria looked away.

With both babies fed and dressed in clean cotton gowns, Gloria went to John William, knelt, and placed a hand on his shoulder.

"MacGregan, wake up now. Time to go."

He was instantly alert, eyes open midsnore.

"How long did I sleep?"

"Long enough."

John William laughed. "Can't argue with that. Are the babies still awake?"

Gloria sighed and rolled her eyes. "Yes, but—"

"Good. Gather 'em up."

"MacGregan, it's late. I really think we should—"

"I'm going to step over that rise for just a minute, then I'll be right back. Get everythin' ready. The Bible's up under the seat."

Muttering under her breath, Gloria went to the wagon seat and pulled out the thick leather-bound book. Then she gathered the babies, sat down, and settled them into her lap. When John William returned, he took Danny into his arms, sat down, and settled the little boy into a semireclined position supported by his leg.

Gloria handed him the Bible.

"Where were we?"

"How should I know?" Gloria said. "That's your book, not mine."

She could tell he was smiling even though he didn't look up. The tiny wrinkles at the corners of his eyes were a dead giveaway.

"It is your book, too," he said. "You should read it."

"I don't read any better than these little ones do," Gloria said. "And I don't understand it any better, either."

"My family will know God's word." John William looked Gloria straight in the eyes, his smile gone. "Now, I think we were in chapter thirty-three."

"We just read when the two brothers met each other again, when they're old."

"Ah, yes. Jacob and Esau reunited. Then we're in chapter thirty-four," he said, and he began reading. "'And Dinah the daughter of Leah, which she bare unto Jacob—'"

"I thought Jacob just had sons."

"Well, I guess he had a daughter, too."

"Why wasn't she mentioned when she was born?"

"I'm not sure—"

"I mean, we heard all about how she bore a son and named him this and she bore a son and named him that,'" Gloria grew more irritated, "why didn't we hear about the daughter?"

"I guess she wasn't important to the story until now," John William said.

"Why is she so important now?"

"Well," John William's voice was full of patience, "why don't you let me read and we'll find out?"

John William continued reading the chapter, but was soon interrupted again.

"What does it mean to have your 'soul clave'?" Gloria asked.

"It means Shechem loved her. The verse goes on, 'he loved the damsel and spake kindly unto the damsel.'"

"So when it says he 'defiled' her—"

"It means he…took her virginity." John William was clearly uncomfortable.

"But he loved her?"

"Yes."

"So why use such an ugly word? *Defiled.*"

"When a woman loses—lost her virginity in this culture…before she got married, she was…unclean. Undesirable."

"And these are God's people?"

John William wouldn't meet her gaze.

"Tell me," Gloria continued, "does God see me as unclean? Undesirable? Defiled?"

"I don't know how He sees you," John William said. "I'm not God."

"Is that how you see me?"

Now, finally, his gaze met hers. "No."

Gloria wasn't sure she completely believed him, but she rewarded him with a smile steeped in gratitude.

"Now," he said, "may I please finish? At this rate we'll be readin' till dark."

Gloria nodded her consent and listened to the rest of the chapter in silence. It had been their habit, a chapter or more each day, beginning in what he called the first book. This in itself had confused her: after all, it was just one book, wasn't it? But she soon caught on, and though she'd never tell him so, she somewhat enjoyed the stories John William read each afternoon.

Today's was especially exciting. Dinah and her lover, the wrath of her brothers, the slaughter of Shechem's family. She had one pressing question, but was reluctant to interrupt the reading again. She filed it away until they resumed their journey.

When John William finished the chapter, he closed the Bible and bowed his head to pray. Sometimes Gloria closed her eyes, too, but not today. Today she looked at John William as he prayed the familiar words—thanking God for the Bible, asking for a safe journey, asking for health and strength—and she wondered if he had felt the same passion for his wife that Shechem felt for Dinah. She wondered if any man would ever put himself in danger because of a love for her. She wondered if she would have known her father if she'd been a son instead of a daughter. She wondered if she was undesirable. Defiled.

John William's deep, reading voice always put the children to sleep. Now, as a continuation of the routine, Gloria tucked them into their little crates in the back of the wagon while John William hitched up the team. He helped Gloria up into the seat and settled himself next to her.

"I'm still a little beat," he said. "Think I'll ride a while."

He slapped the reins softly against the horses' flanks and made a clicking noise with his tongue. The horses began their plodding stride.

"Dinah was lucky," Gloria said after they'd been riding in silence for a while.

"How do you figure?"

"I was…defiled…when I was thirteen years old." Some part of her had been dwelling on the memory since John William first read the word, but the voicing of it seemed to be out of her control. "It wasn't anybody who loved me. We were in California. My mother was extremely ill. We were kicked out of the house where she…worked. We found a room in a building on the edge of town. Cheap, but not cheap enough."

While she spoke, John William stared straight ahead. For a second she thought about just how much time he spent not looking at her. Then she continued.

"We had nothing. Just a few dollars and the clothes on our

backs. The owner of the building took one look at us and knew what we had. What we were."

The horses were taking them through a green, lush valley. The sky was clear, the air was sweet. But as Gloria spoke, she was in the small, stuffy room at the mercy of Stan Corsetti.

"We didn't have enough money for rent," she said. "But my mother would not be turned away again. I remember she grabbed Mr. Corsetti's arm and said, 'Look at her. She's beautiful, isn't she? Wouldn't you like to be her first?'"

"Dear God," John William whispered, still not looking at her.

"So, right there, with my mother in the room, Mr. Corsetti defiled me. I don't remember much, only that he stank, and I was worried that I would smell like him." Gloria gave a short laugh. "*Unclean.* After that, he visited regularly to collect the rent, and he sent up a few of his friends so we could…live."

"I'm sorry, Gloria," John William said, still not looking at her, but looking down. "I'm so sorry."

"So when I think about how I have never been loved even once," Gloria said, "I can't help but think that Dinah was so lucky."

John William cleared his throat. "I s'pose," he said.

"Did you love your wife?"

"Yes, I did."

"Done anything for her?"

"Of course. I took up minin' because she wanted me to."

"Did she love you?"

"I hope she did," he said. "I tried to give her everything. Do everything."

"I hope she did, too," Gloria said, never envying a woman more than she did the late Katherine MacGregan. Not because John William had loved her, but because somebody had.

"Any other questions?" John William asked. "Or can we give the horses a break from all this chatter?"

"Just one," Gloria said. "What's 'circumcised'?"

John William turned to look at her, his face puzzled. "I beg your pardon?"

"Circumcised. That's what caused all the problems in the story today. What is it?"

"It's…well…" John William stammered through a definition, breaking eye contact once again and, as far as Gloria could tell, blushing. When he finished, he gave a short laugh, looked at her, smiled, and looked away.

"What's so funny?" Gloria asked, a little embarrassed herself, but amused at his obvious discomfort.

"It's just…" he began.

"What?"

"I figured, if anyone should know…" His voice trailed off as he shrugged a gesture in her direction.

"I never looked," she said. "It was easier that way."

They retreated into silence again, an oddly comfortable silence that gave Gloria a sense of the beginning of healing. The feeling intensified when John William reached over and covered her hand with his own.

"That's all behind you now, you know," he said, giving her hand a small squeeze.

"It's never really behind you," Gloria said, drawing her hand away.

"It can be, with God."

"I know what God thinks of me. I know what I am. I just never had a word for it until today."

hey had never traveled this late before. Normally by this time, John William had scouted ahead for a suitable camp space. But this evening, though their shadows stretched up the rolling hills that bordered their path, John William said nothing about setting up camp for the night. He walked just ahead of the wagon, one hand resting lightly on the neck of one of the horses.

"When are we stopping?" Gloria asked. She leaned forward on her bouncing seat and repeated the question when he didn't immediately respond, but he seemed lost in thought. In fact, for the past week, besides the obligatory bits of conversation and the daily Bible reading, there had been nothing but silence between them. He had even been more subdued with the children, opting to hold them close rather than spin them, squealing with delight, high above his head.

Now, the team plodded forward, and John William's eyes remained focused just ahead of his boots.

"MacGregan, answer me! Do you plan to walk all night?"

"Do you see that?" he said, pointing to a small pointed rooftop at the edge of the horizon. "That's Fort Hall. We should get there before full dark."

Gloria pushed her bonnet off her head and stood, straining to make out the details of their destination.

"Sit down," John William said, still not turning around, "else you'll fall."

She wondered how he'd known she was standing, then noticed her elongated shadow. She stretched out her hand to give a little wave before complying with his request.

"That seems pretty far," she said.

He said nothing.

"I can't imagine we'll make it before dark."

"We'll be fine."

"But what about—"

"I said we'll be fine." John William turned to look back at her, and his expression left no room for rebuttal.

Fort Hall was not the bastion of civilization that John William was expecting it to be. He had been told of an impressive structure, a bustling environment of fur trade frequented by trappers, manned by soldiers. This should have been a place to get supplies for the final push into Oregon. What he saw instead in the final moments of daylight was an adobe wall still standing to mark the perimeter of the fort, but in disrepair.

On the surrounding land, a dozen wagons stood in makeshift campsites, their contents spilled out around them. Clothing hung on lines strung from the top of their bowed frames to the intermittent boards bracing the walls of the fort. Children scampered about, climbing on the beds of abandoned freight wagons and daring each other to stand on the marked gravesites when the full moon was up.

He searched in the waning light for someone who might have some authority, but the closest he found was a boy of about thirteen who paused in his taunting of a terrified little sister long enough to point toward the heavy wooden gate in the middle of the wall.

"You can leave your rig out here," the boy said. "An' for a nickel I'll unhitch your team and take 'em to water."

He smiled at the boy and fished into the little money pouch he kept stored under the wagon seat. Seeing how closely the boy eyed his actions, he made a great show of returning the pouch to his pocket before helping Gloria down. They each carried a child in a sling carrier and made their way to the gate.

John William was surprised to be greeted by a sentry in uniform, even though both the soldier and the uniform bore the same evidence of disrepair.

"Your business here?" the soldier said, seemingly unaware of the trickle of tobacco juice drizzling through his beard.

"Hopin' to get some supplies," John William said. "Make camp for a few days."

"No tradin' till the morning. Inside's full up, but you can make camp out there with the other'n."

John William nodded and turned to go back to the wagon.

"You and the woman might want to step inside for a spell, though. Huntin' party come back today and there's a feast happenin' in the old mess hall."

"I don't think—" he started, before Gloria's hand clutched his sleeve and yanked him toward the gate.

"Looks like somebody wants some supper," the soldier said, pushing the gate wide open.

When John William and Gloria walked into the old mess hall, Gloria had a sense of familiarity she had not felt since leaving Virginia City. The room was large and dark. Rough-hewn tables and benches lined the walls; square tables and chairs dotted the center of the floor. A dim cloud of cigar smoke padded the air, and the stench of whiskey—poured, spilled, and belched— was just as thick. The clink and clatter of glasses and bottles punctuated the constant rumble of male voices. Occasional raucous laughter bounced off the corners, and Gloria craned her neck in an effort to hear the joke.

John William merely scowled.

"Let's go," he said, taking her elbow and speaking close to her ear. "I don't like this place."

"What's not to like?" Gloria shrugged herself from his grip.

"It's no place for the children," John William said, raising his voice.

"They don't even know where they are."

"I know where they are, and they're not stayin'." He grabbed Gloria's arm. "Let's go."

Gloria spun on her heel and looked him straight in the eye. "I'm hungry. I'm tired. And I'm not too good to be in here."

"That's not what I—"

"So take Kate and go, but Danny and I are going to sit here for a while."

John William laughed.

"What's so funny?"

"You're holding Kate."

"So take her." She stood with her hands on her hips, the full weight of the baby falling on the back of her neck.

"I will." He stepped close and scooped his daughter out of the sling. As she did with every contact with her father, Kate gave a little squealing kick of delight as she was lifted to his strong shoulder.

"Give me Danny," Gloria said, holding out her arms.

"No. He's leavin' with me."

The heated exchange had not escaped the attention of the crowd, and soon they were standing in the center of halted conversation. John William shot one more glare, and she countered with her own. Without another word, he left.

Gloria casually reached around the back of her neck, untied the sling's knot, and lifted the cloth to rest, shawl-like, across her shoulders. She spied an unoccupied table in the corner and made her way to it.

Once seated, she allowed herself only furtive glances around the room. She saw a few tables hosting exhausted men and women with equally bedraggled children, but mostly there were men. Like the sentry at the gate, they wore some vestige of a military uniform seemingly more out of habit than duty. There were also several wild-looking men dressed in buckskin and fur. What she didn't see, though, was any proof of the glorious feast promised by both the gatekeeper and the lingering aroma of roasted meat. It must have been finished off by the crowd, and the only reason she had for staying was to prove to John William that this is where she belonged.

"You up for some supper?"

Gloria looked over her shoulder and saw a tall, thin man wearing an apron splattered with equal parts grease and blood.

"Is there any left?"

"Not sure, but what there is will cost you seventy-five cents."

"I don't have any money."

"Well, don't you worry about what you don't have," he said, punctuated by a salacious wink. On his way out of the room, he stopped and spoke with several of the men, gesturing vaguely toward her. As he left each encounter, the man he'd been speaking to turned to give Gloria a full, curious stare.

Let them stare, Gloria thought. *I've been stared at before.*

Slowly, imperceptibly, Gloria uncurled from her huddled, protective posture and sat higher, straighter. Her hands still clutched the corners of her shawl, but now they stretched behind her, draping the shawl over the back of the chair. She brought one hand to rest lightly on the table. Her other hand found a stray family of curls, estranged from the loose gathering at the nape of her neck, and worked slowly, methodically, twisting the hair around and off, around and off her finger.

She kept her gaze fixed somewhere above the crowd. Not on the ceiling, exactly, but far above any other set of eyes. That's why she didn't see him coming before he was actually standing there, both palms planted on her table.

"Well, Glory-be, it's Glory-A." This followed by stinking, wheezy laughter.

No. No. No. No.

"By gum, it's you! What in h—"

"Do I know you?"

"I don't know if you know me, but I sure know you." He'd grabbed Gloria's hand, stopping it midtwirl. He was filthy. Small. A full beard obscured his face. A stained hat sat low over his eyes. He smelled of beer and sweat and stable.

"Virginia City." His voice had taken on a dreamlike quality. "Best five dollars I ever spent."

"Get away from me."

"Yep. You came highly recommended. Sent you a few of my buddies, too."

"I said—"

"That was what…two, three years ago?"

"Don't touch me." Not demanding, really, but not pleading.

He let go of her hand only to slide another chair over, sitting in it, trapping her.

"Saw you walk in with that baby. Thought I recognized you. Then it hits me—Gloria." He scooted his chair a little closer, leaned in, as if he were telling a secret. "That my kid?"

The rancid laughter returned. Gloria's mind and stomach reeled at the possibility. She frantically searched her memory, desperate to connect the face to a house, to a time, a year, a month.

His laughter took on a self-conscious air before dissolving completely in Gloria's icy silence. He fidgeted a little, mustering all the dignity available to a pile of rags and whiskey. Gloria felt something close to amusement, to victory.

"So you was really rakin' it in back then," he said, trying to assume an air of casual conversation. "Now you don't have six bits for supper."

"I—"

"And I figure, what kind of man would I be to let an old *friend* go hungry?"

"I'm not a friend and I'm not hungry."

"Then, if it ain't too much trouble," he was touching her arm now, squeezing and unsqueezing a little path from her wrist to her elbow, then sliding back down. "I got me a little setup on the back wall. Got a little money," he leaned close, his beard touching her face. "Got all the money you want."

Gloria went perfectly still. Now this was familiar. This was her life. The friendships forged at Jewell's house, the birth of her son, the months with John William and Kate—all of it disappeared in one breath. This stranger was every man she'd ever known. This embrace was every touch she'd ever felt. She recognized the din of this crowd; she'd grown up with the stench of this room. This proprietary grip on her arm was far more familiar and fitting than a small, warm head nuzzled in her neck or a strong hand helping her to stand.

He'd scooted a little closer. His breath engulfed her. His beard skittered on her skin. There was a time when this man would have given her a sense of power. She would dangle her charms, elusive, enticing, just outside the grasp of such desperate starvation. She would have laughed at his need for her, squeezed him for every drop of his money and pride. In her view, she emerged from every encounter victorious. Now, though, she merely sat, motionless, indefensible to his invasion. His voice droned on, a putrid flow of promises and threats, recalling and predicting details that made her body fester with shame. She felt herself disappear a little with each vile caress, dissolving under the stream of his words. The joy of her son, the comfort of John William, the delight of Kate—all faded behind the sour speech of this stranger.

Then, as suddenly as he appeared, he was gone.

"I said, get away from her." The familiar voice of a growling bear.

Gloria glanced over, saw the chair next to her now empty. She turned around and saw the man against the wall behind her, eye level with John William. When she looked down and saw his feet dangling six inches above the floor, she wanted to smile.

A crowd immediately migrated to this end of the room, men eager to witness a fight. Witness any spectacle, really. And it seemed that they would be rewarded. John William's face glowed with rage. He held it, nose to nose with the filthy little man, breathing heavily through clenched teeth. Gloria had never seen him like this. When the pathetic little man attempted to wiggle free, John William slammed his forearm against the man's chest, bringing forth a wheezing gasp.

Gloria stood and laid a tentative hand on John William's sleeve.

"MacGregan," she said.

The little man tore his terrified eyes away from those of the giant who pinned him and looked at her. "What'd you call him?" he asked, his voice devoid of air.

"John William, put him down, now. He didn't do no harm."

The only sound in the tavern was that of John William's rhythmic breath. Somewhere behind the crowd a mother ushered her children outside, admonished her husband who wanted to "stay and see this."

"My money's on MacGregan," shouted a voice in the back. There was a spatter of nervous laughter, a few isolated words of agreement, and a change in John William. At once, he loosened his grip, allowed his prey to drop to the ground, and stepped away.

"I'm sorry," he said, holding his hands up in surrender to his victim. "I'm sorry."

The man held up his own hand even as he fought for breath. "You kiddin'? How many men can say they made it through a fight with John William MacGregan?"

"I know a few who can't," said another voice in the crowd, which responded with raucous laughter.

John William stood in the middle of them, staring at the floor. His breath was deep and even; his shoulders quivered with each exhalation. Gloria took a step closer and looked into his eyes.

He was disappearing, too.

The rotten little man reveled in the attention. He danced little circles around them, throwing air punches. He reached up to give a slight push on John William's shoulder, saying, "C'mon, now. Not so ready to fight now, eh?"

Laughter and taunts from the crowd became a call to violence. In the midst of the rancor, Gloria marveled that so many of the men were able to call John William by name.

Gloria reached up, took John William's face in her hands, and forced him to look at her.

"MacGregan," she said, "where's Kate and Danny?"

"I'm sorry," he said.

"The children—Kate and Danny. Where are they?" She spoke louder to overcome the cries of the crowd.

"They're all right. They're fine. There's an Indian woman looking after them."

"Let's go," she said, softly. "Let's go to the children."

Gloria grasped both of John William's hands in her own and turned toward the door, leading him like a yoked beast.

The crowd jeered their loss in a common voice, but one comment rang out above the din.

"Go on and take 'er, MacGregan," crowed the unmistakable voice of the seedy little man. "Just try and save some for the rest of—"

His last words were lost in a shatter of jaw and teeth. He hit the wall he had previously been pinned to and sank to the floor.

Gloria looked at the man, then at John William, then back at the man again. She brought a hand to her mouth, but soon found it lost in John William's giant, bloodied grip as he tugged her through the newly silenced crowd toward the door.

She kept her gaze fixed firmly on John William's wide back, seeing it slapped by hands from the crowd and the occasional shout of "Nice going there, MacGregan," and "Never thought I'd live to see the day…"

She feared some would follow them, but no one did. Just a few steps into the crisp night air and the scene inside became a murmur.

"I did some tradin'," John William said.

"I though he said we couldn't until morning."

"Indians."

"Oh. Good," Gloria said.

"Got some supplies. Should last us for a couple of weeks."

"Fine."

He was still holding her hand, the little man's blood sticky on her fingers. They rounded a corner. Against a crumbling adobe wall, an Indian woman sat—a heap of softness and skirts—holding Danny. Baby Kate lay in the folds of her lap.

"I asked her to watch them," John William said. "I had to find you."

"Your son," the woman said. Her soft, leathered voice slipped from a brown folded face sporting a four-toothed smile. She held Danny out to Gloria.

"And, your daughter," she said as she handed Kate to John William. "Beautiful children."

That's when Gloria realized that, rather than the bright brown eyes of every Indian she'd ever met, this woman stared through watery gray clouds.

"Thank you," Gloria said, "for watching them."

"Beautiful children. Not born together, these ones. But made to be brother. To be sister."

"Yes," Gloria said.

"Away," the woman said, gesturing vaguely toward the fort's gate.

"We are," John William said. "At first light."

❧ 13 ❧

Once the children were fed and sleeping, John William and Gloria sat next to the dying embers of their fire. The moon was full and casting shadows. Though it was late, neither made a motion to bed down for the night. The silence was a comfortable one, though charged with questions. John William poked at the fire, causing a sputter of spark and new flame. Gloria tucked her skirts closer and spoke into the night.

"What happened in there?" Gloria asked.

"I could ask you the same thing," John William said, tossing his branch into the fire.

"But you didn't. Tell me."

"What do you want to know?"

"Those men, they knew you. They recognized your name. How?"

John William looked at his hands, clenching and unclenching his fists until finally bringing them together, one fist cupped in the long fingers of the other hand. When he finally spoke, he spoke to his hands.

"I used to be a boxer. A few years ago. Used to go to different towns. Different camps. I had a manager who set it all up. Brought the men in, charged a fee, took bets."

The blue light of the moon mixed with the sporadic light of the fire, and Gloria took the opportunity to study his features. The tiny little imperfections took on new meaning. When John William glanced up, catching her eye, she felt as if she'd been caught sifting through his life. She waited for him to look away, to look ashamed, but instead he smiled.

"Not very pretty, eh?" he said.

He brought his hand up to rake back his hair and turned a profile to Gloria. She had never seen his ears, had always wondered why he wore his hair so long. Both ears—but the left one especially—looked like lumps of flattened biscuit dough.

"That's why, sometimes," he said, letting his hair fall back to cover his disfigurement, "I don't hear so good."

"So, did you win?"

"You saw me," John William said, turning inside himself again. "I won. I always won."

"So why did you stop?"

"Sometimes, you can hit a man too hard."

"How hard?"

"I was in Boston. Guy there had a whole setup. We were fightin' in a ring. The take at the door was nearly five hundred dollars—hundred of that went to the winner. I think I cared more about that money than anythin'. It's like everythin' else just…"

"Disappeared?"

John William looked at her, and understanding fueled the fire between them.

"Exactly. I didn't hear anythin'. Didn't really feel anythin'. I know my opponent was landin' punches, but I didn't feel them. It's like I was…"

"Numb," they said in unison.

"He was a little guy. Not like this one tonight, but shorter than me. We were an even match in strength, but his face was just the right level. I didn't have to reach up, you know, to land a punch."

Gloria looked at him, more than six feet of man bent to sit beside a fire, and wondered how any man could match his strength and size.

"So I just kept hittin'. Kept landin' punches. I heard people cheerin', screamin'. His face was all broken, all bloody. It was like poundin' meat. Bits and pieces of it got stuck between my fingers. Then there was one last hit. I felt that one, but I don't think he did.

He just sort of stared at me and fell down. I think he was dead before he hit the ground."

There was silence then, nothing but the crackling of the fire, spitting sparks. Gloria's eyes never left John William, but he didn't face her. His head drooped and he bounced it, lightly, on his gripped hands. She noticed his knuckles, swollen and bruised. Never in her life had Gloria felt any desire to touch a man. Now it was all she could do not to reach out to John William, to comfort him. She remained silent, waiting for him to invite her voice.

"I thought for sure that would be the end of my boxin'," he continued, "but it wasn't. If anythin', it brought in bigger crowds. Bigger fights. I got a manager who started takin' me all over the country, callin' me 'The Killer.'" He gave a short, bitter laugh. "Sometimes I was takin' in more than five hundred dollars a night—"

"Now *there's* something we have in common."

Gloria was rewarded with a slight smile before John William resumed.

"And I was beginnin' to feel like the most powerful man in the world. Then, one night I was in a saloon, just like this one tonight. Was drinkin' every round, and some guy comes up to me and says, 'Hey, Killer, wanna take a shot at me?' I tried to back off, but he just kept pushin' and pushin'. He took a swing at me, and I let it pass. Then he took another, and I let it pass."

Scenes from earlier this evening played in Gloria's mind as John William supplied the details of that night. The jeering crowd, the shouted taunts.

"Then I hit him." He looked up. "And I killed him."

"Oh, John," she whispered.

"And I went to jail."

"But it was an accident, wasn't it?"

"I don't know," he said, and once that sank in he added, "neither did the sheriff. He locked me up long enough to wait for the circuit judge to come for a hearin'."

Gloria knew the stigma and the stench of prison. She'd spent months at a time in crowded, dank cells. She couldn't understand why now, at this point in the story, John William's face beamed.

"It's where I met Katherine," he said.

"Oh?" Gloria said, smirking. "What was she in for?"

John William chuckled. "Well, she wasn't exactly *in* prison. It was just over in South Pass—"

"I passed through there."

"And the jail there, the courthouse in front, they use it as a school when there's no court in session. Katherine was a teacher."

"So she was a genius, too?" Gloria said.

"I don't know about genius, but she was a fine teacher. Mornings, just after the children got settled down, she would read a chapter of the Bible to them. I heard some of it growin' up—Irish Catholic, you know—but it never meant anythin' to me until I was sittin', trapped in prison."

"Was it the same that you read to me?" Gloria asked.

"Some of it. But I remember one day, she'd been readin' about Jesus and His trial, His death. What they did to Him…they beat Him," he explained. "Whipped him. Katherine told the children about the scourge—strips of leather with bits of stone and glass to cut the skin. She told them about nailin' a man to a cross. The wounds and the blood and the pain."

Gloria shuddered.

"And I thought about myself there in prison. Comfortable, warm. Fed. And this was after killin' a man with my bare hands."

Gloria listened hard, but the life and death of Jesus was little more than the subject of ranting street preachers and weeping women. Still, she shied away from appearing even more ignorant to John William. But he must have sensed her confusion because he paused, took both of her hands in his, and spoke slowly, clearly, directly.

"Don't you see? Jesus went through all of that for me. To save my life."

"Your life?"

"Yeah, my life." John William still held her hands. He moved his grip to encircle her wrists and turned her hands so that the palms faced up. "We think our lives are in our hands," he said, "that we're in control of everythin'. But we're not. God is. And someday we'll have to answer to Him for every sin. Every wrong." His grip tightened. "You need to know that."

Gloria just looked down at his fingers overlapping as they grasped her wrists. His last words were punctuated with little tugs, but something tugged inside her, too, telling her to listen, to understand.

"I spent months sittin' there, regrettin' every punch I ever threw. Wishin' I could take back every fight, every drop of blood, and it hit me. It didn't matter if the world called me a killer. It mattered if *God* called me a killer. And while I could never take back all the wrong that I did, I knew that God would forgive me for all of it. If I just asked Him to."

"But that wouldn't change anything."

"Oh, but it does," John William said. "It changes everythin'. I killed two men, sent them to their maker, and I started to wonder about what would happen if *I* was sent to *my* maker. I thought, what if I hang and die and have to tell God what I did? I wondered how I would tell Him that I was sorry and wished I could take it all back."

Slowly, John William had been drawing Gloria closer to him. Their eyes were locked as tightly as their fingers when John William broke his gaze away and bowed his head, resting it on their joined hands. She sensed that his lips were moving, but she heard nothing, not even a whisper. Something in her wanted to prompt him, to urge him on, but something else told her to be still and silent and wait for his next words. Before they came, he raised his head, released her hands, and drew away.

"I was scared to death of dyin'," he said. "Every day, Katherine had the children say a Bible verse. That day it was John 3:16."

Gloria looked at him, blankly.

"'For God so loved the world, that he gave his only begotten

Son, that whosoever believeth in him should not perish, but have everlasting life.'"

Gloria tried to wrap her mind around the words, but their meaning remained distant, blurred. She sensed John William's reverence for it, though, and gave a tiny nod of understanding.

"Jesus died so that I could live. Forever, in heaven," John William said. "And if I didn't believe that, then His death was for nothing. I was already responsible for two meaningless deaths."

"So, you believed."

"I believed. And I prayed. I asked God to forgive me, and He did. That minute I knew my life was saved. That I had changed."

"Changed? How?"

"First, I promised I would never fight again. I asked Katherine if she would leave me her Bible to read in the evenings after school. I read every word of it, and by then it didn't matter if I would spend my life in jail or hang. I knew my soul was safe and my body was in God's hands."

"But you didn't hang."

"No. The judge ruled it an accident. Said I wasn't a murderer. When I was released, I knew that the best way to keep the Bible was to marry the woman who owned it."

"How romantic," Gloria said, smiling.

"It just shows how God puts us where He needs us to be. I don't know if God led me to Katherine or Katherine led me to God, but right now I'm wonderin' the same about you."

"Don't worry trying to figure that out," Gloria said. "God doesn't lead me anywhere. Never has."

"You can't believe that."

"Yes, I do. I've been in places a lot worse than a schoolhouse, places no God would ever take anyone."

"He would if it brought you here, to this moment."

"This is one moment," Gloria said. "It's not a lifetime."

She looked at the fire, now down to mere embers. At some point the evening had become quite chilly.

"I'm tired," she said, standing and stretching. "You must be, too."

He stood with her. "Gloria, you have to—"

"I wish I could believe all of this."

"I wish you could, too."

"And it doesn't bother me to know."

"Know what?"

"About the killing. The prison."

"I didn't tell you as a confession," John William said. "I just wanted you to know the truth."

"It doesn't change anything."

"It should." He crossed behind her to reach into the wagon and pull out his bedroll. He shook it out and laid it down a safe distance from the dying fire.

Gloria sat on the wagon's back step, unlaced her boots and let them drop to the ground. "Well, good night," she said before climbing into the wagon to the nest of blankets in the back. She thought she heard his quiet "night" behind her, but didn't turn to acknowledge it.

She lay there, looking at the canvas above her, imagining the stars above that. John William's words echoed in her head. So many words. He'd never talked so much at any one time. She tried to piece them all together, but they wouldn't form. She tried to remember his face, his mouth in speech, but she only saw his eyes, piercing, sincere. Pleading with her to listen, to hear. Bits and strands came back. A life taken. A life saved. For God so loved...what? The world? Believe. Forgiven. A promise.

A promise.

Gloria sat up and turned her body, careful not to jostle the sleeping Kate and Danny, worming her way to the opening at the back of the wagon. She peered out and saw him lying on his back, hands folded behind his head.

"MacGregan?" Gloria whispered to the darkness.

"Gloria," his voice floated back.

"I'm sorry."

"For what?" His form shifted, and she imagined he was turning toward her.

"You were in a fight."

"I know."

"I made you break your promise."

She thought she heard him smile.

"You didn't make me do anythin'," he said, his voice full of warmth.

"But you were protecting me."

"No, if I was protectin' you, he wouldn't have had a chance to talk to you in the first place."

"Well, thank you anyway."

"You're welcome."

"MacGregan? Are you still…"

"Still…"

"Still…safe?"

"What do you mean?" He was sitting straight up now.

"You promised God you wouldn't fight again, but you fought tonight."

"Don't worry." John William stood up and walked over to Gloria, his features getting clearer with each step. "It's like I'm God's child. He won't abandon me."

"My father abandoned me," Gloria said.

"I know, and I'm sorry. But God won't."

"I'm going to leave Danny."

"You haven't yet."

"But—"

"Listen to me," John William said, his voice close and serious. "My life is secure not because I made a promise to God, but because He made a promise to me. Do you understand the difference?"

"It doesn't matter."

"Of course it matters."

"Not to me."

"Maybe not to you, but to God. And to me. Now let's get some sleep. It's late. The babies'll be up in a few hours."

He dropped the canvas flap leaving Gloria in her cocoon. She lay back again, resuming her study of the canvas and her vision of the stars. Once again she tried to recall the conversation.

Nobody had ever cared about what she believed. Nobody had ever given her anything to believe in. But now everything was different.

Jewell's warning about John William, the danger, his secret— tonight everything was clear and defined. If nothing else, she could believe in him. She had never considered the value of a man's knowing God, but tonight she saw that it made him different. Made him better, kinder, steadier. John William would never let himself be like all those others. This was a man who could make a promise and keep it.

Until he met her.

*T*he next morning John William woke to the sounds of life bustling around him. Muted conversations drifted through the dark morning as his fellow campers loaded their wagons and harnessed their teams in an unofficial race to be the first to ferry across the Snake River.

But John William felt no need for such haste. Getting Gloria to move in the mornings was a daily battle under the best of circumstances. Last night they stayed up talking long past midnight, and he thought he'd heard her up with the babies even after that. This morning he'd do well to get her out of the wagon at all, let alone to rush around and break camp and wait with fifteen other families for their chance to cross the river. No, today would be a day of leisure. They hadn't spent one single day in the same place since leaving Silver Peak. As long as they stayed outside the adobe walls of Fort Hall, last night's ugly business could be forgotten; most of the witnesses would be ferried away by noon.

Perhaps today he would follow Gloria's decadent example and sleep past dawn. The ground here wasn't any more comfortable than the ground anywhere, but he turned on his side, shifted around a bit, and waited for the noise around him to drift away. Maybe this was the morning she would get up first, get the coffee going, walk over and nudge him awake with the toe of her little black boot.

He opened his eyes for one last look and realized something was wrong. He raised himself on one elbow, rubbed the last of the bleary sleep from his eyes. Maybe it had been just a trick of the shadows. He sat straight up and looked again. Gloria's boots were gone.

He flung off his blanket and walked over to the back of the wagon.

"Gloria?" he whispered through the narrow canvas opening, just as he had countless mornings. But this morning there was no grumbled reply. He drew back the flap and looked inside. She wasn't there. He placed one foot on the step and leaned in, reaching into the dark until his hand landed on the soft head of one of the babies, warm with sleep. He groped around until he found the other, also sleeping. Left undisturbed, they might not wake for a couple of hours.

John William took up his bedding and snapped it, scattering particles of dust and grass, before rolling it up and tucking it just inside the back of the wagon. He built up a small fire and got some water boiling for coffee—she would want a cup when she came back—and took down the basket of Indian flat bread he'd traded for last night. Between each little chore, he alternated between checking on the babies and scanning the area for any sight of her, nodding a silent "good morning" to anyone who chose to do the same.

He'd been up for nearly an hour when he saw the boy who had offered to water his horses the day before. This morning the boy was hitching teams and seemed uninterested in coming over to John William—obviously not in need of his services—until John William held up one impressive silver coin.

"Ya need something, mister?" he asked, never taking his eyes off the coin.

John William bent his knees until he was eye-level with the boy. "Go down to the ferry landin'. Find out if they've made any crossin's yet this mornin'."

"That it?"

"For now."

The boy took off toward the river. John William checked in on the children one last time. Confident they were soundly sleeping, he headed toward the fort's large wooden gate. Just as there had been the night before, a slovenly soldier reclined at his post.

"State yer business here," the soldier said, giving John William a disinterested sideways glance.

"You been here all night?"

"Mostly."

"You see a woman come in here? Maybe a few hours ago?"

The soldier cocked back his head to look John William straight in the eye and smiled. "What kind of woman?"

"Blonde hair, wearin'"—he closed his eyes "—a blue dress."

"Blonde hair, blue dress? Nope. Think I'd remember that."

"And you been here all night?"

"Like I said. Mostly."

He was lying, John William was sure, and nothing would feel better than to slam him up against the crumbling wall of the fort and pound the truth out of him. His fists clenched and unclenched at his side, but the memory of Gloria last night, distraught at being the cause of his violent outburst, quelled his anger. Without another word, he returned to his wagon to wait with the children.

Danny was awake first, as usual. He wasn't crying, but when John William lifted the flap, he noticed the boy's feet kicking through his covers, and when he whispered "Good mornin', Danny boy," the infant turned and looked straight at him. "Your ma's not here right now, son, but I've got you."

He lifted the child out of the wagon, sat down on one of the campstools, and relieved the baby of his soaking diaper. For a few minutes it was just the two of them seemingly alone in the world. John William looked into Danny's brown eyes and wondered how Gloria could ever bring herself to abandon this child. "Don't you worry son," he said. "I'll find her." Then he closed his eyes and prayed, *Father, let her be safe.*

"Hey, mister?" John William opened his eyes and saw the

freckle-faced boy standing, breathless, as if he hadn't stopped running since being dispatched on his errand. "The first ferry's just now leavin'."

"Thank you." John William gave a curt nod and stood.

"But she weren't on it. I asked, and the captain said there wasn't no ladies goin' alone. And she ain't standin' around waitin' on the next one, neither."

"How did you—"

"I saw you was walkin' around like you was lookin' for somethin'. Didn't see her, so I figured that was it. Now I gotta go or my pa'll skin me!"

John William cradled Danny in one arm and reached the other out to grab the boy by the shoulder. "Did you talk to anyone else?"

"Nah," the boy said, shrugging. "Don't figure it's any of their business."

"Thank you, again," John William said. He let go of the boy's shoulder and extended his hand. Beaming, the boy took it, and they solemnly shook hands before he turned and tore back toward the river.

So she hadn't crossed. And she was nowhere in the surrounding campsite. John William looked at the worn path that led up to Fort Hall. Certainly she wouldn't have gone off on foot; Gloria could be coaxed off her wagon seat for only about a half a mile a day. He smiled, remembering her laziness, now grateful for it. There was only one answer, and he wouldn't ask the guard at the gate.

The same blind Indian woman was sitting just inside the gate when John William barreled through, a baby clutched in each arm.

"You have come for your woman?" she said, causing him to stop dead center in front of her.

"What did you say?"

She beckoned him to come closer, and as he leaned toward

her, she reached up and took Kate out of his grasp. When she was settled in the woman's lap, he handed over Danny.

"Now you can go get her."

"Is she safe? Is she all right?"

The old woman shrugged. "I just hear talk about the pretty lady. Not good talk."

"Where should I look?"

"The big cooking fire."

John William stood and looked around the inside of the fort, seeing it for the first time in daylight as the sun was just now streaming over the eastern wall. There was no fire, but in the far southeast corner of the fort he did see a large ring of stones containing what must be the charred wood and ashes from last night's feast. The wall behind it was lined with a long, narrow two-story structure made of tightly fitted logs. Every few feet, the logs had been hewn to accommodate a door, and a wooden walkway, suspended by ropes attached to the walls, allowed passage to the single door on the second floor.

A small crowd of men stood just outside one of the doors, laughing and jabbing each other. John William headed straight for them. With each step their conversation became less animated, and when he was fully in their midst, they did little more than stare at their boots.

"I'm lookin' for the woman I came in here with last night," John William said.

"Ain't seen no woman," one of the men said, not looking up from the steaming mug he held in his hand.

"She has blonde hair. Wearin' a blue dress."

"Don't tell me she's your wife," another man said, sending the others into a fit of laughter barely stifled behind their dirty hands.

John William stepped back from the group and surveyed the building. "Gloria!" he shouted, fully expecting her to come to one of the doors. When she didn't, he stepped back a little farther and shouted a little louder, "Gloria!"

"Ah, now ain't that a shame," the man with the steaming mug said. "He ain't taught her yet to come runnin' when he hollers. He oughter try whistlin' her up a bit." He brought his fingers to his lips, but before he could produce the first shrill note, John William shoved him aside, knocking him and his mug to the ground.

John William knocked exactly once on the first door before grabbing the handle and throwing it open. Inside, the walls were lined with bunk beds, stacked two high, and nothing else. He strode to the next door, opened it, and found it to be identical, except for the one man sleeping on the bottom bunk who cursed the intrusion and turned his back to the door. The third room was the same, empty, as was the fourth. He had reached the end of the building and was standing underneath the wooden stairs that led to the second floor. He took to the stairs, grabbing the handrail to steady himself as he felt the flimsy structure sway beneath his heavy step. The walkway proved to be equally unstable, and he feared that ripping open the door would send him falling over the railing. Instead, he gripped the latch tightly and pulled; this one was locked.

"Gloria!" he shouted again, leaning one hand on the wall to steady himself as he pounded the door with the other. "Open this door!"

He continued to pound, not caring about the pain shooting through his hand each time his fist hit the wood. He hated the ridiculous little walkway that held him there, suspended, unable to rush at the door and break it down. All he could do was stand and shout and knock, the strength of his voice and his fist soon depleting.

John William was just about to deliver another blow when the door swung open, barely giving him enough time to stop his fist from colliding with the pale young face of the man who stood on its threshold.

"Listen here, fellow," he said, holding up his hands in a gesture of surrender, "she didn't say nothing about being nobody's wife."

"Get out," John William growled. He stepped aside to allow the man through the doorway, before going into the room.

This one was larger than the others downstairs, running the entire length of the building. Four square windows were cut into the longer walls, and though they were covered with ragged shutters, piercing streams of morning light shone through. Bed frames, probably long unused since none of them had any sort of mattress or bedding, lined the walls. Up against the short wall at the end of the room, just behind the door, was another bed. Still no pillows or blankets, but there was a mattress. And Gloria was on it.

"Go away," she said. She was lying with her back to him, and she didn't turn when she spoke.

"What are you doin' here?"

"What does it look like?" She sat up and turned to face him. Her hair was loose, not soft as it usually was in the mornings, but as if it had been torn from the remnant of the braid that trailed down her back. Her lips were swollen, her whole face somewhat distorted—partly due to her sneering expression, but there was something else, too. The blue dress was wrinkled, the top buttons undone and the skirt matted as if—

Hours ago he was sitting with this woman, holding her hands, praying for the right words to speak to her soul, praying in the next breath that God would keep his thoughts pure, guard him from ever thinking of her like this. He felt bile rise up his throat, and he turned and spat on the floor.

"Those men down there," he said, choking on the words, "were they already done with you? Or just waitin' their turn?"

"Do you really want to know?"

"No. No, I don't." He went to one of the windows that faced the interior of the fort and opened the shutter, bathing the dark room in new light. "They're all gone now, anyway." He walked back to her and held out his hand.

"I'm not leaving, MacGregan."

"Stop talkin' such nonsense."

"Don't sound so surprised," Gloria stood to face him. "This is what I am, MacGregan. This is what I was born to be. You saw that last night. I wasn't alone for two minutes before that man knew exactly who I was. What I was."

"Exactly, Gloria. What you *were*. In the past. But this," he waved toward the bed, "this was your choosin'. This wasn't no mother forcin' you to sell your body, or some piece of dirt bringin' up bad memories. This was you, Gloria. This was you walkin' away from your child. Tradin' everythin' I've tried to give you. And for what?"

"To show you the truth."

"What truth?"

"That people don't ever really change, John. I can't ever be anything different."

"Oh, for heaven's sake, Gloria! I've told you, with God's help—"

"Stop with that!" She balled up her fists and hit him square in the chest, surprising him with her strength. "Just stop it! You proved it last night. God never really changes a person."

"Don't say that."

"He doesn't! You said so yourself. You promised never to fight again, that God had changed you. And then last night…"

"I explained—"

"All it took was me. You abandoned a promise you made to God because of me. How can I live with that?"

"And how am I to live knowin' I brought you here?"

"You can't save me, John. You never could."

He looked at her, standing in the perfect square of morning light, and realized she spoke the truth. He'd taken her away from Jewell's, treated her with respect, fought for her honor, and the first chance she got, she'd thrown it all straight back in his face.

"I won't force you to come with me, Gloria."

"You couldn't if you wanted to."

"And Danny?"

"You made a promise to me, remember?"

He did. Now, John William searched Gloria's face for some hint of the same defiant spirit that had fueled her that day in Silver Peak when she had bargained so valiantly for the future of her child. But it was gone. Though her gaze held his, her eyes were devoid of their usual spark of humor. Her face was set in a grim, passive expression, lips closed but not pursed. It seemed the few hours spent in this room had slowly drained the life out of her, and her outburst against him was her final gasping breath. If, after all he'd done, she could resign herself to this fate, so could he.

"Good-bye then." He opened the door and stepped out onto the suspended walkway, finding it much easier to hold his balance when he wasn't striding in a blind rage. The crowd gathered at the foot of the stairs had dispersed, but had not disappeared, and John William found himself the subject of scrutiny and whispers as he walked toward the gate.

The old Indian woman was still there, holding her court at the fort's entrance, but she was not alone. Danny lolled contentedly in the woman's lap, and several little naked, brown children scampered all around and over her. Next to her sat a younger woman, beautiful with her rich black hair and distinct Shoshone features, with a colorful blanket draped over her shoulders.

"You are back?" the old woman said at the sound of John William's footstep.

"I am."

"And did you find your woman?"

"I did."

The old woman closed her eyes and nodded her head. "This," she said, gesturing to the younger woman beside her, "is my granddaughter. These are her children."

"And Kate? My daughter? Where is she?"

The old woman reached over and pulled the blanket from

her granddaughter's shoulder, showing her to be bared to the waist, with Kate nursing at her breast.

John William averted his eyes, turning his head toward the barracks behind him just long enough to see Gloria's face disappear from the window.

"She was hungry," the old woman said.

John William ventured a glimpse through hooded eyes and, seeing the blanket fully in place, offered his thanks to both women, amazed at how quickly the Lord provided.

Gloria watched the whole scene unfold from the little square window cut into the barrack wall. She was surprised when John William hadn't come for her at the break of dawn. And when she first heard his voice calling out her name, she was even more shocked to hear the level of anger in it. The pounding on the door, now that was to be expected, though she had hoped to see the man in the room with her thrown out over the walkway's railing. But she was prepared to settle for a simple toss out the door before John William scooped her up off the bed and carried her back to the wagon.

Instead, he politely stood aside and let the man go. He offered her no pity, no chastisement. Only his pious disdain and then…acceptance? Almost as if he wasn't surprised at all.

She watched him now, still walking. Not one glance over his shoulder. He meant to leave her here.

Gloria leaned against the window and drew back in pain. Hours past time for her to nurse, her breasts swelled uncomfortably against the fabric of her blue dress.

John William was now at the gate, talking to that same old Shoshone woman who cared for the children last night. She saw one of the babies—Danny, she thought—nestled snugly in the woman's lap, but Kate was nowhere to be seen. Then the old woman whisked the blanket off the shoulders of the younger woman next to her, and Gloria grabbed the open shutter to keep from collapsing. Even from here she could see Kate's tiny pink mouth latched onto the Shoshone woman, and the sight of it brought a new rush of milk to her already engorged breasts. For a brief moment, John William turned, looked straight at her, and Gloria knew she had been replaced.

She crumpled to the floor. The room, though full of fresh morning air and quite chilly just a while ago, was suddenly insufferably hot. She had to get out. She crawled over to the little green case she'd brought with her and took out her hairbrush. Loosening her braid, she raked her fingers through the plait and brought the brush up to smooth the curls. Lifting her arms above her head proved too painful, however, so she settled for two long braids resting over her shoulders.

"Like a little Shoshone myself," she said, dropping her brush back into the case and snapping it shut.

Gloria grabbed the windowsill and pulled herself up. She bent to pick up the green case, stood straight again, and realized it hurt much less to slump a little. She gripped the door latch, took a deep breath, and let the door slowly drift open. The first step over the threshold was fairly simple, once she grabbed the handrail to steady her step. She continued down the walkway and the stairs, ignoring the comments from the men gathered underneath.

At the last step, she set a straight course for John William and the babies, never looking back.

The old woman must have heard her steps, for she said something to John William, who turned and met her gaze, pulling her toward him with what she hoped was a genuine smile. He was holding one of the little Native children, and as Gloria drew closer, the child reached out and touched one of Gloria's braids.

"Pretty, isn't it?" John William said, and all the lewd comments of last night and this morning disappeared.

"Please," Gloria said, dropping her case at John William's feet and reaching for Danny, "I need my son."

The old woman smiled and held Danny up.

Grimacing, Gloria shifted Danny's weight to one arm and reached into the pocket of her skirt. The old Shoshone woman's hands were still outstretched, and Gloria placed a handful of coins in the open palm. "Here," she said. "For your trouble."

John William returned to the wagon, holding Kate in one arm and Gloria's green case in the other. Strapped to his back were the supplies he'd just traded for—flour and coffee, potatoes and salt pork. Enough to last them a few more weeks, anyway. He stopped short when he got to the campsite, a little surprised himself at the comfort he felt at the sight of Gloria's boots dropped on the ground. He deposited his bundle right next to the boots before picking them up and placing them on the wagon step.

"Is that you, MacGregan?" her voice called from behind the canvas.

"None other." He lifted the flap a bit and peered inside.

She looked better, rested. Danny was sleeping, curled up against her.

"Is this what's goin' to happen then, Gloria? Am I just goin' to wake up every mornin' or so and wonder where you're off to?"

"I'm so sorry."

"I was worried."

"I know."

He dropped the flap and started to open the bundle of supplies, but her voice beckoned him again. He couldn't make out the words muffled through the canvas, so he stood straight and opened the flap.

"What did you say?"

"I asked if you would ever forgive me."

"You don't have to ask that, Gloria," he said. "It's not for me to forgive."

Let not conscience make you linger,
Nor of fitness fondly dream,
All the fitness he requireth
Is to feel your need of him.

～ 15 ～

The coffee was weak, but John William took no notice. He sat on his little campstool, as he had for countless mornings, surrounded by this latest variation of God's creation. He'd had breakfast in the shadows of mountains and had slept beside lapping lakes and roaring rivers. But this morning, this landscape, was different.

Gloria hadn't roused yet, and he felt no compulsion to call her from her slumber. The sun was not quite up; the silence settled his soul.

Well, not complete silence.

The sounds of the Umatilla River had lulled him to sleep, and now it serenaded him across the dawn. Umatilla. "Rippling water." The Indians named this land for its sound. After years of whistling Wyoming wind and months of heavy-summer-air silence, the sound of the river called to him and gave him the message he'd been waiting to hear.

Home.

He'd left Silver Peak with a vague notion of Oregon. He knew about the floods of people fighting their way across the country to make a home in this new Promised Land. He himself felt the thrill of accomplishment at the first step after crossing the Snake River. But he hadn't arrived with a plan. He had no destination in mind. He likened himself to Abraham, content to journey with faith and diligence until God saw fit to tell him to stop. This morning, the song of the Umatilla River and the gray outline of the Blue Mountains served as God's missive.

John William set down his coffee and went to his knees, elbows braced on the seat of his campstool, immersed in prayer. Silent, at first, but at some point he spoke aloud.

"Lord, I ask for your guidance. Give me direction. Give me wisdom. Give me—"

"Coffee," her voice invaded.

"Patience," he finished. "Amen."

She hadn't yet emerged from the wagon, and by the time Gloria popped her head through the canvas opening at the back, John William was back on his feet, waving his cup under her nose.

"Does it ever occur to you to pray to yourself?" she asked, her voice cranky and dry.

"Good mornin' to you, too."

"G'morning," she said with a self-conscious smile, her crankiness apparently short-lived this morning.

"Get up," he said. "I have good news."

"Is it coffee?"

"It might be, if you get up. But there's not much left, and I'm feelin' a little greedy."

Gloria scowled and dropped the tent flap. Moments later she emerged, her hair pulled back and loosely tied at her neck. She brought with her a snuffling, stretching Kate, who was immediately traded for a steaming cup of coffee. Gloria inhaled its fragrance, took a sip, closed her eyes, smiled and sipped again before turning her full attention back to John William.

"So what is it?" she asked. "What's the good news?"

"We're here," he said, beaming a smile back and forth between his daughter and Gloria.

"Where?"

"Here."

"Where exactly is here?"

"That," he said, cupping his ear to indicate the sound of the river, "is the Umatilla River. We are, according to the last map I looked at, in Umatilla County. We're home."

"Home? *Home?* You can name a county and decide it's home?"

"I don't decide," John William said. "God told me."

"Really? I must have slept right through that. All I heard was you mumbling a request for directions."

John William started with an equally sharp reply, but stilled himself. For just a moment, he allowed himself to feel flattered that she listened for his voice. He settled himself down on his stool with Kate in his lap.

"It's a feelin' I have."

"A feeling?"

"Yes. It's hard to explain, but I've been prayin' so hard for so long for God to show me where to go. Every other mornin' I've had this restless feelin', like I can't wait to get hitched up and movin'. But this mornin', there was just a feelin' of…"

His voice trailed off when he saw the look of dumbfounded incredulity on Gloria's face. She looked like someone had just whacked her in the head and told her that black was white, and had been all along.

"Am I to understand," Gloria said, speaking slowly, deliberately, "that you get this *feeling,* decide that it's the voice of God, and just like that we've arrived?"

"Yes."

"No hint of civilization. No town."

"There must be something," John William said. "We passed two homesteads yesterday."

"Hmm," she murmured through a sip of coffee before she turned away from him.

"What did you expect?" John William asked. "Did you think we were going to roll into another Virginia City?"

"I don't know what I thought."

"Gloria, we're in a new territory. A new country, really. It's a place to start life over. Nobody knows us, who we are. What we are."

She turned to look at him again. The sun was just coming up, and she stood, bathed in new light, the Blue Mountains a stunning backdrop behind her. John William's breath left him, and he was grateful when Kate demanded his attention by grabbing a handful of his hair and yanking with all her tiny strength.

"It's a new start," he concluded, his voice lame and flat, distracted by his efforts to wrest his hair from his daughter's fist.

Gloria crossed over to John William and took Kate out of his arms. Gracefully holding her coffee aloft, she sat cross-legged, nestling Kate against her. The baby turned to nurse, but Gloria entertained her by twirling long blonde locks across the baby's face. "So, what does God's voice sound like?"

"This morning, it sounds like the Umatilla River," he said. "Listen."

And she did. At least she seemed to. John William was faintly amused at the serious, concentrated look that came over her face as she listened.

Lord, he prayed silently, give her somethin' too, please. Somethin' to hear. Give her—

Music.

Just over the horizon, voices carried across the morning.

"Come ye sinners, poor and needy,
Weak and wounded, sick and sore."

The song grew stronger as a wagon, pulled by a fine-looking team of horses, came into view. The first thing John William noticed was that this wagon lacked the familiar canvas cover that graced nearly every one he'd seen since leaving Wyoming. A young man and woman sat upon its bouncing seat, and the small heads of children peeped just over the open box.

While they were still several hundred yards away, John William stood and waved his hat.

"Hello, there!" he called.

"Shhh," Gloria said, the crankiness returned to her voice. "They'll come over here."

"It's called being neighborly. If this is our home, then these are our neighbors."

"I'm not even dressed!"

"So close a few buttons," John William said over his shoulder. "They're a ways off. You have time."

They were the Logan family: David, Josephine, and their children James, Eliza, and Charles. Months on the trail made it nearly impossible to distinguish one day from another, but this family said it all: Sunday.

David Logan wore a calico shirt so starched that its creases nearly crackled; Josephine wore a crisp straw hat adorned with a wide blue ribbon tied just below her chin. The Logan children were scrubbed raw. Wet comb marks ran furrows across the boys' pink scalps, and Eliza's hair was drawn back into a crisp blonde braid. These were the cleanest children John William had seen since his days peeking through the prison bars. He wondered what the fans of Killer MacGregan would think if they saw their hero getting almost weepy at the sight of a wagon full of shiny children.

"John William MacGregan," he said, after meeting the Logan family. "And this is Gloria and baby Kate." He was acutely aware of Gloria's disheveled appearance and his own unshaven face.

"Pleased to meet you," David said. "You folks passing through or planning to settle?"

"Wasn't sure until this mornin'," John William said. "Been waitin' on the Lord's word on that, but I think this is where He wants us to stay."

"It's beautiful country," Josephine said, speaking directly to Gloria, but when Gloria failed to meet her gaze, she turned to John William. "And it's growing, too."

"Will you join us in church this morning?" David asked.

"There's a church nearby?"

"Just north about three miles, in Middleton," David said.

"Middleton," John William said, turning toward Gloria. "So there is a town?"

"Town's stretchin' it a bit," David said. "A post office, general store."

"And a church," John William piped in, his voice full of wonder. He'd spent many Sunday mornings apologizing to Katherine for taking her away from a civilized congregation.

"It's quite a small gathering, really," Josephine said. "About ten families. But we do enjoy our time together. Won't you come?"

"We've been travelin'," John William said, gesturing around him. "We haven't had a chance to even wash up."

"Well, you're not far from the river," David said. "Go splash around in it a minute."

"Yes," Josephine chimed in. "Surely Mrs. MacGregan would—"

"Gloria. Call me Gloria."

"Of course." If Josephine was taken aback by Gloria's abruptness, she showed no sign of it.

"And we have two babies to wash up," Gloria continued. "This one, and another asleep in the wagon."

"Oh, my," Josephine said. "Twins?"

"A little boy, Danny, and the girl," Gloria said. "So you see, there's no possible way we could join you this morning."

An awkward silence settled over the little gathering and stayed there until the youngest Logan child, Charles, stood up in the back of the wagon and dangled a basket over its side.

"Wanna doughnut?" he asked.

"Yes, please have one," Josephine said. "I fried them last night, but they're still rather fresh."

"No, thank you," Gloria said, her eyes never leaving the basket. "I was just about to make our breakfast."

John William stifled a laugh.

"Please," Gloria continued, "don't let us keep you any longer."

"It's only an hour's ride from here," David said. "We've got plenty of time."

Gloria started to speak again, but John William strode to stand between her and the Logan family. "Give us just one minute," he said to David, then he turned to Gloria. He towered over her, and she rose to her feet.

"We're not going," she said.

John William sensed the uncomfortable shuffle of the people in the wagon behind him. He thought he heard the oldest Logan boy giggle.

"You do not speak for this house," John William said, raising his voice to an authoritative pitch.

"In case you haven't noticed," Gloria said, shifting Kate to her other hip, "this isn't a house. And there has never been a time when I didn't speak for myself. So I suggest that you remember who I am and why I'm here, or I'll just pack myself back home."

"You couldn't make your own way across the creek," John William said. "Now get yourself washed and dressed. We're going to church."

"No."

"Gloria." He attempted a threatening tone.

"No. Listen, MacGregan, do what you want, go where you want. I'll be here."

He bent to her, his forehead resting on hers. "Gloria, you are my family now," he said in a voice he was certain the Logan family could not hear. "I haven't had a chance to go to a church in years. I want to go, and I want you to go with me."

He sensed a change in her breath, a synchronization with his own.

"I...can't," she said at last.

"You can," he said, reaching for her, but caressing Kate's soft cheek instead.

"I won't."

"I'm going," he said.

"Go."

"I don't want to go alone."

"You won't be," Gloria said, stepping away from him and offering a consoling smile. "You have your new friends to take you." She shouldered baby Kate and turned to the Logan wagon.

"It was nice to meet you all," she said before passing Kate through their wagon's canvas flap and following her inside.

John William turned to face ten boldly staring eyes.

"May I ride with you?" he asked, his tone light, if forced.

"Of course," Josephine said.

"Just give me five minutes to wash up."

John William splashed his face with the icy water drawn from the barrel strapped to the side of the wagon. Lacking a comb, he ran his fingers through his hair, careful to keep his disfigured ear covered. He was wearing his cleanest shirt, which he smoothed with his damp hands and tucked into his pants. He grabbed his Bible from its place on his bedroll, dropped his hat on his head, and turned with a cheerful, "Let's go!"

When John William climbed up into the wagon box, the dumbfounded children scuttled to make room for him, and he felt enormous sharing a space with such little people.

David Logan clicked to his team, and the wagon started its bumpy journey. John William turned back frequently to see if Gloria would emerge, but she didn't. And after only a few minutes of travel, the rolling foothills made any sight of her impossible. When he turned back, sighing, he felt a tug on his sleeve.

"Wanna doughnut now?" Charles asked, offering the same basket.

John William gave what he hoped was a friendly smile and reached under the towel to pluck out a pastry. When he popped it in his mouth, the smile became one of pure joy. There was just a hint of crispness left in the fried bread. It had been dipped in sugar, and the sweetness was almost overwhelming. There was little need to chew; the morsel seemed to melt against his tongue.

Gloria would have loved this.

"The journey is hard on a woman," Josephine said, her voice full of compassion. "I'm sure your wife just didn't feel at her best."

"I think she's very pretty," the small voice of Eliza Logan lisped through two missing front teeth.

"I think you're very pretty," John William said, and her blushing smile warmed him.

"I dunno," James said. "She sure seems like a wild one."

John William burst out in a heartfelt guffaw, and David, too, gave a hoot and a giggle.

"James!" Josephine turned in her seat to reprimand her son. "That was not a kind thing to say."

"But true, eh?" David said over his shoulder. "A real little scrapper?"

"Brother, you don't know the half of it," John William said.

As they rode, the full force of what he had taken on hit. Until now, he and Gloria and Danny and Kate had been their own little family, isolated in the middle of this huge country, owing nothing to anybody.

But now…this might be their home. His home, anyway, and he was entering it under a canopy of lies. He wondered what David Logan would do if he knew the stranger in the back of his wagon had killed two men with his bare hands. He wondered how comfortable the Logan children would be if they knew he had once watched children through the bars of a jail cell. Would Josephine make such overtures of friendship to Gloria if she knew she was a prostitute dragged along to nurse his dead wife's daughter alongside her illegitimate son?

Then he looked into the earnest, clear-eyed faces of Eliza, James, and Charles as they offered to share with him their treasures of ribbons, buttons, and rocks. Periodically, Josephine would turn around to check on her children and would include him in her reassuring smile. David filled the silence with occasional details about the land, the crops, the promises of this new country. Maybe, he thought, none of it would matter after all.

"Hey, Logan," he called, "will you have me back before dark?"

"Should be. Worried?"

"Yeah," John William said. "She doesn't know how to start a fire."

❀ ❀ ❀

Gloria watched the Logan's wagon disappear over the horizon. As far as she could tell, John William never looked back.

"Have a wonderful day," she called into the wind. "Don't you worry about me here. All alone. With two babies."

The far-off lapping of the Umatilla River was her only response.

"Oh, no. I'll be fine, just fine."

Both Danny and Kate were awake now. Their lusty cries declared breakfast long overdue. She lifted each child down and removed the night's soiled diapers. She wrapped a fresh one around Kate, but allowed Danny to roll around naked on the blanket while he waited his turn.

"I'm feeding your daughter," Gloria called in the general direction of the long-vanished wagon. "I'm feeding your daughter and I haven't had a bite to eat for myself yet."

The babble of brooks blended with the babble of babies while Gloria sat, staring and dreaming of doughnuts.

There was no bell tower, no church bell, just a man standing in front of the small whitewashed building, shouting a welcome. John William heard the thin thread of his voice before he could make out any discernible features.

"Good morning! Good morning! God bless us today."

The voice belonged to a tall, gaunt man with a stunningly shiny bald head and gray beard.

"That the preacher?" John William asked.

"Yep," David Logan replied. "Reverend Fuller. Thomas Fuller."

"Oh, he's a wonderful preacher," Josephine said. "Of course we've only heard him a few times, but those few times were wonderful. Just wonderful."

"He talks a long time," James said. "Sometimes for hours and hours."

"Now stop that," his mother said, a warm lilt to her chastisement. "You are exaggerating, and that's as close to lying as I ever want you to get."

"Yes, ma'am," James said, but he caught John William's eye and made a face of excruciating boredom, crossing his eyes and lolling his head against the wall of the wagon bed.

"You've only heard him a few times?" John William said. "How long have you been settled here?"

"We've been here a while," David said, without turning around. "But Fuller just started up the church about a year ago. And he don't just stay right here. He goes all over the territory— preaches here once a month."

"Yes," Josephine said. "It's a pity, too. I do miss having church every Sunday."

"Guess I was lucky to make camp when I did," John William said. "Else I might have missed it."

"Mama says luck is man's word for God's perfect timing," Eliza said with a heavy lisp.

"I think your mama's right." John William looked at Eliza and wondered what his own Kate would look like, all grown up with ribbons and shiny shoes. "I think every day we find ourselves right where God wants us to be."

"Well, today," David said, pulling his team to a halt and setting the brake, "God wants us to be in church. And if we don't stop all this gabbing, we're going to be late."

The last flicker of the breakfast fire lost its will to live, and by the time Gloria thought to fan the flames, there was nothing left but a pile of cooling ashes and charred sticks.

Her stomach rumbled as she thought about the little plate of last night's cold beans, the remnants of the morning coffee, yesterday's rock-hard biscuits. Furious and starving, she muttered a furtive curse.

Instinctively she looked up, looked around, awaiting the glare of disapproval. But there was no one to disapprove, just Danny and Kate who were too involved with their little feet to pay her any attention.

Gloria stood straight and cursed out loud.

No sense of reprimand.

She reared her head back and screamed profanity to the vast Oregon sky.

No response, although Danny and Kate were jarred enough to tear their attention from their toes and give her a four-eyed blinking stare.

"Do you see?" she said, granting the infants a bitter smile. "They'd never let me in a church."

Reverend Fuller stood on the step of the little shack-of-a-church house. He spoke to the milling crowd in a voice that proved to be much gentler than the one used to summon his flock.

"Brothers and sisters," he said, "we have a new member here with us this morning. Please join me in welcoming John William MacGregan to our church."

Each member of the congregation greeted John William before entering the building. It wasn't an arduous process. There were three other families besides the Logans. The children mixed and mingled so much it was impossible to tell which set of parents each belonged to. And while John William tried to concentrate on names, he found himself distracted having to repeat the story of Gloria, back at their camp, with two small children too young to come this morning. His mind scrambled around the word *wife,* answering questions with nods rather than statements, careful not to lie outright, hoping his representation of the truth would satisfy even Josephine Logan's intolerance for untruths.

There was an abundance of bachelors—he counted five—in the congregation. Some, he would learn, were homesteaders. Others lived in modest cabins and hired out their labor on neighboring farms. However, there were two women there who seemed to be alone.

The first was a tall woman whose copper-colored hair was arranged in a complicated fashion that made John William think of a massive coiled rope. She had full lips, tinted to match her hair, and a look that he recognized from his boxing days. It was the look shared equally by hungry opponents and hungry women, both itching for a victorious encounter. In the old days, he would have answered such a look with a grin that said, "You don't stand a chance with me." But now, facing such a look from this woman in this place, he found himself scrambling for a defense.

"I'm Adele Fuller," she said, her voice husky with promise. She'd peeled off a glove to offer John William her bare hand. "Reverend Fuller's daughter."

"Not his wife?" John William said, amazing himself at the stupidity of the statement.

Adele Fuller brought a slim hand up to emphasize a short, coy laugh. "Oh, no, I'm not anybody's wife. You here all alone?"

"No, no. Gloria…she's back at camp, with the babies…" His voice trailed off as he searched within the tiny room for David Logan to come and rescue him.

"Adele Fuller," came a sweet, bird-like voice from somewhere near his elbow, "you just leave this man alone and take your seat before your father sees you behaving so shamefully."

Adele gave John William a slow smile. "We don't have many hymn books, so you're welcome to share with me if you want." She walked past John William, allowing the skirt of her dress to glide against his leg.

John William turned to meet his savior, saw nobody, then looked down and saw a mass of wild gray curls surrounding a soft smiling face.

"You better watch that one," the tiny woman said, her dancing brown eyes following Adele. "Her mother died about ten years back, and her father's so busy travelin' he don't have much time to look after her."

"That so?" John William said.

"I'm Maureen Brewster, and if you're going to share a hymn book with anybody, it'll be with me."

The basket was oval shaped, nearly four feet long and two feet deep. A gift from Jewell, something she used to haul washing. Gloria remembered when both Danny and Kate seemed to get lost in the vastness of it. John William had attached a handle made of rope, and these days it served as a mobile cradle. Now Kate protested its confines as she rode, jarred and bumped against Gloria's leg, on a trek to the river's bank.

Gloria struggled with the basket in one hand, Danny clutched in the other arm. John William had not set up camp right at the river's edge; there was a brief thicket of trees between the clearing where the wagon rested and the song of the lapping water. Gifted with the rare opportunity of time alone, one thought crossed Gloria's mind.

A bath.

Nestled in with Kate was a blanket, a relatively clean change of clothes for each of the babies, Gloria's cotton sleeping gown, and the only intact linen towel. A small wooden box held the remains of what had been, at the beginning of their journey, a substantial cake of soap. Much of it had been used laundering the endless supply of diapers, stretched across the wagon's cover to dry in the daily sun. But there was a small cake of it left, and Gloria had mixed in with it the last drops of her lavender oil, intending to pamper her and the children with a full all-over bath.

The first bare step into the cold river water sent painful jolts up Gloria's legs. Her breath was stolen by the initial shock, and a sharp squeal accompanied each step toward submersion. Kate remained within the basket on the river's bank; Danny was clutched firmly in Gloria's arms. His sun-warmed soft baby skin felt delicious in contrast to the icy water lapping around her legs. He cooed, his tight, toothless grin creating a face of pure adoration. The expression changed to one of wide-eyed gaping surprise when Gloria brought a palm full of water to dribble down his bare back.

"Is that cold, baby?" she said in response to his swift gasps. "I'm sorry, Danny," she continued in a soothing voice. "It'll get better."

As she lowered herself into the water, Danny's little feet hit the surface, then his chubby knees. Each inch converted his initial shock and discomfort to squealing joy. He kicked wildly and slapped at the river's surface with his hands.

"Well, you're a regular little water rat, aren't you, Danny boy?" Gloria said, enthralled with his joy. She wondered if her own mother had ever held her like this, exposed together in a moment of pure happiness.

She'd placed the wooden box of soap on a large rock jutting from the shore. Now, Gloria moved in slow bobbing steps over to it. She held Danny tight in one arm and with the other hand reached in, scraping off a layer of soap with her fingernails and used it to cleanse the glistening folds of her son's soft skin, then gave him a final rinse with the river's clear water.

After allowing a few more minutes of playful splashing, Gloria brought Danny to shore and dressed him in a clean, sun-warmed shirt. She laid him down on the outspread blanket. She draped the waist of her discarded skirt over the lip of the basket and extended the material out, creating a makeshift tent to protect the babies' sensitive skin from the sun. The pleasure of the bath met the warmth of the afternoon, and by the time she finished taking Kate through the same process, Danny was fast asleep. Kate, too, succumbed to the ritual, and soon Gloria found herself looking at her son and daughter—no, *his* daughter—sleeping like angels.

She thought about the Logan children—clean, combed, ribboned—and wondered if she would ever see these two so groomed and proper. Quite the little family. Gloria sat on a river rock, her hands folded demurely in her lap.

"Children, time for church," she said out loud, trying to

capture the soft sweet cadence of Josephine Logan's voice. "Come, Kate, let mother comb your hair. Why, Danny, how handsome you look!"

Gloria pictured the stark comb marks in the Logan children's hair. Such discipline. Such cleanliness. So prim and pure. The product of a lovely perfect mother.

She waded to the depths of the river one more time and plunged beneath the surface, then emerged to claw a handful of soap, work it to a lather, and attack her scalp. She grabbed still more, and soon red tracks marked the passage of her nails across lavender-scented skin. She threw herself backward, allowing her hair to rinse as it dangled in the water.

Gloria wondered what would happen if she fell asleep right now. Would she roll over and drown? Maybe the river's current would just take her away, far from Danny and Kate. She pondered, for a second, which would be worse. She realized she really had no idea how long John William and the Logans would be gone. What if that happy little wagon pulled up right now? What a sight she was, the naked water nymph floating on the surface of the sacred Umatilla River. She pictured John William's face, shocked and ashamed. She heard Josephine Logan's voice, softly surprised yet kind.

The thoughts poured through her head as she poured rivulets of water across her stomach, once again flat and firm, all traces of having carried a child lost. Forever.

Gloria righted herself and walked to shore, wringing her sodden hair over her shoulder. She stood on the bank and wrung until no more droplets fell, then ran a wide-toothed wooden comb through the wet tresses before wrapping her head in the towel she'd used to dry the babies. Although the sun felt glorious on her clean dry skin, a nagging bit of propriety insisted that she don her loose-fitting cotton sleeping gown, sleeveless and cut to just below her knees.

Suddenly a nap on the river's bank seemed irresistible. She stretched herself out on the blanket, her head just parallel to the triangle of shade she'd created for the babies. She took one last look at their sleeping forms—Danny on his tummy with his little face half-smashed against the quilt, and Kate on her back with her arms flung open to the world. Gloria curled on her side, facing them, and closed her eyes.

She was just making her way to the edges of sleep when she heard the buzzing. She brought her hand up to send halfhearted slaps toward the sound, but it wasn't until one of her fingers made contact with something that she actually sat up, fully awake and aware.

Bees.

At least a dozen of them swarmed around her, landing lightly on her skin. She leapt to her feet crying, "Shoo! Go away!" slapping her hands together, successfully crushing two of them between her palms.

She swept the towel off her head and whirled it through the air, feeling little fuzzy bodies make contact. When the bees refused to leave, she grabbed the towel by its corners and furled it into a tight coil which she snapped, whip-like, killing two or three more in midflight.

She had no idea how long she waged battle, but at some point she stopped to catch her breath and realized that the air was clear. The bees were gone, and she was full of an exhilaration she had never felt before. This instinct to protect, this animal-like passion to drive the wolves from the nest made Gloria feel alive and proud. So proud, in fact, that her only regret was that nobody had been there to witness the feat. The very lives she was protecting napped through the valiant display.

Then she saw it. A tiny red welt just beginning to swell on Danny's left cheek.

"Oh God," she said, calling out a plea that surprised her. She fell to her knees and gathered her son into her arms, bringing him close to put her lips on the red, hot flesh. "Danny, Danny, I'm so sorry, baby. I'm so sorry."

Still holding Danny close, she scanned every exposed inch of

Kate's sleeping body and was relieved to see that her flesh was milky white and unmarked.

"I could never let any harm come to you, Kate," she whispered as she gently ran a finger down Kate's soft cheek. "If I did…he wouldn't need me any more."

The voice of Reverend Thomas Fuller filled the tiny church. True, any voice would fill the space—barely four hundred square feet—but Reverend Fuller seemed to attempt to reach every corner without overwhelming the congregation.

John William sat on a bench at the back of the church. The wood was smooth and varnished to a gleam. Maureen Brewster sat next to him.

Early in the service, Reverend Fuller led them in songs of worship. Adele had been right about the sparse number of hymnals: there were exactly five. But the reverend led them through songs the congregation knew by heart, and John William felt months of spiritual reserve chipping away as he raised his strong baritone to join the others. Maureen's voice, as diminutive as her body, quavered somewhere around his elbow, and often during a song he looked down and she looked up as they shared both a note and a smile.

Now the sermon was in full swing, and John William was thrilled to hear God's Word spoken by a man who'd studied it and knew its full meaning.

"We are all newcomers here," he was saying, his hands gesturing to encompass both the congregation and the outlying countryside. "We are all strangers in a strange land, and we will determine whether or not this will be a land for God."

John William thought about the places he'd lived, places he'd seen. Wild towns built on gold and promises, fueled by whiskey. Men driven by a quest for fortune. Women…

"So we must commit our lives to this land just as we commit our lives to our God. We must take root and grow a society that will be pleasing to His nature."

Living in fancy hotels or tents. Or four-walled shacks that let the winter snows blow right in. No place for a family. No place for a daughter. Or a son.

"And so I have decided to make Middleton my permanent home."

A unanimous gasp went up from the congregation followed by whispered joy.

"I will be sharing my itinerant duties with a minister in Centerville, and will hold church services here the first and third Sunday of every month."

The elation of the people expanded into applause. The excitement of Maureen beside him made John William feel comfortable to join in the celebration of these strangers. It wasn't until the ruckus died down that he noticed the intent gaze of Adele Fuller, turned fully around in her front seat, fixed on him. He returned a polite smile, but was so startled by the boldness of her expression that he didn't hear what Maureen said.

"What was that?" he asked, bending his large frame to better hear her.

"I said, if we're going to have a proper church, maybe I'll stay after all."

John William wanted to inquire further, but Reverend Fuller was leading them in a prayer of dismissal.

The sky was full of horses and pantaloons. At least that's what the clouds looked like. Gloria sat on the little campstool gazing at them, having gathered the children up and brought them back to the wagon site to finish their nap. Now awake, Danny and Kate inched their way around the blanket spread on the ground at her feet, periodically being scooped up and brought back to safety when they came to near the blanket's edge.

She had dabbed Danny's face with cool river water, and the swelling was down considerably, but the area was still red with a tight raised bump at its center. She held him now, and he rooted against her, hungrily searching out her breast.

"You know, son, I haven't eaten anything today yet, either," she said. "Guess it's beans, beans, beans."

Gloria, still in her nightgown, set Danny back on the blanket, stood up, and wallowed in a luxurious stretch and gratifying scratch before wandering over to the wagon's larder. One bowl of beans. Cold. She knew John William would be able to do wonders with these, given just a slice of salt pork and half an onion, but neither of those was available now. Not that she would know what to do with them. She knew even the smallest fire would return them to a more palatable temperature, but the thoughts of gathering wood and assembling kindling and striking a match seemed a bit overwhelming on such a warm, lazy summer day. So she took the bowl, grabbed a fork, and returned to the blanket.

"Now this," she said out loud, gesturing with the fork, "is what that Sabbath commandment is all about." She stretched one leg out to caress Kate's soft cheek with a toe. "Who needs church?" She allowed a bean to linger in her mouth, warm up a little, before sending it to join the others.

"And I'm saying that because I know," she continued, giving her heavy, damp hair a shake off her shoulders. "I've been to church before."

What she didn't say out loud was that the minute she'd walked through the doors, the minister pointed at her and shouted that a whore such as this had no place in the house of God.

"I even talked with the minister once." The previous evening when she'd refused to perform the favors he demanded. "So I know what we're missing," she said to the babies, who were now each propped up on their little elbows, staring at her intently. "And we're not missing much."

Because the church met so infrequently, the better part of the day was devoted to worship, fellowship, and teaching. After the initial time of song and sermon, the congregation split into Sunday schools. The children were grouped together for classes: the girls led by Adele Fuller and the boys by Reverend Fuller. The women gathered to discuss the focal passage among themselves, as did the men. John William soon learned, though, that the Middleton men's Sunday school class would not be a great source of Bible study. Almost immediately the conversation turned to crops, weather, and farming.

"I'm telling you, MacGregan," David Logan said, "you've never seen land like this for growing things. Looks like I'll be harvesting near twice what I did last year."

"Yep," said another Middleton neighbor, Phil Jasper. John William learned that everybody called him Big Phil, and his imposing girth gave the obvious explanation why. "I got a quarter section of corn coming in, wheat looks good. This is God's country for sure."

"I can see that," John William said. "And a town startin' and a church. I think we can make a life here."

"You might want to talk to Maureen Brewster," David said. "Her husband died last spring, just after getting the crop in. She's been wanting to sell and move back East."

"Now why would he want to do that?" Big Phil said. "He can get himself his acres from the government for free." He turned to face John William. "One square mile, six hundred forty acres, and the same for your wife if you don't mind havin' it in her name."

"Well, yeah," David said, "but the Brewsters was one of the first families to settle these parts. If he buys her place, he gets land that's been cleared, house built. Buying the Brewster place'd be like buying ten years worth of labor."

"Gentlemen, gentlemen please," John William said, laughing and laying a hand on each shoulder. "Let me have some say in the matter. Besides, just during church she said she might not leave at all."

"I wouldn't wait too long to make a decision if I were you," Big Phil said. "Mrs. Brewster's a land-owning single woman. If she don't leave, she'll be married off before the wheat sprouts."

John William looked over at the crowd of women gathered in earnest conversation. Maureen Brewster was one of the oldest there, her gray frizzled hair hardly the markings of an object of desire.

"You sure about that?" John William said.

"Listen here," David said, "women here are scarce. Men can't be too particular about age and beauty and such."

Just then Adele Fuller turned slightly and gave the men a stunning smile before returning to her conversation.

"Then how come that Adele Fuller ain't married yet?" John William asked.

"Aw, she can afford to be particular." This from a slick-looking young hand named Lonnie. "She could have herself any man she wants. And she don't want a farmer."

"Judging by the way she's looking at you," Big Phil said to John William, "you'd better get yourself a farm as soon as you can."

"I'll talk with Mrs. Brewster when I get a chance."

"No better time than now," David said. "It's time for the dinner."

There was a bustle of activity as boxes and baskets were unloaded from the wagons parked around the church building. It was a tradition of the congregation to share a generous potluck dinner, each family contributing what it could. The fresh dough-nuts brought by the Logans were just the tip of their contribution. Mrs. Logan also had two-dozen corn muffins, sausage links, a jar of pickled beets, and cold potato cakes.

Planks were laid across the wagons creating long tables loaded with dishes, bowls, pots, and plates. The bachelors of the congregation brought kegs of fresh water and cider. There were kettles of baked beans, cooked overnight and wrapped in towels to keep warm. One family brought a smoked ham from a pig that had to be slaughtered early, another a huge pot of venison stew. There were jars of pickles, cans of oysters, loaves of bread, dozens of biscuits. Apple, cream, and fresh berry pies were lined up and guarded closely. But the greatest treasure of all was isolated and revered: Adele Fuller's chocolate cake.

John William stared, openmouthed. He'd never seen such bounty in his life. He felt a plate being placed in his hand and looked down to see the now familiar face of Maureen Brewster.

"I couldn't," he said. "I didn't bring anythin'."

"Nonsense," Maureen said. "There's plenty here. Now fill your plate and come sit with me."

"Yes, ma'am. You're just the person I want to talk to."

Mae had given her the magazine just as Gloria was loading her things into the wagon before leaving Silver Peak. "Just a little something to pass the time," she'd said, and Gloria had spent many hours flipping through its pages, largely ignoring the pages of elusive text.

But she did enjoy the pictures, especially the styles that John William told her the magazine heralded as "the latest from Paris." Four of the pages were devoted to hairstyles—complicated labyrinths of braids and loops. For Gloria, who had never done much more than restrain her curls in a single thick braid, they presented the challenge of civilization and sophistication.

Still wearing the sleeping gown she'd put on after her bath, Gloria sat in fierce determination to achieve success. The magazine lay open beside her, a small rock anchoring the pages against the slight afternoon breeze. John William's shaving mirror was propped up on an overturned crate, and next to it a small dish contained every hairpin Gloria owned. Seven. It was hardly enough to recreate the crowning glory from the picture, so she improvised using strips of cloth to anchor sections, tucking and hiding the ends within the mass of hair.

Three thick sections were wrenched into a twist along the back of her head. The hair remaining loose at the side of her face was divided, plaited into twelve tiny ropes—six on each side— which were meant to crisscross over the large twist and create a profile not unlike the prow of an ancient ship.

After what she estimated to be an hour's worth of hard labor,

Gloria had a sheen of sweat across her face, aching arms, and a disaster on her head. Up close, the shaving mirror allowed her to see only a quarter of her face and head at a time. Each step she took away from the mirror gave a fuller view. When she finally had a chance to see the complete picture, the only resemblance to the reflection in the mirror and the picture in the magazine was that both depicted a woman with hair.

"I think that's a better use for that hairbrush," Gloria said, looking at baby Kate chomping hungry little gums on the brush's wooden handle. "It certainly didn't do me much good here."

Kate took the brush out of her mouth long enough to emit a gurgly giggle.

"And what about you, young man?" Gloria said, turning to Danny. "What do you think?"

But Danny was absorbed in the creation of spit bubbles. Gloria couldn't even get him to look at her.

"Men," Gloria said. "Women torture themselves trying to look beautiful for them, and they don't even notice." Not that she had any man to look beautiful for, of course. John William always took extra pains not to look at her at all.

Unfortunately, the undoing of the creation proved to be just as unsuccessful as the style itself, and soon she was left with a mass of half braids, tangles, and wild, frizzed tresses.

Perhaps it was the flurry of activity around her ears, perhaps it was the mumbled cursing that accompanied her task—whatever the reason, Gloria failed to hear the approach of the Logan's wagon. She was, in fact, quite unaware of their presence until she heard John William say, "Gloria?"

She whipped herself around, brought one arm up to cover her uncorsetted breasts and the other to unsuccessfully cover her hair.

"You're back," she said. "I…I didn't hear you."

John William's face was a mixture of concern and amusement. David Logan turned beet red and quickly averted his gaze. Josephine looked like a woman who had just discovered a wounded puppy in a rosebush.

"Can I help you with that, dear?" she asked in that sweet voice Gloria found enviable and annoying.

"No, no, it's fine," Gloria said, frantically trying to pat the mess down.

"Nonsense," Josephine said. "These styles are nearly impossible, especially without a proper vanity table or mirror." Within seconds she was out of the wagon and at Gloria's side. She cleared the shaving mirror off the crate and guided Gloria to sit on it. "Let's just see what we have here," she said, stooping to take the brush from baby Kate's grip.

"Come on, MacGregan," Logan said. "Let's leave the women to their talk."

The men jumped down from the wagon and walked toward the river.

Gloria submitted herself to Josephine's ministrations. She felt gentle tugs on her scalp as Josephine loosened the anchored braids.

"The children are asleep in the back of the wagon," Josephine said. "These Sundays just wear them out."

"I can imagine," Gloria said.

"Your little ones seem wide awake. Did they just wake up?"

"A while ago."

The women lapsed back into silence as Josephine worked with Gloria's hair.

"Let me know if I'm hurting you," Josephine said.

"You're not."

As each section came free, Josephine spread the hair across her palm and smoothed the tresses with the brush.

"Thank you," Gloria said.

"Of course," Josephine said. "What are friends for?"

Gloria looked up at her with questioning eyes.

"At least," Josephine said, "I hope we'll be friends."

"Me, too," Gloria said. She thought about her late night talks with Sadie and the other girls. What in the world would she talk to Josephine Logan about?

Josephine gathered all of Gloria's hair into one hand and brushed the lot of it. The women were silent, lulled by the whoosh of the bristles.

"You have beautiful hair," Josephine said. "The curls, the color. It's just beautiful."

"Thank you," Gloria said.

"Would you like me to braid it for you?"

"No, no thank you," Gloria said. "You should probably be going."

"Of course." Josephine set the brush down on the crate and cupped a hand to her mouth. "David!" she called. "It's time to go!" Then she stooped to give each of the babies a tickle on the tummy before climbing into the wagon to wait for her husband.

As the Logans drove out of sight, John William turned to Gloria and offered her a big smile.

"You seem to have enjoyed your day," he said, looking her up and down with amusement.

"We went to the river, took a bath, came back. Ate beans."

"And the hair?"

"Don't ask. Boredom makes you do crazy things."

She'd taken the time to pull a skirt and blouse over the sleeping gown, but her hair remained full and loose and clean.

"How 'bout you, big fella," John William said, bending to pick up Danny. He hoisted the boy up into his arms, took one look at the child's face, then turned to Gloria with a concerned look. "What happened?"

"He got stung. By a bee."

"What about Kate?" His voice was full of panic, even though the obviously healthy child rolled around at his feet, the only immediate danger being his own boots.

"She's fine. See?"

"Thank God," John William said. "But this poor little one—"

Gloria bristled. "Is fine, too."

"How could you let this happen?" By now he was on his knees, having set Danny back down, and lifted Kate into his arms. He held her aloft, looking over every inch of her, bringing her little feet up close to his eyes and lifting her gown to check the skin underneath.

"I told you she's fine. I handled it."

John William brought his daughter close to his face, inhaled, made a face, and brought her close again. "What is that smell?"

"I haven't had a chance to change her."

"That's not what I mean." He sniffed the child again. "She smells like...flowers?"

"It's lavender. I mixed some of my lavender oil with the soap. Otherwise, it's just so—"

"What were you thinkin'?" John William stood to his full height, still clutching Kate protectively. "Turnin' my daughter into one big flower, then layin' her out in a field! Of course the bees came swarmin'. You're lucky they didn't eat her alive."

"Oh, no," Gloria said. "I didn't even think—I'm so sorry!" Gloria reached out to touch baby Kate's cheek, but John William brusquely turned, taking her out of reach.

"You just have to be careful," he said, his voice softening a little. "It could have been bears."

"I would have fought them, you know."

John William turned to look at her again and, to her immense relief, a smile tugged at his eyes.

"You know, I believe you would have."

Gloria reached for the dishtowel hanging on a hook on the side of the wagon. "You should've seen me with those bees," she said, whirling the towel into a rat's-tail whip. "They never stood a chance."

"Really?"

"Yep. I *snapped* them." She punctuated the word with a flick of the towel. "Killed them in midflight."

"So bath, beans, and bee-killin'? You have had a busy day.

Well, I had a busy day, too. I'll tell you about it over supper."

"Supper?"

"Yes. My surprise."

Gloria hadn't paid any attention to the basket John William brought out of the wagon, but now she eyed it with curiosity. "What's in there?"

"It is…" John William whisked the large cloth napkin off the top of the basket, "a feast!"

Gloria peered inside. "Is that chicken?"

"It is indeed. There's a family here, the Jaspers, that brought two or three fried chickens and a chopped egg and vinegar salad."

Gloria felt her mouth water as the contents of the basket were unloaded onto the overturned crate. Slices of ham, sweet potatoes, fried onions, beans.

"I'm afraid it's all cold," John William said. "If you like, I'll build up a fire so you can heat it up."

"No, no, it's fine," Gloria said, her mouth already full. "I'm starving."

"Can't you say a blessing first?"

"Oh, all right, go ahead."

"Thank you, God," he prayed, "for the generosity of our new neighbors. Bless this food. Bless our new home. Amen."

Gloria was staring at him when he opened his eyes from prayer.

"New home?"

She worked her way through the contents of the basket while John William told her about his conversation with Maureen Brewster.

"She's a wonderful woman," John William said. "Very sweet. Her husband died about three months ago. She's ready to sell and move back East."

"Is that what you want to do?" Gloria asked.

"It just seems like God's perfect timing. She needs to sell, we need to buy. The land already has a house, a crop."

"What is she asking?"

"We didn't discuss price today," he said. "We're going over tomorrow to talk in detail. I need you to—"

"Be on my best behavior?" She used her sleeve to wipe the stream of bean juice that dribbled down her chin.

"After today, I'll be happy if you'll just comb your hair."

"I'll do better than that," Gloria said. "If she offers me tea, I'll lift my pinkie like this." She clutched a biscuit delicately, littlest finger extended, before shoving half of it into her mouth.

"What more could I ask?" John William said with mock appreciation.

Gloria finished off the biscuit and licked her fingers one by one. "That was the best meal I have ever had in my life." The last word was lost in a very unladylike belch.

"Didn't save room for dessert?" he asked.

"Oh, don't tease like that." Gloria leaned back against the wagon's wheel. "I couldn't eat another bite."

"Really? Are you sure?"

"Positive."

"Because I have another bite," he said in a playful tone.

She sat up straight.

"It's not much, you know, just a little somethin'…"

He reached one hand behind his back and brought it back holding a small plate. The sun was nearly set and the little camp was bathed in shadows, so Gloria couldn't see exactly what it was. He held the plate in front of her face, moving it back and forth slowly, causing her head to follow its movement.

"Chocolate?" she said in a tiny, hopeful voice.

"Cake."

"For me?"

"Well, I don't know. After all, it was a church dinner, and really only the people who go to church ought to get to eat."

"But you let me eat all that other food," Gloria said, not caring that she sounded whiny and weak.

"That's because you were starvin' and pathetic. Now you're full. I'm not sure you deserve this."

He picked up the slice of cake and brought it slowly toward his mouth.

"Please!" Gloria called out. "Just a bite. I don't need the whole thing, but I haven't had chocolate since Virginia City. Just a bite? Please?"

"This cake was made by the preacher's daughter herself. What kind of person would I be if I gave it to some person who doesn't even have the decency to listen to her father's sermon?"

"Just a bite and I'll go to church next time."

"Yes, but what about the time after that?" John William had returned the cake to its plate. "How about this? You go to church for every bite you get."

"All right," she said. "One visit to church for every bite. Now give it."

She reached for the plate, but John William snagged it away from her. Holding the plate in one hand, he used the other to pinch off a corner of the cake. Gloria marveled at how such huge hands could maneuver such a tiny morsel from the plate to her open, waiting mouth without dropping so much as a crumb.

"That's one week," he said, smiling.

"Now wait a minute." Gloria's protest was silenced by yet another pinch of chocolate.

John William laughed at how her eyes crossed as his hand approached, so she closed them and kept them closed. Bite after bite, she tried to focus on the flavor, but could only feel the texture of his fingers as they brushed against her lips. The delicious morsels may as well have been sawdust. She clamped her lips shut and opened her eyes.

John William was ready, staring right into them. Yet another pinch from the half-eaten cake was held suspended between them.

"How many was that?" she asked.

"I lost count."

"It doesn't matter." She opened her eyes and took the remaining piece from the plate and plopped it, whole, into her mouth. "I'll go as long as I'm here with you."

John William studied the pinch of cake he held in his fingers before popping it into his mouth.

"That's all I ask."

16

*T*hat's the house?" Gloria asked.

"Must be," John William replied. "Mrs. Brewster said the place was about three miles north of town. She said it had a house, garden, single slant-roof barn." His voice filled with promise as he listed each attribute.

Just behind the house, if she stood up in the wagon and craned her neck, she saw a blanket of green.

"Wheat," John William said. "Acres and acres of it."

"The house looks big," Gloria said. "Did she have a lot of children?"

"None."

"Then why the large house?"

"I don't know. Maybe they—"

"And look at the door. It's beautiful!"

John William chuckled. "Yeah, you sure see that comin'."

It was painted a bright blue and, next to the sky, was the bluest thing Gloria had ever seen. She couldn't imagine anything more inviting, until the door opened and Maureen Brewster walked onto her porch, smiled and waved.

"That's her?" Gloria said.

"That's Mrs. Brewster."

"She looks nice."

"She is. I think you'll like her."

"Why?" Gloria asked, genuinely puzzled.

"Because deep down inside, you're nice, too."

The kitchen was perfect. A large eight-paned window looked out to the company path. Just underneath it, a hand pump drew well water into a galvanized sink. Tiers of shelves stocked with an orderly assortment of spice tins and pretty blue crockery adorned the wall on both sides of the window. The workspace counter rounded the corner of the room, creating a convenient L-shaped surface. A length of calico hung from its edge, and Gloria felt an overwhelming urge to take a peek underneath it. A crystal vase full of fresh flowers sat in the middle of a round table; the cuts in the glass cast a pattern of rainbows on the glossy wooden surface.

"It's beautiful," Gloria said, her voice little more than a breath. She carried Danny across her shoulder.

"Thank you," Maureen said. "We've been very happy here."

"Why would you ever leave?"

"Now, Gloria," John William said, his voice chastising.

"No, no," Maureen said. "Believe me, it's not an easy choice. But I can't work the place alone, and my sister and her husband have a place for me back in St. Louis, so…" Her voice trailed off in sigh accompanied by a shrug and a shake of her head.

"Yes, well," John William spoke into the awkward moment. He held Kate, the baby's back against his broad chest, and the little girl pointed a soggy finger toward the flowers on the table. She emitted a gurgly gleeful sound, and every adult in the room welcomed the distraction.

"Yes, aren't they pretty?" Maureen said. "They're violets. Here."

Maureen reached into the vase and pulled out a purple stem. She ran it lightly across the little girl's face before placing it in the waiting chubby fist. Kate immediately put the flower into her mouth, made a face, and pulled it out again.

"She's always hungry," Gloria said.

"Can't imagine where she gets that from," John William said, smiling.

Gloria shot him a face that equaled Kate's in its sour displeasure.

Maureen laughed and said, "Let me show you the rest of the house. This, of course, is the kitchen. I'll bet you're glad to see a proper stove again."

"Why?" Gloria asked.

"She's not much of a cook," John William said.

"I see." Maureen pulled back the material that skirted the countertops revealing shelves full of clean, empty jars. "Just about ready to put up what's in the garden. And there's a creek in the south corner of the property with some wonderful blackberry bushes. Makes the best jam you've ever had."

"I can't make jam," Gloria said.

"Of course not, of course not. We'll divide up the job. You can pick the berries, I'll make the jam."

"I've—"

"Never picked berries?" John William interrupted, smiling.

"Now you stop." Maureen gave John William a slight slap on the arm. "Everybody's picked berries."

I haven't, Gloria thought.

Maureen led them into the parlor adjoining the kitchen. An imposing fireplace dominated one wall. A line of dainty figurines graced its mantle, as did a cheerful ticking clock and a sepia-toned daguerreotype of a much more somber Maureen with her hand resting on the shoulder of a serious-looking man.

"We had that made last spring," Maureen said, running a finger along the gilded frame. "Just about three months before he died."

"He was very handsome," Gloria said, though most of his face was obscured by his heavy whiskers. She glanced over at John William and the full beard that months of growth had produced. She secretly wished he'd shave.

"These are stones taken from the Umatilla," Maureen said, stooping slightly to stroke the hearth. "And my husband made all the furniture himself."

A long cushioned high-backed bench sat against the wall adjacent to the fireplace. Two chairs of a similar style created an inviting view of the flames. Gloria ran her hand along the back of a chair. Someone had sanded the wood to silk. The third wall housed a window that looked out to the garden. Underneath the window was a wicker basket full of mending and a willow rocking chair.

"You thoroughly capture the morning sunlight there," Maureen said, pointing to the chair. "It's perfect light for sewing."

"I don't sew," Gloria said. Danny was beginning to fuss a little, so she repositioned him.

"Well, I can see we'll need to have a long talk about just what it is exactly that you *can* do. Now, let me show you the bedroom."

Gloria opened her mouth for a smart remark, but the look on John William's blushing traumatized face stopped her.

There were two bedrooms. Their combined space took up nearly half of the square footage of the house. The first was the room Maureen Brewster shared with her beloved Ed. A large bed took up most of the room, the thick mattress nestled between ornate head and footboards. It was covered with a cheerful quilt and piled high with pillows. On either side were two small tables, one of which had a kerosene lamp and a well-worn Bible. A curtain ran the length of one wall, concealing a series of hooks on which Maureen hung her other clothing. A large chest of drawers stood against the wall opposite the bed, and next to it sat a washstand.

"I'll probably leave the bed," Maureen said. "Leave all of the furniture for that matter. If there's one thing we learned on the journey here, furniture's not suited to travel."

Neither John William nor Gloria spoke. There was an overwhelming sense of true, lasting love in this room, and when they did happen to glance at each other, their expressions mirrored a mixture of humility and shame before they quickly looked away.

The second bedroom was bare, though not empty. It contained the furnishings of its function, but there was no sense of life in it. Much smaller than the first room, it had a narrow bed tucked into a corner and a large wooden trunk on the opposite wall.

"The bed's actually fixed to the wall," Maureen said, pulling back a corner of the quilt to demonstrate. "Ed figured it would be easy enough to just put a railing around the two open sides. That way when we didn't need a crib any more, we'd just have a bed. We kept the rocker in here for a while…"

Something happened to her voice as she spoke. It was as if Gloria and John William had left the room and she was left talking to the ones who lived, or should have lived, in the house with her.

"You never had any children?" Gloria asked. She'd been carrying Danny this whole time, and now she clutched him a little closer.

"Gloria, don't—"

"Ed and I married late in life," Maureen said. "I was thirty-two, he was almost forty. We wanted children, prayed for them. I figured if God could give a miracle to Sarah—"

"She's the one who laughed," Gloria said.

"Yes, she did," Maureen said. "But I wouldn't have. Every day, from the day we married until the day he died, I prayed that God would send us a child. I guess He just didn't see fit."

"You would have been a wonderful mother," Gloria said. "I can tell."

"Thank you, child. And who knows? I'm only fifty. Maybe I'm still just too young."

There was a ripple of laugher.

"Course I'd have to find me a husband first."

There was another ripple of laughter, but this one distinctly thinner.

"Mrs. Brewster?"

"Please call me Maureen."

"Maureen, then. I need to feed the babies. May I go somewhere and sit down?"

"Of course, dear. Go on into the parlor. Sit in the rocker. That's what it was made for, you know. Never been used to nurse a babe…" Her voice started to drift again.

"Maureen," John William said, "I'd like to take a look at the property, if you don't mind. The barn, crops."

"Certainly. I've had a few neighbors over to help, just to keep the place up, you know. Ed has—we have—I have everything you could need as far as tools and equipment. Livestock, you'll see."

"Are you coming with me?"

"No, no, son. You just go on. I'll just take this little one," she took Kate out of his arms, "and talk with Gloria. She can tell me all your secrets." Maureen delivered this comment with a jaunty wink, and John William seemed amused by Gloria's shocked expression.

"She might at that," he said. He walked toward the doorway of the tiny bedroom, but before leaving he turned and said, "You know, they say confession is good for the soul."

Nothing, Gloria thought, had ever felt as good as sitting in the willow rocker, staring out at a budding garden while feeling the rhythmic tug of a baby at her breast. She was nursing Kate who, as usual, had been too impatient to wait for Danny, who lay on a blanket near the hearth, contentedly mouthing a silver spoon. Maureen was in the kitchen putting a pot of leftover stew on the stove to heat and sliding a pan of bread into the oven. The faintest aromas were just beginning to drift through the house.

This could be a home, Gloria thought. This could be my home.

Maureen came into the room, wiping her hands on her apron. She settled her tiny frame into the chair to the right of where Gloria was sitting.

"Well, I must say," she said, "I feel like a regular lady of leisure sitting down in the middle of the day. There's plenty I should be doing, but I think it would be nice to sit and chat for a while."

"Yes," Gloria said, a bit uncomfortable. Chat meant questions and questions meant lies, and though she had known Maureen only for a matter of hours, she knew she could never bring herself to lie to this woman.

"Your children are beautiful," Maureen said, looking wistfully at Danny, who was now engrossed in shifting his spoon carefully from one hand to another.

"Thank you," Gloria said. She dislodged Kate, now sated, and closed her blouse. She brought Kate to a sitting position on her lap and began rubbing and patting her back.

"Twins," Maureen mused. "What a blessing."

"Mm-hmm." Gloria focused intently on a tiny spot on the back of Kate's neck. A single little freckle. She'd never noticed it before.

"I have cousins who were twins, but they were both boys. Not identical, but they did favor each other."

"Really."

Since they left Silver Peak, babies in tow, Gloria had heard this same conversation countless times. Every family they encountered—at supply stops, river crossings, well-traveled roads—had something to say about the "twins." People commented on how much they looked alike, how very different they looked, their own twin siblings, cousins, children. They sang little rhymes, made dire predictions, quoted superstition, and through it all, Gloria and John William shielded the truth with silent nods and mumbled appreciation for the stories.

Maureen was still speaking, a cheerful friendly patter, but Gloria hadn't heard a word. Somewhere in the middle of hearing the exploits of Maureen's adventurous twin cousins, Gloria looked at her and said, "They're not twins."

"What?"

"Danny and Kate. They're not twins. They're not brother and sister at all."

Maureen didn't look as surprised as Gloria thought she would.

"John William and I, we're not—"

"It's all right, child."

Maureen got up from the chair and sat on the floor at Gloria's feet. She put a comforting hand on Gloria's knee.

"This is John William's daughter," Gloria said, handing Kate down to Maureen's lap. Maureen held the little girl close, and Gloria got up from the chair, gathered Danny, and settled in to nurse him.

"And this is…Danny is my son."

"Gloria, darling, you don't need to tell me—"

"Please. Please let me."

She locked her gaze with Maureen's, and even though the older woman nodded a smiling consent, the words just wouldn't come. So she looked into the earnest contented eyes of her son and let the words flow out of her.

"I was born in California…"

And then it was so easy. Her mother, the men, the migration from one mining camp to another. She told stories that should have racked her body with sobs, but the steady suckling of her son kept her grounded. Kept her still. She placed her thumb in Danny's soft palm and gathered strength from his grip.

"After Mother died…"

Her own legacy. Her migration. Dubious fame and tainted fortune. And pregnancy.

"I still don't know why I went to Jewell…"

She could have stayed in Virginia City, had an abortion, given it away. But she'd worked for Jewell before, felt a connection.

"She reminded me of a mother," Gloria said. "Not my mother, but *a* mother. She always took care of us girls."

Maureen sat, still and soft at Gloria's feet. She said nothing except the occasional, "Poor child."

"And then I met John William."

Silver Peak. The birth, her death, the deal. Leaving. All of it, every mile, every hardship, every test of patience and fortitude. Everything that led up to this moment, this conversation, this…smile.

It was the first time Gloria chanced to look at Maureen's face, and she was shocked to see the wide smile that infused the older woman's face with unblemished youth.

"I think you may be the strongest woman I've ever met," Maureen said.

Gloria squirmed under the admiration in her voice. Danny had fallen asleep, his warm milky mouth was slack, and she felt the tiny puffs of his breath against her bare skin. She shifted him gently, just enough to close her blouse.

"I just wanted my baby to have a father," Gloria said. "I always wanted a father. Dreamed of having one. I used to wait for him to show up and take me away from my mother and…everything."

"Child, child." Maureen reached up to clasp Gloria's hand. "Don't you know that you have a Father?"

"No, I don't."

"But you do, Gloria."

"You mean God?" Gloria gave a scoffing laugh. "A lot of good He's done for me."

"Can't you see how He has taken care of you? Guided you?"

"Taken care of me? Weren't you listening?" Gloria's voice was rising. She dislodged herself from Maureen's grasp and stood up, laying the sleeping Danny back on the folded quilt on the floor. "Why would anyone who loved me want me to have that kind of life?"

"Just because that's the life you had doesn't mean that's the life He wanted for you," Maureen said, her voice gentle.

"And what does He want for me?"

"For you to have peace. And joy."

"Well, He certainly never gave it to me, did He?"

"Didn't He?" Maureen remained sitting on the floor. A drowsy Kate listlessly chewed on her finger. "I listened to your story. Watched you as you spoke. And your face changed, your voice changed when you talked about leaving that life."

"I haven't left *that life,*" Gloria said. "It's all I know. It's what I am."

"But it doesn't give you peace, now does it? Not like you feel here."

"The peace I feel now is for my son," Gloria said. "All that matters is that he'll be cared for when I leave. When he doesn't need me anymore."

"And just when is that? When does a child stop needing its mother?"

Kate was now fully asleep, and Maureen laid her gently on the blanket next to Danny. She rose and stood next to Gloria, who was looking out the window, past the garden to where John William could be seen walking in the field.

"When it has a father," Gloria said. Her throat was raw with the threat of tears. "A real, live father on *earth,* not some spirit in the sky who just watches while you live your life scared and hungry and torn. A father who will pick him up and read him stories and sing him songs. A father with big strong arms to hold him so he can curl up in his lap when there are storms. A father with a deep voice who can tell her that he loves her, that everything will be all right. That she's safe."

Gloria began to shake, then. She clutched her arms to herself and willed her body to stop, closed her eyes to stop the tears, but the cleansing relief prevailed, fortified by the two small arms wrapped around her, a curly soft head resting on her back. They stood there, together, until their synchronized breathing brought a stillness to Gloria's body, even though tears continued to stream down her face.

"He's an excellent man, you know," Gloria said.

"He seems so."

"He's not perfect."

"Nobody is."

"But he's so gentle with the babies. Sometimes I think he loves Danny as much as he loves his own child."

"I talked with him for a long time yesterday," Maureen said. "Danny is his child."

"I didn't love Kate at first, you know."

"That's understandable."

"Maybe because I knew I was taking another woman's place. Maybe he could love Danny because he didn't have to worry about filling anyone else's shoes."

"Neither do you, Gloria." Maureen turned Gloria around, her two small hands firmly gripping Gloria's arms. "Can't you see? It doesn't matter what you've been or how you've lived.

Look at what you have now. What God has given you. A son. How can you consider walking away from a gift like that?"

"How can I stay?" Gloria said.

"What are you afraid of?"

"I'm afraid of him."

"Who?"

"John William," Gloria said. "I'm afraid of disappointing him. Not being what he needs me to be. We had a deal, you know. I'd take care of his child, he'd take care of mine. But I can't help but feel like he got the losing end of the stick."

Maureen laughed. Slight, at first, but then she reared her head back and let loose with deep, glee-filled noise.

"What are you laughing at?"

"Child," Maureen said, "you really don't see, do you?"

"See what?"

"You are a beautiful woman."

"I hate that."

"You hate it because of how others have seen you. But let me tell you," she brought a hand up to caress Gloria's cheek, "I'm talking about the beauty I see on the inside of you. The way you love your children. The way you admire John William. The way you open up to me."

"I've never met anyone like you before," Gloria said.

"You're being given a chance at a new life, Gloria. Don't dwell on the old one, and don't go back."

"But I don't know how to *do* any of this new life."

"I'll teach you."

"But you're leaving."

"I'll stay."

Gloria could tell that Maureen hadn't considered staying until that moment. And when the realization hit both women, they burst into smiles and fell into each other's arms.

"You'll really stay?" Gloria said. "You'll take care of the children?"

"No, I'll take care of you. For now. Until you can take care of yourself."

Just then the door opened and John William's heavy steps entered the kitchen.

"Smells wonderful in here," he called out. He crossed the room to take a peek at the children, then glanced up to look at Gloria. "Are you all right?"

"I'm fine," Gloria said, hastily wiping the last of her tears.

"You're sure?" he asked.

"I'm sure."

"We've been talking," Maureen said. "Gloria and I had a long talk. She told me everything."

The weight of that word landed in the middle of the room. John William took off his hat and ran his fingers through his hair.

"So you know," he said, "that we're not—"

"I *know*," Maureen said, "that we are all in a state of flux right now, and maybe we better take a deep breath before doing anything hasty."

"So you're not going to sell?"

"Oh, I'm going to sell. And it looks like I'm going to sell to you. I'm just not going to leave."

Gloria beamed silently at her side while the news sank into John William. His face registered shock at first, then acceptance, then a mysterious amusement.

"So, shall we discuss this over dinner?" Maureen said, all business.

"Yes," Gloria said. "I'm starved."

They walked together into the kitchen. Maureen directed Gloria to the cupboard that held the dishes; John William pumped water from the faucet to wash his hands; Maureen busied herself dishing the stew into bowls and slicing the bread. When they sat around the little round table, John William bowed his head to say a blessing.

"Oh, come now," Maureen said. "Let's do this right.

At her bidding, the three joined hands, and John William's deep voice filled the room. He thanked God for the food, the friendship, the family gathered in this place. Gloria felt his calloused fingers gripping her right hand, while her left enveloped the diminutive hand of Maureen. She wondered briefly which held more power, before the room echoed with "Amen," and she bit into her first meal in her new home.

17

I t was as if they'd been a family forever. John William built a partition in the second bedroom, dividing it into two smaller rooms. Maureen found the unused railings, and once attached, Danny and Kate shared the biggest bed they'd ever known. The mattress from the wagon was stuffed with fresh hay, giving John William a bed in the newly created third bedroom. Maureen worried that a straw tick on a bare floor would be terribly uncomfortable, but John William declared that, after months of sleeping on hard, rocky ground, this felt like wafting toward heaven on clouds of feathers.

Gloria shared the bedroom with Maureen.

The days here started just as early as the days on the trail. Any thoughts Gloria had of lounging in the feather-stuffed mattress were dashed the first morning that Maureen's chipper voice woke her up, saying, "Gloria, dear? Rise and shine! Come see the new day God has given us."

Although she was grumbling on the inside, Gloria pasted on a smile and did her best to greet the morning. By the next day, the smile was genuine, even though she quickly learned that Maureen would not cater to her.

"Listen, dear," she said the first time Gloria plopped herself down at the table and waited for coffee, "you'll never learn to take care of yourself if you don't try. Now, our first lesson will be biscuits."

At Maureen's instruction, Gloria carefully measured, mixed, rolled, and baked. They were edible, if not airy, and as John

William added an extra spoonful of gravy, he declared them the best she'd ever made.

The days were a blur of chores. After the monotony of sitting in a wagon all day, Gloria welcomed the activity. Every piece of clothing that she, John William, and the babies owned was washed and hung to dry. Their few tools and utensils were assimilated into Maureen's household. The garden was bursting with the earliest of its generous yield, and afternoons were spent hoeing weeds along its rows.

The noon meal was a time of great camaraderie. Maureen assigned part of the meal's preparation to Gloria—even if it was merely slicing the pickled beets—and the three of them joined around the table, just as they had that first afternoon. It was often a rushed affair, as there were always a hundred things left to do, and the conversation was centered on the workings of the farm.

"I never worked a spring wheat crop before," John William said one afternoon. "Ain't it a bit late to be bringin' it in?"

"We'll be the last ones to be sure," Maureen said. "But before you came along, it was just me, and all the crews are already working. I couldn't get anybody to come on until that last week in August.

Then John William and Maureen's conversation turned to numbers—how many acres, how many machines. Gloria listened to all of this, but contributed nothing to the conversation. She liked it best when they would talk about the crew—who worked hard, who was shiftless. Names of men and women, people of the church and the community floated around the table.

The afternoons were busy, too. Of course there were dishes to be cleaned and put away. The floors were swept. There seemed to be an endless supply of things to wash or repair. John William worked on creating the larger corral necessary to accommodate his horses. Gloria returned to the garden, finding a new love among its tidy rows of promise. It also allowed her, with just the slightest turn of her head, to watch John William work.

The babies flourished. Gloria and Maureen took the canvas cover from the wagon and spread it on the ground for Danny and Kate to lie on while the women worked outside. They rolled from one end to the other, and frequently either Maureen or Gloria would have to rush to rescue someone in danger of rolling straight through the onions. At mealtime, the babies sat on laps around the table and experimented with whatever the adults were eating. Maureen soaked cubes of bread in milk and sugar, much to Kate's gummy delight. They also had tastes of cooked carrots and soft cooked noodles. Gloria's heart skipped a beat with each little mashed bite. The day would come when they wouldn't need her at all.

Then there were the evenings. The hours after supper and before bed were Gloria's favorite of the day. Supper was usually a light fare—perhaps soup or stew that had been bubbling through the late afternoon—which made a quick and easy cleanup. Then everyone settled into the parlor. The lamps on the mantel and small table made a cozy glow in the room. Maureen taught Gloria a simple stitch, and soon she set herself to making what she hoped would be a scarf. John William sat on the floor, his long legs stretched in front of him, and played with the children, letting each take a turn grasping his fingers and stretching to early, tentative steps.

And the conversations, the stories. The little parlor brimmed with laughter and thoughtful silences as, hour by hour, Maureen and Gloria and John William shared their lives with each other. This is where Gloria learned that John William grew up in Illinois. His father, an immigrant from Scotland, married a lovely Irish girl who died when John William was just five years old. He was a hired field hand who never owned his own farm. He drank heavily, much to the shame of his family, and John William's first fights were an attempt to defend his family's honor.

He told Maureen about his days as a boxer, about the death of two men at his hands, about prison. Gloria sensed his acute shame as he told the story, and she longed to reach out and comfort him. But as he told of his "salvation," his voice took on a tone of triumphant joy, and Maureen muttered a tearful, "Praise God." Gloria felt a little like an outsider, like someone who didn't quite understand the language of the room.

At some point, after the babies were fed for the final time and sleepy, the long day's work wore on everyone. There were yawns and stretches and declarations of being asleep before the head hit the pillow. Every night, starting that first night, John William bent low to kiss Maureen's soft cheek, then stood and nodded good night to Gloria before going outside to check on the livestock one last time. Gloria and Maureen went into their room where, over the course of changing into nightgowns and brushing and braiding hair, the conversation continued to flow.

When Gloria finally sank into the softness of Maureen's feathered pillow, she lingered awake but silent, respectful of the prayers of the friend beside her. She listened until she heard John William come back in and latch the door. She waited for the soft thump of the second boot, the rustle of straw. She tried to wait for the familiar buzz of his snore, but often fell asleep before she heard it, wondering if he were praying, too.

One evening there was a dazzling sunset that washed the farm in brilliant color. Gloria stood at the kitchen window, mesmerized, her hands wiping dishes. Behind her, John William sat at the table, jotting down rows of numbers that had something to do with the amount of seed needed to expand next year's crop. Maureen was out in the yard keeping the babies amused until Gloria was finished tidying up.

"She really loves the children," Gloria said, looking over her shoulder at John William.

"Mm hmm."

"You shouldn't tip that chair back like that, you know. You'll crack your skull."

"Mm hmm."

Gloria sighed and returned to the task at hand. She remembered a conversation with the girls back at Jewell's, about the deep satisfaction of doing dishes. Right now, she thought she'd really rather be outside playing with the babies, but that stemmed more from the frustration of being ignored.

"You know," she said, amused with the prospect of annoying John William with her talk, "when I was at Jewell's, we had a thought about doing dishes. I said that I actually liked doing them because it was like getting a fresh start to the day. Then Biddy— I'm not sure you remember her; she was so young and so…sad."

Gloria allowed her voice to trail, wondering if John William would follow it. When he didn't, she simply picked up a cup and resumed.

"Well, Biddy said that she thought what would be even better than that would be having your own home and doing your own dishes." She smiled a little at the memory, and sent a wish that Biddy was sharing some of the happiness that she was now. "Then Sadie—I know you remember Sadie—she said…"

Again she left a silent little trail, but this time she simply remembered what Sadie had said, and decided she didn't want to share after all. She set the cup to drain on the countertop and rummaged through the soapy water in search of another.

"What did Sadie say?" His voice was quiet, distracted.

"It's not important. You know Sadie."

"No, tell me." She could tell he was looking up from his papers. Looking at her.

"Well, she said…" Gloria straightened her shoulders and assumed the tall woman's posture and worked her voice around an exaggerated German accent. "Washing in your own home would be *gut,* but what would be *best* would be to have the man of the house…"

"Yes?"

She dropped the accent. "To have the man of the house come up behind you—now remember, this was Sadie talking—come up behind you, give you a little nuzzle on your neck and say, 'Tut, tut love, you look tired. Why don't you go lie down and let me finish up?'"

She'd stayed true to Sadie's words and immediately felt stupid for it. She could have said anything, made up any clever quip, but her mind was not as sharp and witty as her old friend's was, and the silence that followed was unbearable.

Then she heard the sound of two chair legs landing on the smooth wood floor and the scrape of them as he backed the chair away. She sensed rather than heard him unfold his long body from behind the table, felt the footsteps that brought him up behind her.

His breath was warm on the back of her neck, but perhaps she felt it only because her own had stopped. He was leaning in closer, so close that if she were to turn her head, his whiskers would graze her face.

She didn't turn her head. He turned it for her. He brought his hand around her to rest on her chin and turned her face to look straight into his.

"Well now, darlin'," he said, that warm smile on his face. "I don't think you look a bit tired." He brought the tip of his nose to briefly nuzzle the tip of hers, then took the last corn muffin from the platter about to be washed and went outside to play.

~ 18 ~

*Y*ou can't make me go," she said that morning even as she carried the blanket and food for the church dinner out to the wagon.

"You're going," he said, amused by her protest.

"What about the babies?"

"They're fine with me," said Maureen. "Kate oughtn't go out with this sniffle anyway. Besides," she added with a wink, "might be nice for the two of you to have a little time alone."

The morning crackled with the timid chill of early September, a chill that would disappear long before noon. The sun climbed higher with each turn of the wagon's wheels, sending a golden light across acres and acres of ripened wheat ready for harvest. His wheat. His harvest. Or it would be some year. He had enough cash to meet half of Maureen's asking price for the farm; the other half he would pay in labor—taking no share of the profits—until a fair price had been paid. He still wasn't sure who profited from the deal more: Maureen for the opportunity to stay with the life she so dearly loved, or him for having a soft buffer to come between him and Gloria.

"I won't know what to do."

"I'll show you."

Land rolled all around them, soft sloping fields bordered by towering trees. They passed freshly cleared land of new homesteads, drove through cold gurgling streams. Morning dew muffled the horses' hooves and discouraged dust.

"I won't know what to say."

"Say nothin'."

A series of structures dotted the horizon. Middleton. A new, limited general store. A livery stable. A post office. A church.

It wasn't until he reached up to help her down from the wagon that John William realized Gloria's protests were born not of stubbornness but of fear. She was firmly on the ground, but she kept a grip on his arm as if to save her very life.

"They won't like me."

"They don't know you."

"But I don't belong—"

"Everybody belongs in God's house." He tried to adjust his tone from one of chastisement to reassurance, but her frozen expression told him he hadn't soothed her at all. One arm wanted to fold her to him and bring shelter from whatever unkindness she anticipated, the other wanted to yank her through the doorway. Luckily, the warm, welcoming voice of Josephine Logan kept him from doing either.

"Gloria? Oh, Gloria, I'm so glad you could join us this morning."

"G'mornin' Mrs. Logan," John William said, touching his fingers to his hat.

"Mr. MacGregan," Josephine said. She gave an eager look around before asking, "Where are the babies?"

"At home," Gloria said, with more than a little resentment in her voice. "Mrs. Brewster is watching them this morning. Kate had a bit of a sniffle."

"So you are staying at the Brewster place," Josephine said. "How kind of her to stay behind this morning."

"Oh, yes," Gloria said, her voice dripping sweetness. "She is kindness itself."

Just then Reverend Thomas Fuller stood on the top step and called out, "Come and worship! Let us gather in worship!" and the crowd began to move toward the door.

John William cradled Gloria's elbow and steered her inside.

He took them to the last row of seats, right up against the back wall, and settled in with Gloria sitting on the aisle.

"You may leave any time you wish," he whispered in her ear.

Gloria turned and said, without whispering, "I know that."

"But I'd like you to stay."

When the congregation stood to sing, Gloria stood with them, stoic and silent by his side. John William always loved to sing; he rather vainly enjoyed the admiring looks given over the shoulders of the people in front of him. Gloria had told him once that he had a very nice voice, and when he asked her to sing, she'd laughed and said, "The only songs I know would make your ears turn to fire." He'd caught her humming to the children and trilling nonsense verses countless times. But now she made no sound. He held the hymnbook between them, ran his finger along the lines of text, but she just stared at a point on the floor somewhere, and he remembered she couldn't read.

The songs were followed by a time of prayer. At Maureen's, they'd developed the habit of joining hands, so John William reached for her, only to realize that both her hands were folded into her crossed arms. He brought his hand back, allowed one to clutch the other, and bowed his head.

Reverend Fuller was five minutes into his sermon when Adele walked in.

"I'm sorry, father," she said quietly as she passed in front of the pulpit and made her way down the aisle. The smile on her face said she was completely aware of every eye on her. Her wide silk skirt brushed against the pews as she made her way to the back, to the very back where John William and Gloria sat.

"May I sit here?" she said.

John William nodded and slid down the bench.

"I guess she didn't hear me," Adele whispered. At least that's what John William thought she said, for she was sitting to his right, the side with his badly damaged ear. Soon the smell of

Adele Fuller's lavender water engulfed Gloria's clean, soapy scent. Her silk-clad arm brushed against his as she opened her Bible. When he turned his good ear toward the pulpit in order to hear the sermon, his peripheral vision captured the lace ruffle that rose and fell with her breath. So he scooted over one more inch, faced straight ahead, and allowed the preacher's words to disappear.

It was a long ride home.

"Can we go any faster? I'm starving," Gloria said. They'd been riding for nearly thirty minutes, and these were the first words spoken.

"We could have stayed for the dinner."

"I need to get home. I know you're anxious for me to be on my way, but the babies—"

"Who said I was anxious for you to leave?"

"You did. If I remember correctly, we were sitting in the house of God when you reminded me that I was free to leave at any time."

John William sighed. "I meant church. That you could leave church. I saw how uncomfortable you were."

"So you don't think I belong there either?"

"Oh, for Pete's sake." John William slapped the reins causing the horses to lurch ahead. Gloria had to grab the seat in order to regain her balance.

"You said you wanted to speed up," John William said.

A few moments passed before Gloria said, "What was her name?"

"Who?"

"The woman you were sitting with."

"I wasn't sitting *with* her."

"What was her name?"

"Adele Fuller. She's the reverend's daughter."

"Ah," Gloria said.

"You didn't move with me," John William said. "You just sat there."

"I didn't know I could move."

John William laughed out loud. "Didn't know— That's the silliest thing I've ever heard. When someone comes in you move down. Make room."

"And how was I supposed to know that?"

"It's common sense," he said, and immediately wished he hadn't. Nothing about this was common to Gloria. He'd made her feel abandoned and alone—exactly what she had been afraid of all morning. Transferring the reins to one hand, he brought the other over to touch her arm, but she bristled and pulled away.

"If you remember," John William said after a while, "I also sat in the house of God and said that I'd like you to stay."

"That was before."

"Before what?"

"Before she came in. Before she sat down."

Then it hit him, what this was all about. An intense, amused warmth spread through him, bringing with it a triumphant smile. He pulled the reins to bring the team to a halt and turned to face her.

"Gloria," he said, "don't tell me you're jealous."

She wrinkled her nose and scoffed. "I most certainly am not jealous. I am simply a practical woman—"

He laughed out loud at that.

"And as a practical woman, I realize that Adele Fuller is perfect for you."

"Really?"

"Of course. She's pretty and clean. She's the reverend's daughter so she probably knows the Bible backwards and forwards…" Gloria gestured nervously as she spoke. "Can we keep driving, please?"

John William clicked to the team and let the reins fall gently on the horses. Their pace was now a leisurely one, perfect for allowing thoughts to settle in.

"Plus," Gloria said, "it's obvious that she wants you."

"Obvious, is it?"

"There were other seats, but she headed right for you."

"I wonder why that is?" John William said, assuming a tone of true curiosity.

"Well, she must think you're handsome."

Handsome. He let the word sink in, enjoying the sound and thought of it.

"You really think so?"

"Well, *I* don't think so, of course."

"Of course."

"I mean, your hair's so long, makes you look like an Indian or a gypsy."

"Maybe I'll ask Maureen to cut it."

"I know you're concerned about your ears," Gloria said, "but they're really not horrible. Take off your hat."

For some reason, he complied.

"Now, let's see." Gloria raked his hair behind his ear. "There, that's not so bad. Maybe if we trimmed it just to here…" Her finger grazed just below the swollen mass. "And the beard covers up some of the scars, but maybe you could trim it just a bit so you don't look like some wild mountain man."

"Maybe Adele Fuller likes wild mountain men," John William said, plopping his hat back on his head. He turned to Gloria and grimaced and growled, getting close enough for the longest of his whiskers to graze her skin.

"Stop making jokes," Gloria said. "It's been six months since your wife died. It's time you start thinking about…"

"Another woman?"

"Not just a woman. A wife. And I just thought that since Adele—"

"Stop," John William said. "I don't want to hear another word about her."

"But she's—"

"She's nothing."

Over the course of their months together, John William had mastered the tone that would end an argument. He used it now, and the only sound was the clomp of the horses and the rattle of the harness. The occasional rut in the road urged a groan from the wheels, but other than that there was silence.

Maureen's property was in sight, the bright blue door beckoning. He tried to picture making this trip with Adele Fuller, tried to envision her riding beside him in this wagon, but as long as he'd owned this rig, Gloria was the only woman who had ever shared it with him. Somehow Adele's silk and lace just wouldn't seem right against the rough wood seat. She'd make them ride in some fancy black buggy.

"I hate them things," he said out loud.

"What things?"

"Nothin'."

He wondered if Adele Fuller had ever held a child. Would she laugh if Kate tugged at her perfect curls? Would she let Danny amuse himself by making paste with a bowl of flour and a spitty hand? Would she let them roll around, healthy and brown, wearing nothing but diapers? He pictured walking into the parlor, both children dressed in little white lace gowns, sitting perfectly still and straight, tied to the chairs.

"They're just babies."

"What about the babies?"

"Nothin'."

Then, before he could stop himself, he was thinking about Adele herself. The woman. He conjured her face, but no matter how hard he tried to hold the image, Adele's cat-like green eyes became soft and round and blue. Her cunning smile became one of openmouthed joy. Her complicated auburn coif softened, became the color of ripened wheat, and fell around her face, tumbled down her back. Soon, she wasn't a pristine preacher's daughter sitting beside him at church, but an earthy temptress, fresh from sleep, looking at him through a canvas flap, a blanket draped loosely about her bare shoulders. In his mind's eye, he reached out, slipped one finger underneath the blanket, felt the glide of her skin as he—

"Finally." They were stopped in front of the house, and Gloria was already standing up, getting ready to step down from the wagon. "I didn't think we'd ever get here."

John William reached out a hand and grasped Gloria's arm.

"Gloria," his voice choked on the word. "Let me—"

"I can manage just fine, thank you," Gloria said, wrenching her arm from his grasp. She reached a foot down to step on a wheel spoke, but when she swung the rest of her body around, a portion of her skirt was caught in the seat spring, and a resounding ripping sound accompanied a large tear in the fabric.

"Oh, no," she said at first. Then, when she saw the extent of the damage, she let forth a stream of curses.

"Don't talk like that. It makes you sound like a—" By the time he got to the end of the sentence, he was on the ground looking at her.

"Like a what?" Gloria's hands were planted firmly on her hips. "Like a whore?"

"I've never called you that."

"But you haven't forgotten that's what I am," Gloria said. "You can dress me up and take me to church, but that's not going to change what I am inside, is it?"

"Have I ever," John William said, measuring his words, "ever treated you like a, like a…"

"Whore!" Gloria opened her arms wide and screamed the word. "You can't even say it, can you? You can't face that part of me."

"That's not how I see you."

"Of course it is."

He had never in his life raised a hand to a woman, but now he grabbed Gloria's shoulders and turned her so that her back was pinned to the wagon. He released his grip and planted both palms on the wagon bed, hemming her in. She need only duck under his arm to escape, but by sheer will he forced her to stay and meet his gaze.

"Do you really want to know how I see you?" he asked. He took her silence as consent to hear an answer. "I see you, God help me, as the mother of my children."

"Child," Gloria said. The spite behind the word shocked him.

"No, Gloria, children. Katherine was the mother of my child. But I've come to think of Danny as my own, and I've seen how you've taken to Kate. And for the life of me I can't imagine them without you."

"You make it sound like something horrible."

"No, Gloria, *you* make it sound like something horrible. Every day you talk about leavin'. I can tell that every time one of 'em takes a bite of food you're countin' the days till you can go. And now, today, you're talkin' about dumpin' Adele Fuller on me. Well, maybe I don't want Adele Fuller."

He took three full breaths before his next words tumbled out.

"Maybe I want you."

For just one heartbeat, he expected her to melt into a smile and throw herself against him. He loosened the tension in his arms in anticipation of an embrace. But Gloria remained steel.

"You don't want me. You told me, back in Silver Peak, that you wouldn't need me forever. That you wouldn't want me for a wife."

"And you're clingin' to that? That was months ago, Gloria."

"So I'm good enough now?"

"I don't know." John William ripped his hat off his head and ran his fingers through his hair. "No one's ever good enough for anything. We just do the best we can."

Just then the blue door flew open and Maureen emerged with a fussy Kate on her hip.

"Back so soon?" she said, jostling the baby. "You must not have stayed for dinner."

"No," they said simultaneously.

Thankful for the diversion, John William turned away from Gloria and took his daughter into his arms.

"Well, then," Maureen said, looking from one to the other. "I'll fix us something."

"I'm not hungry," Gloria mumbled. She breezed past Maureen and disappeared inside. John William tried not to look at the exposed petticoat peeking through the torn skirt, but his eyes would not obey.

Maureen caught him looking, and a mischievous grin spread across her face.

"You two have a quarrel?" she asked.

"You might say that."

"What about?"

He sighed, tried to think of an explanation, and decided to go with the truth.

"Adele Fuller," he said.

Maureen laughed. "Hoo, boy. Nothing like a redhead to light a fire under a woman, is there?"

John William gave her a sideways scowl.

"I think it's a good thing we got the harvest coming on," she said. "You look like you'll need something to occupy your mind."

"My mind is fine," he said. He looked through the kitchen window and saw Gloria slathering a slice of bread with blackberry preserves. *Not hungry*, he thought, smiling.

"She's a beautiful woman, isn't she?" Maureen said.

"She is at that."

"But sometimes she seems almost…well, like a child."

"She's scared."

"Yes, I suppose that's it. Tell me, about this bargain between the two of you. Do you really think she'll leave?"

"I didn't think so until today."

"And just when did you decide you wanted her to stay with you?"

He held his daughter close and searched for an answer. Kate had ten grubby fingers tangled in his beard. She tugged and giggled and tugged some more, and his mind flashed back to that first night, the chilled, lifeless little body he had carried into that tiny warm cabin.

"The moment she held Kate, I suppose," he said. "Is that awful?"

"Awful? Why would it be awful?"

"Because Katherine, Kate's mother, she was just…had just…"

"And you were doing what you had to do for your child. There's no shame in that."

Until that moment, John William hadn't realized just how much shame he felt, leaving his dead wife in the early dawn, handing their child over to this woman Katherine held in such disdain.

"Now let me ask you this," Maureen said. "When did you fall in love with her?"

"I'm not—"

"Now there's no shame in that, either. I know I loved her the first time I met her. She gets to your heart, doesn't she?"

"I guess you could say that." John William took another glance through the kitchen window where a seemingly satisfied Gloria licked the remnants of jam off her fingers. "But I've prayed for God to guard my heart. My thoughts."

"And it's a good thing you did, all that time alone together, just the two of you in the middle of nowhere half the time."

"You know I never, never touched her."

"I know, son," Maureen said. "But things have changed, haven't they?"

"Not so much."

"It's all right, John. It's only natural. She's a beautiful woman, she's mothering your child. God brought you together for a reason."

"She's not seekin' God's will."

"Maybe not. But she is seeking God, don't you think?"

"I don't know," he said. "Sometimes I think she realizes how lost she is, and other times she just seems so bitter."

"Not bitter. Scared."

"But I've tried to tell her. Tried to protect her and make her feel safe."

"I know you have, John." Maureen reached up to put a hand on John William's shoulder. "But be patient with her. Let her come to God. Then she'll come to you."

They stood there for a moment, the three of them connected.

He'd been watching Gloria through the window this whole time, but she just now returned his gaze. He smiled and took up Kate's hand to offer a little wave. Gloria blew a little kiss to Kate, then met John William's eyes and stuck out her tongue before standing up and flouncing away from the table.

John William laughed. "Maureen? You asked when I fell in love with her?"

"Yes."

"I think just now."

This he gives you, this he gives you,
'Tis the Spirit's glimm'ring beam;
This he gives you, this he gives you,
'Tis the Spirit's glimm'ring beam.

19

*T*he first day of harvest started long before dawn. Maureen was putting a third pan of biscuits into the oven when Gloria, bleary-eyed, came into the kitchen to help her.

"You get on over and start stirring that gravy," Maureen said, directing Gloria to a large saucepan on the stove.

"You're trusting me to make gravy?"

"No, I'm trusting you to *stir* gravy," Maureen said. "And mind you don't let it scorch, or you'll have a bunch of angry workers on your hands."

The crew showed up at dawn. Six men and a young boy piled out of the back of a wagon hungry for Maureen's famous biscuits 'n' gravy.

"Now you all just hold your britches," Maureen said, walking out to the front yard to greet them. "Get out your cups. Breakfast'll be up soon."

The men stood in a line, mugs held out ready for a steaming cup of coffee. Maureen made her way down the line, greeting each man in turn.

"Ron, good to see you again. This your son? Looks just like you, don't he...Bill, looks like you've put on a few pounds...Sam, now didn't I tell you that woman would be no good?"

Each man shifted his feet, muttered a reply.

"Norman, have you had a doctor look at that? Lonnie, you just get more and more handsome...Big Phil, I'm still using Anne's cream pie recipe."

Gloria watched all of this through the kitchen window, fascinated by Maureen's transformation. Normally sedate, almost matronly, she became flirtatious and coy. The men continued to shuffle and blush until finally one of them—Lonnie, she thought—reached out to take Maureen's hand.

"Won't seem right workin' these fields without Ed," he said. "He was a good man."

"Yes, he was," Maureen said.

"This new man, you sure he ain't just after your land?"

Maureen laughed and gave him a nudge in his ribs. "Lon, I *know* he's just after my land."

"Aw, Maureen, you know what I'm talkin' about. He ain't just takin' it out from under you."

"Don't you worry," Maureen said. "We hit on a fair price. Some he's paid cash, the rest he's working off. He gets a working farm, I get to stay on a bit and have help while I'm staying. I love this place, Lon. Ed and I worked hard here. Trust me, I wouldn't hand it over to just anybody. John William MacGregan's a good man."

Just then, John William came around the corner from the barn.

"Speak of the devil," Gloria muttered to herself, forgetting to stir the gravy.

He strode across the yard, seeming taller, stronger than Gloria ever remembered. He clapped his hands together and rubbed them in apparent anticipation of the day's work ahead. She heard him holler "Mornin'!" to the crowd before making his way down the line of workers, offering each a hearty handshake. When he got to Maureen, he engulfed her in a brawny hug and planted a kiss on her gray curls.

"Let's get to work!" His voice boomed into the morning, and the men raised their cups in agreement.

"Let's have breakfast first," Maureen said, earning an even louder cheer. She turned and looked straight at Gloria through the kitchen window. "Gloria, bring on the biscuits! John, you go on in and get the gravy. That skillet's heavy."

The gravy!

Gloria turned her attention back to the stove and used the wooden spoon to break apart the skin that had formed on the top. Then she dipped it into the creamy mass, gingerly touching the bottom, testing for the soft sign of scorching.

"Gloria?" It was the first he'd spoken to her since their argument yesterday after church. "I'll take that outside now."

She whirled around to face him, and smiled at what she saw. "You trimmed it," she said.

"Yes." He brought his hand up to his newly trimmed beard. It was cut close to his face, each line and contour clearly visible. "But I didn't cut the hair."

"So I see."

His hair was pulled back and secured with a strip of leather at the nape of his neck. His ears, bulging and disfigured, were clearly visible. She noticed that he seemed to make an effort not to bring his hand up to cover them.

"The gravy?"

"What?"

"Maureen asked me to take the gravy outside. You're to bring the biscuits."

"Oh, yes. Of course."

They stood there in the half-dark, oven-warmed kitchen. The last time they spoke, he said he wanted her. She wondered if he still did. His gaze was unsettling, her breath uneven, and the gravy was *blopping,* sending splatters to sizzle on the hot stove.

"The gravy," they said simultaneously.

She handed him a tea towel to wrap around the hot handle, and he reached around her to lift the pan off the stove. She stepped aside before his arm could brush against her.

"I'll be right out with the biscuits," she said. "Tell Maureen I'll put more coffee on."

Try as she might, Gloria could not ignore the hired hands' appreciative looks as Maureen introduced her to them one by one. Even though no one said more than, "Nice to meet you, ma'am," each pair of eyes peered out from under a sweat-stained hat brim

214 ❧ ALLISON PITTMAN

and lingered just a little too long on her face. She declined to shake hands after the one named Sam deposited a sweaty glaze.

The oldest of the bunch, Big Phil, was a portly man with a ruddy face and a ready laugh. He took one look at Gloria, then one look at John William and said, "Now, MacGregan, I swear. I don't see how a man with a mug as ugly as yours could get himself a beauty like this. Just don't seem right."

"Maybe he hasn't quite got me yet," Gloria said, smiling slyly. "After all, we're new here. I had no idea I'd have so many choices."

The men let out a hearty laugh, and Big Phil grabbed Gloria around the waist and planted a meaty kiss on her cheek.

"You'd better hold on to this one, MacGregan," he said. "Reminds me of my wife. She's a spunky one, too."

"Yes," John William said. "I'm truly blessed."

"It's like they say," Maureen said, "there's a lid for every pot."

"Well, this lid's going inside," Gloria said. "I've got a baby calling me."

John William marveled at the power of the reaper, pulled by a team of horses, as its blades cut the wheat stalk close to the ground. Ed Brewster bought the machine after his most profitable harvest, an investment Maureen had said was long overdue. Two of the men, Big Phil and Lonnie, owned their own reapers even though Big Phil didn't have a crop to bring in, and Lonnie didn't even own land. Each would collect a rental fee on top of the pay for their labor. John William had to convince Maureen to lay out the extra cost. But with three machines and five men—well, four men and one strong boy—working to bind the stalks, he figured they would be able to harvest nearly fifteen acres a day. With just over three hundred acres—half of Maureen's section—he expected it wouldn't take more than three weeks to get the whole crop in.

This harvest was a far cry from the fieldwork he'd done beside his father, a hired hand much like the men he employed today. He remembered endless days of swinging a sickle and stooping to gather bundles of wheat. Now it was near noon, and already he and his team had done what would have been a full day's work in his childhood.

"We gonna take a break soon, boss?" Big Phil's good-natured voice called from behind.

"Don't call me that," John William said over his shoulder. "You all know more about this than I do." He shielded his eyes and looked up toward the sun that sat in the full center of the sky. "I expect the women will be bringing dinner out soon."

He was right. Within minutes he heard Maureen's voice, clear and sweet, carrying across the fields.

"Sing to the Lord of harvest
sing songs of love and praise
with joyful hearts and voices
your alleluias raise."

She was pushing a small handcart through the newly formed paths left by the reapers. Gloria followed, carrying Kate on one hip and Danny in a sling wrapped around her back. Her face was hidden within the tunnel of the sunbonnet, and he found himself wishing she would push it back and refresh him with one of her smiles.

Maureen broke off her song to announce "Dinner's on!" and a hearty cheer erupted from the men.

The contents of the cart were covered by a threadbare quilt that John William snapped in the air and laid in a place of newly cleared land. Then he took Kate out of Gloria's arms and lifted her to a giggly height before bringing her back down for a nuzzling nose rub.

"Men," he said with pride, "this is my little princess Katherine Celestia MacGregan. We call her Kate."

Big Phil removed his hat, took her tiny hand and bent low over it, planting a solemn kiss.

"And if you'll take her, sir," John William said, handing

Kate over to Big Phil, "I'll introduce you to my son." He lifted Danny out of the sling, untangled Gloria's thick braid from his grasp, and took him through the same ritual of big lifts and soft kisses.

"And this is Danny, my son," he said. "Think we can put him to work today?"

Baby Danny giggled, then everybody else did, too. The men took turns passing the babies from hand to hand, each offering a special greeting, except for Ron's son who busied himself pouring water from a barrel into a galvanized tub for the horses.

Meanwhile, Maureen and Gloria set out the noontime meal. There were three loaves of bread cut into hearty slices and a cool crockery bowl of butter. Half a round of cheese was given over to Lonnie to slice into chunks. A basket of apples appeared, and each man dove for one to bite into, except for Ron's son who decided he'd rather give his to the horses, if that was all right with everybody. There was a jar of pickled beets and onions, and when it was empty, the men poured shallow puddles of brine to sop up with the bread. Four jugs of gingered water were passed from man to man, each drinking his fill.

Before long, every crumb was gone, and seven men and one boy lounged on the ground under the sleepy sun. Danny and Kate rolled in the available space, making tentative inching progress using their elbows and knees. Maureen and Gloria busied themselves packing the dirty dishes back into the cart.

Big Phil rubbed his substantial stomach. "Delicious as ever, Maureen."

"Wait and see what I got in store for you this evening," she said.

"How 'bout you, Miz Gloria?" Lonnie's lazy voice slithered out from under the hat that fully covered his face. He propped himself up on one elbow and lifted his hat. "You cook good, too?"

John William sat up and turned his full attention to the young man. "She's learnin'."

Lonnie tapped his boot against John William's boot and said, "I guess there's more than one way to keep a man satisfied then, ain't there?" He laughed and looked around for the other men to join in. No one did.

"I think you owe the lady an apology," Big Phil said.

Before Lonnie had a chance to say anything, John William was on his feet. He reached down and grabbed the front of Lonnie's shirt, bringing him to an abrupt standing position.

"And I don't know if I want to hire a man who would say something like that about my—"

"John William MacGregan!"

Gloria's voice stayed the hand that was drawn back in a fist.

"You let him go," she said. "Remember what happens when you lose your temper."

Lonnie's eyes grew wide, and he looked back and forth between John William and Gloria. "What happens?"

"Guess," John William said through his teeth.

"Darling, we don't want any trouble here, do we? Not when we're just making friends."

"Listen to her, MacGregan," Lonnie said. "We don't—I don't want no trouble."

By this time all the men were on their feet. John William continued to breathe through a face of fury, but by now the expression masked his amusement at Lonnie's fear.

"You really think I should put him down?"

"Yes," Gloria said, and the others agreed. John William released his fistful of blue cotton, and Lonnie stumbled a bit regaining his balance.

"I didn't mean nothin'," Lonnie said, straightening his shirt.

"Let's just get back to work," Big Phil said.

There was an uncomfortable shuffling as the men dusted off their backsides and went to harness the horses to the reaping machines. The last of the dishes were packed in the cart, and when the blanket was folded and put on top of the pile, there was plenty of room to place the babies inside for a ride home.

"There you go, big man," John William said, swooping Danny up from the ground and settling him into the cart. "I think she can ride, too." He took Kate from Gloria's arms and sat her down beside Danny.

"Come on, MacGregan!" Big Phil called. "Kiss the little woman good-bye and let's get back to work."

"You heard the man," John William said.

Gloria looked up. Her face, still shielded within the generous brim of her bonnet, registered an expression of impending doom. With one hand, John William tugged the bonnet string and pulled it from her head. With the other hand, he encircled Gloria's waist, drawing her to him. Claiming her.

"My little woman," he said.

"Little woman, my—"

But he trapped her words in his kiss.

Her lips were full and soft, softer than anything he'd ever imagined. He felt her hands braced against his chest, not pulling him closer, but not pushing him away, either. Somewhere in the background, he heard the men whooping and hollering. Encouraged, he tightened his grip around her waist and brought his other arm around to envelope her in a full embrace. He crushed any chance she'd have to pull away. His lips smiled against hers, amused at her squeaks of weak protest.

When he reluctantly released her, she staggered a little on her feet, and he felt greatly rewarded by the dazed expression on her face. She looked flushed, a little sleepy even. It didn't last, though. Almost immediately she was stone still, alert and angry. Those same lips that had been so soft seconds ago now barely moved as they spoke her command.

"Give me my bonnet."

The whooping and hollering became a low, amused rumble. John William looked around, egged on by his comrades, and held the bonnet high, just out of Gloria's reach.

"How bad do you want it?" he asked, his voice teasing.

"What?"

"One more kiss, and it's yours."

"That so?" Gloria held her hands behind her back and sidled

up to him, as near to him now as when she was locked in his embrace. She tilted her face high; he could feel her breath on his neck. Her eyes closed, her lips moist and ready, she smiled and said, "Keep it. I'll risk the burn."

She stepped away, grasped the handles of the cart, and started down the path toward the house. "Come on, Maureen," she called over her shoulder.

He still held the bonnet, and when he brought his hand up to cover his laugh, he caught the sun-warmed scent of her hair.

"Here," he said. "Take this to her."

Maureen had been standing, openmouthed, throughout the ordeal. Now she offered John William a wide wink, took the bonnet, and turned to follow Gloria. "See you all at supper!" she called.

John William walked the gauntlet of jeers and backslaps to take his place in the reaper's seat.

"Looks like it's gonna be a cold night tonight!"

"Whew! Anybody else feel that frost?"

John William just laughed it off. "All the more reason to get this crop in," he said. "Looks like an early winter for this farm."

Long after it was over, the kiss consumed her.

She thought about it all the way back, trying to ignore Maureen's amused silence. She thought about it all afternoon as she stirred pans of cornbread batter. Throughout the day, the trace of his lips, the ghost of his embrace warmed her like a fine residue until she shook it off, remembering her irritation.

But the memory came back when the men did. It rode on the sound of the reaper's blades, drifting in on the wave of masculine conversation. It wrapped around her hands as she served up supper and snaked across her cheeks as she attempted to smile and socialize. She tried to tuck it away when the men bedded down—some in the barn, some in the back of their wagons, some on a tarp under the stars—but it crackled along with the hairbrush she dragged through her curls, and it tossed on her pillow as she tried to sleep. She thought she'd leave it behind if she left her bed and settled in the parlor's rocker for a while, but it followed her there, too.

In fact, it walked right in, in lockstep with John William's bare feet.

"Gloria."

It was the first he'd spoken to her since the kiss. She stood and walked toward him, and when she was close enough to smell his scrubbed skin, she balled up her fist and landed a resounding blow square on his jaw.

She hadn't expected him to laugh. She didn't know just what reaction she did expect, but the wry smile and low chuckle never figured into it.

"I guess I deserved that."

"I guess you do," she said, her anger tempered a bit.

He brought one hand up to rub the spot where Gloria's fist connected.

"You've got a good right hook there."

"So I've been told."

He laughed again and settled his large frame on the parlor sofa.

"Let me see," he said, taking her hand and drawing her down to sit next to him. She uncurled her fingers, and he ran his thumb softly along the reddened knuckles. "You're probably going to bruise."

Gloria brought her other hand up and ran a finger along his jaw.

"So are you."

They both laughed at that, and Gloria drew her hands away to fold them gingerly in her lap.

"You had no right to…to do that to me," she said, combing her fingers through the fringe of the shawl she'd thrown over her nightgown.

"I'm sorry," John William said. "It was just a kiss. I didn't think—"

"I'd mind?"

He said nothing.

"You think I've been kissed so much it wouldn't matter?"

"I didn't think anythin'."

"Because it does matter."

She wanted to say that his kiss bothered her in a way that no man's touch ever had. She who had earned thousands of dollars with hundreds of men, whose body had been wagered and won at gambling tables, felt violated by a simple kiss under a blazing noonday sun. The paradox drew a bitter laugh from deep within her.

"It matters," she repeated.

"I didn't mean to hurt you," he said.

Another bitter laugh. "You didn't hurt me. You disappointed me. I thought you were different."

"Different," he said, blowing the word out in disgust. He stormed up from the sofa and walked to the window, turning his back to her. "I'm a man, Gloria. Flesh and blood. And you're a beautiful woman."

"You didn't kiss me because I'm beautiful. And I wouldn't care if you did. In fact," she leaned back against the arm of the sofa, "you could kiss me again right now. You could come on over and take me right here, and I wouldn't care. Because at least I'd know you were doing it to please yourself."

He turned, took in her pose, and averted his eyes. "What's that supposed to mean?"

"You weren't acting out of lust this afternoon. You were acting out of pride." Gloria got up from the sofa and stalked over to where John William stood. "You were kissing me for them. The more they cheered, the better it was for you."

She leaned closer and closer with each word, trying and failing to trap him into looking at her. She needed to see his eyes, needed to know that this was the man to whom she could entrust her life and the life of her son. But the more he evaded her gaze, the more he looked like every man who had ever used, raped, beaten, and sometimes even kissed her. She paused, silent, waiting for the kind word that would reassure that she was safe and wanted. Instead she got a downcast, shuffling mumbling mass of man. Just like all the others.

"I'm just tired of the lies."

"Lies?" Gloria said. "You've handed me nothing but lies since you met me."

He took her arm in a grip that sent waves of bruising comfort. "What lie have I ever told you?"

"You told me it didn't matter." His grip demanded more. "You've always told me that it didn't matter who I was or what I did. You've said that I could be a new person, that God could make me a new person. That I didn't have to feel ashamed. That you didn't see me that way."

"I don't."

"Yes you do!" She tore her arm from his grasp and stepped back, out of his reach. "And even if you didn't, it wouldn't matter. Because nobody will ever see me as anything different. I can put on a bonnet and play the little farmer's wife, but there will always be a Lonnie who will remind me of what I am."

"Who cares what Lonnie thinks?"

"You care!" Gloria said, her voice too loud for the sleeping family. She hazarded a glance toward the doors leading off the parlor, then continued in a thick whisper. "You care, and don't try to deny it. You weren't defending my honor today, you were defending your own."

John William's head snapped back more violently than it had when she hit him, his face registering first anger, then something else. He stepped past her, sat down in the willow rocker, and buried his face in his hands.

"You'll never really be able to forgive me for what I've been," Gloria said, gently now, following John William and placing her aching hand on his shoulder.

"It's not my forgiveness you're needin'," he said, looking up. His face was an expression of desperation, a pleading that Gloria couldn't understand. He looked stricken, vulnerable, and she found herself so entranced that she forgot her anger. She felt his hands grasp her waist and allowed this embrace to guide her until she was kneeling on the floor, her face level with his.

"I've got no reason to forgive you," he said. His hands were now on her shoulders, his thumbs fairly digging into soft flesh. "I've got no reason and I've got no right. You've never done me any wrong, you see? Since I've known you, you've never done nothin' against me."

"But before I knew you—"

"I don't care what you were before. It's a new life you have with me. You need to put your past behind you."

"It's not that easy," Gloria said. "I can't just forget what I've been."

"No, you can't. And neither can I. But God will, Gloria, if you'll let Him." He softened his grip but did not let her go, and she found herself unable to look away. "You can't imagine what it feels like to allow God to forgive you, to know that there's no price left to pay for what you've done."

"Price?"

"Yeah," he said, releasing his grip entirely. "We pay for our sins. Shame, guilt."

"That's just it," Gloria said. "I've never felt ashamed of myself before. Not really."

"And you don't have to again." John William's face broke into a smile of pure joy. "Because when Jesus died, He took all of that shame on Himself, you see? So God can take it away from you. So all that's left for you, darlin', is to ask Him to. Tell God you know you've done wrong. Tell Him you believe that Jesus died for your sins. Accept that forgiveness that He offers you."

"It can't be that easy."

"But it is, Gloria, it is. I spent so long hatin' myself for what I done. Not just the men I killed—yes," he stopped her protest, "killed. But when I think of the ones I hurt, humiliated. When I think of how many men took money meant to feed their families and used it to bet on the fact that I'd beat the other guy. There's no way I could go to each of them and say, 'Forgive me. I've changed now.' The only way to have any peace with my past was to let God grant it for me. And He did, but not until I asked Him to. So you see," he concluded with a shrug, "you don't need anythin' from me."

"Oh, but I do." She reached up to take his face in her hands. "I need you to take care of my son. To raise him right, so he'll be as good a man as you are."

"You know I will."

"And I need to know that you'll protect Kate, keep her safe from men like Lonnie."

"Did you not hear anythin' I just said?"

"I heard you," Gloria said, standing. "I heard you say that God can make me a new person, but you and I both will always know what I really am."

He closed his eyes. "God help me." He opened his eyes and looked up at her. "If only you could see. If only you could see what God has to offer you. How He loves you. Then maybe you could see how much…"

The little mantel clock ticked. And ticked. And ticked.

"How much?"

And ticked. He stood up, holding Gloria's full gaze. "I'm only goin' to ask this," he said. His voice no longer had the pleading passion from earlier. It now had an edge she recognized—the one that told her his patience had run out. "I'm askin' you to stay. With me. To be my wife."

"I can't. Not as your wife. That wasn't our agreement."

"Gloria—"

"I'll never forget us in my little cabin and you telling me plain as day that you didn't want me for a—"

"Enough about th—"

"Good enough for that baby of yours," she said, her voice a hoarse whisper, "but not quite good enough for you."

Gloria felt a pounding in her throat and eyes. She folded her arms tightly across her chest and turned her back to John William. When she felt the slight touch on her shoulder, she took a step closer to the window and rested her head against the cool pane.

"That must have hurt you," he said.

Gloria concentrated on the feeling of her face against the glass.

"But my wife had just died. I didn't want to be—"

"Stuck with me?"

"What's that?" She felt a tug on her arm and allowed John William to gently turn her around. "I can't hear if I can't see your face."

"I said you didn't want to be stuck with me."

John William tossed his head back and laughed. "No avoidin' that, now was there?" He brought his hands up to cradle her face and bent her head forward to place a tiny, almost imperceptible kiss on the blond curls at the top of her head. "But if you're not my wife," he spoke into her hair, "I got no claim to you."

Gloria stepped out of his embrace and raised her eyes to meet his. "You can't *claim* me, John. I'm not a piece of land you can improve and own."

"That's not what I meant."

"Every place I've lived, all those houses were full of girls just waiting for some man to come along and make them a bride. Take them straight out of the whorehouse and down the aisle. But I never wanted that. It was never my dream."

"What was your dream?"

His voice, so soft it skittered on the edge of hearing, asked a question no one had ever asked before. When she was young, she dreamt of a father who would show up at her mother's door and take Gloria to his home—a beautiful, three-story mansion with terraces and garrets sitting in the middle of a lush green meadow where a beautiful woman, his lovely wife, would throw her arms wide and welcome this battered little girl who would become her own child. Later the dream changed to an older gentleman in a quiet brick house full of lush carpets, pipe smoke and books, who relied on his long-lost daughter to provide him comfort and conversation in his old age. But never in the idle hours between men did she waste her time fantasizing about a husband. She'd spent her life in and out of beds giving men what was expected from a wife. What was her dream? To live a life free from the life she'd lived. To protect her son from the sins of his mother. To never again be a part of a man's desire; to never again be on the other end of a man's touch.

That is, until she felt lips in her hair asking about her dreams, and absolute terror at not having the right answer.

"Why did you marry Katherine?"

"What?"

"Did you want to claim her? Rescue her? Or was it mad, passionate romance?" She clasped her hands to her breast and fluttered her eyelashes, mocking the emotion. John William responded with a smile and a slight shake of his head.

"She was a good woman," he said. "She taught me about Christ, gave me a Bible. I guess some part of me thought that marryin' a good woman would make me a better man."

"So you think marrying me would make me a better woman?" A sly, taunting smile tugged the corner of her lip.

"Well," John William said, shrugging, "I don' think it could hurt the cause."

Gloria emitted an exaggerated gasp of horror and punched his arm playfully—nothing like the blow she landed earlier. John William grasped his arm and staggered to a half-sitting, half-lying position on the sofa. Barefoot and in her nightgown, Gloria attempted to flounce past him and into her room, but his hand caught hers before she could get away, and there was something in his grip that kept her from taking another step.

"Gloria, look at me."

She did, and as she did, their fingers intertwined.

"I've got strong feelin's for you," he said, looking at their hands rather than her eyes. "Feelin's that just aren't right without you bein' my wife." He looked up at her, briefly, then looked away again.

"I can't make you a better man," Gloria said. "Making me a wife isn't going to erase my past. It isn't going to change me. Think about what I am, John, and tell me that it's something you want to claim." She felt his grip loosen and let her fingers go slack, but the connection remained.

"I'm leaving, John. Just after the harvest."

He smiled. "Now, darlin', we've been through this before."

"That was different. I didn't know then what kind of future Danny would have. But now…"

"What's changed?"

"Look around. I'll always be able to picture him in this home, growing up, going out into the fields. With you."

"And Kate?"

"That little girl owes her life to me, but I don't owe mine to her. Or to you. Good night, John."

She turned her back on him and padded away. She thought she heard him say her name one more time, but the rushing in her ears made her unsure if he had said "Gloria," or "Good night." She wouldn't acknowledge either.

She crawled into bed with Maureen, who appeared to be asleep. She lay awake, waiting for the sounds of John William's settling into the bed in the room next door, but heard nothing.

When the sky outside beckoned her to leave her bed—after an unnecessary rousing from Maureen—she half-expected to find John William still splayed out on the couch, and in her mind she reclaimed the dangling hand, brought it to her lips, and spoke to him the promises he'd asked for last night.

But he was gone. The next time she saw him he was up—dressed and scrubbed—swigging coffee and slapping backs, ready to get the harvest under way.

hile there had never been any discernible affection between John William and Gloria, they now took incredible pains to avoid each other. John William roused early, grabbed whatever cold food he could find in the pie shelf, hitched a team, and was well into the wheat before the rest of the hands had their first cup of coffee. Gloria begged off taking a noon meal out to the men, claiming the afternoon sun was too much for the babies and that she would be of much better use staying back at the house washing and slicing the vegetables from Maureen's garden in preparation for preserving and pickling. When the men came back at dusk, John William tended to the livestock while Maureen and Gloria served the crew a hearty supper. At his request, Maureen fixed a plate and took it to him in the barn.

If anybody picked up on their avoidance of each other, nobody remarked on it. Maureen attempted a few worried questions, but neither would offer conversation. Big Phil made one joke about sensing an early winter on an occasion when Gloria and John William passed in the yard, but a withering look from John William stopped the comment from escalating into banter. The sheer rhythm of a farm in autumn, the harvest of the field and the bounty of the garden, provided a work-filled haven from idle conversation.

Then came Sunday.

During harvest, the idea of Sunday as a day of rest seemed unreasonable. Despite the perfect stretches of clear crisp days, there was always the threat of frost or storm—any agent of the God they worshipped that could take away a year's worth of work and profit in a day. So when Sunday morning came along, the men had to make do with warmed gravy over cold biscuits and no guarantee of a second cup of coffee, as Gloria and Maureen confiscated one team and a wagon to take themselves and the babies to church.

"No argument this time?" Maureen asked as they bumped along the road.

"Hm?" Gloria was mesmerized by the passing landscape.

"I'm just remembering the last Sunday you went to church." The cheerful chortle that lurked just behind all of Maureen's words grated on Gloria's nerves, just as it had all week. "You kicked up quite a fuss. Thought that man was going to have to hog-tie you to a pew." She bubbled into full laughter that died out after a few self-conscious moments.

"Just feels good to get away," Gloria said after a while.

"That it does. Those men might feel the need to work on the Lord's day, but not me. He gave me a day of rest, and I intend to take it."

Gloria glanced over her shoulder to the babies in the back of the wagon. Nearly six months old, neither Kate nor Danny would settle for being packed away in a blanket-lined basket as they had been for their journey from Silver Peak. Now the entire wagon bed served as a traveling crate, the bottom made soft and smooth by no less than three quilts. Although Danny showed no interest in ever bringing mobility to his little body, Kate had taken to grabbing anything she could get a grip of and pulling herself to stand on her stubby, sturdy legs. Gloria checked frequently lest Kate stand up and get bounced right out of the wagon.

"They all right back there?" Maureen asked

"Fine."

"Think they're warm enough?" There was a slight chill in the autumn morning. Both babies wore woolen pants and sweaters, gifts handed down from Josephine Logan.

"I'm sure they're fine."

After a while, Maureen transferred the reins to one hand and reached the other over to cover Gloria's own.

"Child," she said, and only that, while the occasional squeezing of Gloria's hand communicated with more warmth than her most cheerful voice ever could.

Gloria broke the silence. "How long do you think it will take?"

"To get to town? About an hour."

"To bring in the crop."

"Ah," Maureen said, withdrawing her hand to gain better control of the team before they veered off the narrow path. "When it was just me and Ed and a sickle, it could take nearly a month. And that was with only ten acres planted. But that was before there was anyone to help. Just every farmer for himself. Now that the country's growin', why there's all kinds of men here just to hire out as hands. Pocket full of cash, no responsibilities. Course, Big Phil's just being neighborly. He's got a place of his own, but he's takin' to start an apple orchard, so he don't have a crop this year, except hay, and there'll be plenty of time for that after the wheat gets in."

"How long for *this* crop?"

"I talked with John last night," Maureen said. "He thinks they're about half through."

"Half?" Already?

"Well, they got eight men working, two reapers, a team going behind each machine tying up the sheaves."

"That's just another week."

"Until it's all cut. Then of course the stalks have to dry—"

"How long?"

"A few days. Then it all gets loaded and driven to Centerville. They've got a mill there—"

"Is that far?"

"About three days. Maybe five with the wagon loaded down. But that's a blessing. Time was we had to thresh it all by hand."

"And then what will he— What's after Centerville?"

Maureen turned and gave Gloria a full smile. "Why, it's time to put up the seed wheat for the spring and start bringing in the hay."

Gloria turned around to check on the babies again. Kate lay on her back, madly gnawing at the sleeve of her sweater. Danny was on his stomach, valiantly holding his head high until the next gentle jolt of the wagon made his elbows give out and his little head bomped down on the quilt. He was frustrated—not hurt— and Gloria sent him a sound of sympathy in the midst of her calculations.

One month.

"A lot can happen in a month," Maureen said, a sly song in her voice.

"What do you mean?"

"Just that a month is a long time." Maureen's voice oozed innocence. "Seems to me that this time next month, little Kate might be able to walk herself to church."

Gloria laughed at the exaggeration, then said, "When *do* babies start walking, anyway?"

"Whenever they decide to. One day they're just crawling around, hands and knees filthy from the floor, and God just hands down the strength to get up, find a balance, and take a step. After that, walking just comes natural."

Gloria took a sidelong look at the woman who had grown to be so dear to her. "How do you know all this? You've never had—" She stopped herself too late, but the older woman's chuckle set Gloria's mind at ease.

"Good heavens, girl," she said, "you don't have to have children to know they get up and walk." She turned then, and seemed determined to stare until Gloria rewarded her with a smile. "As for the *when* we walk, why there's nothin' to knowing that either. It's in God's timing—just like everything else. Nothing on this earth ever happens until God gives His hand to it. Crops don't grow, babies don't walk. We can make all the plans we want to, can try to make people fit and fill our lives, but there's not a thing we can do outside of His power. Funny how sometimes it's the people who love God the most that are the worst about lettin' Him do His work, and the ones that don't care the least are happy driftin' along, not even knowing they're under His hand.

"Men—well, human beings—can be just so stubborn. They feel the need to force *their* desires, *their* vision. Staying up nights, worrying…"

The pause hung between them like a worm dangling from a hook, but Gloria refused to take the bait.

"And just how are *you* sleeping these nights, Maureen?" Gloria asked.

Maureen turned and gave her a wink. "Some nights better than others," she said before clicking to the horses and turning them toward town.

John William felt a bit hypocritical not going to church that Sunday. All the wheedling and convincing he'd done to bring Gloria to church for the last service echoed in his ear. What a blessing it was to be near a congregation. How important it was to forge ties in the community, to obey God's command to assemble together.

None of his crew members seemed disappointed to be working on the Lord's Day—although Big Phil declared he would miss the after-service dinner—and he considered leaving them to their labor and accompanying the women and babies. But the long ride to Middleton with Gloria was not an idea he cherished. Moments of silence in passing were one thing, but hours of ambling non-conversation were quite another.

"Men," John William said before the first stalk of wheat was cut, "seein' that it's the Lord's Day today, let's say a prayer before we get started this mornin'."

There was a series of uncomfortable mumblings and shufflings, and nearly a full minute elapsed before Lonnie caught on that he should remove his hat. John William's request for a volunteer to lead sent eyes darting to the dust, except for Big Phil, who launched into prayer before John William's eyes were fully closed.

"Our Father God in heaven," Phil's voice boomed into the

morning, "we labor here today to Thee. We ask Thine hand of safety upon us."

John William moved to put on his hat and head to work before he realized that Phil wasn't finished.

"And for this bounty that we harvest, for this Thine blessing Thou has broughtest forth from Thy earth, we truly praise and thank Thee."

Shuffle…

"Though we know we toileth not for our own selves, but for the benefit of our brother and new neighbor, we know he shareth our gratitude. May he findeth rest here easy. May his family be at peace here in our midst."

A few men mumbled "Amen," but Phil pressed on.

"And *finally* Lord, we thank Thee for Thy love and bounty. And mostly for Thy wisdom in our lives." Pause. "In the name of Thy Son Jesus Christ, the Savior of our souls, we offereth this prayer to Thee." Pause. "Amen."

"Amen!" echoed the hands. John William sensed the movement around him, but he remained head bowed, eyes closed in prayer.

May his family be at peace here in our midst. He wondered if Phil would pray for God's blessings if he knew the nature of his "family."

Forgive me, Lord, he prayed silently, both for deceivin' my friends and for allowin' such discord in my home. I'm givin' that woman over to You and Your wisdom. You sent her to save my child, and for that I give thanks. Renew my strength to resist temptation, and help—

"Amen, MacGregan!" Phil said, giving a hearty slap on his back. "Are we workin' or havin' a prayer meetin'?"

John William opened his eyes to see the smiling face of his new friend, this older, portly man who, in a single innocent prayer, managed to bring him a path of peace for the discord in his home. He kept his hat gripped in one hand and extended the other to shake Phil's.

"Thank you brother," John William said, pumping Phil's hand. "That was a powerful prayer."

"Well, if we don't get to work soon, we may as well have gone to church."

They shared a laugh as they made their way toward the waiting men and horses.

Gloria entered the small Middleton church for the second time in her life. This morning had a distinctly different feel to it. Absent were the gatherings of hands-in-pockets, dirt-stamping husbands. No crowds of rowdy boys ran circles around screaming packs of little sisters. There was only Reverend Fuller, dressed in his somber black suit, to lend a baritone voice to the gathering crowd. He did so poised on the steps of his little church, ringing its bell, calling the group of women and young children in to worship.

Gloria remembered seeing several of the women the previous week, but John William had not taken great pains to introduce her. Maureen, however, made her way across the lawn and through the crowd of longtime friends, holding baby Kate in one arm and the other stretched behind her, leading Gloria by the hand. "This is Gloria," Maureen said to one smiling, bonneted face after another, "and her son Danny and daughter Kate. I kept them back at the house last week..." Gloria followed, silent behind her, with a tight-lipped smile and downcast gaze accompanying each greeting.

Both Danny and Kate were looking especially bright-eyed and beautiful this morning, and Gloria steeled herself for an onslaught of oohs and ahhs, for torrents of admiration and questions. But nearly every woman she met had her own beautiful baby in her arms or clinging to her skirts, so Gloria's babies were hardly given more than a passing glance.

"Well," Maureen said, turning to Gloria with a smile, "shall we go in, then?"

"I suppose so," Gloria said, truly wishing she had a choice.

The women ascended the small set of steps that led to the

open church door where Reverend Fuller stood greeting his congregation.

"Good morning Mrs. Brewster," he said, extending a warm handshake to Maureen. "And who is this lovely child?"

"This is John MacGregan's daughter, Kate, and his son, Danny. And you met Gloria last week."

"Of course I did." His voice was soft, Gloria thought, and wrinkled. "Good morning, Mrs. MacGregan." He extended his hand, and Gloria allowed his fingers to grip hers, but she did not meet his eyes when she mumbled "Good morning," before passing through the door.

She breathed again after passing the threshold. The same rows of benches as last time. Some of the same faces. Same rays of sunshine pouring through the glass windows. Same muted conversations. Same smell of sawdust and leather and soap.

Maureen walked just ahead of her. As she passed each row, heads looked up and women smiled, then returned to their conversations. Nobody seemed shocked to see Gloria in the room. Nor did they seem elated, disappointed, or outraged. Gloria, mute and musing, followed behind Maureen to the bench in the last row on the left-hand side. Where they'd sat last week. Maureen gestured to Gloria to slide in first.

"John William said you'd be more comfortable in the back," Maureen whispered as Gloria slid halfway down the bench. "I usually sit third row from the front," she pointed to where another older lady was turned, offering a white lace wave across her shoulder, "but back here's nice, too." She used Kate's hand to return her friend's wave.

"She looks familiar," Gloria said, offering a guarded smile to the woman in the third row.

"That's Big Phil's wife, Anne," Maureen said.

"That's why she looks familiar. She looks just like Phil."

"Well, they've been married nearly thirty years. They say after a while you just start to look like each other."

Gloria brought Danny's fist up to her mouth and grazed his

little fingers across her lips. She tried to picture herself thirty years from now with a misshapen nose and a cauliflower ear. She smiled into the eyes of her son and thought, what better reason to leave?

A familiar brood slid into the bench in front of them. Josephine Logan settled two of her children—Eliza and little Charles—beside her before turning around to offer Gloria and Maureen a warm smile.

"Just look at these babies," Josephine continued. "I can't believe how fast they're growing!"

Gloria surged with pride at a compliment given by such a successful, accomplished mother. She searched for a wise, insightful response, but Josephine's attention was commanded by Charles, who seemed determined to yank off his shirt buttons. There was no other opportunity for conversation after that because Reverend Fuller had taken his place at the front and was attempting to bring a congregation full of women and children to attention.

"Good morning. Good morning," he repeated until the room was brought to a hush. "Let us raise our voices in song to our Lord." He reached into his breast pocket and produced a pitch pipe. A subtle humming filled the room as the women found the note before the tiny church erupted in song.

> *"There is a name I love to hear,*
> *I love to sing its worth;*
> *It sounds like music in mine ear,*
> *The sweetest name on earth. "*

Gloria had heard Maureen sing this song countless times as she puttered around her kitchen. They'd sung it last week, too, though the song sounded lighter without the rich male tones. She felt the words bouncing through her brain, felt the tune at the back of her throat. The lyrics of the verses eluded her, but when the chorus came around for the third time, Gloria found herself mouthing the words.

"Oh, how I love Jesus,
Oh, how I love Jesus,
Oh, how I love Jesus,
Because He first loved me!"

When the final "Amen" came, she was coming as close to singing as she ever had in her life.

Reverend Fuller invited them to sit. Just as the rustle of skirts and petticoats died down, Adele Fuller walked through the door. Gloria scooted closer to the wall, dragging Maureen with her.

"We can move down to make room," she said with a slightly authoritative air.

"All right." Maureen caught Adele's eye and patted the bench beside her.

"Well, I can see by the faces here that we are well into the time of harvest," Reverend Fuller said. "I considered canceling our services this morning, but then who am I to deny such lovely ladies an opportunity to worship?"

A soft ripple of laughter affirmed his decision.

"You know, if a stranger were to walk into our little church for the first time today, he might get the idea that we were a community devoid of men, wouldn't he? A stranger just might look at the faces of these precious children here and mistake them for poor, fatherless orphans."

Yes, yes, bonnets nodded in agreement.

"But in truth there's not a one among us who doesn't have a father."

That's right, the bonnets concurred.

But Gloria held her head still as stone, her eyes locked on the old man at the front of the church.

"For we are all children of God. We can all claim the same Father as did His Son, Christ Jesus, can we not?"

A surge of passion coursed through the little crowd as delicate gloved hands were raised to half-mast affirmation. Gloria gripped her son tighter than she had just moments before.

"Now I know there are those among us who live without the guidance and comfort of an earthly father." *Yes, yes.* "And some of us have lived a life abandoned. Maybe unloved." *That's right.* "I look back there," he gestured toward the last row and panic surged through Gloria, "and see my lovely daughter." The bonnets turned to dip in acknowledgment. "And most of you know that she and I don't always see eye to eye on everything." Soft, soprano chuckles. "But there is nothing she could do, no ambitious business decision, no extravagant silk gown that could make me love her any less."

"Amen." Adele's throaty voice coaxed a ripple of giggles.

Gloria cut her eyes to the right, but Maureen and Kate blocked her view of the reverend's daughter. She wanted to lean forward—just a bit—to get a glimpse of this woman who lived the life Gloria had always longed for. She didn't envy the latest gown specially ordered from New York or the acres of land she owned that allowed her to buy such luxuries. Gloria would have lived her life in rags in a sod house teeming with vermin if she could have done so with this man. From her vantage point, she could see only Adele's skirt—pumpkin-colored silk with black velvet piping. She focused on that swatch of skirt and shot mental accusations. *If I had such a father I would live a life to please him.*

"I have always looked to the Scriptures to know how to be a good father," Reverend Fuller continued, "to know exactly how to discipline. How to provide. How to love." Gloria could feel Adele beaming. "What is just as important, though, is to look to the Scriptures and know that we can be more than just imperfect children of mortal parents. Jesus called God 'Father,' and He invited us to do so, too. When He taught us to pray, He told us to say, 'Our Father.' *Our* Father."

The restlessness of the opening remarks came to a halt as the women settled in to listen. Gloria shifted Danny to rest against her shoulder, pressing her hand against his back to keep him quiet. And close.

"I am the pastor to all of you in here," Reverend Fuller said, his hands sweeping the crowd. "All of you in here may call me 'Reverend,' but only one of you can call me 'Papa.' But anybody who believes in God, anybody who will receive Him gets the right to become children of God. Galatians 4:6 says that God sent the Spirit of His Son into our hearts, the Spirit who calls out 'Abba, Father.' Do you know what 'Abba' means?"

No.

"Ancient Hebrew children, when they needed comfort and guidance, when they needed love and attention, when they had a heavy heart or a bleeding knee, would run to the man they knew as Abba—Papa—and climb into his lap. Do you know that feeling?"

No.

"Romans 8:15 says that when we receive Christ into our lives, we receive a Spirit of adoption. We become God's child. That's why I can look across this room at each of you, not knowing where all of you came from or what kind of family you had, and say that there's not a one among us who doesn't have a father." Gloria's eyes never left the Reverend, and while his own gaze roamed the crowd, she was sure his voice was aimed directly at her. "All of us in this room who recognize Christ, who will open our hearts to acknowledge Him, have the right to look to the almighty God, creator of the world, and call Him Abba, Father."

On the bench against the wall, Gloria buried her face in the soft warm neck of her fatherless son and whispered the word. "Papa." It was the first time she had ever said the word out loud.

Shortly after the final *Amen* of the final hymn, the women filed out of the little church, pausing to take the hand of their beloved Reverend. There was no real hurry to leave; this was a time of reflective conversation. Gloria and Maureen—babies in tow—

trailed behind the celebrated Adele, who planted a daughterly kiss on her father's weathered cheek. "Wonderful sermon, *Papa*," she said with a grin.

"Such high praise coming from you, my dear," Reverend Fuller said, his tone matching her lightness.

Maureen, following behind Adele, took his hand and jostled baby Kate, saying, "This little girl is just as lucky as yours, Reverend."

"Ah, yes." He took Kate's hand between his thumb and forefinger. "MacGregan seems like a fine man. Everything going all right?"

"Just wonderful," Maureen said. "We're becoming a regular little family."

"Does that mean, then, that you're planning to stay in Middleton after all?"

"It means, *Reverend,* that I like being where I'm needed, and right now I'm needed here a lot more than I am with my sister in St. Louis."

Gloria wasn't sure what she had just witnessed, but the blush in Maureen's cheek was unmistakable, and the glint in the Reverend's eye wasn't there when he greeted any of the other women.

When it was Gloria's turn to share the top step with the Reverend, she found she had nothing to say. She simply extended her hand once again, but this time her grip was strong. His eyes were so kind, but it was clear that if either of them was going to speak, it was going to be her. "Thank you," she managed to say, though she wasn't quite sure what she was thanking him for.

Reverend Fuller released Gloria's hand, gripped her by her shoulders, and pulled her to him, placing a soft kiss on her forehead.

"Welcome to our family," he said.

Outside the church, women were loading themselves and their children into their buggies and rigs. Amidst the flurry of good-byes, Josephine Logan turned to Maureen and asked if she and

Gloria were planning to stay for a picnic dinner on the church lawn. Gloria nodded enthusiastically, still remembering the delicacies John William had brought back from his first visit to the Middleton church.

"But everybody's leaving," Maureen said. Indeed, the crowd had dwindled to just Maureen, Gloria, Josephine and the children. Even Reverend Fuller was gone, having taken his daughter to his home for an after-church dinner. "And I didn't bring anything—"

"*I* did," Josephine said, a note of triumph in her voice. "Not much, but enough to make a nice snack before a long ride home, and give us a chance to talk." This last remark was directed straight at Gloria. For the second time that day Gloria felt warmed by the attention of this woman. "Eliza," Josephine said, "hand down that basket. Charles, you can help spread the blanket."

There certainly was enough for a snack. Josephine had a length of venison sausage, a loaf of bread, and a stone crock of soft cheese. She'd been experimenting with goat's milk cheese and declared this to be her most successful attempt yet. There were half-a-dozen tart green apples, picked too early at her eager young son's insistence.

Like the babies' clothes, the meal spread in front of them was just another example of Josephine's generous spirit.

"I'd say there's more than a snack here," Gloria said as each item was brought out of the basket. "Thank you for sharing with us."

"It's our pleasure," Josephine said, slicing the sausage into thin rounds. "Who's feeding your crew today?"

"I sent them out with some bread and butter," Maureen said. "We're running low on just about everything, feeding those men. I'm hoping they'll come in a little early and maybe get some fish for dinner. We haven't had a good fish fry in a while. Otherwise, looks like beans and cornbread tonight."

They had spread a quilt in the grass beside the church, situating themselves where they could soak in the autumn sun while being sheltered from the autumn breeze. Gloria settled herself at the blanket's edge and leaned back against the church wall. She opened her blouse and brought Danny to her breast to nurse, draping a shawl across her shoulder. Josephine took a plate from the bottom of her basket, loaded it with goodies, and set it within easy reach of Gloria. Maureen gave Kate a crusty bread heel to keep her occupied until Gloria could nurse her. Before sitting down herself, she smiled and produced a small paper package tied with string.

"Here's our contribution to the meal," Maureen said, smiling. "Molasses cookies. I brought them for the ride home."

"Why didn't you tell me we had cookies?" Gloria asked, her voice a mix of delight and petulance.

"Because then we wouldn't have had any for the ride home."

The three women laughed and promised Eliza and Charles that the biggest cookies would be theirs if they ate their meal quietly and behaved. They settled into easy conversation. Maureen reported the status of their crops, the bounty of her garden. Gloria gave a glowing report of the latest milestones of the babies—sitting up, pulling up, sounds suspiciously close to being actual words. Josephine said that David and James would be able to bring in most of their crop. They didn't have much more than what they would need through the winter; David was intending to raise sheep next year. They were expecting to get the start of their first flock in the spring.

"I guess David was just meant to be a shepherd," Josephine said, laughing. Maureen laughed, too, and Gloria was sure there was a joke in there somewhere. She produced a polite chuckle and told herself to remember to ask Maureen about it on the ride home.

"He's wanted to go into ranching since we got here," Josephine continued, "but the opportunity just hasn't been right until now."

"How long have you been here?" Gloria asked.

"Let's see…we were married just before we arrived, had James three years later, he's twelve…about fifteen years."

Maureen shot her a look of surprise. "You married just *before* you arrived? You got married on the trail?"

Josephine blushed a bit and cast down her eyes.

"I've been here since forty-nine," Maureen said. "I thought I knew everyone's story. Guess I missed one."

By now Josephine was fully blushing, and Gloria would have felt sorry for her had she not been so curious about Josephine's story.

"Well," Josephine began, then noticed little Eliza leaning forward. "Eliza, get the water jug out of the back of the wagon and take it to the water pump just over there." She pointed to the blacksmith's building some fifty yards away.

"Aw, ma," Eliza said. "I wanna hear the story."

"Go. And take Charles with you."

"Yeah!" Charles said.

When the children were well out of earshot, Josephine took one delicate bite of apple and began.

"My parents and I came over with a train of other families. About fifteen wagons. David was one of the scouts. I thought he was just about the most handsome thing I'd ever seen. He wore buckskin pants and had a knife strapped to his leg. He had a beautiful black horse named Bullet that he rode in circles around the wagons every evening, and sometimes when we stopped for meals he let some of the little boys ride him. That's how I caught his eye—he was giving my little brother a ride. I'll never forget it. David was sitting up tall in that saddle, my little brother clinging to his back. Well, he smiled down at me and said, 'Hey, little girl. You want to go for a ride with me sometime?'"

"What did you say?" Gloria asked. Danny was finished nursing, and she handed him over to Maureen who, in turn, passed Kate to her.

"I told him that I was not a child, and if he wanted to go for a ride with me, he could just come and court me proper."

"How old were you?" Maureen said, rubbing Danny's back and bouncing him on her soft lap.

"Sixteen. Sixteen and thinking I knew all I had to know about life. Well, my father was not about to let me go off with some wild wagon scout. And we were in the middle of nowhere, so we didn't exactly have any church socials to go courting *to*. So the first time he came riding around our wagon, my father told him that he could just ride himself right off."

"But you didn't," Gloria said.

"Oh, no." Josephine's face took on the glow of the girl she'd been fifteen years ago. "I made eyes at him every chance I got, just a terrible flirt. And he tried just about everything to get to talk to me alone. So one evening, I'm dumping out the dish water, and he comes up to me, leans down real close and says, 'How about going for a walk with me tonight?'"

All three women emitted a sound of delight, as if they had been transported to their sixteenth year, face to face with a dashing young suitor. Even Gloria managed to conjure a feeling of innocent thrill.

"And you said…" Maureen prompted.

"What do you think I said? I waited for my mother and brother to fall asleep in our wagon. My father actually slept outside, so that was a little trickier. I unlatched some of the canvas ties and snuck out the side."

"And he was waiting for you," Gloria said.

"He was indeed. We didn't say a single word. He just took my hand and we started walking. When we thought we were out of earshot of the men on watch, we started talking. Whispers at first, then he said something funny, and we laughed and talked some more. And walked some more, and before I knew it, we were lost."

"Lost?" Gloria's voice was full of skepticism. "What kind of a scout gets lost?"

"The kind that's sparking a pretty young girl," Maureen said.

"All I know is that one minute I looked over my shoulder and saw the fires in our camp, then I looked back and there was nothing but darkness. I was terrified. I just knew we were going to get eaten by wolves or attacked by Indians—"

"Or found by your father?" Maureen asked.

"Especially that," Josephine said. "But it was *pitch* dark outside. I couldn't see a thing. I couldn't see David, and he was right next to me."

"I'll bet he was," Gloria said.

"So he said the safest thing to do was just to stop. Right there. Before we got any further away."

"Good decision," Maureen said. "Sometimes when you don't know where to go, it's best to just stay put." She waited until Gloria was looking right at her before adding, "Besides, you couldn't have been far from the dawn."

"It *seemed* like it at the time. But we just sat down and—"

"Prayed?" Gloria asked.

Josephine sent her a puzzled look. "Why would you say that?"

Gloria shrugged. It just seemed like one of those stories where everybody ended up praying and everything turned out all right.

"Well, we didn't," Josephine said, seeming a little embarrassed. "We just sat together for a while, then he kissed me. It was my first kiss, and I thought to myself right then that if we survived that night, I would want to spend the rest of my life kissing him."

"Aww," Maureen and Gloria said in unison.

"Then he tried something else, and I slapped him, and I decided that if we lived through that night, I'd let my father do whatever he wanted to. And that's when I really got scared—thinking about my father. What was I going to say? How was I ever going to earn his trust or forgiveness?"

"And did you?" Gloria asked.

"I guess I fell asleep—I was crying, you know—and the next thing I knew, I heard my name being called." Josephine cupped her hand to her mouth and, in a deep voice, yelled, "'Josie! Josie girl!' It was just beginning to get light. The sun wasn't up, but the sky had gone from black to that silvery blue. I stood up and called, 'Daddy? Daddy!' I wanted him to come and find me, but he didn't. He just stayed right there in the camp and called and called so we could follow his voice. David and I walked together—he was much better about following the sound than I was—but as soon as I saw my father, I broke away from him and ran and ran."

"You weren't afraid that he'd be angry?" Gloria asked.

"Not anymore. Not once I heard his voice."

"What did he say?" Gloria had long forgotten about the baby at her breast.

Josephine's words caught in her throat a little. "He didn't say anything. He just held out his arms, so grateful that I hadn't been killed or…worse."

"I'll bet he didn't hold out his arms for young David, though, did he?" Maureen said.

"Oh, no." Josephine's humor was back. "He greeted David with a shotgun barrel, and I had to do some pretty fast talking to convince him to put it away, even though there was a part of me that thought he deserved to be shot."

"But you still married him?" Gloria said.

Josephine shrugged. "That's the power of a kiss. You have to admire a man who would take that kind of a risk just to get one little kiss."

The afternoon turned out to be a warm one. Gloria took Kate and Danny out of their little woolen suits and tucked them snugly into quilted cocoons for a nap on the ride home. She felt herself feeling drowsy in the sunlight, and more than once during the ride home her head bobbed in sleep.

"Where you goin'?" Maureen's voice seemed far away.

"Hmm?"

"Do you have a plan? A place to go?"

Gloria was fully awake now. "I don't make plans. Never have. When it's time to go, I just pick up and leave."

"Just like your mother?"

"I am *nothing* like my mother. My mother dragged me through her life. Made me a part of it. I won't do that."

"So you think leaving's your only choice?"

Gloria said nothing.

"Because it's not, you know. You could *choose* to stay. Stay and make the kind of life you wouldn't mind sharing with your child." Her voice got softer. "The kind of life you wanted, all along."

"And what?" Gloria said, turning toward Maureen. "Just set myself up in some other woman's house?"

"For now." Maureen in turn faced Gloria. "Besides, haven't you always lived in some other woman's house?"

Gloria bristled and turned away. "And I'm supposed to keep on pretending to be *Mrs*. MacGregan?"

"No," Maureen said. "Become her."

Gloria thought back to the first Mrs. MacGregan. Cold and withdrawn, the type of woman who hated women like Gloria.

"You know," Maureen continued, "not everybody has a story like Josephine's. Not all women are lucky enough to ever be young and in love. So if that's what you're waiting for—"

"It's not," Gloria snapped. "I don't even know what that is."

"I loved Ed Brewster," Maureen said, her face and voice softening, "but I didn't marry him because I loved him."

"So why did you?"

Maureen reached over to pat Gloria's hand. "Don't think that you're the only woman to feel like she doesn't have a choice. I was twenty-six years old. I'd spent my whole life taking care of my parents—when they died, I was just so alone. I'd known Ed for a while, and when he said he was pulling up stakes to move out west and wanted someone to go with him, I went.

"John William's a good man," Maureen continued. "He's strong, and handsome in his own way. Most important, he's a godly man who cares for you a great deal."

"He told me once that he thought God brought our paths together," Gloria said. "But I think he was just talking about Kate. What I did for her."

"Maybe so. Maybe you were meant to save Kate, but you know what I really think? I think God sent *Kate* along to save *you*."

The idea hit Gloria like a horseshoe to the head. "Why would He do that?"

"For the same reason that Josephine's father would stand at the edge of their camp and call out to his child. He brought you to safety."

Safe. It was the very word to describe how Gloria felt every minute with John William. The first day she met him, he'd protected her from the barbs of his wife. The first night in her cabin, when he entrusted her with his daughter, not even his imposing size and demand intimidated her. They'd journeyed together for countless miles, and even in the wildest country she'd felt protected. Sheltered. He steered conversations with strangers away from incriminating questions, and built her up to be a natural, welcome part of his life. She had never felt as valued as the night he destroyed the detestable little man at Fort Hall. Then there was the day, just one month ago, when together she and John William drove this very path, rounded this very corner to the pretty house with the welcoming blue door. She'd felt at home. Not just then, but ever since the day she'd put her foot in John William's hand and he lifted her up into this wagon.

"All my life," Gloria said, her voice barely above a whisper, "I've wanted two things. A father, and a home. And the minute I knew I was pregnant, I promised myself that my child would have those things."

"And he will," Maureen said. "But girl, there's no reason to deny them for yourself, too."

"But I told him I was leaving. He said he didn't care."

"He said no such thing." Maureen answered Gloria's questioning look with a smile. "I was awake, remember?"

"Well, that's what I heard."

"That's what you wanted to hear."

"What *did* he say?"

"That he cares for you. That he has feelings for you. He wants to marry you and take care of you and your child."

"But he didn't ask me to stay."

"No, child, he's asked you to choose."

They drove into the yard, stopping just a few feet from the front door. Gloria turned around to check on the children and smiled at their ability to slumber through bouncy roads and conversation. Off in the distance, she heard the sound of the men's voices as they worked. They were singing. The actual words were lost in the distance, but John William's voice rose slightly above the rest.

"But what will I tell him?" Gloria said.

"Don't tell him anything. I'll just stand on the porch with a shotgun waiting for him to show up."

21

*G*loria didn't say another word about leaving.

Each morning seemed to be a little colder, and while there was no threat of an imminent frost, a sense of urgency prevailed. John William was anxious to get his wheat to the miller in Centerville, not only to have his own supply of flour and grain set aside for his newly acquired family, but also to pay the wages earned by the crew he'd hired to bring in this first crop. Each day, the men worked past the threshold of darkness, returning to the house too exhausted for their accustomed evenings of supper, drinks, and card games.

After the second week, four of the men John William hired left to fulfill obligations to other farmers, leaving just Big Phil and Lonnie to help bring in the remainder of the crop.

Just after breakfast one morning, John William stood in the kitchen doorway, hat in hand, and announced that he needed a favor.

"What?" Gloria asked suspiciously.

"Now, John," Maureen said, casting a disparaging look at Gloria, "we're all family here. Asking for help isn't like asking for the moon. What do you need?"

"Another set of hands."

"Gather up as much as your hand will hold," John William said, demonstrating by filling his palm with a generous bunch of newly cut wheat.

"Like this?" Gloria held up a scrawny bunch—probably no

more than twelve stalks—clutched in a hand that seemed to mirror her sullen attitude.

"Only if you want to make this last till it's time to plant again." He reached over to unclench Gloria's fist, placed his own cut bunch into her grasp, and curled her fingers around it. "There. About like that. Enough that you can get a grip on it, not so much that you're gonna let any drop."

"I think I have the idea," Gloria said with an exaggerated tone of understanding.

"Good. Now transfer it under your arm, hold it tight against you. Just like that. Now, take another handful, hold it with the rest until you have a nice big bundle. Good, now take a piece of twine," he reached into his pocket and pulled out a length of string, "and wrap it 'round."

"Then tie it off?"

"No. If you hold it tight enough, you'll just need to tuck the end under, like this…no…here, let me…" John William leaned in and helped Gloria guide the end of the binding twine under and around itself. It was the first time he'd touched her since the night she'd said she was leaving, and he half-expected her to flinch. He was pleased when she didn't.

"And we'll do this all day?"

He chuckled. "Time will fly. You'll see."

For this day's labor, John William had given up his seat driving the reaper and chose instead to walk behind the machine. He had cheerfully handed the reins over to Big Phil, who seemed only too eager to climb up and master the rig. Lonnie worked behind them, cutting the missed stalks with a scythe and bundling them in seemingly one motion.

"See him?" John William said, gesturing toward Lonnie. "Before you complain about the labor, look at that and realize it could be a lot harder. I spent my childhood workin' alongside my father. Hired out."

"There's worse ways to spend a childhood," Gloria said.

The newly formed sheaves were unceremoniously dropped

in the wake of the reaper, but when three or four were formed, John William showed Gloria how to stand them together, each supporting the other, so they could dry.

"You see why you need to make the bundles strong?" John William said. "They need to be able to support each other."

On they worked throughout the morning, stopping only for swigs of gingered water from the stone jug that rode alongside Big Phil on the reaper's seat. At the first break, there was some hemming and hawing and searching for a suitable cup so that Gloria, too, could drink, but thirst overwhelmed her and she simply grabbed the jug from John William's hand and swigged away like the rest of them. She followed her swig with a satisfied swipe of her sleeve across her chin.

Then they were off to work again. They made an interesting crew. Big Phil rode the reaper, occasionally looking over his shoulder to share witticisms and wisdom.

"Know why some dogs just won't hunt?" he'd ask. And just as the others braced themselves for some great truth, he'd answer, "'Cause they're lazy."

This made Gloria laugh and John William groan and Lonnie grumble that if he had half a dollar for every time he heard someone fall for that one, he sure wouldn't be here choppin' wheat alongside no potbellied philosopher and greenhorn farmers.

Somehow, John William's prediction about time passing quickly proved to be true, but by noon every inch of Gloria's body—from the tips of her fingers rife with tiny cuts to her blistered feet—called for a time of respite. The ache in the small of her back intensified each time she stooped or stood, and her right arm was sheathed in pain. The decision to leave Maureen home to tend to the children had been made with the understanding that, come noon, Gloria would walk back to the house to nurse Danny and Kate. But now such a trek seemed far too heroic an effort, and her breasts felt none of the heaviness she associated with mealtime. Instead, she dropped her last bundled sheaf and asked, "Can we eat now?"

"Hungry, are you?" John William flashed her a smile full of

understanding. "Maureen sent somethin' with us. I guess we can break."

He called out to Big Phil, who willingly called a halt to the team and jumped down, bringing Maureen's wicker basket with him. Lonnie swung his scythe through one more handful of wheat, bundled it, and steadied it against the sheaf Gloria had just dropped to the ground.

John William took the familiar frayed quilt from under the reaper's seat and spread it, flinging weeks' worth of grass and dirt into the air. The massive noon meal of that first day of harvest had diminished, being replaced by a loaf of bread, a crock of sweet apple butter, and cheese, but to Gloria it seemed a feast.

"Cheer up, darlin'," John William said, mistaking the exhaustion on her face for disappointment. "When I saw Maureen this mornin', she was pickin' out a chicken I suspect she's plannin' to fry up for supper."

It didn't take long for the last morsel to disappear. Lonnie unhitched the team of horses from the reaper and took them to drink from the creek at the far edge of the field. He wasn't more than five steps away when Gloria saw the real reason he volunteered for the job—a silver flask he'd been sipping from all morning. Big Phil sat propped against the overturned basket and declared he would rest his old eyes for just a minute while the horses got watered.

"I thought we were all so desperate to get this done," Gloria said. "If we all have enough time to take a nap, then maybe you can just finish up without me."

"Calm down, darlin'," John William said. "The body has to rest a bit if it's to be any good at all. And since we have to wait for the horses to get back anyway..." His final thought trailed into silence as he stretched himself out on the quilt, flat on his back with his hat covering his face, just as he had every afternoon of their journey together.

So, just like every afternoon of their journey, Gloria was left alone with her thoughts as she sat, bolt upright on another corner of the quilt. Just next to her was a little patch of some wildflowers that had miraculously escaped the whirring of the blades. She picked one, then another, and worked their ends together. She picked another and another, finally making a chain long enough to fit over her head, like a necklace. She lifted one of the blossoms and scrutinized the color. Lavender. Maybe he would notice that it just matched her eyes.

Until now, it always seemed as if life was like this chain—each moment, each man, a link stretching on and on until suddenly it was over. That had certainly been true for her mother. The final link, the final cough.

But now Gloria wondered if life wasn't a little more like what she'd lived this afternoon. Maybe people didn't pass through your life, weighing down your past like so many rings of iron. Maybe she and Danny and Kate and John William and even Maureen had been scooped up by some giant hand—maybe even by God—and brought together, held close and tight and wrapped and tied. Maybe life wasn't a chain of moments and people strung along, but a bunch of them, tossed together chaotically and imperfectly to be set against one another, leaning, depending, pulled from the safety of their soil and roots to become something better.

The thought of it made her smile. Made her want to stay, because though her body ached and her fingers bled and her skin was soaked with sweat, she felt today like she *belonged*. Like she had never belonged anywhere ever before. She wanted to stretch her foot and nudge John William right now, to announce her conclusions and ask him to let her stay, but the imposing figure of Phil snoring softly nearby stilled her impulse.

She sat quietly, staring at the wheat, wanting desperately to talk to him. About anything. She missed him.

Had this been an afternoon on their journey, John William would have roused himself from his nap and settled in for a Bible reading, and the remaining stalks of wheat bowing in the breeze reminded her of one of the stories he'd read, about a man who'd had a dream about wheat. His name was Jonathan? Jehoshaphat? Jericho?

"John?" she asked, softly at first, then repeated it until she got a grunt in reply.

"What was the name of that man in that Bible story who had the dream about the dancing wheat?"

John William brought his hand up to tip his hat away from his face—just enough to give Gloria a puzzled, impatient look. "Dancin'?"

"Remember, all the wheat was dancing around all the other wheat—"

"It wasn't dancin'," he said, propping himself up on one elbow. The look he gave now was one of affection and indulgence. She loved the thought that she had pleased him.

"It was Joseph," he continued. "And the wheat was bowin' down to him because he was about to rise up in power over his brothers. They weren't happy about that, so they—"

"All right, all right, I don't need the whole story. I just couldn't remember the name."

"Why were you wonderin'?"

"No reason," Gloria said, shrugging. "The wheat just reminded me of it, and I couldn't remember."

"All right." He gave her one more suspicious glance before lying back down and balancing his hat over his face.

The afternoon was tinged with just a bite of autumn, and the last of the summer insects droned along the margins of the clearing. Phil's snores added to the symphony, and John William's breath was heavy and regular. After a few moments, Gloria felt her own eyes growing heavy. Half of the quilt was there—empty and inviting—and it wasn't until she was stretched out, lying on her stomach with her face buried in her arms, that she realized this was the most intimate position she'd ever shared with John William. Truth be told, this was the most intimate position she'd ever shared with any man. At first she was tense, worried about what he would think, worried that she would offend him, but soon sleep edged its way in to quiet her thoughts.

Then she heard his voice.

"Hmm?" she said, taking her turn at giving him an indulgent yet cranky glance.

"I said I had a dream about wheat once."

"Really."

"It had to be a few years in the future, because Danny and Kate was old enough to be walking, but not too big. And the wheat was grown high—'bout up to my waist."

"That's high all right," Gloria said.

"And I guess they wandered off or somethin', because I couldn't find 'em. They wasn't tall enough to be seen over the wheat, and I was just tearin' through the fields, callin' for 'em."

"Did you find them?" Gloria still refused to lift her face from the nest of her arms.

"I woke up and walked straight over to make sure they were all right."

"Were they?"

"Of course."

"That's good."

A silence settled around them once again, and Gloria dozed in and out. At some point she felt like a spectator in John William's dream, saw him striding through the fields, searching, calling. And then she wondered.

"Was I there?" she said.

"Where?"

Gloria propped herself up on one elbow and turned her body toward his.

"In your dream," she said. "Where was I?"

She watched him sigh before he brought his hand up to lift his hat from his face. He turned his body to mirror hers. His brow furrowed before giving way to a full and joyous smile that drew Gloria to him like no embrace ever could.

"You were right beside me, darlin'," he said, "callin' out their names."

It was a moment, Gloria thought, that should have taken her breath away. Such affirmation. Such invitation. Instead, she felt it settle within her.

"What do you think it means?" she asked

Big Phil interrupted with a yawn befitting his name and a satisfied belly scratch. "If you ask me," he said, grunting as he hoisted himself off the ground, "it means that you two better keep them kids on a leash once they're old enough to walk."

John William and Gloria had been smiling at one another, and now they burst into comfortable, relieved laughter. In the distance, the soft jingle of the horses' harness signaled an end to the noon-time break. Rested and revitalized, they roused themselves to resume the day's work. There were, after all, only three acres left.

The harvest was in before dark.

I will arise and go to Jesus,
He will embrace me in His arms;
In the arms of my dear Savior,
O there are ten thousand charms.

22

*G*loria sat in the willow rocker exchanging gurgling giggles with a very happy Danny. It was a rare moment stolen from the endless work of the field and garden and kitchen. But the cellar was stocked with vegetables, and the cupboards were full of things pickled and preserved. A glimpse out the window showed Big Phil and Lonnie in the distance, pitching the bundles of wheat into John William's wagon, its sides framed high to contain the sheaves. Gloria's eyes searched the distance for John William—seeking him as she seemed to these days—and became so engrossed in her search that she failed to see his face grinning at her from the other side of the window until his knock on the glass caused her to jump.

"Dah!" blurted Danny, his chubby finger pointing.

John William smiled and wiggled his fingers at Danny before beckoning to Gloria. "Come outside," he said, his voice muffled.

"What do you want?"

"Just put the baby down and come outside."

Gloria sighed, heaved herself and Danny up from the willow rocker, and went to hand the child off to Maureen.

The season had definitely turned. The afternoon held a bracing chill as John William and Gloria made their way through the newly shorn fields.

"It looks sad out here," Gloria said.

"Sad?"

"Dead. Finished."

"You can't look at it like that, darlin'," John William said. "You've got to look at the ground and see the promise. It'll be a new crop next year, more, even. I hope to put in at least another fifty acres of wheat, maybe corn."

"What does Maureen think of all these great plans?"

John William was quiet for a moment. "She's signin' it over to me in the spring. It'll all be in my name. It's gonna be ours."

Ours.

They continued walking farther from the house, across the fields, their feet sinking into the soft soil, heading toward the grove of trees that bordered the field.

"Where are we going?" It was the third time she'd asked since leaving the house, each request more petulant than the last.

"You'll see," he answered.

John William's long stride covered nearly twice the distance of each step of Gloria's, and she scrambled not quite behind him, determined to keep up. Once or twice she stumbled on the uneven ground, and she reached out and clutched John William's sleeve. When her ankle twisted in a particularly deceptive hole, John William caught her around the waist and steadied her.

"All right?" he asked.

"Fine."

"Good. Come on."

Somehow her hand ended up clutched in his, and she left it there, content now to walk behind him, following in his footprints as he half-led, half-dragged her across the field.

A small running stream, maybe ten feet wide, created a border between the edge of the wheat field and the grove of trees.

"What do we do now?" Gloria asked as they came to a stop at the water's edge.

"What? Can't you swim?"

His amusement seemed to infuse his body, from the twinkle in his eyes to his smile to the slight squeeze he gave before dropping her hand, plopping to the ground, and pulling off his boots.

"You're not serious," Gloria said. She looked at the stream, trying to gauge its depth. "It doesn't *look* deep."

"Guess we're wadin', then." He whistled a little as he rolled up his pants legs.

"I am not walking through that river."

"Now, darlin', it's hardly a river."

"Have you ever had to drag yourself around in a wet skirt and petticoat?"

"Do you really want an answer to that?" His smile was infectious now, and Gloria found herself wanting to play along.

"Oh, all right," she said. "But you undo the laces."

"At your command." He bent down on one knee in front of her. Gloria put her foot on his leg and steadied herself with a hand on his shoulder, enjoying watching his fingers work the intricacies of the hooks and laces on her boots.

"Stockin's, too?"

"Of course not," Gloria said, a false haughtiness to her voice. "I am, after all, trying to become a lady."

When the second boot was loosened, Gloria stepped behind John William and reached under her skirts to untie her stockings just above her knees. Then, her palm firmly planted on the top of his head , she lifted first one foot, then the other, pulling off boot and stocking in one fell swoop.

"Let's go, then," John William said when the second boot hit the ground.

"Just one second." Grumbling, Gloria gathered handfuls of skirt and petticoat, bunching it all up gracelessly just above her knees

Together they took the few remaining steps to the water's edge.

"Give me your hand," John William said. "The rocks might be—"

Her foot gave way beneath her, and she landed on her backside on what had to be the hardest boulder in Oregon Territory. Somewhere through the water's splashing and the curses flying in her head, she thought she heard deep throaty laughter. Then one strong arm wrapped itself around her waist and hauled her to her feet; another hooked itself behind her knees and swept her off them. They were well into the middle of the stream before Gloria could speak.

"Put me down."

John William laughed that big laugh of his. "You've already been down. Now let's work on getting you across. If you wiggle, I'll lose my balance and we'll *both* take a tumble, so be a good girl."

Gloria relaxed and dropped her head against his shoulder, leaving it there until they were safely on the other side.

"What about my shoes?"

"What about them?"

"They're on the other side."

"I guess they are."

"I'm supposed to walk barefoot?"

"Unless you want me to carry you the whole way."

She did.

"Is the ground soft?"

"Soft enough."

"Then put me down."

He hesitated for just a moment before gingerly lowering her to the ground. Still, his hand lingered on her waist, and neither made any move to budge it.

"What are we doing?" she asked. "I mean, where are we going?"

"I want to show you something."

She felt the slightest squeeze of her waist before he took his hand away and started walking. The ground was soft and covered with layers of dead leaves and grass. It seemed as if they were going to be walking through dense forest, but within just a few seconds they'd stepped into a clearing.

"What do you think?"

In the middle of the clearing was a little house made of rough-hewn logs stacked snugly together. It was long rather than square, and the facing wall had both a small window and a narrow door hung on leather hinges. The roof was made of smooth planks laid from one end of the cabin to the other, forming a modest peak around a stone chimney that crawled up and out of one end wall. There was a small, fenced-in square of earth that had clearly been a garden.

"What is this?"

"Let's look."

He took her hand and led her across the soft grass of the clearing to the very door. A wooden latch held it closed, and John William grasped the protruding stake, dislodged it from the wall, and pulled the door open.

It took a moment for Gloria's eyes to adjust to the darkness; the only light came from the little square window. But soon it infused the cabin with enough light for her to see the details. A white plaster had been spread between each log, leaving no gaps. The wall at one end was dominated by a rock fireplace, the floor in front of it a semicircle of black.

Gloria curled and uncurled her toes, expecting to feel the grit of hard-packed earth, but the coarseness beneath her feet was merely a layer of dirt on a rough wood floor. On the long side of the room, a large plank protruded perpendicularly from between two logs and was held up by yet another log at its end. A table. Two low benches were similarly engineered on either side. As her eyes further adjusted to the light, she saw that the wall opposite the fireplace extended only about three-quarters of the way across, creating more of a divider than an actual wall, leaving a doorway into what must be a second room.

"This is the first house he built for her."

"Who?"

"Edward. For Maureen. This was their first home. When they realized the main road to Middleton was going to run along the opposite end of their property, he built the new place so they'd be a little closer to town."

"How did you find it?"

"Maureen showed me."

Gloria stepped farther into the little house, and John William followed her, allowing the door to hang open on its leather hinges.

"It's so small," she said.

"Compared to what Maureen's living in now, yeah. But at the time, for them, it was enough."

"For them."

"For us."

Gloria had been gliding over the floor, but she stopped mid-step and stood in the center of this little house that seemed to be growing larger with every breath.

"We need to start our own life, Gloria. If you're to be my wife, we can't just go on livin' with Maureen."

"There's no stove."

"You don't cook." He laughed and then added, gently, "I'll get us a little one to go just over here." He took her elbow and turned her to look at the corner where the rock met the wood. "See? There's a hole cut in the roof for a stovepipe already. She had one here."

"What about the babies?"

"Just for this winter we'll keep their little beds in this main room. I'll build them something small that we can stash away during the day."

"What about us?"

"Come here," he said. He'd been saying that all afternoon. Follow me. Walk this way. In truth, he'd been saying that since they'd left Silver Peak together, and she'd always obeyed. So when he once again took her arm—loosely, just above her wrist—there seemed no reason not to go along.

He led her to the little doorway that divided the cabin into one small room and one smaller one and pulled her across the threshold into total darkness. There was no window here, nothing but the sweet scent of raw wood, the sharp scent of him, and the sound of his breath. And hers. The lack of orientation made her dizzy and she put her hand in front of her steady herself and found the sturdiness of his body to hold her up.

"We'll need to steal a lamp," she said, surprised at the thinness of her voice. "And dishes for the table."

"Of course." His voice sounded closer. His breath in her hair. "And maybe a—"

Her last suggestion was lost as his mouth covered hers, his lips soft against her own. She wondered for just a moment how he had landed the kiss so perfectly in such perfect darkness, but the thought was a fleeting one as she disengaged her hand from his and snaked it up around his neck. He brought his arms around her, pulling her fully to him.

"Oh, Gloria." He took his lips from hers to say her name, then trailed more kisses across her cheeks, dotting her nose before claiming her mouth again.

She ran her fingers through the length of his hair, grazed her thumb against his misshapen ear and ached as he flinched against her touch.

"Shh," she said, bringing her fingers to his face and tracing—even in this utter darkness—every scar.

He caught her hands in his and she felt his mouth against her palm—first one, then the other. Then she felt her face caught in the warmth of his work-hardened hands, his thumbs against her cheekbones, her ears nestled between his fingers. He kissed her again, releasing her from his grip once their mouths were engaged. She felt one hand at the small of her back, the other caught in her hair. He moved her a few tiny steps back until she felt the log wall press against her.

This was new, this feeling of melting, this sense of embrace. She'd never felt so powerless, left to the whim of her desire. Truth be told, she'd never felt desire. And that's what it was, that need to pull him closer. She wrapped her arms around his back, loving this feeling, enticed by this thrill. This was nothing like their first kiss. There was no audience, no glaring open light. Only the two of them.

Together they shuffled one step, then two, and she felt something press against her calves, the coldness of her wet skirts sending a chill up her legs. The bed. Gloria's legs buckled underneath her until she was sitting on the wooden plank and then, further still, until she was lying on her back, trapped beneath the weight of John William above her.

This, now, was familiar. This she knew. She'd been here countless times before. The only difference was that there was no money on the table, no sick and dying mother in the next room, no one else waiting outside the door.

Soon the feel of his mouth on hers was too sweet, too intimate to bear, and she turned her face violently away. She tried to remember the tricks she had used to make herself disappear. In the old days she used to imagine that she was actually standing in the corner, watching the whole thing. But she couldn't imagine herself away from this. This was MacGregan. This was John William, and that hand that groped her thigh was the same hand that had gently lifted her into a wagon and into another life. It was the same hand that unbuttoned her shoe, held her son, touched her hair. This was the same man who read Bible stories and prayed.

And at the same time, he wasn't. The gentle nature of his earlier embraces was gone, replaced by an urgent intrusion she was all too familiar with. Every second under his touch brought her closer and closer to the woman Gloria thought she had left behind. But worse, it brought him closer to becoming just another man she would despise.

She brought her palms up and braced them against his broad chest, pushing him away.

"John," she said.

But he didn't hear, and Gloria found her body flushed with fear—adolescent and virginal—that threatened to crush her resolve.

"John, please."

There was a moment when everything stopped. A rustle of movement and he was sitting up, his long legs draped over the edge of the bed. Gloria's eyes had adjusted to the darkness, and she could just make out a familiar profile. John William with his head bowed, his fingers raking the hair from his face, his massive shoulders hunched as if in defeat or prayer or both.

"I'm so sorry, Gloria. God, forgive me."

His penitence broke her heart. She stretched out her hand only to feel him brush against it as he headed for the thin triangle of gray light that marked the threshold to the front part of the house.

"John," she spoke into the darkness, then followed him into the light.

He was standing in the front doorway, filling it with his body, one hand on each side of the frame, his head hanging down. She brought her hands to his shoulders, urging him to turn and look at her.

He didn't. She let her hands drop.

"I have to know. Is that why you brought me here?"

He spun on his heel and turned to her then, his face unreadable. "How can you think that?"

"I'm sorry. I just…I couldn't let you—"

"I brought you here to show you that we can have a home. Together. A life together. I brought you here so you could see that you're no different than any other woman. Any other wife. That you could marry me and we'll have a little house. Just like—"

"You had with Katherine?"

John William charged at her, making the same big bear noise he made when he played with the children. He gathered her up in one massive embrace that lifted her off her feet and squeezed every possible protest out of her. He held her there, aloft, her arms pinned to her sides, her face floating just above his. For once he had to look up at her.

"You make me crazy." A comic growl underscored his words.

"So I see. Put me down."

"Not until you hear me. Now yes, I loved Katherine. She was my wife. She was the only other woman I've ever loved."

"So how could you—"

"Shh. You listen. Now, we've talked around this and danced around this enough. I'm a good man, Gloria. I'm a patient man, but I am a man and I cannot, will not wait longer for you."

"You don't have to—"

"So we'll go, today, now, to Reverend Fuller. Just him. Just us."

It sounded perfect, simple. He offered so much and asked for so little. But even the little he asked seemed a world away from what she had to give.

"John," she said, her voice taking on the quality of a chastising parent, "put me down. Now." When she felt her feet touch the ground, she took a step back, stood an arm's length away from him, letting him hold her hands so loosely that the slightest flinch would break them apart. "Tell me, John, would you want me if things were...different? I mean, if it weren't for Kate. If you just saw me one afternoon..."

"I could ask you the same thing, couldn't I? But why waste our time on such questions?" He brought her fingers to his lips and grazed kisses along them. "We've waited long enough. I've waited long enough."

Gloria twisted her hands from his and began smoothing her hair away from her face, nervously tucking the strays behind her ears.

"I can't today. Not now." She turned her back to him and smoothed her skirt. "I have to get back to the babies. It's—"

"It's all right." He wrapped his arms around her and drew her back into his strength. She felt his chin rest on the top of her head, just for a moment, before he bent to touch his rough cheek to hers. "It's all right," he said again, reassuring. "We won't do anythin' today. We'll wait till Sunday. That's just five more days. But come Sunday, we're goin' to church, and we're talkin' to Reverend Fuller and havin' him marry us right there, right then."

John William planted a quick kiss on her cheek before releasing her entirely. He walked through the open door, out into the afternoon sunlight, turned and stretched his hand across the threshold. Without hesitation, Gloria placed her hand in his.

They walked in silence, hand in hand, until they reached the running stream. Once there, John William swooped Gloria up in his arms and was about to wade into the water when a distant sound, faint and unfamiliar, caught his attention.

"Did you hear that?" he asked, gingerly setting Gloria down.

"Was that Maureen?"

Then the sound was unmistakable. It was Maureen's voice, raised in an anguished scream.

"Stay here," he said before leaving her and crossing the stream in two massive strides.

"John, wait," she called, but the urgency in Maureen's cries would not allow him to so much as look back. Frustrated, she gingerly made her way through the icy water, and once on the other side, picked up her boots and stockings and ran, barefoot, all the way back to the house.

"I don't know what happened!" Tears streamed down Maureen's face as she handed baby Kate over to John William, whose arms were outstretched for her from the moment he passed through the gate. "All of a sudden she just started coughing, then wheezing and then…"

John William took Kate into his arms, and her body seemed possessed by a stiffness that stretched her arms and legs. The longer he held her, though, the more she relaxed against him, and he was acutely aware of the shallowness of her breathing.

"Maureen, what happened?" Gloria said just behind him.

"I don't know! I don't know! I brought the babies out here with me when I came out to finish up in the garden. They were just over there," she gestured toward the quilt where Danny still lay, clutching his toes to his mouth, "and all of a sudden she was just screaming. And then she just—"

"What's on her face?" John William asked, running his knuckle along Kate's soft cheek that was covered with some sort of sticky substance.

"I was stirring molasses into my tea, and she reached for the spoon. I let her lick it. Oh, God," she brought her hands up to her face, "do you think that's what's made her sick?"

John William studied his daughter's face, and then recoiled at what he saw. There were at least five of them that he could see— tiny mounds swelling, each with a nearly invisible prick in its center: one at the corner of her eye, one near an ear, one at the corner of her upper lip, two on her neck. Clutching Kate's gasping body close to him, he strode to the wooden overhang over the front door. One glance up confirmed his suspicions.

Wasps. The nest wasn't large enough to have attracted attention before; it was fairly small and tucked away. Maureen had followed him and stood now beside him, her hands still clasped to her mouth in disbelief. "Oh, John. I didn't know."

He caught one of Kate's tiny hands between his thumb and forefinger and brought it to his lips, just as he had that cold rainy morning she was born. And, just as he had that morning, he worried she wouldn't live through the day. Each tiny breath grew shorter and shallower, and he longed to fill her with every breath he would take for the rest of his life if doing so would bring back her little smile. As it was, her face held an expression of faint surprise—wide-eyed and openmouthed—and the only sound was the tiny squeak that accompanied each labored gasp.

"Ah, Katherine," he whispered, hugging her close, "my beautiful, beautiful girl." He closed his eyes, blocked out her desperate gaze, and prayed, "Lord, God my Father, don't take her from me. Father, you can heal her. Sweet Jesus, I beg you…"

He fell to his knees. Behind the veil of his closed eyes he saw her healthy and whole, newly born, nestled in her mother's arms. He felt a hand on his shoulder and heard Gloria begging him for a chance to hold her, but the mother in his vision had long black hair tied with a scrap of blue cloth and a thin, gaunt face.

After a time, and God alone knew how long, the faint spasms of Kate's breathing ceased and she became perfectly still, her eyes still open and staring.

John William lifted his face to heaven. "God, give me the strength to get through this." He covered Kate's face with his palm, and when his hand was lifted her eyes were closed.

"Gloria?" he said, looking up and around for the first time.

"She's gone inside," Maureen said. She was still standing on the porch. "Is Kate…?"

"She's safe now. She's with her mother."

23

*G*loria had never visited the low swelling hill along the southern edge of the Brewster's property, but she had seen Maureen up there often enough, kneeling beside the simple headstone that marked the grave of her husband. A small picket fence formed the perimeter of the grave itself.

Two days after Kate's death, a small crowd gathered at the newly turned earth. A tiny white coffin sat beside the open grave, its lid covered in a layer of roses from Josephine Logan's garden. The entire Logan family was there, each child scrubbed to perfection, their parents apologetic for their obvious health. Big Phil stood with a protective hand holding his wife close to his side. Adele Fuller was resplendent in a sweeping black crepe de chine dress; the veil suspended from her smart black velvet bonnet divided her perfect face into a series of diamonds. Reverend Fuller clutched his worn black Bible in one hand and with the other took Maureen's arm in a comforting gesture.

John William stood apart from the crowd, his arms hanging straight down at his side. His face was covered with a three days' beard, his hair loose and lank, every inch the image of a man mad with grief.

All of this Gloria witnessed from the front porch of Maureen's home. She hadn't exchanged a single word with John William since their conversation in the tiny cabin. Baby Kate's body was laid out in Maureen's parlor while funeral arrangements were made, and during that time, Gloria barely left the room she shared with Maureen. John William hadn't stepped a foot inside the house. He'd been sleeping in the barn, washing at the pump, and as far as either of the two women could tell, not eating at all.

Gloria held Danny close to her side, bouncing him gently. He cooed and grasped at the loose tufts of hair that escaped the twist at the nape of her neck. She wore the dark brown skirt Mae made for her back in Silver Peak and a brown blouse sprigged with deep red poppies. As she dressed this morning, she had bemoaned the fact that she had no proper black dress to wear, although Maureen assured her that the brown would be fine. Now, though, she couldn't help notice the outline of Adele Fuller's perfect figure creating a stark silhouette against the autumn foliage and could only hope that her own outfit would help her blend in and disappear.

John William looked up and their eyes met across the yard. He gave a barely discernible turn of his head, nodding toward the small crowd, and looked back at Gloria, clearly a directive for her to join them. But Gloria clutched Danny closer and held her ground. John William raised a single eyebrow, but still she did not move. Finally, he squared his shoulders, appeared to excuse himself to those standing around him, and made his way across the yard. He walked slowly and purposefully, and when he reached the porch he placed one foot on the bottom step, grasped the rail, and leaned in to speak quietly.

"You comin'?"

"I've never been to a funeral before."

"Not your mother's?"

"No."

"You didn't go to your mother's funeral?"

"I woke up. She was dead. I left. I don't know if she had a funeral."

She unwound a clump of curls from Danny's soggy fist and gave him a corner of her shawl to clutch.

"Well, this is different, Gloria. This is Kate, our baby girl."

"She was your baby girl, John. And like you said, she's safe now. With her mother. She doesn't need me anymore, does she?"

"I'd like you there, Gloria, to be with me."

He held out his hand. How easily she'd taken it the last time it was offered to her as they left the little cabin that was to be their home. It seemed impossible, now, to think of a life together.

"Nnn-dah! Nnn-dah!" Danny said, reaching both arms for John William. Gloria held him tighter, but his little arms continued to flail. Soon two massive hands were reaching for her son, and before she knew it, John William lifted the boy high above his head, jostling him until the giggles drew the attention from the people across the yard, then drew him close.

"Ah, Danny," he whispered. Without another word, he turned and began to make his way toward the little crowd gathered at the grave. He left her alone, just as he had that afternoon at the creek's edge, walking away and not looking back. And, just as she had that afternoon, Gloria followed, alone, just steps behind him.

Reverend Fuller's face seemed softer today than it was on those Sunday mornings behind his pulpit. His Bible lay loosely open in his hand, and the same breeze that rustled the pages picked up his words and carried them effortlessly to each person gathered.

"When the child King David fathered with Bathsheba fell ill, David went into a period of mourning," Reverend Fuller said after a short opening prayer. "He shut himself off from the rest of his household, not eating, not sleeping. He was in such a state of mind that the servants of the house were afraid to tell him when, after seven days, the child did die. They thought the news of the child's death would be too much for him to bear.

"But, in fact, the opposite happened. When they went in to him, he asked, 'Is the child dead?' and they answered, 'He is dead.' And something amazing happened." Reverend Fuller turned his full attention to his Bible and read, "'Then David arose from the earth, and washed, and anointed himself, and changed his apparel, and came into the house of the LORD, and worshipped: Then he came to his own house; and when he required, they set bread before him, and he did eat.'

"Of course, his servants were amazed. They couldn't understand how he could be so grieved when the child was ill, yet fully composed after the child died. But listen to what David said."

Gloria was standing on the other side of John William, and she leaned forward, drawn into this story as she found herself drawn to every story she'd ever heard from this book. She stole a quick look at Maureen, who stood just across from her on the other side of the open grave, and the woman sent over a quick smile.

"David said," continued the reverend, "'While the child was yet alive, I fasted and wept: for I said, Who can tell whether GOD will be gracious to me, that the child may live? But now he is dead, wherefore should I fast? Can I bring him back again? I shall go to him, but he shall not return to me.'" He kept his finger in the book to mark the page, and looked up. "Children are, indeed, a gift to us by the graciousness of God."

At this, Gloria once again looked up to catch Maureen's eye, but the older woman's face was bent low to the ground.

"I only saw the child a few times," Reverend Fuller continued, "but she was, I'm sure, a gift treasured by all who loved her. And though her death was sudden and tragic, let us turn our hearts to the joy she gave while she was alive. What a blessing it was that these parents had no knowledge that the last days they spent with their daughter were to be the last days she would spend on earth. What a tragedy to spend the last days together in mourning rather than simply in loving and caring for the child."

Gloria sensed John William nodding his head. She glanced over and saw that Danny's head was resting against John William's strong shoulder. She reached out a hand and touched the little boy's soft cheek and was rewarded with a slight lazy smile from his soft parted lips. As she drew her hand away, John William caught it with his own. Her first instinct was to jerk it away, but she allowed his fingers to close around her clenched fist and returned her attention to the reverend, who was speaking directly to her and John William.

"Parents, do not believe that King David's actions meant that he wasn't deeply grieved at the passing of his son. But know that no amount of sadness or gestures of mourning will ever bring your daughter back to you. Rather, rejoice in the fact that you will be reunited with her someday. For, as David said, 'I shall go to him, but he shall not return to me.'

"Christ tells us in Matthew 6:20 to lay up our treasures in heaven, 'where neither moth nor rust doth corrupt, and where thieves do not break through nor steal: For where your treasure is, there will your heart be also.' Kate is a treasure now in heaven. She will never be sick. She will never be sad. She will never suffer disappointment or pain."

All around her, Gloria heard whispers of "Amen" and saw Maureen and Josephine Logan nodding and smiling. Big Phil and his wife exchanged a smile. Their seeming peace nearly drove her mad.

I could have kept her from sadness! I could have kept her from disappointment and pain. Why wasn't I enough?

"But most of all," Reverend Fuller said, "she is a part of the treasure stored expressly for you in heaven. For it is there that, by the grace of Jesus Christ, you will be reunited with your little girl. In the meantime, you have each other and," he reached out to lightly stroke Danny's arm, "you are blessed with this little one here. Let him be a comfort to you at this time.

"Finally, the Scripture says that David went to his wife and comforted her. So should you two turn to each other at this time and comfort one another. Let us pray."

Gloria bowed her head and closed her eyes with the others, but she didn't hear a single word of the prayer. Instead her head reeled with the words he'd just spoken. Her stomach churned with the dishonesty and deceit of the family she and John William presented to their community, even more so with the comfort these people offered to her as the mother of this deceased child. She hadn't shed a single tear, a fact that caused Josephine Logan to hold her close and say, "You poor, poor dear. It's such a shock." In fact, all afternoon as their neighbors arrived, her stony front was met with gushing platitudes by all the women, and a sense of relief by the men who were obviously more comfortable with a silent grieving mother than a hysterical one.

And now everyone thought she was going to take solace in the idea of being reunited with Kate in heaven? She wasn't sure if heaven even existed, and if it did, it was a place where she surely wouldn't be welcome. Besides, what comfort could be there? Suppose she did find her way to heaven only to stumble across the little girl, happily gurgling in the lap of the cold, dismissive woman who gave birth to her. The thought of it was bitterly amusing, so much so that Gloria must have emitted a short laugh or snort, because the next thing she knew John William was squeezing her hand mercilessly hard, and when she opened her eyes to look at him, he was scowling.

When it was time to lower the tiny coffin into the ground, John William handed Danny over to Gloria and joined Big Phil, David Logan, and Reverend Fuller to take an end of one of the ropes looped around the casket. Adele Fuller moved to the foot of the grave and, clasping her hands demurely in front of her, began to sing:

> *"God is love; his mercy brightens*
> *All the path in which we rove;*
> *Bliss he wakes and woe he lightens:*
> *God is wisdom, God is love."*

Hand over hand the four men lowered the casket into the open grave. One by one, those in attendance picked up a handful of the moist earth and dropped it in. Gloria heard each grain hit the wood and, unable to bear it, turned her ear to Adele's voice.

> *"E'en the hour that darkest seemeth*
> *Will his changeless goodness prove;*
> *Thro' the gloom his brightness streameth:*
> *God is wisdom, God is love."*

As the final note was carried away with the autumn wind, John William cleared his throat and said, "Thank you all for comin'. We'd like to invite you all to stay to dinner."

"Yes, please," Maureen said. "You all have been so generous. Please stay."

The women began to make their way back to the house to set out the food they had brought; the men, including John William and Reverend Fuller, stayed behind to fill the grave and place the marker—a simple wooden cross—at its head. Gloria lagged behind. Perhaps Danny's impending naptime would be an excuse from setting up platters of meat and slicing bread. She could quietly go into her room to nurse him and put him down.

"Katherine Celestia MacGregan." Big Phil read the inscription with a bit of a chuckle. "That's a big name for a little girl."

"Yeah," John William said, his voice equally amused, "that's what her mother said."

Gloria stopped midstep and turned on her heel. "No she didn't," she said, barely unclenching her teeth.

All four men stopped and stared at her, David Logan holding the shovel aloft.

"Her mother was dead before that child had a name. I was the one who said she had a big name for a little girl. Remember? It was cold and it was raining and she was starving and you came to me?"

"Gloria, please." John William walked to her and put his hand on her arm, but Gloria shrugged him off violently.

"Don't touch me. You have no claim to touch me. You have no claim on me at all."

Danny was jolted from his dozing reverie and let out a half-hearted wail at Gloria's raised voice.

"Phil, would you take Danny inside?" John William said over his shoulder.

"Sure thing," Phil said, his voice full of relief. "Why don't you come with me, Logan?"

"Right behind you." David Logan dropped the shovel and

fairly trotted behind Big Phil as the two men made their way back to the house.

Once Danny was out of Gloria's arms, John William grasped her elbow and no amount of flinching or twisting on her part could release his grip.

"Shame on you," he hissed into her ear after pulling her close.

"Let me go!"

He jerked her arm again. "What are you thinkin' makin' such noise?"

"I said let me go!" Gloria brought her free hand up, but he easily caught her wrist.

"Woman, if you ever raise your hand to me again I'll—"

The gentle sound of Reverend Fuller clearing his throat brought them both to an uncomfortable silence, and they turned to face him, their hands still clasped together. Reverend Fuller stood calmly, looking first to one and then the other, and after a time the pounding in Gloria's heart and her head soothed as she looked down and stared hotly at their entwined fingers.

"We was," John William shuffled his feet like a child caught in a lie, "we was goin' to talk to you on Sunday. To see about gettin' married. You see, my wife, Kate's mother, she died and—"

Reverend Fuller held up his hand, and John William lapsed back into silence.

"This is neither the time nor the place for this discussion." Reverend Fuller's voice rang with authority, and the Bible he grasped only added to the weight of his words.

"I just didn't want you thinkin'—"

"Please, Mr. MacGregan. Let us remember the reason we are all gathered here today. Let us respect the solemnity of the occasion."

With that, he brushed past them and walked back to the house. Once alone, John William dropped Gloria's hands and raked his hair off his face in the gesture of frustration and despair Gloria had grown so familiar with.

"John, I'm sorry," Gloria said. "It just seemed that these past days you've forgotten I'm here. That I was ever here."

A bitter laugh escaped John William's lips, a sound chilling to Gloria's heart.

"Forget you?" he said. "I doubt there's a man out there who could ever forget you."

"Stop it."

"Do you know why King David's son died? Ah, look who I'm askin'. Of course you don't."

"I know a little," Gloria said.

"David lusted after Bathsheba. Desired her. So much that he forgot the kind of man God wanted him to be."

A sudden burst of wind brought a smattering of autumn leaves to rest along the hem of Gloria's skirt. She folded her arms tight against her chest and bent her head against the chill.

"God took his child away." John William brought a finger to Gloria's chin and forced her to look up at him. "To punish him. Because he lusted for this woman. Because he murdered her husband."

"What does that have to do with all of this?" Gloria said, gesturing toward Kate's open grave.

John William turned his back to her, casting her into shadow. Gloria felt a tightening in her throat when she saw the defeated stoop of his shoulders; the same man who once frightened her with his physical power now appeared utterly crushed.

"Reverend Fuller talkin' about our last days with Kate," he said without turning around. "Her last hours."

His shoulders convulsed once, twice, and then he turned to face her. Gloria braced herself for the sight of tears on his scarred face, but nothing could prepare her for the twisted expression she encountered, and the bitterness in his next words made her flinch.

"How do I forgive myself for where I was, what I was doin' while my baby girl was…"

"What's to forgive, John? How could you possibly have known?"

"But if I hadn't been there with you—"

"You'd have been out in the field. Or in the barn. Or to Centerville."

"But I wasn't any of those places, was I?" John William turned again and took a few steps farther away. He flung his head back to face heaven straight on as he shouted, fist in the air, "I was with her! Lustin' after this woman after tryin' so hard—"

"How dare you!" Gloria said, grabbing his upraised arm and forcing it back down to his side. "After all you've told me about God and his forgiveness? Is this God who is supposed to love me the same God that would kill a child? Out of spite? To teach you a lesson?"

"That's not what I'm sayin'."

"You think this is my fault?"

"If you had been here—"

"What? What could I have done?"

An endless moment passed as she waited for him to answer. She thought about that summer afternoon on the shores of the Umatilla River when she fought off the swarm of bees. Would Kate have died there, on that afternoon, if a bee had found its way through Gloria's defenses? If she had, would Gloria be here now? Would she have been a part of this home?

The late afternoon sun crept behind the small grove of trees, casting shadows across the little white grave marker. The smaller branches waved in the ever-present breeze, creating a pattern of motion across the little girl's name—Katherine Celestia MacGregan—one moment in sunshine, the next in shadow.

Still Gloria held onto his arm, until his coiled muscles relaxed and she was drawn into an embrace, his arms encasing her utterly. "I suppose this changes everything," she said, her face pressed against the rough texture of his woolen shirt. She felt his cheek come to rest on the top of her head, felt his lips move against her hair.

"Not so. If anythin', Danny's more precious to me than ever." He dislodged her from their embrace and held her at arm's length, oblivious to the large, cold stone he had just lodged somewhere inside her. "God blessed David with another child. Danny's the blessin' given to me."

"What about me, John? What about Sunday and Reverend Fuller?"

"I don't know," he said. "I've got to finish some threshin'. Get a load of wheat into Centerville. I planned to be there and back by Sunday, but now…"

"Are you saying not this Sunday? Or ever?"

"I don't know." He wouldn't look at her.

When they walked into Maureen's parlor, the only sound was Danny's insistent cry. Gloria made her way past the curious stares of her new neighbors and collected her son to take him into the bedroom to nurse. Nobody said a single word until she was well out of the room, and then all she heard was Adele Fuller's honey-sweet voice offering John William a piece of her famous chocolate cake.

~24~

*J*ohn William worked one finger through the twine and unbound the sheaf, sending hundreds of stalks to fan around his feet. He stood on the canvas tarp, unbinding one after another, until the surface of the tarp was covered with about ten inches of ripe wheat. The afternoon was cool and dry with just enough of a breeze to enable him to sift the grain.

The flail he used was yet another example of Ed's extraordinary handiwork. Two and a half inches in diameter, and honed to perfection, the flail rested easily in his hands, the two sections of it connected with a leather strap. He held the handle in his hand and paced the circumference of the wheat, trying to gauge the direction of the wind and decide just where to begin. A movement caught the corner of his eye. In the distance, Gloria and Maureen were heading out to the old cabin, Maureen pushing her little handcart and Gloria following with a broom. He hadn't seen Gloria since their conversation at Kate's graveside. She'd taken Danny into the bedroom and refused to come out again, even after the guests had departed.

This morning as he awoke from a chilly and uncomfortable sleep on his bedroll in the barn, Maureen was standing over him with a steaming cup of coffee and a plate of breakfast that included slices of the ham David and Josephine Logan had brought.

"We're going out to the cabin today, Gloria and me," she said. "Going to get the place cleaned up. There's no use you sleeping in a barn when there's a perfectly good home just waiting."

"You don't need to bother with the cleanin'," he told her. How could he tell her that the layers of dust weren't the reason for his choice. He had actually walked back there the night Kate died, bedroll and blanket in hand, but the memories of those brief moments with Gloria brought home that the barn was where he belonged.

"Suit yourself," Maureen said, stooping to put the plate of food by his side. "But eat up and get your strength. I want you to thresh enough of that wheat to get me some straw to stuff a tick. There's going to be a nice clean home with a good fresh bed for somebody."

Now he stood straight, watching them—watching Gloria—wondering if she would turn around and offer a smile, a wave, any acknowledgment. But even though she was well within earshot, he didn't call out.

"Wheat's not going to thresh itself, you know."

The voice of Big Phil came from just behind him. The greeting was accompanied by a hearty clap on John William's shoulder, and then the big man sat on the ground and reclined against the barn wall.

"Good mornin' to you, too, my friend," John William said, forcing a good-natured tone to his voice. "What are you doin' here?"

"Maureen asked Anne to come over this morning and watch the baby. Seems she and Gloria have some work to do. Thought I'd come see what I could do for you."

"You'll be sure to let me know if my labor interferes with your mid-mornin' nap."

"Don't worry about me," Phil said, pulling the rim of his hat low on his face. "I could sleep next to one of those big steam machines."

John William bent at his waist, held the flail above his head, and sent it crashing to the tarp. The highly satisfying *thud!* sent the grains of wheat flying from their hulls and sifting down through the straw. Without hesitation, he hoisted the flail and brought it down again, repeating the process over and over, taking tiny steps around the circumference of the carpet

of wheat. The pure physical exertion of it felt good, reawaken-
ing muscles in his back and shoulders he hadn't accessed since
his work in the mines.

Thud!

Why would God test his strength with a woman like that?

Thud!

A woman who had seemed to be an answer to a prayer to
save his daughter's life.

Thud!

And then take his baby girl away the minute he—

Thud!

"Remind me never to pick a fight with you, son." Big Phil's
voice sounded drowsy.

"Why's that?"

"Because I have a sneaking suspicion you're picturing some
poor fellow's face hiding underneath all that straw."

"Just my own, Phil." *Thud!* "I've got no quarrel with anybody
else."

John William continued to work; Big Phil continued to
watch.

"You know," Phil said after several minutes, "there's a machine
up in Centerville that can do all that. Get the whole crop done in
just a few days."

John William paused in his labor and stood straight. His hair
had worked itself out of the tie at the back of his neck, and he
brought his hand up to rake the loose strands off his face.

"Them machines," he said, turning to face his friend, "don't
do much more than save some time. They crunch up the straw,
make it so it can't be used for nothin'."

"Ah," Phil said before he disappeared into the barn and came
out with a pitchfork. Careful to keep himself clear of the working
flail, he dug the fork under the wheat already threshed and lifted
it several inches off the ground, shaking it a bit to separate the
stalk from the grain. He then dumped the stalks in the soft green
grass that grew in the barn's shadow. "This for a new bed?"

John William did not reply.

"Yep," Phil continued, "nothing makes a sweeter bed than a fresh straw ticking."

John William thought of a reply, then thought better of it. *Thud!*

"Better than feathers, that's what Anne and I think. A man doesn't have a claim to feathers, but when you and the wife settle down in the straw, it's like falling asleep in the fruits of your labors."

Thud!

"Don't know if I'm bound to settle down with no woman any time soon."

"That so, MacGregan? Reverend Fuller seems to think you two will be showing up on Sunday for a wedding."

"That was the plan at one time." *Thud!*

"And plans changed?"

"Of course plans changed, Phil." John William continued to circle the wheat, crashing the flail down in an irregular rhythm. "I buried my little girl yesterday. How could I be thinkin' of—" John William dropped his arm and closed his fingers in a fist around the wooden stick in his hand and turned to Phil. "Why was Fuller talkin' about any of this?"

"Now, son—"

"Are you tellin' me that while my baby girl was lyin' in her grave, all of you were inside discussin' whether or not that woman was my wife?"

"Of course not." Phil lowered the pitchfork and eyed the heavy wooden stick in John William's hand. "Reverend Fuller would never allow that kind of gossip. Not even from the women."

"I've been honorable to her, Phil," John William said.

Big Phil chuckled and scooped up a forkful of straw. "Well, God bless you for that, son. Course I always figured you two had some unfinished business."

❦   ❦   ❦

"We were very happy here, you know," Maureen said.

"From what you've told me," Gloria said, "you two would have been happy anywhere."

They stood in the middle of the little cabin's front room, armed with a broom, buckets, and rags. The door stood open, as did the window, filling the house with chilled fresh air.

"It seems a bit drab now," Maureen said, smiling warmly at Gloria, "but you'd be amazed at what a good cleaning can do. Then, we'll get some curtains for the window, a cloth for the table, a bright quilt on the bed—sure as shootin' this'll feel like a real home."

"I wouldn't know," Gloria said, tying a square of cloth over the top of her head. "I've never had a real home."

"Then, missy, it's high time you did."

Maureen positioned herself in one corner of the room and began sweeping with grand strokes across the wooden floor. The clouds of dirt kicked up were enormous, and Gloria was glad to have left the baby back at Maureen's house under the careful supervision of Big Phil's wife. How suspiciously convenient it was, Gloria thought, that the elderly couple happened to show up for a visit this morning.

"Now don't you just stand there doin' nothin'," Maureen said, her voice full of affection. "Go on down to the creek and fill up that bucket. We'll give this place a good scrubbin', make it look like new."

Gloria continued to stand listlessly in the middle of the room until Maureen took her hand and gave it a quick squeeze. "Come child. There's nothing like hard work to help a heart to heal."

For the entirety of the morning and into the afternoon, Gloria did nothing without Maureen's explicit instruction. She swept where and how Maureen told her to, shaved as much of the soap into the bucket as instructed, and emptied the wash water only when Maureen deemed it too filthy to be doing any good.

Slowly, the tiny house took on new life. Cobwebs were

cleared from the highest and lowest corners. Every surface was swept, scrubbed, rinsed, and scrubbed again. When the initial layer of grime was removed from the window, Maureen used a mixture of water and vinegar to wash it again, bringing in the sunshine with gorgeous clarity.

Through it all, Maureen kept up constant chatter about the history of the little cabin. How Ed had made the table and benches a permanent fixture to the walls because he had an irrational fear that the Indians would steal their furniture. How she had lived there three years without any cookstove, preparing all their meals over the fire in the fireplace, just as they had on the trail. How the first roof on the house was the canvas from their wagon and how it kept them just as dry as any shingled roof ever had. How Ed's desire for privacy led to the construction of the wall dividing the one-windowed cabin, creating a bedroom that was in perpetual darkness.

"I know," Gloria said absently.

Maureen paused midscrub and looked over at her. "You do?"

Immediately, Gloria blushed—*blushed!*—and said, "Yes. John showed me the day—the day we came here."

"Did he, now?"

"That's why he's so angry with me. He says that's why Kate—that if we hadn't been—"

Maureen dropped her cleaning rag and held her arms out to Gloria, who walked straight into them, bending to rest her head on the little woman's shoulder.

"Child, child," Maureen said, patting comfort onto Gloria's back. "Men can say truly awful things in the face of grief. They feel like sadness ain't enough. They got to be angry at something, too, and they'll just turn on whatever's closest."

Gloria disengaged herself from Maureen's embrace and sat down at the table. "He blames me," she said, staring at the wrinkled fingers she clutched in her lap.

"He blames himself."

"He doesn't need me anymore, Maureen. He doesn't want

me. I have a feeling he's going to send me away. Or send me…here."

Maureen propped her hands on her hips and assumed a posture of indignation. "Now what's wrong with *here,* might I ask?"

Gloria looked up and smiled at her friend. "Nothing. It's lovely. But I hoped to be here together. As a family. I don't think I could go back to being the woman stashed away at the back of the property."

"Nonsense," Maureen said. "Besides, my first mind is to set John William up here. Get him out of my barn. What must people think of me?"

Gloria tucked a stray curl back under the kerchief on her head. "I can't stay where I'm not wanted."

"I want you, child. I've grown so fond of you."

"But he doesn't."

"He does. I know it."

"You didn't see the way he looked at me yesterday."

"Maybe not, but I've seen the way he's looked at you every other day. Just give him some time."

John William scooped up the last of the grain in the wide shallow bowl and tossed it up into the air. The breeze caught it midair and blew the chaff away, the grain making soft little *ticks* as it fell back into the bowl. He repeated the process again and again until the grains were clean enough to suit him, then he poured them into the grain sack propped against the wall. He took the pitchfork from Phil, used it to pitch down more of the wheat piled high in his wagon, picked up a sheaf, loosened its bundling, and spread the stalks on the tarp, repeating the process until the canvas was once again covered.

He held the flail out to Big Phil and offered to trade jobs, but Phil declined.

"I don't have the right muscles for that job," Phil said, running his hands across his ample belly. "You're the strong one."

"Trust me, my friend, this flesh is weak."

"All the more reason to have a wedding." Phil picked up a piece of straw, placed it between his teeth, and leaned against the barn wall.

John William merely scowled and attacked the grain. "You know," he said, speaking between blows, "I do care for her."

"Of course you do, son. That's why you need to make an honest woman out of her."

"It'll take more than marryin' her to do that."

"You do your part here," Phil said, "and let God take care of the rest."

"She has a past, and she's havin' a hard time puttin' it behind her."

The leather thong joining the two sticks was threatening to come loose, and John William stopped to tighten the knot.

"How about you?" Phil said.

"I try not to let it bother me, but sometimes—"

"What I meant was your past. You got yourself quite a story, don't you?"

John William paused in his task and turned his better ear toward Phil. "What did you say?"

"I saw you fight in Saint Louis," Phil said, as calmly as if he were mentioning having seen him in the feed store last Tuesday. "Back in '59."

John William felt his very breath slammed out of him, as if Big Phil had taken the flail and struck it square on his spine. He turned away and tried to absorb himself in repairing the flail.

"Beautiful match. Think you took him down in seven rounds. Long enough to make it worth watching, not so long to make it a bloodbath. You were like some sort of an artist in that ring."

"If you're callin' me an artist, you need to see more paintin's." John William waited for Phil to join him in his nervous chuckle, but the older man was looking at him through narrowed eyes that seemed far from laughter.

"After that match," Phil went on, "they offered twenty dollars to the man who would go just three rounds in the ring with you. Remember?"

He did.

"We was all standing around, thinking that you had to be pretty tired out, and if you could have heard us all talking, wanting more than anything to get in that ring and take down Killer MacGregan. You recall what happened next?"

He didn't.

"Young kid came up. Couldn't have been more than twenty. Probably pretty drunk, too, from the looks of it. But strong. Been bragging all day about pulling stumps up bare-handed. Said he was going to use that twenty dollars to buy a ring for his girl."

John William's memory came clearer with each detail, and when Phil once again asked if he remembered what happened, he had an answer.

"I dropped him with three punches."

"Kid didn't know what hit him." The tone of admiration was gone. "And the funny thing was that the same guys who was wanting to see you drop, cheered just as hard when that kid hit the canvas. Lust is lust, I guess."

"I guess so," John William said quietly.

"Know what I remember next?" Phil stood up and began to take steps toward John William. "I was at Boyd's Saloon—the missus never liked me drinking, but I never found much in the Bible to say a man couldn't toss back a few with his friends—and they brought you in. A crowd of men—and quite a few, er, ladies— brought you up to the bar like you was some kind of a hero. Some fancy fellow was with you—"

"My manager."

"—and he said 'A round of drinks on the Killer!' And we all started cheering again, never mind that he was buying drinks with our money lost betting against you."

"Shoulda known not to bet against me." John William offered a feeble smile, then turned to raise the newly repaired flail high and resume threshing the wheat. When he tried to bring it down,

however, he could not. Big Phil stood behind him, his hand gripping the handle. John William released his own grip, and Phil
held on to the stick, holding it close to John William's face in a
manner that, had Phil not shown himself to be a friend, could
have been seen as a threat.

"I was standing," Phil said, "right at your elbow when you
lifted that drink. You had money pouring out of your pockets.
And blood crusted in your knuckles."

"Why didn't you mention this when I first met you here?"

"Because," Phil said, taking a few steps back, "you didn't
introduce yourself to me as Killer MacGregan. I looked at you,
your family, and decided it was something you'd put behind you.
You seemed happy—more than I can say about you when I saw
you drinking that night."

"Why are you tellin' me all of this now?"

"Let me ask you a question. What would it take to get you
back in that ring?"

The memory of what he used to do—what he used to be—
filled him with such distaste that he hearkened back to the taste
of his own blood in his mouth and was overcome with the desire
to spit it out, which he did, causing Phil to take yet another step
backward.

"I could never go back," he said, staring at his boots. "I made
a promise to myself. To God. I paid my price for what I did. For
the men I hurt. Killed."

"Maybe so," Phil said, holding the flail out to John William,
"but you got to remember that you didn't kill that little girl of yours.
And neither did Gloria. You don't have to pay any price for that."

John William looked into Big Phil's bright blue eyes and realized
he'd never seen such wisdom and compassion in a man.

"Now I don't claim to know the details of Gloria's past," Phil
continued, "but I can make a pretty good guess at it. And don't
you think she's made a few promises of her own?"

"I don't know. I suppose she has."

"Sending her away'd be like putting yourself back in that

ring," Phil said, picking up the pitchfork and preparing to sift the straw on the canvas. "And it won't bring your baby girl back."

Gloria threw out the last of the wash water and dropped the soiled rags inside.

"Neat as a pin, now, isn't it?" Maureen's cheerful voice hadn't lost its spirit or cadence despite the long afternoon's work.

"It's perfect." Gloria set down the bucket and, with her hands pressed to the small of her back, stretched back.

The handcart Maureen had brought from the house held a wealth of treasures beyond the cleaning supplies, including a bright blue cloth for the table.

"When John William goes to Centerville for the milling, he can look for some matching fabric to make cushions for the benches," Maureen said as she lofted the tablecloth over the slab of wood. From her own home she donated a matching butter dish, creamer, and sugar bowl to sit in the middle of the table.

The shelves above the little workspace held the few dishes Gloria and John William had in their wagon. The frying pan hung on a hook in the wall; the cooking pot stood ready in the fireplace.

"And of course," Maureen said, "you can borrow from me anything that you need."

Crisp, starched white curtains hung at the newly clean window, and the narrow shelf below it housed a pretty collection of glass jars.

"For herbs," she'd said. "The light here is perfect for them."

Gloria had simply followed behind her, running her fingers over each item.

"I think I'll have you take the rocking chair from the parlor— you have so much more need of it than I do," Maureen said, her hands on her hips as she surveyed the room.

Then she walked into the little bedroom at the back. "I still have the old ticking for this bed." Her voice carried from the room. "Hopefully by tomorrow John William will have threshed enough to have some good, fresh straw to stuff it with. Ed never did like sleeping on ropes—always wanted a firm foundation to sleep on—so you'll need plenty of cushioning because that slab of wood is woefully uncomfortable." Her head appeared from behind the wall just long enough to treat Gloria to a wink. "But I guess you already know that."

"Maureen, please," Gloria said. She'd been tapping the broom against the open doorway to shake off the last of the dirt and gave a resounding *smack* as the woman's cheerful chatter went beyond the point of bearing. "How can you talk like that after Kate…"

"Oh, now dear," Maureen said, leaning against the dividing wall, "you and John William shared Kate's life. And you shared her death. But your life—yours and his together—it isn't over."

"I don't know that we ever had a life together. Not like you and Ed had, anyway. You started together with nothing. You built this place together. But John and I…"

The fatigue of the day's labor took its toll and Gloria sank onto the bench at the table.

"You and John what?" Maureen asked.

"Do you know what I am? I'm King David's woman. Bathsheba. Bringing the great man down to sin."

"Well, I'm sure it wasn't anything…*completely* improper. After all, I believe John William to be a man of great restraint."

"Of course you do," Gloria said, her voice full of disgust.

"Now wait a minute," Maureen said, walking into the room and sitting on the bench opposite Gloria. "Are you telling me that he tried to force—"

"Nothing like that. He would never, never force himself. In fact, when he first touched me, I was perfectly willing…but after a while, well, it just seemed…wrong."

"Ah."

"It was just awkward and…humiliating. And it's the reason God took Kate away."

Maureen took Gloria's hand in her own tiny one. "Now child, is that what you really believe?"

"It's what John believes."

"You know he's out of his head right now."

"You know what I wish?" Gloria said, surveying the room. "I wish the same thing could happen to me as what we did to this little house."

"What do you mean?"

"It was just so easy. A few hours' work, some soap and water, and just like you said—spankin' new." She adopted Maureen's characteristic singing tone. "Fresh as a daisy."

Maureen laughed at the imitation.

"I wish there was just some way to do that to me. To my life. Because that's why I couldn't stand for him to touch me. I just felt…dirty. And I know that's what he—"

"Now, Gloria, darling—"

"He—and you—always talking about God and forgiveness. Is that what happens? Is that how it feels?"

"Yes, child, it is."

"How? How do you know?"

"Just think about King David. He committed a great sin, arranging the death of a woman's husband so that he could have her as his own. Even though he was God's own, he was not protected from sin."

"God's own," Gloria said, whispering.

"Yes. And because he did have a heart for God, he recognized that what he had done was terrible, and he cried out for God's forgiveness. Wait here, I have one more thing for you."

Maureen got up from the table and left the cabin, returning within minutes with a package wrapped in clean white paper.

"I was going to save this as a wedding gift," she said, "but I think we need it now. Open it."

Gloria took the package and untied the pretty blue ribbon wrapped around it. Carefully—savoring the rare occasion of opening a gift—she unfolded the paper to reveal the present within. A Bible.

"Every home needs God's Word," Maureen said.

"John has a Bible."

"You need your own."

"I can't read," Gloria said, handing the Bible over to Maureen.

"You'll learn. For now, just listen."

"Are you going to read the same story Reverend Fuller read at the funeral?"

"Not quite."

Gloria watched with envy as Maureen flitted through the gilt-edged pages. She leaned forward, breathing in the smell of a new book, preparing herself to understand the words that were often so confusing.

"Here it is," Maureen said. "Psalm 51. This is what David wrote just after that great sin of his. 'Have mercy upon me, O God, according to thy lovingkindness: according unto the multitude of thy tender mercies blot out my transgressions.'"

"Transgressions?"

"Sins," Maureen said, looking straight into Gloria's eyes. "All those mistakes we've made. Now, he goes on, 'Wash me thoroughly from mine iniquity, and cleanse me from my sin.' See? Just like you were saying. He's asking God to wash it all away."

"Show me," Gloria said, suddenly greedy to see the words for herself.

"Of course, dear." Maureen turned the Bible toward Gloria, her finger leading her eyes to the place on the page where she had been reading. "Here."

Gloria's eyes raked the page, the print largely meaningless. But the odd moments spent looking over John William's shoulder brought a few words to clarity, and she struggled to bring them to life.

"Ag—in—st thee on—lee have I s—sin—sind…"

"'Against thee, thee only, have I sinned,'" Maureen said,

sending Gloria a proud smile. "That means that yes, we have all sinned. But it's God and God alone that we sin against. You see? Not against each other. Not against our children. I know your heart is badly broken now, my dear, and there's nothing we can say to make any of that hurt go away. Not really. Only God can do that for you."

Gloria slid the book across the table to her friend.

"Read it to me," she said. "All of it."

"All right." Maureen began reading again at the beginning of the psalm.

Much of it, still, was lost to Gloria's comprehension. She remembered the night of Danny's birth, and how the rush of blood in her ears blocked so many of the words Sadie spoke, but bits and pieces of the ancient writing of a sin-ridden king fell upon her heart.

"For I acknowledge my transgressions: and my sin is ever before me…"

With every waking breath. In every dream.

"In sin did my mother conceive me…"

Mother. What if you had a chance to hear these words? How would your life have been different? And mine?

"Purge me with hyssop, and I shall be clean; wash me, and I shall be whiter than snow…"

White. Pure. Virgin. Can it be?

"Create in me a clean heart, O God…"

Because now, I feel I have no heart at all.

"Cast me not away from thy presence…"

So many others have thrown me away. Left me alone. If I become Yours, will You keep me?

"For thou desirest not sacrifice; else would I give it…"

I would. I would give anything.

"The sacrifices of God are a broken spirit…"

Broken.

"A broken and a contrite heart…"

Broken.

"O God, thou wilt not despise…"

How could You not despise me? When I so despise myself.

"Then shall they offer bullocks upon thine altar."

Maureen stopped reading, letting the final phrase hang in the air. So many thoughts and questions fought against each other in Gloria's mind, but she couldn't share them now. They were too new. Too raw. But the last words of the Scripture begged an answer.

"Bullock?"

"It's an animal. A bull used as a sacrifice to God."

"But he just said that God wants no sacrifice."

Maureen smiled warmly. "You have a quick mind, Gloria. Yes, God requires only that we offer the sacrifice of our hearts, ourselves. But King David lived in a time when God still required a blood sacrifice—the killing of an animal. But when Jesus Christ, God's Son, died on the cross, He became the final sacrifice. No man would ever again need to shed blood in order to seek forgiveness from God."

"His Son."

"You know the pain of losing a child, Gloria. Imagine if the only way to save the life of someone was to take away the life of your son. Sweet little Danny. Imagine how much God must love you that He did that for you."

"'For God so loved the world…'" John William's words from so long ago crept through her memory.

"The world, yes. But you, too, dear. God loved *you* that much."

"It's not believable."

Maureen giggled and gave Gloria's hand a squeeze across the table. "It seems that way, doesn't it? But, dearie, all He asks is that you *do* believe. Believe that Jesus died for you and that He will forgive you, and He will."

The little cabin was growing darker with the afternoon waning. Maureen had been holding the Bible closer and closer to her face with each verse, and now there was not enough light to continue reading, even if Gloria's head and heart had the stamina to go on. The effort of the day's labor infused her entire body, her head throbbed with questions, her stomach felt tight with hunger and something else she couldn't quite identify. It was long past time to nurse Danny.

But she didn't want to leave this place. There was magic here at this little table, two friends talking, words of Scripture lacing their conversation. A longing had been satisfied here in this cozy little room. Everything she had ever been seeking—peace, a home, a mother—all of it was wrapped up in these solid four walls, simple and new and given so freely.

"Thank you, Maureen," Gloria said softly, her voice barely a whisper. "I never expected when John—when he brought Kate to me, when he asked me to—I never thought I would have so much. I can't bear the thought of losing it all now."

"Let me tell you one more thing, dear, before we head back." Maureen's tone was serious. Imperative. "You could have all of this—a home, a man who adores you, beautiful children. But unless you pray, my child, until you free yourself from this burden you have, you'll never really enjoy it. You cannot truly love or *feel* truly loved without giving yourself over to God and *His* love."

Gloria loved this woman—loved her to bursting. She looked at the soft, warm face—just on the verge of wrinkles—and wished she had grown up in her loving care and wisdom.

"I wish you were my mother," Gloria said, and her voice trembled with the fear of rejection.

"Oh, my child," Maureen said with a sigh. "You had a mother, for good or for ill, and she made you what you are today. Not what you were in the past, but the strong, seeking woman you are right now. I cannot be your mother, but, in Christ, I can be your sister." The most beautiful smile Gloria had ever seen spread across Maureen's face. "Wouldn't you like for us to be sisters?"

"I'd love it. I—I love you," Gloria said, her speech nearly impaired by the unfamiliar words.

Maureen stood up and walked around the table to place a soft kiss on Gloria's forehead, then on each cheek, before folding her into the softest embrace.

"I love you too, my child," she said.

❀   ❀   ❀

They could hear Danny's petulant cries when they were still yards away from Maureen's house.

"Poor baby must be starving," Maureen said.

"I know how he feels." Gloria's stomach had been loudly rumbling for much of the walk back.

"You go straight to that baby, dear, and I'll fix us a snack."

Although it was just late afternoon, dusk had settled around the farm. Gloria looked, hoping to get a glimpse of John William, but there was no light coming from the barn, and she was certain he wasn't in the house. He hadn't stepped across the threshold since the funeral. Also, the wagon and team were gone, although it was much too early for the horses to be put up for the night.

"He's gone."

"What's that dear?" Maureen's voice betrayed how tired she must feel.

"John. He's gone. He's taken the wagon."

"Certainly not. He didn't say a word about it."

Maureen and Gloria had reached the cheerful blue door and were greeted by the full-out screaming of Danny, who was being jostled on Big Phil's lap. Anne was at the stove, stirring a pot of something that smelled wonderful.

"Do something with this baby!" Big Phil said good-naturedly.

"Now, Phil, stop that," Anne said. "He's been a perfect angel until just a few minutes ago." She turned from the simmering supper and smiled at Gloria. "He just needs his mama right now."

Gloria reached down and scooped her fussy son from Phil's grip. She brought him close for a hug and kissed his red, wet cheek. "His mama needs him, too," she said before leaving the cozy kitchen and taking him to the rocking chair in the parlor to nurse.

"I've made soup!" Anne's cheerful voice called from the kitchen. "It'll be ready when you are."

"Thank you," Gloria called back.

The muffled sounds of conversation filtered from the kitchen, and though Gloria longed to hear every word, she contented herself to see to Danny and relax, rocking, staring out the window into the early evening sky. Danny's frantic sucking eased into a comfortable rhythm matched by the rocking of the chair. Soon she allowed her head to loll against the back of the rocker and shut her eyes. Bits and pieces from the voices in the kitchen floated her way.

"He went to Centerville…to the mill…"

"Just after noon…he'll camp tonight…"

"…tried to tell him, but he wouldn't wait until tomorrow…"

"Saturday evening…wants to be here for church on Sunday."

So she was right. He was gone.

But he was coming back.

*S*he wiped the last plate over and over with the now-dampened rag, staring out the window, willing her eyes to see despite the darkness.

"Relax, child," Maureen chided behind her.

"He said he'd be here this evening. It's evening."

"He's fine, dear. I'm sure of it."

She reached from behind and took the plate from Gloria's hand and exchanged it for a very fussy Danny, who had been crying all evening. Gloria dropped the rag on the countertop and brought her son to her shoulder, bouncing and shushing him as she walked the circumference of the kitchen. Maureen returned the plate to its place on the shelf beside the window before lifting the basin from the countertop to toss the water out the door.

"It's cold outside," Gloria said, turning her body to shield Danny from the chill that rushed into the room. "Did he take a coat?"

"I'm sure he did. He's a sensible man."

The two women retired to Maureen's cozy parlor. A fire burned in the fireplace, casting a warm glow throughout the room. Gloria sank into the rocking chair, opened the buttons of her blouse, and brought the cranky baby—now nearly screaming—to her breast. Danny fell immediately into contented silence.

"I think he misses his sister," Maureen said softly. "He's been much fussier since she…"

"I think so too," Gloria said, looking into the little boy's half-closed eyes. "You know, the first night he brought her to me, we—well, I—thought she was dead. But the minute I first heard her cry, I just had this *need* for her."

"And she needed you."

Thirty minutes passed and Danny fell asleep. Gloria gathered him up and laid him in the bed he had shared with his sister.

Maureen's little clock continued to tick, tick into the night, emitting its low chime every half hour. The darkness outside became deep and complete, the light inside flickered with the flames of the fire.

"Well, we won't do any good sittin' up and worrying," Maureen said. "All kinds of things might've happened—a delay at the mill, a broken wagon wheel. He may have stopped for supper with Anne and Phil."

"He wouldn't do that." Gloria spoke with certainty. "He knows we'd be worried."

Maureen had no reply, and the two sat in companionable silence until the clock struck again.

"We should go to bed, child," Maureen said finally.

"You go on," Gloria said, her eyes fixed on the window where they had been all night. "I won't be able to sleep."

"He wouldn't want you up worrying, you know."

"Do you think he would stay up worrying about me?"

"That he would, dearie. But he'd be praying for you, too."

"So pray."

"Come join me," Maureen said, patting the seat of the couch beside her. "Come, Gloria, and pray with me."

Gloria got up from the rocking chair and crossed the little room to sit beside Maureen. Maureen turned towards her, their knees touching, and took Gloria's hands in her own.

"Father God, we pray Your guiding hand on John William tonight, that he is safe on his journey, traveling under Your protection."

We pray? Gloria had never prayed for anybody. She'd been an observer of many prayers—for safety, for blessed food, for healthy children—but she'd never been named as an active participant. How cold was her heart, she wondered, that this prayer for John meant nothing more to her than those other ramblings? How could she not join Maureen's sincerity, her obvious ability to be an agent of safety between John William and the evils and dangers that awaited him? She remained lost in this reverie until one phrase of Maureen's prayer startled her back to attention.

"And please, dear Lord, bring him back to Gloria…"

Of course. Back to Gloria. Back to that sin-filled woman who could only bring him to the brink of lust? Back to that woman who would steal his thoughts away from the godly woman who died giving birth to his child? Back to that woman who has known more men than she could ever count? That woman?

Maureen had stopped praying at some point, and in the settling silence, she gave Gloria's fingers a slight squeeze.

Gloria sat, still as stone.

"Gloria, dear, would you like to pray now?"

"I can't."

Maureen opened her eyes and met Gloria's gaze. "Why do you think that?"

"Because I've never…I just don't feel it. When I listen to you, I know I should feel *something*, shouldn't I? And it just seems that if I don't feel anything, He doesn't hear anything."

"I think He hears more than you can ever imagine."

Gloria took her hands from Maureen's grasp and began twisting a lock of her hair. "Go to bed, Maureen," she said, smiling softly. "I think your prayers would be more powerful without me."

"Oh, child. I'll go to pray alone, but I leave you in here to do the same."

She kissed Gloria softly on one cheek, then the other, and took herself off to the bedroom.

Gloria saw the dim line of candlelight coming from under the door for a few minutes, and by the time the clock struck again, she heard little snores coming from Maureen's room.

The rest of the righteous.

She put another log on the fire and stood beside it, watching the flames take hold.

Pray, pray, pray, she willed herself, but the words would not come. She tried them in her head—*Dear Father, Heavenly Father*—but the concept was still out of reach. She wrapped her mouth around the words, "Dear God, Dear Heavenly Jesus," but the use of His name in reverence was still too tainted by the years of coupling it with curses hurled through filthy streets.

She sat back on the sofa and tried to access memories of her innocence. Surely she had prayed as a child. She remembered kind women talking to her and her mother about Jesus Christ before her mother brusquely sent them away. She remembered the mission churches in California—their imposing crucifixes and the tragic figure of a dying Jesus—and wondering who was that man and why did He have to die like that.

Now she knew. He did it for her. He died for this miserable prostitute. For Gloria. For her sins. Confess them, Maureen had said. Confess them and be made clean. Be made new.

But where to begin? Perhaps it was the night the thirteen-year-old girl—under her mother's watchful eye—felt her body seared in pain, felt her own blood drip through her torn flesh. Had she sinned that night?

Gloria slid off Maureen's sofa, falling to her knees beside it. She clutched at her body, feeling anew the pain of that night, the shame of it all. How, she thought, could she face the God who would allow that to happen? Why should she ask forgiveness for something that had caused her such pain? In her mind and in her heart she was back on that filthy mattress on the floor, back with the landlord who raped his rent, wishing she could scream and kick and send him flying straight to hell.

Here, this night, on her knees in Maureen's home, her body contorted in the pain from that first night, from every night, from the men who beat her, from the ones that held her throat, bound her wrists, cut her flesh. Her skin crawled with their filthy touches. Her mind filled with their faces, their breath hot and rotten on her face. For a moment she thought that if Maureen were to walk into this room right now, she would see them—ghosts all—and she felt a need to beg forgiveness for allowing them into this house.

But then, no.

God, she prayed. Holy Father God. Forgive me for allowing them into myself. Into your creation.

In her mind she saw her outstretched hand, covered in silver, the wealth derived from peddling her charms. Then, one by one, the coins were taken away, dissolved and scattered like sifted sand, leaving only her palm, tainted with the stain of them.

I give it all to you, Father. Wash me. Make me clean.

She saw her hand disappear within another. This hand, covered in blood, held her own—tightly, as if for dear life. And just when she felt she could endure the exquisite pain of this embrace no longer, it released its grip, leaving her skin soft and without stain.

Thank you, Father, for the blood of Christ Your Son.

So this was peace. This was the comfort she'd heard about. This was the reason John William had said that Kate was safe, and now Gloria believed it, too, because for the first time in her life God was real and heaven existed and Gloria knew with a certainty that she would see the baby girl again. The power of her love for that child while she lived was just a hint of the powerful love a Father in heaven had for her now, and would have for an eternity.

The grip of her own mother's indifference, the blame and resentment Gloria had carried for so many years, melted, replaced with a brief and gentle mourning for the woman's own wretched life.

Tears, like she had never felt before, streamed unchecked down her face as Gloria released the despised life she had lived, making way for new visions, new direction and desire. Her hands clenched and unclenched, clutching the fabric of her skirt; her forehead rested on the cushion of the sofa.

So engrossed in her prayer was she that she didn't hear the creak of the door opening in the kitchen. Didn't hear the heavy footsteps cross the room. Was unaware that the strong arms that embraced her weren't the arms of Christ Himself, holding her tight and keeping her safe as she leaned against those strong shoulders, saying, "Father. My Father."

Later, she would open her eyes and turn to look at him, and he would know, they would know, that she wasn't the same woman.

Reader's Guide

1. *Ten Thousand Charms* contains the stories of three very different courtships: Gloria and John William; Josephine and David Logan; and Maureen and Ed Brewster. Which courtship most closely matches your idea of true love and romance? What aspects of each lay the foundations for a life-lasting relationship?

2. One of the aspects of God that draws Gloria to Him is the concept of Him as a Father. How is that relationship—that of a father to his child—important in the life of a Christian?

3. Both John William and Gloria have an unsavory past. How does his life as a boxer parallel hers as a prostitute? What can both of these stories tell us about the sacredness of our bodies and ourselves?

4. The idea of the importance of home is a recurring theme in the book. What does "home" mean to Gloria? What does "home" mean to you?

5. Gloria interacts with and reacts to many different women throughout the course of the story: Jewell, Sadie, Maureen, Josephine Logan, and Adele Fuller just to name a few. With which of these women do you most identify? Which one is most likely to be a friend of yours?

6. Coming to the knowledge of God and an acceptance of Christ is a process. What were some of the points in the

story where you saw Gloria's heart beginning to open? Where does it seem that she is being touched by God?

7. Imagine you were giving Christian counseling to someone like Gloria—someone who felt unloved and unworthy of God's love. What passage of Scripture would you be most likely to share with that person?

8. First John 3:2 (NIV) says, "Dear friends, now we are children of God, and what we will be has not yet been made known." The story leaves Gloria at the moment of becoming a child of God. What predictions can you make about her eventual walk with the Lord?

9. What influence do you think Gloria's leaving Silver Peak will have on the friends she made there? What will become of Biddy? What will be the impact of leaving Sadie the $1,000?

10. The title *Ten Thousand Charms* comes from the lyrics of the hymn "Come, Ye Sinners, Poor and Needy," several stanzas of which head the different sections of the book. What is your favorite hymn or praise song? What do the lyrics inspire in you? What memories or feelings does it invoke?

An excerpt from *Give to the Wind*,
Book 2 in Allison Pittman's Crossroads of Grace series:
(Available March 2007)

Five Points, New York City

*E*very Sunday Mr. Maroni built up a fire right on the corner of Mulberry and Bayard. After hauling out the big black cauldron from the back corner of his grocery, he tossed in the odds and ends of unwanted food—potatoes with black spots, limp carrots, turnips gone soft, greenish meat. To this, he added water and whatever broth could be salvaged from the meat boiled for his own Saturday night supper. All this he set simmering in the predawn hours of the city's day of rest. By the time the first church bells rang, a perfectly respectable soup (or stew, or hash, depending on the ingredients and consistency) was available to the public. Mr. Maroni stood at the pot with a ladle the width and depth of a blacksmith's fist, ready to serve anyone who came with a bowl and a penny.

On chilly autumn mornings like this one, the line formed early—sometimes before Mr. Maroni even had a chance to settle the pot over the flames. The drunks showed up first, reeling from a night full of rotten whiskey.

Then came the rowdy street boys, arriving in line as they moved through life, together. They whiled away their time in line knocking each other upside the head with battered and rusted tin cups. They taunted Mr. Maroni with threats of violence to his wife and his children if their serving was watery or thin, detailing just how they would torch his entire grocery if they found another cockroach at the bottom of a cup.

Sometimes a mother would show up with her entire brood and a handful of pennies—one for every ladleful dropped into her bucket. Later she would gather her children and divide the contents according to each child's age and hunger, until, as it happened every week, there was only the barest broth left for herself.

Then there was Kassandra. Small and slight, she lingered at the edge of the crowd clutching a blue porcelain bowl. It had a tiny chip at its rim and a picture of a sparrow perched on a branch painted in its center. The bowl was deep enough to hold two servings of Mr. Maroni's soup, a fact not lost on the rowdy boys who elbowed each other in front of her in line.

"Better have yourself two pennies for that," one said, his beady eyes staring hungrily at Kassandra's bowl as he patted his own piece of broken pottery nervously against his leg.

"Aw, leave 'er alone," said another boy. Taller than the rest, his red hair sprang from his head like tiny curled flames. "She's so scrawny, looks like she needs an extra bit."

Kassandra herself said nothing, but clutched her bowl to her body and shuffled her bare feet closer to the bubbling cauldron. It would be the first meal she'd had in days, and the endurance of a few boys' teasing seemed a small price to pay. She kept her attention focused on Mr. Maroni's ladle as it sloshed its contents into the cups and bowls and jars of the men and women and children in front of her. Kassandra felt today would be a lucky one, that her place in line was just perfect. Too close to the front or too far back and you might get nothing but broth.

Soon, only the redheaded boy stood in front of her. He held his bowl out, dug a penny from his pocket, and dropped it into the grocer's outstretched hand. Two heartbeats later, Kassandra stood in front of that same outstretched hand, holding her bowl up until it was just level with her chin, focusing her large gray eyes on Mr. Maroni's deep brown ones.

"Penny?" said Mr. Maroni.

Kassandra shook her head from side to side, then held her bowl a little higher.

"No got a penny?"

Kassandra shook her head, no.

"Well, then," said Mr. Maroni. He balanced his ladle across the top of the soup pot and crouched down until he was eye-level with Kassandra. He brought one long brown finger and tapped his right cheek. On command, Kassandra leaned forward and planted a tiny kiss, feeling the edges of his moustache tickle her lip.

"And again," said Mr. Maroni, tapping the opposite cheek. Again Kassandra leaned in to give a little kiss.

"And here." Kassandra had to go a bit to her toes to land a kiss on Mr. Maroni's forehead, just between the bushy eyebrows almost equal in density to his moustache.

"Now, you want soup?" he said, flashing a smile.

Kassandra nodded her head and tightened her grip on the blue porcelain bowl. She closed her eyes and leaned forward one more time, placing her own lips on Mr. Maroni's. He tasted, as always, of olives, and she called on all her strength not to shudder against the bitterness.

"Now, *bella*," he said, "give this to me."

He reached for her bowl, hooking one dirty thumb over the rim and cupping it from the bottom in his large hand. Within seconds, the bowl was full of two steaming helpings—plus a delightful little piece of fat floating on the top—and she offered a small curtsy as the prostitutes behind her in the line laughed and tried to negotiate their own price for a free meal.

Kassandra gathered up her skirt using the thin material as a shield against the hot bowl. She brought the bowl to her lips and allowed herself one tiny sip of the broth—just enough to burn the taste of Mr. Maroni from her mouth—before heading through the streets to find a quiet corner to savor her meal. Her body had grown dull to its hunger, but that little taste brought it to ravenous life again.

Lately she'd been sleeping in a large building up the street where the peddlers parked their carts for the night. Now, as she looked around, she saw them singing their songs and hawking their wares. The warehouse would be abandoned and quiet, perfect for a leisurely meal and a good sleep to follow.

When the heat of the soup began to seep through the fabric of her skirt, Kassandra quickened her pace slightly, careful not to let one precious drop slosh over the side. The anticipation was often more delicious than the soup itself, and she smiled thinking of the little sparrow on its branch waiting for her at the bottom of the bowl. Somewhere in her blanket at the warehouse was half a sourdough roll she'd found just yesterday. Left alone it was a flour-crusted stone, but Kassandra intended to plop it into this broth, then mash great moist bits of it into her mouth.

Without breaking stride, she brought the bowl to her lips. Had she not been so engrossed, so hungry, she probably would have seen the carriage careening down the street toward her. If nothing else, she would have heard the terrified cry of the horse as its driver pulled desperately on the reins to avoid running over the little blond girl with the blue bowl of soup in the middle of the street. Instead, her first knowledge of the carriage or the horse came as something hit the bottom of her bowl. She felt the porcelain rim clink into her teeth and bump against her forehead. She got one quick glimpse of the sparrow sitting on its branch before two ladlefuls of Mr. Maroni's Sunday soup flew into her wide eyes.

She was surprised to hear herself scream. She thought her voice had completely closed up within her, it had been so long since she'd uttered a single sound. Yet here she was, her face alive with pain, as she fell to her knees, then straight to the ground. Some of the broth had gone up her nose and now choked in her throat. She writhed on the street, calling *"Muter! Muter!"* although the memory of when such a call would bring her mother to her side was a memory all but lost.

She felt a hand take both of hers in its grip and another cradle the back of her neck. Kassandra had been touched enough to know it was a man, and she stiffened against his ministrations.

"Hush now," a gentle voice said. "Hush little one. It's going to be all right."

Kassandra let her body go limp. Tears welled up in her closed eyes as new waves of pain throbbed inside her head. She sensed a crowd had gathered, heard muttered conversations and a few hurled, angry words. The gentle hand that held her own released its grip, and the voice that had been so gentle in her ear now spoke loudly above her.

"She's calling for her mother! Does anyone know where her mother is?"

Kassandra wanted to tell him that she had no mother, but when she opened her mouth to say so, she could only whimper.

"Well, then," said the voice, "where does she live? What is her name?"

She knew nobody could answer him. Nobody knew her name, and she didn't live anywhere. She wanted to tell the voice all of this, but before she could she was weightless, lifted by one strong arm under her legs and another around her shoulders. Then she was flying through the air until she finally felt soft solidity beneath her. She tried to open her eyes, but the effort seemed too great and an onslaught of pain a promise, so she contented herself to enjoy the comfort of what must be a cushion.

She felt her body shutting down, felt uncontrollable drowsiness take over. She thought to herself that maybe she was dying—she'd never felt quite so comfortable and tired ever in her life. Maybe the arms she'd felt were the arms of God Himself, lifting her to this upholstered heaven. Her mind filled with a sense of relief. What perfect timing this death would be. After nine (or ten? eleven?) years on this earth, how convenient to be taken at her hungriest. Before the winter came to find her without shoes.

Her reverie was interrupted by the voice speaking softly just to her. "*Haben Sie nicht Angst,*" it said, telling her not to be afraid.

And strangely enough, she wasn't, even as her body lurched forward into what was surely a journey into the next world.

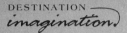

Next stop...
Britain!

Win a trip for two to England and Scotland!
Visit us at **http://fiction.mpbooks.com** for more details.

Each Multnomah fiction title featured in the
DESTINATION *imagination* program entitles you to
an additional contest entry.

Passport Code: TTC106

Multnomah® Publishers · *Keeping Your Trust...One Book at a Time*®